VERADEL

VERADEL

GUARDIANS & MONSTERS VOLUME 2

MARIAH MONTOYA

GRACE PEARCE

Cover design and illustration by Wavyhues

Internal design and illustration by Aethrastic Designs

Map by Shepengul

ISBN: 979-8-9998419-2-6 (paperback)

ISBN: 979-8-9998419-3-3 (hardcover)

For everyone who wants to spark change.

LUCAN

At more than two hundred years old, I can confidently say that time is fucking weird.

Sometimes, like during the slow, rainy days when trails of water crawl down the windowpane and the world breathes as if it's sleeping, time *trickles*. At others, like when the blood-tinged moon anchors itself in the sky and I can smell all of the humans being Chosen as sacrifices on the other side of the Wall, time bolts ahead, faster than I can catch it in my jaws.

Right now is one of those times.

I practically beg time to slow down. Delay the moment Saskia hits the ground.

Give me more time to find a way to save her.

But it doesn't. Rebellious as ever, it speeds up, as if gravity wants to claim her faster than I can even register her body—her real, physical body—falling through the mist above my head.

Her scream slices through the woods cloaked in sunset, vibrating in my heart right where our connection usually stirs. I'd howl back at her if I was in my other form, but I'm human now, so all I can do is maneuver myself right below her hurtling figure and hold out my arms.

It doesn't matter if I catch her. The Wall is too high, her fall too great. Her bones will still crack in my arms upon impact, and her lungs will explode, just like all the other Chosen Ones who jumped before her.

But I won't let her hit the ground anyway. Even though this is the end before we could truly begin, I told her I've got her.

That won't ever change.

A red film of grief and anger clouds my vision as she gets closer, her hair sailing above her, her arms and legs flailing, her scream still fracturing what's left of my soul into a hundred tiny, jagged pieces. The Guardians always told their citizens they threw transgressors over the Wall as fodder, that the Monster would be waiting at the bottom with an open maw and deadly teeth.

I'm waiting now, but this is a woman I would have devoured in a completely different way if I'd had the chance.

In another life. Another reality. Another world.

Now, her death is going to eat me alive. Consume me until I'm nothing but a skeleton alongside her.

Closer, closer, closer, Saskia falls, and I grit my teeth, bracing for the impact of the end of both our lives.

Then...

Her weight crashes into me, slamming against my arms, but I don't let my knees so much as buckle when her scream cuts off, the sound dying from her lips and her eyes flicking shut.

Her *eyes*. Such beautiful hazel eyes, speckled with green, that I caught a glimpse of before they closed forever. And her *eyelashes*.

Hauling in deep, shuddering breaths, I sink to my knees on the forest floor and marvel down at them, so dark and thick surrounded by the light sprinkle of freckles I wish I could have an eternity to count.

I cradle her tightly against my chest and run my fingertips lightly down her cheek, amazed at how intact her body still is. I briefly wonder if it's because she was already part-stone—if her injuries are all internal...

Tucking a strand of her hair behind her ear, I lift my eyes as they fill with tears I didn't even know a Monster like me could shed. I try to blink them back, reel in my emotions. She deserved more than this.

One teardrop falls against her neck.

And—

Wait.

Fucking *wait*.

Slowly, as if my entire future depends on it, my gaze slides down Saskia's neck, where the tear zigzags along her skin... and a pulse flutters with life.

More quickly now, I slide even lower, to her chest. Her *moving* chest. The vial filled with my grandfather's blood bobs in rhythm with her breaths, unbroken as the rest of her.

Inexplicably, miraculously, my little nightmare is perfectly whole in my arms.

As my whole world reorients itself, resuming its spin around us, her eyelashes quiver.

She sighs.

And opens her eyes.

SASKIA

T o my surprise, the afterlife feels nice. Someone is stroking my hair.

And I'm being held. Cradled. It reminds me of my childhood, in the arms of my mother after a particularly nasty nightmare. Except the fingers that graze my forehead now are much too large, the skin too callused, to belong to her.

They also tremble, as if brimming with barely-restrained strength.

I crane my neck, a happy sigh leaving my lips at the thought of those hands curling around my throat, and open my eyes.

A gasp shoots out of me at the face that blooms in my vision.

Striking amber eyes pierce me with an intensity that makes me feel impaled in the best of ways, pupils wide and all-consuming as they race up and down my body. Thick, furrowed brows frame his golden bronze face, his dark hair mottled with waves of lighter brown. His strong jaw clenches, his powerful neck muscles tightening as I let my gaze travel down the length of him, to the muscled arms holding me against his heaving chest.

His heaving *chiseled* chest.

This is, without a doubt, the finest male specimen I've ever laid eyes on, even in the thinning light of dusk. And I think I know who he is, even though I never could have imagined the Monster looking this way in any form. There's just something about the tether pushing and pulling between our locked gazes that feels completely foreign and completely familiar all at once.

"Lucan?" I whisper up at him.

An awe-struck expression clouds his face. "Yes, baby?"

Scratch that. The afterlife isn't just nice... it's *heaven*. Even though I know this isn't the real Lucan—he couldn't have possibly followed me into death so quickly—my imagination is doing a phenomenal job at conjuring up a fantasy version of him that already makes heat flood through me, tingling my nerves. That voice, such a rough, deep tone, settles right between my thighs.

Smiling now, I reach up a hand and run my fingers along his jawline, marveling at the sharp shape of it. Lucan's eyes widen even more, then close briefly at my touch.

"You," I breathe, "are even sexier than I could have ever dreamed of."

One of those thick, gorgeous eyebrows cocks up, and his mouth twitches.

"Is that so?"

"Yes." I nod up at him fervently, content to lie against his chest forever. "To be honest, I didn't even know if the afterlife was real. But if I could come back to life and preach to everyone about it, I'd tell them dying isn't so bad, actually." I finally manage to rip my eyes from his face for two seconds to glance at the scenery around us. "I mean, look at all these trees! The smell is invigorating." I take a big inhale, and a giggle escapes me. "And I'm more turned on than I've ever been in my *life*. I mean, *look* at you."

"More than in the bathtub?" Lucan teases.

His mouth stretches into a genuine, smirking smile, and I inhale sharply at the flash of canines. That's strange.

The inhale filled my lungs with air so quickly, it hurt.

Almost like my ribcage is bruised.

But the afterlife shouldn't hurt, should it? Out loud, I say, "Death feels more real than I thought it would."

"You're not dead, little nightmare," Lucan says, his voice grazing me in all the most sensitive places again. "You're just outside the Wall for the first time in your life."

The smug glint in his eyes tells me he's never going to forget my comment about him being sexier than I could have ever dreamed of. Or the turned-on thing. Or...

"Wait, wait, wait." I try to scramble out of his arms, swearing under my breath when an ache shoots through my ribs again. But Lucan's grip doesn't relent, and I go still, caught in his snare without a chance of escape. "I'm..." I crane my neck to catch a glimpse of the Wall rising up behind me, of the mist overhead. "I'm alive? I didn't..."

Splatter into a bloody heap on the forest floor? I can't get out.

"No." Something carnal and ferocious seems to swirl in the amber of Lucan's eyes, but his throat bobs as he swallows it gruffly down. "I don't know how you survived, Saskia, but you did. I caught you. And you're just as alive as I am."

For a moment, we stare at each other. Every part of my body heats and tightens, true sensation flooding through my system again as I realize...

I'm not dead. And this isn't even a dream.

Lucan—the Monster—is here, in the flesh, pinning me in place with those eyes, his body so physical and rock-hard against me that I can barely breathe.

Then embarrassment creeps up my cheeks as I remember what I told him. How I traced his jawline with my hand. How he's holding me against his chest like I'm the prey he's finally caught. And when his lip curls up in another smirk, my eyes snag on his canines again. They're not as sharp or needle-like as Arad's, but longer, thicker, and somehow more masculine.

Those canines wouldn't pierce my skin or make me bleed, but they would bruise.

And why is that exciting me even more? Maybe I did knock my head a little too hard.

"Put me down, Lucan," I try to say confidently, but the sincerity leaks out of my voice before it can even take root. In actuality, I don't want this male to ever put me down again.

Lucan cocks his head down at me.

"No."

"I said—"

"And I said *no*, little nightmare." He only tightens his hold, crushing me against him. "This is the first time I'm able to touch you, and I'm not letting you go so quickly. Not when I can smell your desire to stay right here."

I squirm in his hold—to no avail, of course. The effort is half-hearted anyway. "I know you have a good sense of smell, Lucan, but I don't think strawberries and roses are capable of giving you any indication of my desires."

"I'm not talking about strawberries and roses, Saskia. Not this time." Lucan's voice dips. "I'm talking about that sweet wetness pooling between your legs right now, drenching you through your clothes. I was never able to smell it with a Wall between us, but now..."

His nostrils flare, and my cheeks practically sizzle with mortification. I got so comfortable talking to him mind-to-mind that I forgot what a powerful, threatening force he actually is. He might not look like the Monster right now, but he's sure acting like it.

"Well, I can feel *your* desire through your pants, so we're even," I bite out.

It's true, actually. With my hip nestled up against Lucan's groin, his hardness stiffens against me, and I actually have to suppress the moan building in my throat—and the urge to grab him.

I just fell from the Wall, I remind myself sharply. *Arad is probably listening to the murmur of our voices from above. The people of Xantera are still in danger. Now is not the time.*

Or the place. One more swift glance around me tells me how truly out of my element I am out here. Whereas I've always lived in perfect structures under bright fluorescent lights or in the palace surrounded by extravagant furniture and decorations, *this* is absolutely wild.

And somehow, breathtakingly beautiful at the same time.

Pine needles sprinkle a russet dirt floor beneath me, but we're in the only bald spot as far as my eye can see—as if Lucan's constant treading here stamped out any undergrowth. But otherwise, ferns spring up between trees, moss cloaks the trunks all around us, and branches reach for each other with scraggly arms that create an intricate web of wood among the mist.

When I look up, a single drop of water plops against the tip of my nose and rolls down.

"C'mon," Lucan says, his expression hardening over into something unreadable. His jaw clenches again, as if he's biting back a million different words, but that glint of amusement still shines through. "Let's get you inside before you get even more wet."

Inside? Where are we even going? Is he taking me to his own house? Right now?

For some reason, the thought sends nerves shooting into my belly. Not because I'm afraid to be alone with him, but because I'm afraid I might finally meet the others he so rarely talks about. His fellow Monsters who can also shift between forms.

"I'm fine," I try to say, even as more droplets sprinkle us from above.

"Maybe." Lucan's already spinning and striding into the forest, away from the Wall, with me still pressed up against his chest. "But I just watched you fall from a one-hundred-foot height, so I'm not taking any chances letting you stay out here and catch a cold."

"That's not even how colds work," I argue.

"And you're not walking yourself," he continues, ignoring me completely. "Not until I get our medic to look at you and make sure you truly didn't break anything."

"I'm a healer!" I protest. "I'm pretty sure I would be able to tell if my own bones are broken." I squirm, my hip knocking into his hardness again. "So you can put. Me. Down. Right. Now." I push against his chest fruitlessly.

Lucan stops abruptly, the shadows of the woods pressing in on us. Dusk has bled into nighttime, and hardly any moonlight streams through the gaps in the trees and mist above, but I can still see the lift of his lips again as he stares me down, eyes two slits of glinting yellow in the darkness.

"I can carry you like you're a princess, Saskia, or I can carry you like you're a wicked little nightmare," he purrs. "Your choice. But until I know for sure you're safe and unharmed, I'm not setting you down. So which is it? What do you want to be right now?"

All my pent-up frustration and anger over the last several months seem to home in on him. Not because he's the cause, but because he's the outlet. And I swear, his eyes track the way my own spark up. I *want* this fight. Need to let it out as surely as my heart needs to beat.

And he knows that. He's ready for every part of me.

So in response, I squirm and twist and kick.

"Nightmare it is," Lucan snorts, and hoists me over his shoulder until I'm hanging down the length of his back, the necklace swinging beneath me, his hands clamped around the back of my upper thighs. His fingers so close to the spot that pulses for him that I swear he probably feels that wetness he gloated about.

I shriek and scrabble at his back, but he just lets out a low chuckle that rumbles through each point of contact and lengthens his stride.

And that's how the Monster carries me away from Xantera, into whatever lies beyond.

By the time Lucan bursts through a clearing some ten minutes later, I'm panting so hard from the continuous effort of trying to break free that I almost tip over when he flips me forward and sets me on my feet.

"Easy," he murmurs into my ear, planting his hands on my hips to steady me. A retort bubbles on my lips... until I look up and realize where we are.

A dirt road stretches out before me, forking off in different directions and bordered by derelict wooden housing units. Only, these housing units don't look anything like what we have in the complexes, smashed together like perfect blocks. These have individual pointed roofs with lopsided shingles like crooked teeth and strange, narrow brick structures climbing out of them. And the windows—all in different places, giving each house something like a... personality.

My gaze skates across the nearest one, which has a window shattered in and a door that hangs off its hinges. But the house beyond it has light flickering in the window and smoke curling from the opening in the brick structure at the top.

Up and down the road, curtains flutter in the lit windows, and I swear I sense the weight of eyes pressing in on us from between the gaps.

"This is where you live?"

For some reason, despite Lucan telling me he lived in an abandoned town, my mind could really only conjure lairs and caves. But something about this place bites me with a nostalgia I didn't even realize I had, a kind of yearning for cozy comfort ingrained in my bones.

"This is where *we* live," Lucan says, his tone tightening as three figures exit one of the houses at the end of the dirt road and streak toward us.

I tense at the sight of them, glad that Lucan let me have the dignity of standing on my own two feet for the moment I meet the others of his kind.

"Lucan, we heard a scream, but we weren't sure... oh."

The middle of the trio, a female with short, dark brown hair and a heart-shaped face, cuts herself off as she finally comes to a halt before me. Her eyes, amber like Lucan's, widen as they land on me. Even though she's technically smaller than me, her lean muscle and willowy, ethereal grace make me feel like she could hold her own.

"Hello," she tells me nervously, confusion warring with excitement on her face.

"Vivian, this is Saskia," Lucan says curtly. "Saskia, this is my pack. Or at least, some of them. Vivian, Merrick, and Soren."

His pack? The word sounds strange, but it fits, somehow. The way all four of them react to each other's body movements, like they're connected through their very blood, even without the use of a necklace. A pang of longing, of wishing I could be one of them, flashes through me unexpectedly.

The male to Vivian's right—Merrick—gives me a friendly nod that is the complete opposite of how a Monster should greet you. He has a rich, dark skin tone, his black hair braided back in several rows, and broad shoulders like Lucan. Meanwhile, the male to Vivian's left—Soren—has a slightly narrower build, with olive skin and light brown hair cropped close to his head.

When he notices me staring at him, Soren flashes his canines in a smug smile. "Glad to finally meet you in person, Saskia. This asshole—" He nods at Lucan. "—has been insufferable ever since he fell i—"

"Saskia's going to need some more clothes," Lucan cuts him off, directing that statement to Vivian, who nods with an eager bounce on the balls of her feet. "Gather a variety of them, please. And I'm going to need you to go get Taika." He turns his glare onto Soren, who shoots him a conspiratorial grin. But before he can obey, an older, gruffer voice permeates the night behind us.

"No need. I'm here."

I whip around to find a gold-badged man limping toward us, leaning heavily on a gnarled cane topped with a carved wolf head. Of course, he doesn't actually wear a badge pinned to his chest, but the silver of his hair reflects the first moonbeams that peek through the clouds up above.

"Taika," Lucan says, and I can feel some of his tension loosen on an exhale. "She fell from the Wall. I need you to look her over, make sure there's no internal bleeding."

Soren cocks an eyebrow, and the others visibly glance at each other in question. Up until this point, the surprise of seeing a human in their midst has kept their confusion at bay, I'm sure, but now I can practically see the questions brewing in their eyes.

How did I even get to the top of the Wall? Why did I jump? How did I survive the fall?

I can answer all of them but that last one. Because the truth is, survival should have been impossible. I shouldn't be breathing, glancing uncertainly between Lucan and the old man with the cane in a ghost town where dozens of curtains still flutter from lit windows.

Taika is obviously thinking the same thing, what with the way his eyes—again, amber like Lucan's—squint at me with inquisitive assessment. But after a long-bated breath, he nods.

"Right this way, then. Follow me."

The others disperse, making way for us as we turn around and follow Taika back to one of the first houses at the end of a short, rocky lane. This one looks noticeably different from the others, with a wider roof, double door, and ramp leading up to a wooden deck. The ramp creaks as we walk up, Lucan's arm a steady anchor around my waist, and I glance at some faded lettering barely visible on the front windows: *F M LY MED CAL C NT R.*

My spine ripples with even more foreign nostalgia as an old bell dings above our heads when we shuffle in, entering a waiting area with moth-eaten sofas, frayed carpet, and peeling wallpaper. The silence in here breathes down my neck, but I know what it is.

A miniature Healing Center. An ancient one, judging by the musty smell, but a Healing Center all the same. Did there used to be more than one back before the vampires took over and trapped us all within the Wall? How long has it been since this one was used?

As if he can sense all the questions stirring within me, Taika shrugs off his coat and drapes it over the nearest armchair.

"Before we were exiled from our kingdom, I was the king's physician, so I found this an... appropriate home for me after the war," he explains. "I've kept all the medical equipment as sharp and clean as I can, and I try to keep our medicine cabinets well-stocked with herbs and oils I can find in the forest." He chuckles. "No more antibiotics, not that we need them that often, but I do have plenty of garlic, ginger, and honey."

I cock my head, all the adrenaline and fight within me giving way to excitement, curiosity, and maybe even awe. Back during my healing apprenticeships, our instructors touched lightly on the science behind medications, but I was never chosen to be one of those who actually invented or created them. I could learn so much from Taika, if he'd teach me.

Lucan clears his throat. "Less talking, please. More examination."

"This way, then," Taika sighs, but shoots me a small smile.

He leads us out of the waiting room, down a hall, past a patient-room-turned-bedroom, from the looks of it, and into an office lined with cabinets and a counter cluttered with supplies. He gestures for me to sit on the ripped padded recliner, while he lowers himself carefully into a metal swivel chair with squeaky wheels.

Lucan himself just crosses his arms over his chest in the corner, his attention drilling holes into the room with its intensity. It takes everything in me to look away from him and focus on the medic in front of me.

"Arm, please," Taika says gently, grabbing a handheld blood pressure monitor from the counter. This one isn't hooked up to a machine like I'm used to but made of a leather strap and strange rubber bulb. When I stick out my arm, he wraps the cuff around me and pumps the bulb several times until it tightens just like the ones at the Healing Center do.

"Interesting," he muses, squinting at the needle on the attached dial.

"What?" Lucan asks sharply. It's so strange to hear his voice, not in my head, but out loud. In person. A physical sound that grazes against my skin.

"Lower blood pressure than I'd expect."

My heart drops, and I can practically feel Lucan's fury sizzle outward, washing the room with white-hot energy. The venom is already at work, then, slowly fossilizing my insides. Will my transformation to stone take longer than the other Chosen Ones, now that there aren't any vampires around to continue biting me? Will I have more than ten years left? Or will I still find myself bedridden before I know it, even though I don't feel lightheaded or dizzy like Odette did?

"Nothing to be too concerned about though," Taika says, sitting back.

A rumble stirs in Lucan's chest. "Check it again."

His tone leaves no room for debate, and Taika takes one glance at him seething in the corner before he nods.

The silence stretches as the cuff tightens around my biceps and Taika listens and times my pulse again. "Still the same," he says, talking to Lucan with his eyes trained softly on me.

"What about her heart—" Lucan says impatiently, but Taika's already reaching for a stethoscope, shaking his head and clearly trying to hide his amusement.

Like the blood pressure cuff, this one looks slightly different than the instrument I'm used to: made of wood and rubber rather than plastic and metal. But it must do the trick, because when Taika presses it to my chest, he nods.

"Well?" Lucan demands.

"No stutters. A strong heart. On the slower end again, but strong."

That's funny. I feel like my heart has done nothing but race since I laid eyes on Lucan. But the venom must be slowly hardening that organ as well. Great. By the tic of Lucan's jaw, I'm guessing he thinks the same. Slow heartbeat be damned, my pulse seems to thrum at the sight of that stormy expression. Not being able to read his thoughts makes my toes tingle in anticipation.

Lucan crosses the room in two long strides. "I want to hear."

Taika looks to me for permission, and I laugh.

"Like you said earlier, I'm alive," I assure Lucan, "but feel free."

Now my heart decides to gallop as Lucan, whose eyes latch onto mine intensely, takes the stethoscope from Taika and inserts the earpieces into his own ears.

"See?" I joke. "Not dead yet."

Lucan ignores me and asks Taika gruffly, "What about internal injuries?"

Taika clears his throat. "Would you feel comfortable lifting your dress so I can check your abdomen, Saskia?"

"Oh, of course."

Lucan doesn't say a word as I gather up the hem of the dress I put on what feels like an eternity ago, but I can sense his focus pummeling into us, assessing with narrow eyes, as Taika begins to press against my stomach and ribcage.

"No lumps. No swelling. No bruises."

"Really?" I ask, surprised. I could have sworn I'd be black and blue, but now that I think about it, the pain in my lungs has already evaporated.

Lucan latches on to that, concern leaking from his voice. "What do you mean 'really?' Does it hurt?"

"No," I say. "I promise." *It did, but not anymore. I feel like I'll never be in pain again now that I'm next to you.* Thank goodness he can't read my thoughts right now, because my cheeks are already warming in embarrassment.

Taika nods with furrowed white brows. "It's rather impossible, actually. Are you sure you're human? Not a were—"

"Taika," Lucan interjects immediately with a tone that makes me jump.

"A what?" I ask, frowning between the two of them.

"A..."

Taika doesn't finish. Instead, he glances at Lucan uncertainly, who sighs.

"Their knowledge of the outside world has been extremely limited," he offers. "But yes, she's human."

"Hmm." For a moment, Taika leans back in his chair, his eyes scouring my face as if for any signs that I'll keel over sideways and drop dead right in front of him. When I remain seated, blinking at him awkwardly, he says, "Well, if you feel any dizziness or weakness, notice any swelling, or vomit any blood, come right back here. For now, though I'd say you need to rest and recover from... whatever happened. But in the morning..." Here, he turns his gaze back to Lucan. "The pack will be expecting some kind of explanation. We've been locked out here for five hundred years, trying to get back in without any kind of breakthrough until now. This is the first living human I've seen since the war and the first human many will have seen in their entire lives. They will have questions."

Lucan gives a curt nod, and I suddenly realize what all those fluttering curtains were about. Vivian, Merrick, and Soren were the only ones who wanted to come and meet me. The others... are they wary? Hesitant? I'm pretty positive Lucan won't let them eat me at this point, but will they accept me?

The questions subside when Lucan puts a firm hand beneath my elbow, helping me back to a stand. "They can wait until then," he says, no room for argument in his voice.

Taika nods and grunts to a stand as well. "There's an extra room above—"

"No need," Lucan interrupts. "She's staying with me tonight."

I whip my head toward him, my heart thrumming again. "I am?"

"Yes. I'm not letting you out of my sight." Lucan pauses. "In case."

"You don't trust Taika's examination?" I tease.

Lucan raises an eyebrow. "I trust him with my life. But I won't trust anyone except me with yours."

My heart skips. If Lucan's trying to keep me alive, he may need to change tactics before I die of a heart attack.

"Don't worry," he adds. "I'll sleep on the floor."

And there goes my fluttering heart dying of dismay. What if I want him to sleep in the bed with me?

"Are you going to throw me over your shoulder again to get me there?" I ask with a teasing edge, trying to soften the deadly lines in his face. I might be turning to stone, but for now, I'm alive. I'm free. And I want to forget everything that came before this moment for just one night before I have to face reality again. Want him to forget, too.

"No," Lucan says seriously, his jaw still set. "Now that I know you're fine, you can walk yourself."

A bit of disappointment sinks in my chest before his hand reaches up and covers the vial sitting against my chest until it's sandwiched between our skin. I suppress a gasp when a burst of electricity shoots through me, and his presence invades my mind just like it does when he's in his Monster form.

Unless you beg me, his thoughts croon into my ear. *Then I'll do whatever you ask of me, little nightmare.*

I jolt and give a little cough as his hand drops again, his mind leaving mine as he turns to look out the window.

Taika clears his throat, then lowers his voice so low I have to pause to piece together his words. "Before you leave, I have to ask..." He holds out a little pouch filled with herbs—like a teabag—that I didn't even notice him retrieve. "Would you like something to prevent... pregnancy?"

The heat of embarrassment whooshes through me before I stutter out, "I... I have to?"

Taika blinks with a mortified expression. "What? No, of course not. I'm not forcing you, Saskia. It's completely up to you. I just..." He steals a glance at Lucan's turned back. "Though rare, it's possible for werewolves and humans to conceive."

"Oh," I whisper, dissolving into a puddle on the spot as I reach out and take the pouch. I might as well. Just in case. I don't have any expectations, but I know what *I* want.

"Just brew it like tea," he tells me, back to a modicum of professionalism.

"Thank you, Taika." I glance around at all the medical equipment again, noting the scale in the corner, a glass thermometer, and a variety of other tongs or scalpels. "Maybe..." I begin hesitantly. "Maybe I could help you, in the future. If someone's sick or injured or just, you know, if you need someone to polish..."

I'm rambling now, but Taika just bows his head with a smile.

"It would be my pleasure, dear. I've greatly missed having an apprentice."

LUCAN

When we finally get to my house, Saskia stops in front of it with her mouth agape.

I halt alongside her, painfully in tune with each of her movements, the way her fingers rise to her mouth, and how her eyes skate along every feature I've never looked at twice.

A wooden porch wraps around the stone structure, every hole and crack repaired by me over the last few hundred years. Wild creepers twine along the railing. Two wicker chairs sit by the front door, although I've never lounged in either one of them. They used to belong to my parents, but my mother insisted I take them after my father died.

Saskia's attention grazes the chairs, then raises up to my second floor, where my bedroom door leads out to a small, rounded balcony that looks out over the whole town.

"I can tear that down," I say quickly, noting how pale her face looks, "if it bothers you..."

I have half a mind to leap upward and rip the balcony off my house here and now, on the chance that it will remind her of the Blood Moon Palace balconies she had to wave from. I told her she's sleeping where I can monitor her, but if any part of my house triggers her...

"No." She shakes her head, wrapping her arms around herself. "It's just... what do you even use that balcony for?"

I blink at her, a twisting kind of heat coaxing out my inner beast at the question. But in this moment, I push it back, remaining calm for her.

"On clear nights, I lean over the railing to look at the stars."

"The stars?" she asks, and glances up at the cloud-smeared night sky.

That's when I remember her only experiences of the nighttime before now have been the Choosings and the catacombs, and my anger rears its head again. I swallow. Flex my fingers.

"I'll show you how beautiful it can be the first cloudless night we get. But for now, let's get you warm." I don't dare touch her again. Not yet. As soon as I do, I know I'll lose every fraction of control I've managed to maintain since she opened her eyes, so I just lead the way up the porch and push open my front door.

Inside, Saskia once again takes her time on the first floor, observing every seemingly mundane thing. But to her, it's not. When we pass through my kitchen, she trails her fingers along my wood-burning stove, gaping at it like it's the most fascinating thing in the world.

"Are you hungry?" I ask, my voice tight. Controlled. "I can make you something."

"No." She shakes her head. "I just didn't get a chance to look at these things when I was in the kitchen in the Blood Moon Palace. Whoa." Her head jerks up, her eyes widening at my living room beyond the kitchen, where the floor-to-ceiling windows stretch from one side of the house to the other. "What a view."

I glance at the forest spreading beyond the windowpanes before fixing my attention back on her. "Yes, it is." My eyes skate over her body again, trying to unearth any clues that she's in distress or pain, but she just hurries toward my spiral staircase as if wooden banisters are the most exciting thing she's ever seen. Which, considering the hellhole she's been locked in all her life, maybe they are.

I flex my fingers again, trying to contain my irritation at everything and everyone who has kept this beautiful woman locked away from a world that could be equally as beautiful.

"Is your room up there?" Saskia asks, maybe a little eagerly as she traces the lower banister with a feather-light touch. "I mean..." She coughs, her cheeks flushing with the loveliest hue. "Not that I'm trying to intrude. I can sleep on the sofas down here if you want. I was just cur—"

"You're not sleeping on any sofas, Saskia." I nod at the stairs. "Go on up. My bed's waiting for you if you want to go to sleep."

"Oh, I'm not tired in the slightest." She starts up the stairs, and I'm left staring after the sway of her hips for a moment, viciously trying to shove my desires way down, where they can't touch me. After such a long night and such a great fall, she should be hungry and fatigued, not practically bouncing on the balls of her feet, fracturing my restraint more and more with each passing second.

Cursing to myself, I follow her up the stairs, where her wide, hazel eyes scan around the room slowly, stopping on each and every thing that graces my walls. My fireplace still simmering with red-hot coals. The glass door that leads to that balcony we saw from below. My bed, situated on a sprawling, four-post frame I made myself when I was twenty years old.

She smiles at everything as if she didn't almost die a million times in the last twenty-four hours. As if the way she sacrificed herself—fully believing she would perish despite all my attempts to beg her to reconsider—means nothing.

And now my anger simmers, bubbling along my spine as I watch her take everything in, clad in that green dress that I want to rip off her body.

She's fascinated with my things, and I'm fascinated by her. And we're finally alone.

Together.

She's alive, I repeat to myself for the hundredth time. A breathing, walking, talking, deliciously-sweet-smelling human right in front of me.

But I almost lost her so many times.

Saskia whips around like the fury in me lashed out and twisted her body to face me.

The chain around her neck snakes down to where the vial rests between her breasts. I have a hard time tearing my eyes away. They're even better in person than the hazy images through our mind-to-mind connection. Her curves look like they were made for my hands, which flex in response.

For a second, I crave her voice in my head, but *this*? Having her in the flesh, wondering what she's thinking, deciphering her feelings from the expression she wears? This is so much better, because I realize I still know her without having to read her mind.

"What's wrong?" she asks, voice low, one eyebrow hitched. Almost like she senses my battle of pleasure and displeasure pressing in from all sides, and it exhilarates her.

"What's *wrong?*" I repeat. "You almost died. You should be *dead.*"

"But I'm not," she counters.

A growl rises in my throat. I take a step toward her, clenching my fists to stop myself from running my fingers along her smooth skin, from feeling her heartbeat thump under my palm.

I can hear it though—that uptick of excitement racing beneath her sternum, thanks to my exceptional hearing. I pause to take it in, listening closely to the flooding adrenaline rhythmically pumping through her heart.

With a sly smile, Saskia takes a half-step back like this is a game to her. Her back hits my dresser, sending a vibrating thud through the wall. Her hands wrap around the edge, her knuckles going white as she grips it hard.

"You didn't listen," I shoot back. "Running around that palace like you're invincible. You had me worried out of my goddamn mind. And when that *vampire* had his hands on you, I didn't know what he was going to do to you. He was *this* close, Saskia." I take another step into her, crowding around her and caging her with my arms. I drop my voice to a gravelly whisper next to her ear and watch goosebumps pebble along her neck where my words land. "And that made me feel like a helpless fucking *animal.*"

When I pull back to look at her, Saskia's eyes twinkle. Her pupils expand.

The warmth from her body curls around me like a trap, even though she's the one who couldn't squirm out of the position I have her in—if she wanted to.

I tip my head down, hovering my mouth over hers. Baring my canines only elicits a thrill, not fear, in her eyes.

She tilts her chin up. And after a sharp inhale that tugs at my lips, she breathes out, "So, punish me then."

SASKIA

My gasp sticks in my lungs as Lucan drags one finger from my cleavage to my feet with lightning speed.

I blink, and my dress falls to the floor—like he sliced right through it with ease.

But when I inspect his index finger, it looks human. Although his hands are larger than any man's I've ever witnessed before.

His eyes rove down my body, now only clad in undergarments, with a hunger that makes me feel more exposed and vulnerable than ever. My eyes drop to make sure my skin is even still intact, but there's not a single mark on me.

Now I can't keep the grin off my face, the rush pulsing through my body. In another lifetime, I'd have been terrified.

But this? This menace of a male towering over me, looking so fearsome despite the fact that I know he'd never hurt me? It just makes me pulse between my legs.

Lucan crouches and gathers the fabric he's torn to shreds into his arms before he calmly walks over to the fireplace and throws my dress into the simmering coals. Right before my eyes, the fabric catches fire and flames crackle to life.

When he turns back to me, a look of depraved satisfaction twists across his face. "You're not wearing anything else picked out by any more Guardians ever again."

I nod, my body suddenly aching to obey him just from the tone of his voice.

He cocks his head, eyes dark. "You want to follow orders now, little nightmare?"

A small smile plays on my lips as I consider it, make him wait for my answer. Back in the palace, I was in charge of myself, with other people counting on me. The thought of how I failed at saving them makes the smile slip off my face just as quickly. I failed, and just for one night, here in this bedroom, I don't want to have to take control anymore. I need someone I trust to take charge—of my body, of my mind, of my soul.

I nod.

"Fair warning..." Lucan's eyes gleam. "I don't know how to *not* be intense."

I nod again, eager to experience it *all*. "I know."

I think it's my favorite thing about him—how he's just himself.

He inhales through his nose, steps closer, and wraps his hand around the vial again.

I stay still despite the tingle that connects down my spine. His presence fills my mind again, silently this time, like a dark shadow exploring every recess and trying to find something.

Understanding settles into me. *I'm* not *in pain,* I insist.

A satisfied smile spreads across his lips before he releases the necklace and his two enormous hands drop to my hips, his thumbs digging into the lace of my underwear that skims across my skin.

Like I'm weightless, he lifts me onto his large dresser. Sitting, I still don't even reach him eye to eye.

"Lean back," he commands.

I place my hands down flat on the cool wood and rest my weight on my arms.

He smirks. "Better. Now show me where you want me to touch you."

Using my pinky, I trace my top and bottom lip before I gather all my courage and drop a hand down my body, caressing over my bra and underwear. Honestly, there's nowhere I *don't* want him to touch me. His eyes spark as he watches the path I take. Then he drags his gaze back to mine.

"I can't stop thinking," he whispers, glancing uncontrollably down to my lips, "about that dream."

"Where you kissed me?" I ask with a small smile. I've been pushing away the details of my most recent nightmare, but the way he brought his mouth to mine is the one thing that keeps brimming to the surface of my mind. I never saw his face in that dream, but I felt his lips, and when I woke up, it felt too soon. Like I would long for that kind of touch from him again for the rest of my life.

"But it wasn't real." Lucan pauses, stepping between my desperately widening thighs.

His presence is all-consuming. The way he fits his body between my legs overwhelms my senses. The smell of him, the feel of him, the raw power that emanates from him.

In a fury, his lips press into mine.

The world melts away, and it's just us enduring a frantic storm. Hard. Soft. Nips. Licks.

A real kiss. Frenetic. Starved.

I part my lips, and his tongue fights against mine, both of us eager to taste each other. And fuck, how good he tastes. Like a dark, sweet cherry on the precipice of bursting.

Running my hands through his hair, I claw him into me. If there's any space left between us, I want it gone. Now.

Lucan groans into my mouth, a rough sound that travels through my core, as he grinds his hips. His erection rakes against my clit with a desperation I've never had the pleasure of experiencing. I've never felt so wanted. So free. So wild and crazed. This is pure desire. Pure lov—lust. And I'm a whimpering mess to prove it.

Reaching behind my back, I try to unclasp my bra, but Lucan bites my bottom lip, sending a zing down my spine, and takes both of my wrists in one hand.

Chest heaving, he pulls back with a fiery look. "I don't think so. That's mine to remove. And burn."

His finger swipes at the center of my bra, and it miraculously pops open just like my dress.

I crash my mouth back to his and bite just as hard as he did—maybe harder—into his full lip. Matching his intensity, I squeeze my thighs around his waist. The bitter taste of his blood coats my tongue as I run it over his bottom lip, and my hips squirm against his erection, aching for more friction.

"Fuck," Lucan growls into my mouth before he plants kisses across my collarbone, down my sternum, until his face settles between where my bra hangs sliced open. "I'm not going to survive you."

He tightens his grip on my wrists, pulls down hard to pin my arms. The pressure against my shoulders builds even more heat through my already ignited nerves. My head falls back as a lustful sigh escapes my lips.

"You like the pain, don't you?" he teases me, running a flat tongue between my breasts. "When it's just enough." I nod. "It makes you feel alive."

"Yes," I murmur in confession, my cheeks heating. Maybe I shouldn't be so turned on by it, but I have no control over my body. Maybe Lucan isn't as into it as I am.

But then I forget my doubts as soon as Lucan takes my nipple in his mouth. I moan when he applies light pressure at first, a suction that makes me see stars dart across the ceiling. And then I gasp when his teeth sink into my sensitive skin, positive he loves this just as much as I do.

"Good girl," Lucan coos, circling his tongue to soothe the sting and switching sides. "I want to make you feel alive. I want to be the one that rips you to pieces and the one to put you back together again." His free hand trails along my underwear, rolling over the wet spot that's growing with each word that leaves his mouth.

As soon as he lets my arms free, my hand rests against the back of his head as he looks down, both of us fixated on his thumb running over my clit.

"Lucan," I whimper, out of my mind with bliss.

"Watch closely, Saskia," he says, the amber in his eyes liquid when he locks them with mine. One finger slips under the lace separating us, and before I can blink, a claw tears through the fabric and slashes up to the elastic below my belly button. I suck in a breath. And then he retracts it as quickly as it appeared.

Lucan uses both of his human hands to rip it the rest of the way off before he slides my bra straps down my arms and pulls all of the remaining fabric away from my skin. He turns back to the fire and tosses my undergarments into it, where my dress is already a mixture of green and black and white ash.

His smile flickers wickedly, an orangish glow from the fire reflecting off his face, making his amber eyes spark. "Now there's nothing left of that wretched place."

With that, he spins on a heel back to me, where I'm fully naked now in front of him with only the red-vialed necklace on. Perched on a wooden dresser, panting.

"Spread your legs for me," he commands.

I don't hesitate, even though the action feels so vulnerable. Completely exposed to him in every way possible, I watch as he sinks to his knees before me, positioning his head right between them, and stares at me. Then his eyes flick up to my face, where he locks his gaze with mine and slowly drags his tongue up my center.

My heart nearly bursts out of my chest at the new sensation, and I writhe with a moan, but Lucan just pins my thighs to the dresser with punishing force and continues licking.

"Fuck," he groans against me. Into me. "I *am* a monster. I could ravage you forever and it would never be enough."

Please do. I don't want this torture to end, I think, almost startled that his response doesn't materialize in my brain.

He pulls away from me, lips already glistening from my arousal. "Are you ready to learn a new word, Saskia?"

"A new word?" I repeat, my mind buzzing and confused.

"Yes. This..." He drags his tongue back up my center again, then nips at my clit until I gasp, my back arching. "Is your perfect pussy. And I am going to devour it until your throat turns raw from screaming. Do you understand?"

"Yes," I whimper, clutching the edge of the furniture with piercing fingernails.

"Up," he says, taking a step back.

Mind thrumming with anticipation, my body listens instantly, sliding off the dresser and trembling to a stand.

Lucan is in front of me before I can take in a breath. His rough, warm hands roam my curves, over my breasts, down my hips, across my hips, and then dip between my legs to my... pussy. My legs almost give out when one of his fingers skims through my arousal.

I gather my courage and slip my hands into his shirt. His plane of a chest is like a wall in its own right. Hard angles, rigid lines. Grabbing the hem of his shirt, I push it up higher. Little squares, two on top of two on top of two appear on his stomach, and my mouth drops open, practically salivating.

"Are these your *abdominal muscles*?" I marvel.

"Yes," he chuckles. "Abs."

"Oh..." No one in Xantera is given enough time to ever tone *these*. "I want to see the rest of you," I whisper, standing on my tiptoes to try and get Lucan's shirt off his enormous frame.

"Not yet." He grinds his palm into my clit as his other hand snakes around my throat. With the gentlest of squeezes, he maneuvers me until my legs hit the bed frame. A smirk forms on his lips before he kisses my pout, much too lightly. "You haven't earned it yet, baby. Not until you scream my name."

Then I'm falling back against the soft mattress, surrounded by the pine scent of Lucan's sheets.

"Lie there," he instructs me, "and I'm going to show you exactly what you've been missing." He drops to his knees again like he's about to pray. "They took away every pleasure in the world from you. And it's only fitting that I'm the one to give it back."

I crane my neck to look at him down the length of my body. His face is hovering so close to me, I can feel his breath against my searing skin. His pupils are so blown, I can't tell where his irises start. I shimmy, trying to reach him, trying to feel his tongue on me again.

Lucan pulls back a millimeter for every one that I get closer. When I let out a frustrated huff, he chuckles darkly.

"But only if you're good for me." His eyes bore into mine, as if trying to drill in the memories of all the ways I disobeyed him in the Blood Moon Palace. "Say it."

"I'll be good. I promise," I reply too quickly, no longer caring what I have to do to get that damned mouth back on me.

"Such a greedy little thing," he murmurs happily before working his lips and tongue up my inner thigh. That word—greed—has always felt like a transgression, such a break of the Cardinal Rules. But with Lucan, here, right now, it feels undeniably *right*. "You're going to let me protect you? Keep you safe?" I nod, fisting the sheets as he rewards me with a swirl of his tongue. "You're going to give me all of your depraved thoughts? Secrets?"

"Yes," I breathe out.

"No more walls," Lucan demands, pressing his middle finger into me. "No more rules."

I almost cry out from that alone. How a single finger of his could fill me this much has sent me into other-worldly delusion.

"Fucking hell, baby." He drags it out. In. Curls. "So wet for me. So sweet. Can you take two?"

"Lucan," I plead. "Yes."

Yes. Yes. *Yes*. I could say that one word forever and never tire of it.

Another finger slides in, stretching me perfectly.

His tongue drags across my clit, and this time, he doesn't stop. His fingers and lips and tongue and teeth all work in tandem, building pressure and pleasure, mixing hints of pain and ache.

Lucan's rough hums vibrate against me, adding to every one of my electrified senses. My fingers braid through his hair. My hips grind unapologetically against his face.

Higher and higher, I keep climbing, to a point I never thought was possible. Where I don't have to do it myself. Where the man kneeling before me can't get enough of *me*.

He smiles between my legs, a dark, villainous, upward tilt of his lips that has me falling.

"Come for me, little nightmare. Show everyone how good the Monster devours his prey."

I scream his name.

Until I see black.

"I have no clothes now," I sigh.

It's been over fifteen minutes since Lucan crawled up my body, lay beside me, and let me collapse onto his chest to recover.

Now, he lets his eyes roam hungrily up and down my naked body, gleaming with flickering firelight. "I can't say I'm bothered by that predicament."

"You're going to keep me naked forever?" I raise a playful eyebrow. "Let your friends see me like this?"

I mean it as a joke, but a vicious growl rips from Lucan's throat, and in one fluid motion, he flips me around onto my stomach and straddles my thighs. "I don't share when it comes to you."

His erection—disappointingly still in his pants—digs into me while one of his enormous palms skates down the groove of my spine.

"Well, I can't stay in your bedroom forever," I taunt, eager to explore this possessive side of him... but also testing to see what his possessiveness looks like. Will he lock me away in the same way Arad did, keeping me from the rest of the world?

"You can stay in this bedroom forever if you want," Lucan begins slowly. "Forget everything and let me worship your body for the rest of our lives." He pauses, brushing his lips down the same path his hand just took. "Or you can run far away from here, wander and explore the world you never had the chance to know. But if you do run away, Saskia, mark my words." From the corner of my eye, I see his expression darken. "I will chase you. I will catch you. And I will continue to worship you." He lets out a breath against my spine. "But it's your choice where that takes place. In here or out there or anywhere in between."

My chest squeezes with the significance of those words. Before I can form an adequate response, the weight of his body releases me as he plants both of his feet on the floor.

"Where are you going?" I turn my head and settle my other cheek down against the mattress.

He opens the door next to the bed to reveal a closet, showcasing a variety of female clothes. Brown and black pants, cotton shirts, leather jackets, elaborate dresses, and simple dresses all hang from hangers in two deep rows. After a jolt of unease, I remember how he told Vivian to fetch me some outfits and marvel at how quickly she followed his command.

"Do you..." I clear my throat. "Do you control your pack like how you controlled me in the bathtub?" A flush crawls up my neck at the memory, but the answer feels important, somehow.

Lucan turns to look at me, cocking his head at the warmth in my face. "No. What I did to you in the bathtub was more of a strong, *strong* suggestion. Since you were willing, I was able to guide your hands exactly where I wanted them, but it wasn't actual control. Trust me, little nightmare." His jaw tenses. "If I could truly take over someone's willpower, I would have made Arad slit his own throat every time he put that necklace on."

The air chills at his words, and I shiver as I remember how he threatened to battle me for my own mind to keep me out of trouble in the Blood Moon Palace. He seems to track my trail of thoughts now and massages his temples.

"It was an empty threat, and I never should have made it. I was just so pissed off and terrified that you were going to get hurt, I thought maybe I could accomplish the impossible and force you to change your mind. But in the end..." He lifts his head back up. "What you do with your free will is why I l..." He trails off and restarts. "It's what makes you you. Even with my pack members, I have no desire to actually take control like that."

"But they still follow your commands?" I ask carefully, curious.

"Yes. They can't disobey a direct order of mine unless they're willing to fight me, but I can't actually dictate their muscles like they're puppets—not that Vivian would even *want* to disobey any request involving clothes." He chuckles and gestures at the various items. "Which one do you want to wear?"

"Oh." I blink at the closet. "I can pick?"

His amber eyes burn into mine. "Of course. You have a choice here, Saskia."

"Oh," I say again, blushing at how stupid I sound, even to my own ears. "Okay, well..." I pass over the elaborate dresses with a shudder. I never want to wear something so extravagant again. And the simple pants and shirt remind me too much of living in the city of Xantera, forced to wear the same thing day after day. Instead, my eyes flutter to a simple white slip with thin, lacy straps. It reminds me of my nightgowns, free and flowing.

I've always felt most comfortable in the night, anyway.

"That one," I say confidently, nodding at it.

Lucan doesn't need to be told twice. He maneuvers himself back on top of me, slipping the silk fabric over my head. Then he carefully pulls my arms through, and before he pulls it down over my hips, he bites my glute gently, sending a flurry of butterfly wings through me.

He bends down, the front of his body flush with my back, and brushes my hair away from my neck.

"Okay?" he asks after he kisses me below my ear.

I nod into the mattress. "Okay."

"Good. So now that you have clothes—" He flips me over, runs his hands down my waist, and scrunches his nose in disappointment. "—what else do you choose?"

My desire blooms from the deepest part of my heart, desperate to fill in the blanks, settle the internal debate of my imagination.

"I choose you. And I want to see you..." I trail off, running the tips of my fingers underneath his own clothes to get a taste.

Lucan pulls his shirt off the rest of the way, and my mouth can't keep up with my brain. If I had known that *this* was on the receiving end of the necklace all along, I probably would have been too busy salivating and stumbling over my words to even get to know him. So I'm glad I didn't. I'm glad we got to know each other mind-to-mind before we finally get to explore each other body-to-body.

Now, I want him in every possible way I can have him. My heart thrums. My greedy hands explore everywhere. But a seed of doubt still lingers in the back of my mind, as if the male before me can't possibly be the same one who helped me through the catacombs or listened to me talk about my mother or helped me through my last nightmare.

So before I have him this way, I want one more thing.

"I want to see you in your other form. As the Monster," I amend.

For a moment, Lucan goes rigid, staring at me as if I've just uttered some kind of curse—or prayer. I wish I could read the thoughts racing through his mind right now, but I won't be able to. We won't be connected in that way again unless he shifts.

In a flash, Lucan grabs both of my wrists and pins them above my head. His nose hovers inches from mine.

"Are you sure?" he asks, voice dangerously low.

"Of course." The synapses of my brain snap insatiably as I press my lips to his, then trail across his jaw and down the corded muscles of his neck. I stop over his pulse and nibble his hot skin. "The monster in you is the same monster in me."

And I need to finally face the beast we were always taught to fear.

Lucan nods, then drags me off the bed. "Outside."

"Why?" I protest helplessly around a laugh, even as a bolt of exhilarated fear shoots through me when he tucks me into his chest with that strength I can't comprehend.

"You'll see," he warns.

Once he deposits me barefoot on the soft ground somewhere on the outskirts of the ghost town, the nip of fresh, chilled air shocks me to my core. It's so much more... free here. A soft breeze invigorates my senses, waking up every nerve in my body that isn't already ignited as it whistles through tree branches.

Lucan backs up, and my excitement simmers within me. I wrap a tight fist around the vial of my necklace. Waiting.

He stares as if testing me. Like he's waiting for me to change my mind.

But after a few long ticks, Lucan's shoulders jerk. Every part of him elongates right in front of my eyes: his spine, his arms, his legs. Coarse, dark fur sprouts all along his body, intercepted with streaks of golden brown, just like his hair, and his ears rise until they're two sharp spikes on top of his head, just like horns. His mouth widens, more canines ripping from his gums, his nose melting into a snout. Even more muscles swell, bulging from arms that hit the ground like anchors, massive claws tearing into the ground at our feet.

He has similar features to a... a dog, but everything is so much bigger, deadlier, more monstrous. Not something that would fit within the confines of a house, that's for sure.

But not a Monster, I decide. I just have no other word for him.

A werewolf, he says into my mind, the electricity connecting our brains snapping into place as soon as his shift is complete.

A werewolf.

I repeat the word in my head again. It's fitting.

Keeping myself rooted to the spot as I suck in lungfuls of air, my head snaps back to take in the sheer size of him now. His lupine face stares back at me, amber eyes glowing in the dark, assessing, waiting for me to make a judgment. Letting me process.

This.

This is the dark shadow of my nightmares, finally stepping into the light of the moon. This is what the Guardians always said they were protecting us from. This is the beast they said was starved for meat and bone. *Beware its eyes. Resist its howl.*

But I'm looking him dead in the eyes.

And I can't resist him any longer.

As much as this form of his should terrify me, it doesn't. So finally, I take a single step toward him and place a palm in the center of his chest.

The werewolf—Lucan—visibly relaxes at my touch.

You're not scared? he asks me mentally, while a low growl rumbles from his real throat.

"Of course not," I reply out loud, even though my chest feels like it's hammering once again. But not from fear. No, something about having this massive, monstrous creature before me fills my body with a delicious rush of adrenaline.

Lucan's maw twists into a smile, sensing what I want. What I need.

Then run, little nightmare.

LUCAN

Her heartbeat creates an intoxicating mix of devious frisson, but she doesn't hesitate.

She bursts into a run, heading for the trees, and I have to physically restrain myself from immediately lunging after her and pinning her down.

But no, not in the light of the other houses where everyone is probably peeking through their curtains. I told Saskia I don't share, and I mean it.

Ten... nine... eight... I count out, and she picks up her pace with a shriek. The pads of her feet make little thuds against the packed earth, faster than I could have anticipated.

Only a ten-second head start? Not fair, she argues through heavy inhales and exhales.

Pausing, I let her buy a few extra seconds. She takes one last look at me over her shoulder, her gorgeous red hair blowing in the wind like she belongs here, before she disappears into the tree line.

I know these woods like the back of my hand. There's nowhere she can hide that I won't find her. Between my sense of hearing and my sense of smell, she'll be able to evade me for a few minutes tops.

But the chase is half the fun.

And judging by the electricity in her veins, she thinks it's more than half.

Seven... six... five...

Lucan! she shouts indignantly, but I can sense the laugher, the exhilaration, in her head, too. Her thoughts bounce from large bushes to hollow logs to climbing trees, trying to decide the best course of action.

That's cute that you think you can hide.

No cheating, she protests. *You can't read my mind.*

I don't need to... four. Both of our heartbeats tick up together at the increased anticipation. I dig my claws into the earth, aching to get my hands on her. I should have had Vivian bring two of every piece of clothing for when I inevitably rip this dress off as well. *What do I win when I catch you?*

I think we both win, she says slyly.

Wicked thoughts replace her previous ones, her smile stretching through my chest.

Three... I whisper.

Two... she whispers.

I crouch down, the shadow of my hulking form growing smaller.

Get ready, baby. Your punishment isn't over.

One... we whisper together.

Then I erupt with a howl at the moon—and pounce.

SASKIA

The thump of my own footsteps rattles through my bones as I push aside branches and leap over fallen logs, but I don't slow down—not because I'm afraid of Lucan, but because I'm *free*.

I've never had the privilege of pushing my body to this limit before. Never felt my lungs burn like this. Even when I used to exercise at the Recreation Center, the movement was stiff and practiced, but this... this air cutting against my cheeks and adrenaline shooting through my veins—it's wild and chaotic and beautiful.

And when Lucan howls, I almost do, too.

His presence doesn't just chase after me. It surrounds me. I feel him in every shadow between tree trunks, in the way my hair lashes past my shoulders. Every rustle of the forest has me whipping my head up, my heart ticking as my imagination blooms with all the possibilities. The wind whistles through the trees, creating moving shapes with tricks of moonlight through the leaves.

Scared? Lucan taunts through our connection, the pounding of his chase somehow behind me and in front of me and around me all at the same time.

I laugh through the heaviness of my breaths. *You'll have to try a lot harder than this to scare me, Monster.* In fact, this might be the best nightmare I've ever had. I'm *relishing* in it, waiting for his claws to reach out and snare me.

Over here, he murmurs, and a branch snaps to my right.

I stop short, panting and nearly doubling over. But when I turn, there's nothing there.

Behind you.

Whipping around, again—nothing.

I blink… until Lucan's monstrous shadow steps out between two trees in the distance. With the moonlight shining through the fog, I can't make out anything other than his outline and the piercing glare of his yellow eyes glowing in the dark.

My thoughts aren't coherent, bouncing from incomplete ideas to unformed sentences. His mind twists with mine, and I can't grasp on to anything concrete except the enormous pull between us. The craving. The eagerness. The ache. The both of us trying to climb right into the other's reality. I want to keep running away from him and run *to* him at the same time.

Giving up so soon? he asks, and I can practically hear the wicked smile in his voice.

Hardly. I stand firm, refusing to back away even an inch. *I'm just weighing my options.*

Which are?

Fight, flight, or freeze, basically. But they all end the same way.

A low, hungry growl permeates the dark. *Which is?*

I can't think anymore, my brain conjuring up images instead—lewd, filthy ones that set Lucan over the edge.

With a ravenous snarl, he lunges again... but this time his shadow shifts as he does.

His coat disappears. His torso shrinks. His strong jaw and handsome face return, his body morphing from hulking to upright—all in the span of yards as he barrels toward me.

I grin, and just for the hell of it, whip around and break into another run.

He closes the distance in a few strides, snaking two long arms around my waist from behind me. I shriek. He lifts me off my feet, and then the world spins and tilts and I'm suddenly on my back. Pinned to the forest floor so quickly and painlessly I didn't process the landing.

"Got you," he says, capturing my wrists and locking them above my head.

"You got me," I repeat in a whisper.

The hairs on my arms straighten as goosebumps crawl along my skin. His warmth is magnified, and wrapping my legs around his hips, I pull him closer, heart melting, trying to get him to put his full weight on me.

Clarity starts to return for a moment.

Ferns encircle us, closing us in. Treetops fold over each other, layers and layers of leaves blocking out the night sky except for one slice where a full moon hovers above us. Am I monstrous for wanting this right here, right now? Out in the open, on the forest floor?

"Eyes on me," Lucan says, bringing my attention back to his face. "Right here is perfect. And inside of you is going to be my new favorite place." He drags his canines across the shell of my ear, then pulls my earlobe into his mouth and sinks his teeth into it.

I gasp, the reality of the forest melting away until it's just him and me.

Lucan hums in appreciation, then lets his lips roam down my neck, nibbling and sucking.

"I've scoured your mind," he says against my throat, "but I still have so many things to discover about your body. Like where I can put my tongue to drag the loudest gasp from you. Or which position is your favorite. Or how hard your legs will shake when you come..." Before I can voice my confusion, Lucan chuckles against my skin, applying pressure against me with his hard length. "On my *cock*."

A moan rattles up my throat at the word, how exhilarating it makes me feel. One of Lucan's hands skates down my sternum. My hips press up. His press down, his erection pressing right up against where I burn for him.

I try to squirm against him to get more friction, but he shakes his head with a devious grin and peels himself away, hovering over me.

"You're going to make me suffer?" I breathe out.

He presses his lips to mine, then dips his mouth to the low neckline of my slip and pulls it down with his teeth. "Only the best kind. Besides, gentle isn't in my nature."

A bolt of electricity shoots down to my belly button when Lucan swirls his tongue over my nipples, teasing me as he switches back and forth.

"More," I beg, even though that's always been against the Cardinal Rules, to want more.

But Lucan's eyes burst with pride for voicing what I want. "You deserve it all."

And yet, he still takes his time: edging the hem of my new dress up to my waist, biting into my hip, swiping his tongue in one long drag up me.

I arch into him and reach for his pants, eager for him to bare everything to me, but he pins my arms by my side with a click of his tongue and straightens on his knees.

"You're going to watch, Saskia," he says, unbuttoning his pants, the zipper following torturously slowly, "as I ravage you. No touching me yet. I won't be able to focus with your hands on me. You understand?"

I swallow thickly and nod, nearly out of mind when he reaches into his pants and pulls out his erection.

My mouth waters, imagining my lips wrapped around his shaft, my own tongue teasing the head.

"Let me taste you," I plead.

Lucan strokes himself, eyes blazing as they bounce between my mouth and lower down, where my dress has tangled up around my knees, exposing me. And then his lips curl.

"Not yet." Dragging the head of his cock through my arousal, he lets out a harsh breath. "Fuck. You're so perfectly wet for me, Saskia."

A sharp flame of pure need singes up my spine. "Lucan," I whimper.

"Say it," he rasps. "Say you want the Monster to fuck you."

I can hardly get the words out as he presses his tip against me. "I want the Monster to fuck me."

"Good girl."

Then he drives into me, punishing me with one long stroke without letting me adjust to his size. His hips slam into mine just as my gasp echoes through the forest, and my entire body rages like a wildfire.

"I was right." Lucan holds himself there, his expression crumpling as if the bliss borders on the point of pain. His eyes fasten to where we're joined, the gold in his irises molten. Finally he begins to move, his pupils simultaneously eternally satisfied and hungrier than ever. "My. New. Favorite. Place," he says with a harsh thrust between each word.

Breaths are forced from my lungs. All my senses heighten. Inhaling sharply at the pressure, I arch my back, trying to somehow get closer to him when he's *inside* of me, all the way to the hilt. The intensity on his face makes me want to reach up and trace every line of his desire etched into it, grab fistfuls of his hair, and feel his heartbeat under my palm.

But I obey him and keep my arms above my head, because no touching. That's one rule I can follow. For now.

Lucan's thumb drags quick circles over my clit, and the sensation blinds me. Stars flicker in my vision, and heat builds in my core.

Lucan increases his pace until my legs shake uncontrollably.

"Come on my cock, baby."

With wild moans that carry on the wind, my entire body obeys, shuddering through shockwave after shockwave as I clench around him.

When I go still, Lucan slips out of me slowly, but I'm quickly using the opportunity to wrap my palm around him. The weight of him in my hand. The heat against my skin. The massive size of him.

It all makes me want to wrestle back control.

Releasing a little pressure, I glide my hand up and down his shaft, using soft strokes at first. Then I grip him firmer, smiling at the way Lucan's chest heaves and his abs contract.

He groans when I run my thumb over his head and through the pre-cum beading there before following with my tongue. The deep sound shoots through my core, but Lucan's eyes shoot open.

"Teasing me?" he chuckles. His left eyebrow curves upward along with his smirk. "You *want* to suffer, don't you?"

I nod honestly, my heartbeat stuttering as it waits for my next welcome punishment. With hope in my chest, I part my lips expectantly, but Lucan only chuckles darkly.

"I'm not going to come in your mouth the first time, Saskia," he tells me plainly.

Suddenly, he flips me over, maneuvering my body however he wants with ease. On all fours, I spread my legs for him, desperate for him to be inside me again.

Thankfully, he doesn't waste time.

His cock fills me again, pressing against me with shallow pumps of his hips, until he can't take the slow pace anymore.

His fingers twist into the roots of my hair, before he wraps his palm with the strands of my hair—once, twice.

He tugs my head back, forcing me to look up at the treetops and night sky. Even though he's not entirely gentle, a content sigh leaves my lungs.

"That's it," he coos, his lips against my ear. "You love it when you're mine, don't you?"

I try to nod but his grip is so tight on the roots of my hair, my head can't move.

"Yes," I pant, as my body heaves forward from the force. "I'm yours."

My hips grind back, chasing the orgasm he's building, like the electricity that usually joins us is overflowing beneath my skin.

"Are you going to come with me, Saskia?" he asks, voice low.

But he doesn't need an answer.

His hand settles around my neck, squeezes slightly, as he turns sloppy and his fingers find my clit. Instantly, the pleasure stacks on top of itself, shooting up my core, from each sensation where Lucan is connected to me in some way.

The rhythm becomes chaotic as we both moan out each other's names into the dark. The pleasure building becomes other-worldly, out-of-body, almost as if it's too perfect, too right, too *every-thing*. And maybe I wasn't meant to ever find it, and the Wall was merely a barrier to prevent this cataclysm from ever happening—a higher power interfering, like always. Because how can I feel this *much*?

"I've been starved of you for centuries, little nightmare," Lucan rasps.

And then he sinks his canines into my shoulder, and we both unravel together, like the threads of the very universe coming un-done.

We're still lying here silently over half an hour later, curled into each other and watching the moon through the treetops as the dark clouds drift by.

Every second that ticks by is just one more moment that reality doesn't creep back into our lives. But even when you delay it, time always has a way of yanking off the wool you've put in front of your eyes. Ignorance isn't bliss forever.

So when Lucan finally scoops me off the forest floor, my body spent and poorly fighting sleep, I manage to whisper, "We still need to save Xantera."

I expect him to say we can't. I failed to get the key from Arad, and our method of communicating to those within the Wall still hangs around my neck. There's no way to know if Eleni and Claudia followed through with the plan.

Maybe seconds or minutes go by until I'm deposited onto his soft bed and tucked beneath the blankets. I squint up at Lucan, my vision hazy with exhaustion.

"I know," he finally answers instead, dropping a kiss on my forehead. "And we will."

LUCAN

S askia's even breathing fills my bedroom, and I feel like my chest fully expands for the first time in more than two hundred years as I gaze down at her, her hair already splayed across my pillow. Some deep, primal part of me swells with satisfaction at the fact that her scent is already infusing my room, mingling with mine. Marking us as each other's.

Something else lingers beneath her strawberries and roses smell, though, something I can't put my finger on. My lips curl down in a frown as I inhale, trying to pinpoint what it is, exactly.

She survived the fall off the Wall. She's unharmed. Breathing with a relatively normal beating heart. Safe in *my* bed, in *my* arms.

Yet the hint of something foreign lurks in her veins, right beneath her own scent. A smell of putrid, rotten decay. Like impending death, but—no. That doesn't make sense, dammit. She's got ten more years before she fully turns to stone. Ten more years to share my bed. Ten more years to explore and learn and experience and live.

And yet...

I glance out my window, where I'm sure my packmates are lying awake in bed, waiting for me to explain what the hell is going on, just as Taika said. But I meant it when I said they could wait. For now, I'm not going to let myself slip into dreams when my dream come true is right here, right now, sleeping peacefully under my gaze. What if she has another nightmare?

Or what if, a less rational part of my brain demands, *Arad comes to steal her in the night?*

It must be his venom that I'm smelling. A part of *him* inside *her*. My veins pop, my jaw ticking, and my hands close into clawed fists. The thought of that alone fuels me with enough anger to tear down my own house brick by brick... but I hold myself back, just so I don't wake her.

No. She's *mine*, and I won't let his lingering presence taint that.

But still, I stare down at her, watching her eyelashes flutter as she dreams, and I do not sleep.

All night.

SASKIA

The next morning, I wake up to a new sound.

Not the grating voice of the robotic female on the loud-speakers or the heavy press of silence in the palace, but *music*.

When I peel my eyes open, it's to find a few bluebirds hopping on the sills outside Lucan's window, twittering at us through the glass. Sunlight streams onto the bed, where Lucan and I lie inter-twined, my head on his chest and legs wrapped around his.

And his amber eyes already open, staring down at me.

"Good morning, little nightmare," he says in a rumbling voice that feels like it travels all the way down every point where our skin makes contact.

"Good morning," I breathe back, instantly flushing with heat when I remember last night. I give a little laughing cough and add, "So much for you sleeping on the floor."

"You want me on the floor," he growls, nipping at my shoulder again, stroking his tongue along the marks his canines left last night, "then I'll get on the floor. You want me between your legs, I'll get between your legs. You tell me where to go—either away from you or inside you—and I will obey. Whatever you want to do, I will oblige."

I marvel at the ripple of his muscles as he lifts himself onto an elbow to look at me, at the way his bed frame groans every time his weight shifts even slightly. This behemoth of a male is saying he'll obey *me*. It inflates me with a sense of power I've never felt before, and I bite my bottom lip, thinking about all the things I could make him do.

"Hmmm. I think I want—"

A sharp rap against the door cuts me off.

"Hey, you two love kittens! We're going to go hunt for some breakfast. Want to join?"

Lucan freezes, his entire countenance shifting from adoration to overflowing rage. I have a feeling the term "kitten" is even more offensive to him than all the other curse words combined.

"Why the *fuck* are you in my house right now, Soren?"

"Oh, it's not just me," Soren calls through the peeling wood of the door. "Vivian and Merrick are here with me." After a stretch of silence, he hisses, "Say something, or it'll seem like I'm lying, you fucking idiots. I swear they're with me. They're right here."

Lucan bounds out of bed and nearly rips the door off its hinges, revealing the two males from last night and the female Vivian standing sheepishly between them.

Merrick runs a hand over his hair and grimaces. "Truthfully, we just wanted to make sure you're both okay. We saw you chasing after her in your werewolf form last night and..."

"Weren't sure in which way you destroyed her," Soren finishes for him, smirking and landing his eyes on me. "Well, hello, beautiful. I'm glad to see you're not—"

He doesn't get to finish that sentence. Lucan slams him against the wall by the top of the stairs, and the force of it breaks open the plaster from behind. I jolt upright, my eyes wide, as Lucan snarls, "Call her beautiful again."

"Can't," Soren gasps, his throat pinned by Lucan's arm. "Not when—you're choking—me."

"Will you two cut it *out*," Vivian cries, and moves to wrench them apart. I'm not sure if she has some kind of incredible superior strength or if Lucan finally snaps back to his senses, but he releases Soren, who hacks at the carpet, a huge grin lighting up his face.

"Oh, you *are* in love. This is an incredible development. Gives me even more motivation to save Xantera so that I can find my own woman..."

Merrick groans. "Soren, if you don't want to be buried next to our ancestors, stop talking for once in your life." He flips his gaze to me and asks softly, "Are you hungry, Saskia?"

I didn't think I was, but my stomach growls in response. Lucan flicks guilty eyes onto me and massages his temples. "You don't need to get out of bed, Saskia. I can bring you something."

"No, I... I want to." I jump to my feet, the covers falling off me, and my head swoons. I must be weaker and hungrier than I realized, but the prospect of hunting for my own food sounds both terrifying and gratifying. My whole life, someone has either delivered my meals to me through a slat in the door or, more recently, brought it to me on a tray while I lay in bed. I want to see where food *comes* from. How to pick it or snare it or whatever else you do to obtain it.

Lucan doesn't protest or try to get me to change my mind, like I halfway expect. He simply scans my body with narrow eyes, as if reassuring himself that my physical state is fine, before nodding. And even though he's not in his other form, I swear I'm getting good at reading his thoughts through the microexpressions on his face.

In this case, he's thinking the same words from earlier: *Whatever you want to do, I will oblige.*

But out loud, he says, "We're usually in our other forms when we hunt. It's faster that way. Easier to catch our prey."

I frown, realizing it might be impossible for me to hunt with them. I'm neither fast nor strong. Just a human with no claws or fangs. I would only hold them back.

But a ghost of a smirk crosses Lucan's face as he steps toward me, the other three forgotten behind him as he cups one of my cheeks with his enormous hand and dips his lips to my ear.

"How would you feel," he whispers, "about riding a werewolf?"

I was wrong, before, when I said running felt like freedom.

This feels like freedom, my hands curled into the mottled brown and gold fur of Lucan's neck, the world blurring past us as he leaps and bounds past trees like he's cutting through butter. My thighs burn from how tightly they clamp around his torso, and my eyes sting with tears from the wind rushing past, but I keep them peeled open so I don't miss a single thing.

Aspen trees melt into pine trees the further northwest we travel, away from the Wall of Xantera and up a mountain ridge where creeks gurgle past us, streaking my periphery with winking silver. The other three—Vivian, Merrick, and Soren—follow behind so that whenever I crane my neck to look back, I can see three pairs of amber eyes squinting up at us, wolflike monsters bounding after us.

In her werewolf form, Vivian is lean but strong, with long limbs that easily keep up with the two males beside her. Her fur is a glossy shade of brown, while Merrick's is black, and Soren's is a golden blonde that gleams in the stripes of sunlight flashing through the trees.

Not that I need to see them to know they're there. Now that they're in their werewolf forms, too, my mind suddenly bursts with their thoughts as well as Lucan's. I'm not sure why they never seemed to be connected when I put the necklace on in Xantera, but now a telepathic connection flows between the five of us like intricate strings of a spider's web dangling from the vial on my chest.

What are we feeling for breakfast this morning, kittens? Soren asks, even his internal voice more flippant and casual than Lucan's deep grumble. *Something cute and fluffy or large and vicious? Or something slimy, maybe?*

For fuck's sake, Lucan growls, and I feel a jolt of pleasure at how familiar the cadence of his tone sounds to my mind in the midst of all this newness. *How do you make every possible food option sound completely inedible?*

Are fish not slimy? Soren protests. *Are bears not vicious? Are bunnies not cute?*

Are you not a moron? Vivian spits back without breaking her stride behind us. *Saskia, do you want to eat a moron for breakfast?*

I laugh against the wind. *I think I'll pass for now.*

'For now' being the key phrase, Soren, Lucan warns. *All Saskia has to do is give me the word.*

Maybe you should direct that murderous energy toward the herd of elk a few miles north of here, Merrick cuts in with a chuckle. *It feels good to be back. I can smell them on the wind.*

Apparently, the others can, too, because they all increase their speed, Lucan remaining in the forefront, and soon the chill of the air nips at my skin as we climb higher and higher.

Are you cold? Lucan asks me as we finally slow, the others slinking to crouches on either side of us, all of them trained on something I can't see through the foliage.

No, I say confidently, even though it takes an effort to keep my teeth from chattering.

Lucan huffs beneath me, unconvinced. *We'll just watch for now. You stay on me and keep warm.*

Nodding my understanding, I bury myself deeper into his fur and peer ahead, waiting for something to happen. Beside us, Vivian, Merrick, and Soren are utterly still, their coats camouflaging into the scenery around us. A twig snaps from somewhere ahead. Branches rustle.

And then it steps into view.

A creature unlike anything I've seen before, not quite the size of Lucan but still huge and majestic, with antlers curling into the air like the branches of a tree and four strong legs that end in hooves. Elk. For some reason, my throat squeezes at the realization that this here is like all the animals I've eaten my whole life, always consuming without ever *knowing.*

Now, I know, though. And when the three other werewolves streak past us to pounce on it, I don't stop my tears from falling at the reverberating thud it makes as it falls, too. The way the sound follows the elk's barking wail of alarm that cuts off abruptly when Soren closes long canines around the animal's throat.

Instantly, jets of the elk's blood soak the pine needles baked into the ground. Lucan shifts beneath me as sharp hunger clamps my stomach, but the thought of eating its actual flesh roils in my stomach and makes my head spin again.

Are you okay? he asks me.

Fine. I gulp. *I just think... maybe I need a minute before I eat this kind of breakfast.*

I can feel the flicker of unease that passes between the four of them. Just as quickly, Lucan's mental presence seems to lift up walls around just him and me, so that the others are blocked out. I'd ask him how he does it if my stomach wasn't roiling. *You don't have to eat the elk, Saskia. We can always find something else.*

No, it's not that. I tighten my grip on his fur, desperately hoping I don't sound ungrateful. *I don't... know, exactly. Maybe I just need something a little lighter.*

Lucan's concern ripples into my mind. *I know a spot where there's a huge patch of blackberries just a few more minutes uphill. Would that—*

Yes, I answer immediately. The thought of rich, dark juice bursting in my mouth rather than the meat of a dead animal... it sounds infinitely better at the moment.

Lucan tears down the mental walls around us long enough to command the others, *Take the elk back home. Prepare it for tonight. I'm going to take Saskia a little further up.*

He shutters them out before they can respond, and we're racing uphill again, just me and him, past the gory scene, over a creek, and into a balder spot of the mountain where the pine trees stand spaced apart from each other like lonely statues. Thorny brambles grow in hordes between them, though, and the air swells with a sweetness as my eyes land on all the clusters of berries hanging from their stems.

I slide off Lucan and lunge for them, my stomach grumbling again. Lucan's chuckle rumbles through me for a moment before the connection between us snaps as he shifts back into his human form and comes up behind me, watching me eat with a curious tilt of his head.

"What?" I demand, whirling toward him, knowing my lips are probably already stained dark blue. "You fucked all the energy out of me last night."

"And you," he says, drifting closer and swiping a thumb along my chin, collecting a drop of juice, "are remarkably good at using curse words for someone who's just learned them."

"What can I say?" I shrug and pluck another blackberry from its stem, popping it into my mouth. "I'm a fast learner."

I'm glad Lucan can't read my mind right now, because behind the smiling shape of my lips, part of my chest is caving in at how right all of this feels—well, besides the dead elk. But the *pack*. The way they're all connected. The way they live, so wild and free and in houses that actually feel like homes. I wish I could truly be a part of it, but I'll never be able to run as fast as them, or hunt something like them, or shift like them, no matter how fast of a learner I try to be.

"It's hard to remember," I continue, turning to view the landscape around us, "the Guardians and what they do to the people in there when you're out *here*. I don't know how you always remembered us." I turn toward him, a pinch of admiration twisting my heart. "How you kept fighting for us when everything is so perfect outside the Wall."

Lucan's amber gaze dips from my eyes to my mouth before flitting back up, contemplative. "There's a place at the top of this mountain, actually, where I go whenever I need a reminder. It's the highest point you can get—even higher than the Wall. High enough to see all of Xantera."

My mouth drops open, and I glance upward. "Really? Can you... can you show me?"

I know, realistically, that I won't be able to see individual people from such a great distance away. Not Malcolm or Gaia, and certainly not Eleni or Claudia trapped within the palace. But even just viewing my old prison from above might help me remember that my fellow humans are trapped, dying, and aren't even aware of it. That we still need to find a way to tear down that wretched Wall. That my mother deserves all the vengeance in the world.

"Of course," Lucan says, his expression inscrutable as he studies me. "Remember, whatever you ask of me..."

Ten minutes later, he's depositing me onto a rounded crown of icy snow, barren of trees but circled by slick black boulders. It truly does seem like the top of the world, because when I sweep my gaze all around me, I can see the rise and fall of the terrain in every direction, silver strings of sparkling water winding among the ravines, and the circular disruption of the land that is Lucan's stolen kingdom.

And when I squint over the spikes of the Wall...

Even with my human eyes, I can see the bustling dots of people in the streets—not walking in orderly fashion like normal, but swarming, converging like ants attacking each other. Even though I can't hear them, I swear the wind carries a faint note of screaming.

And flames—those are *flames*, licking toward the sky from various buildings.

"Xantera," I gasp as Lucan goes stone-still beside me. But I can't get the rest of the words out, because I don't know if it means hope or the destruction of everyone in that city. All I know is that Claudia and Eleni must have succeeded in getting incriminating evidence onto everyone's screens in their housing units.

The people of Xantera are rioting.

I cling to Lucan's fur as he barrels back toward town, summoning all of the remaining pack to shift.

One by one, their presences coil through me. Flooding my nervous system, I can tell every werewolf carries a unique feeling, like a mental fingerprint, but it's hard to pick out who's who without knowing them.

One hour, Lucan tells them. *Pack meeting.*

Their thoughts go haywire before Lucan shutters off the unfamiliar voices for me.

Thank you, I say, tucking myself into his fur as he streaks down the mountain with lightning speed, weaving between tree trunks with seamless grace.

Lucan doesn't even sound winded. *You'll get used to it*, he assures me.

Maybe so, but right now I'm thankful for silence because I need to think, and my mind and stomach are twining into knots.

Malcolm. Gaia. Walter. Eleni. Claudia. Even Tristan.

They're all caught in the middle of a riot—that I technically started. Or at least contributed to.

My distraction worked, and Eleni and Claudia succeeded. All of the citizens must have heard my last conversation with Arad, where he admitted everything. I don't know whether my nerves are pride or the need to vomit.

Xantera wants to fight. And I want to help.

Though I don't have long to stew on the fact that I can't help. Not while that Wall is still standing.

And certainly not when we turn back on the main dirt road to find Soren, Merrick, and Vivian already waiting, standing in a row in their werewolf forms like some sort of shield.

Lucan's mental block melts, and there's a tense shift in the air. I'm clueless, eyes churning between these enormous wolves. For a second, I wonder if Lucan has cut me out of whatever is going on.

But as soon as my feet hit the ground, a werewolf I don't recognize, with reddish fur and a long, pointed snout, stalks up from behind them with his teeth bared. *Let's talk now.*

Lucan steps in front of me, and a deep growl echoes in the air and inside my head. The hair on the back of my neck raises along with everyone else's as they all crouch defensively.

I said one hour, Gabriel, Lucan replies, voice hard.

But the male named Gabriel doesn't retreat. *You've been acting strange for months. Keeping us out of the loop. And now a human woman miraculously shows up without any explanation.*

Gabriel's disdain for me seeps into my bloodstream, almost hot with hatred. I've never even heard of him before, yet he already seems to despise me.

Lucan flicks his eyes toward me before cocking his head toward Vivian. *Go with Vivian.*

I blink uneasily, very aware that they can all hear my thoughts and any response I offer. I don't want to leave Lucan alone with someone who's obviously angry about my existence.

Are you sure? I ask.

Gabriel seems to sneer at me. *The human doesn't even follow orders, Lucan.*

The air goes frigid rapidly, and before I can register it, Lucan is mid-air, clashing with Gabriel. Then it's a blur of werewolves tangled on the ground. Limbs flailing and kicking, teeth snapping and snarling.

With two yelps, Soren and Merrick jump into the fight, and now it's a blurry cloud of brown and red and black fur.

Vivian, in human form, sidles up next to me with a roll of her eyes and places her hand on the back of my elbow.

"Bunch of children," she laughs, but does a double take when she sees me staring, eyes wide, like someone's about to get their head ripped off. "Don't worry. They're fine." She assures me with a gentle squeeze and then leads me past the growling twist of werewolf bodies. "They'll work it out."

I nod, trusting her, and follow her up the sidewalk past two abandoned houses until she opens a small, white picket fence and motions up at the most adorable house I've ever seen. Ivy climbs up the white-washed brick, kissing the wooden shingles hanging from the roof.

As Vivian unlocks her light blue door and I step over the threshold, the street goes silent behind me. Lucan's presence cuts out of my necklace so fast it startles me. Looking over my shoulder, I see Soren and Merrick both pinning a now whimpering human Gabriel down by the arms and throat, while Lucan looms over him.

"She answers to no one," Lucan tells Gabriel, dragging him up to his feet and glancing back at us one last time.

"See?" Vivian says as she shuts the door behind her. "All under control."

Vivian pulls me into her bedroom and sits me in front of the most gorgeous mirror.

Framed with a simple white wood, it sits connected to a four-legged table with drawers to my left and right. On top sits little vials and round containers, brushes of all different sizes, glass bottles of pretty-colored liquids.

"What is this called?" I ask, taking in my reflection—my wind-chapped cheeks, tangled hair, and dirt-streaked skin. Unlike Diggory's handheld mirror, this one is large enough to take in all my features at once. Dozens of unfamiliar tools and instruments are scattered on the tabletop beneath it.

Vivian smiles when our eyes connect in the mirror. "A vanity."

A laugh bursts from my mouth. "It's literally named after being conceited?"

"Or a makeup table," she says, winking. "But give me an hour and you'll see why."

"Makeup?" I repeat.

Vivian nods and picks up a hairbrush out of the first drawer. "You'll be obsessed with yourself almost as much as Lucan is."

My cheeks heat. "He's not obsessed with me."

The words somehow die as they exit my mouth, like I don't necessarily believe it myself, or maybe more that I wish it were true. Because I'm certainly obsessed with him. But I have no way of knowing if this... thing between us is permanent or simply an exciting fraction of his centuries-long life for him.

I'm not permanent, that's for sure, not with Arad's venom slowly inching through my organs and turning them to stone. Why would Lucan be so taken with someone he can't have forever?

But Vivian purses her lips in amusement as she starts to brush through my knotted, wind-blown hair. "You know why you couldn't hear all our mental voices before, only his?"

"No," I confess.

"Lucan ordered us not to shift."

"What? Why?"

"He didn't want to confuse you." Vivian snorts. "Or so he said. *I* think he just wanted to keep you all to himself, from the moment he first heard your voice."

I blink at her, even more confused now. "But even that first moment I put on the necklace, I didn't hear any of you. Only him."

"Oh," she says, beginning to play with the edges of my hair with a casual touch I've never experienced from a friend before, "we used to take turns patrolling, stalking around the Wall looking for a way in. Lucan just liked to take as many shifts as he could, especially around the time of the blood moon, so he was on the receiving end of your necklace the night you put it on for the first time." She drops her voice to mutter under her breath, "And every night after."

"So the howls?" I ask, incredulous. "Before a few months ago, it wasn't just Lucan who haunted Xantera... but all of you on rotation?"

"Yeah." Vivian's laugh now is a howl in and of itself. "Could you imagine if it had been Soren on duty that night you first put on the necklace and you'd fallen in love with him instead?"

I scrunch my nose playfully, but the word *love* rattles around in my brain. I'm not sure what the rules regarding that particular emotion are, but I don't think I would have felt the same toward Soren or anyone else. The fact that it was Lucan that night, that he decided to be there every other night after, from the moment he first called me a nightmare...

Vivian's watching my expression in the mirror as if she can see the thoughts racing across my eyes, so I give a little cough. "You and Merrick then?"

She sighs, taking the bait for a change of subject. "Definitely love him."

"How did that... happen?" I ask, unsure how most romantic relationships even begin. Probably not with a blood-infused necklace connecting you to a deep voice that awakens your soul.

"Childhood friends, really, that experienced everything to-gether," Vivian tells me. "When we were kids, life was pretty carefree. We didn't really know we lived in a ghost town that used to border something so much greater, because this was all we'd ever known. These ramshackle houses might as well have been castles, and the Wall might as well have been the edge of the world."

Through the mirror, I watch her gather sections of my hair and begin to twine them together in a beautiful pattern I've never seen before. She continues talking, oblivious of my awe while her fingers work magic.

"Lucan, Merrick, Soren, and I, we all would get into so much trouble. Jumping off cliffs into the river, daring each other to see who could climb the tallest tree. But one day, after finding a ravine north of Eversnow Peak, Lucan and Soren raced off ahead, and Merrick and I made about a hundred trips back and forth trying to find them. By the time night started to approach, we realized *we* were lost. Together. Just the two of us."

"That's romantic," I say earnestly.

Vivian laughs. "I didn't think so at first. Merrick had never been more than just a friend to roughhouse with, but that night, we had to..." In the mirror, her cheeks take on a bit of pink. "Sleep next to each other."

"What?" I ask with a cocked eyebrow. "There was only one cave?"

"We slept on a flat expanse of rock beneath the stars, thank you very much," Vivian huffs, then smiles. "Most beautiful night of my life. We talked until we both drifted off... and then we shared a traumatic experience later on when we found our way back to the town and every single werewolf chewed us out for about ten hours straight."

"Had Lucan and Soren made it back?" I ask, trying to imag-ine the scene she's painting as if I'd been there, too. As if I actually belong.

"Of course. They were about as smug as you'd expect. Back then though, Lucan didn't have all this weight on his shoulders. No one depended on him. Then we got older, Lucan's father, Warren, died, and Lucan took his place. We grew up quickly. Responsibilities shifted. But Merrick and I have always been bonded in a way I can't explain since that night."

Lost in thought for a moment with a far-away smile, Vivian finishes braiding my hair down my back. When she's done, she swivels my chair around and grins. "Not that there are many options in our pack. Only two or three bloodlines, so Merrick's one of the only werewolves who *isn't* my cousin."

"Lucan is?" I ask, eyebrow raised.

"Yeah. Second, technically. And Soren's my first."

As Vivian fusses with the waves of hair that frame my face, a question bursts from my mouth before I can stop it.

"Do I have to worry about the ones not related to him?"

It sounds childish, but Lucan is hundreds of years old. Surely, he's made a connection with another female before he met me. And even after he met me, what if he never thought he'd see me in the flesh and continued to have other relations, believing there would always be a Wall between us? I chew on my lip nervously, and Vivian sighs.

"We're friends, okay? So I would never lie to you," she says. "Lucan's our alpha, and he's definitely not a virgin angel."

"Your what?"

"Virgin angel?" she asks, eyebrows pinched.

"No." I flush. "The other word you just said."

"Oh. *Alpha*." Vivian looks relieved that she doesn't have to explain what a virgin is. "It means he's the leader of our pack. That, combined with his stunning looks I hear enough about—which he gets from my side of the family, by the way—and the few females he's *not* related to throw themselves at him."

My heart feels like it grows bristles sharp enough to puncture my lungs. "Right," I say.

But Vivian calmly cleans my face and picks up a tube of some substance that matches my skin tone. "Werewolves have very good hearing, just so you know," she says, glancing at my chest, where the necklace still lays against my sternum without a connection to Lucan and my heartbeat thumps erratically. "You have nothing to worry about. He's always been too obsessed with bringing down the Wall. And then ever since you found that necklace, he's been too obsessed with *you*."

I try hard to keep the idiotic, immature smile off my face as Vivian applies something to it with a brush. But this is what it must feel like to fall. To care who the person you love is thinking about. To care if they feel the same way as you do. It feels dangerous and messy, yes, but I can only hope it'll be more rewarding than any partner the Guardians could have assigned me to.

"Close your eyes," she instructs me.

They flutter closed to the sound of her little containers snapping open. For a minute, we're both silent while she brushes something across my eyelids, but my own awkwardness builds again.

To keep myself from blurting out any more questions that completely give myself away, I ask, "What else are werewolves really good at?"

"Everything," she says with a smile in her voice as she switches to my cheeks. "Along with our hearing, our sense of smell is amazing. We're exceptionally strong and fast. Great at sex, of course. And best of all, we're loyal. Unlike your Guardians."

My eyes fly open. I shake my head slightly, but Vivian fusses at me to stay still.

"They're not my Guardians anymore," I insist.

"Regardless," she says, pulling out a black tube that she opens and paints over my eyelashes. "We're just as superior as them in every way. Maybe more so. If they hadn't had the element of surprise, we'd have won that damn war. It's the only way they managed to kill our king, and they would have succeeded in killing all of us if Taika hadn't helped our ancestors escape."

I try to open my mouth, but Vivian taps my lips. "No talking while I apply lipstick," she says before dragging a red waxy stick across my upper and bottom lip.

She steps back, admiring my face with a tilt of her head. Reaching up, she adjusts a piece of my hair.

"Anyway," she adds, beaming at whatever she did to my face with her makeup. "Next time it won't be an ambush."

Then she spins me back around to face the mirror, and my gasp echoes through the room.

"Vivian..." My voice trails off. With my mouth hanging open, I'm speechless.

I look like myself, but more exaggerated. My eyelids are a shade darker than my now flawless skin, and my eyelashes are so long I can feel them when I blink. A rosy hue dusts my cheekbones, accentuating the curve of my face. Everything looks natural, just my own face slightly enhanced staring back—except my lips, which are plumped and blood-red.

"This is..." My brain can't process what I'm taking in. "...makeup."

"This is makeup," Vivian says with a nod, looking at me through the mirror with a pleased tilt of her own lips. "Oh, and one more thing!"

She reaches over my shoulder and picks up a glass bottle before she sprays a plume of mist against my neck. I cough at the sweet scent that fills my nostrils, but Vivian only smirks.

"Now you're ready for your first pack meeting. And when every pair of eyes can't stop staring at you, Lucan will go absolutely feral."

LUCAN

We don't have pack meetings often, but when we do, it's usually in the old, crumbling town hall, where there's a room large enough to accommodate all thirty-five of us.

Not all thirty-five of us are here, at the moment, but enough file in that it starts to feel cramped—including some of the younger ones, who huddle in the corner, playing a game with a weighted sock that they bounce around. My father used to tell me that every pack member had their value, no matter how old or small, so I've made an effort to invite and include everyone, even if I can't fathom how they'd aid the conversation.

It doesn't matter what I can fathom or not. The world doesn't revolve around my ability to comprehend it. Another thing my father taught me.

My chest pinches as the reality that he's gone crashes into me all over again. He's not here. And neither is my mother, who decided to stay back in her little house by the meadow when I told her about the meeting. I don't think she can bear to attend another meeting where we talk about everything and go nowhere, but something feels different about this one.

Saskia will be here, for one.

If Vivian would do her job and bring her, for fuck's sake.

My eyes stay glued to the town hall door, waiting for them to show, but every time it swings open, it's someone else. Soren and Merrick. Ashe. Kyra. Gabriel, keeping his eyes lowered as he scrapes out a chair and slumps in the seat. Taika, hobbling in with his cane.

Gritting my teeth, I whirl to look at the clock hanging above my head, wondering if I need to go check on them. Vivian's always late, but never *this* late.

Then the hush of voices becomes a wave of silence.

Even the children in the far corner stop laughing.

I turn around, and my blood turns to fire and ice as my gaze slams into the most beautiful woman in the entire world.

Saskia. It's Saskia, but every feature of hers stands out with startling clarity. Her lips glisten. Her eyes sparkle, fluttering with thick, dark lashes. Even her hair, which is braided down her back, somehow looks more vibrant, like it's soaking in all the crimson hues in the room.

If that wasn't enough, everyone else is staring at her, too. I expected wariness and hesitation from them and yes, maybe even some anger. In their defense, I've been an asshole the last few months. But too many of them are noting her with obvious signs of awe and *interest*.

Hell no. Not on my fucking watch.

As she approaches me, it takes everything I have to stand still and not carve my teeth marks into every inch of her body, mark her as mine, so that there isn't a question in anyone's mind. So they know she walks toward *me*, that she sleeps in *my* bed, that only *I* can touch.

Gripping the back of the chair in front of me so hard I feel it splinter beneath my fingers, I slide it out for her. The legs scratch against the floor like nails on the old schoolhouse's chalkboard.

She smiles hesitantly as she approaches and sits in the chair, unaware of my urge to throw her down on the dining room table and fuck her here and now, just so everyone knows exactly who makes her come. Just in case anyone is daring to think of challenging me for her.

But I can't. Not exactly the time or place for that. All I can do is murmur hello and remain standing behind her to hide how hard my dick is.

"Hello," she whispers back. Then, in such a quiet voice even my superior hearing barely catches it, "Everyone's staring."

I wish I could talk to her mind-to-mind right now, but I settle for a low growl. "Because you walk in here looking like that."

Her already-rosy cheeks deepen their hue, and her fingers rise up to touch the chain of the necklace settled against her chest. "Vivian calls it makeup."

For the first time since Saskia walked in the room, my eyes flick away from her—just for a microsecond—to glance at Vivian. Who smirks at me, of course, as she settles in a chair beside Merrick.

I lower my attention back to Saskia. "Makeup or no makeup, you're incredibly beautiful, and they'd still be staring like this. But if it makes you uncomfortable, I can always rip out their eyeballs." I say that last part a little louder, so that everyone hears and abruptly wrenches their gazes away.

Saskia swings her fist back to lightly punch me in the knee as her heartbeat tries to regain a normal rhythm. "Not necessary. They're going to need all their body parts intact if we want to defeat the Guardians."

Right. The Guardians. The riot. The whole reason I called this meeting. I need to quit fantasizing about fucking her against the Wall so hard that it crumbles.

For now, I lift my head to officially address my pack.

10

SASKIA

I know you're all wondering what's going on." Lucan straightens to his full height and stares around the room, making eye contact with every single werewolf with an intensity that crackles through the air.

I take deep breaths, calming my nerves in the face of so many pairs of amber eyes.

"Well," an older man with graying hair to the left speaks up, "you've been keeping us in the dark for months. We don't know what to think."

"I don't blame you. It's my fault. But I also know you've been gossiping with each other enough to get the basic facts: that Saskia is the first human from Xantera who has ever managed to escape alive, and she's here with us now."

His reassuring hand rests on my shoulder, but it doesn't do much to relieve the weight of everyone's gaze on me, judging, thinking, assuming.

"What you *might* not know," Lucan continues, "is that she also showed the rest of her people the truth about what's happening to them and their Chosen Ones, and now the citizens are rebelling."

Instantly, murmurs swell throughout the room. I shift uncomfortably in my seat, all too aware that the way Lucan phrased that makes me out to be more capable than I really was. *I* didn't show the people of Xantera the truth—Eleni and Claudia did. And we're still no closer to helping them without any way to get through the Wall.

Still, a few of the gazes assessing me turn from skeptically curious to... admirable. Like they think I'm some kind of hero instead of just a human.

But some still don't look convinced of anything.

"How do you know they're rebelling?" a female voice to my right pipes up.

"Saskia and I went up to Eversnow Peak," Lucan explains. "They're fighting in the streets. Buildings are burning."

The one named Gabriel, whose face is already turning a mottled black and blue from Lucan pommeling him earlier, keeps an obvious expression of distrust trained on my face.

"You actually fell off the top of the Wall?" he asks me, cutting through all the muttering until it dies away. "And lived?"

"Yes," I answer quickly, startled. Maybe I shouldn't have spoken, but how else would I be here now? Lucan bristles beside me, but Gabriel's only asking a question, not accusing me of anything, even if the sentiment lurks beneath his actual words. I just don't understand what that accusation even *is*. "But Lucan caught me."

Instantly, dozens of amber eyes flick toward Lucan. Eyebrows raise, and Taika assesses me with a slight tilt of his head from the corner, his hands clasped patiently in his lap. It dawns on me, then, like a fist to my gut, what some of them might be thinking, just as another male leans back in his chair with a scoff.

"How do we know she's not a spy?" he asks the room.

The female sitting next to him nods in agreement. "Maybe she was lowered or let out."

Actually, that sounds more plausible than the truth.

I stiffen and turn my head up to Lucan, but he doesn't need to make eye contact with me to know I'm losing my burst of confidence. Instead, he chooses to stare down the female with such a withering expression that I'm surprised she doesn't crumble to dust under the weight.

"I *caught* her, Kyra. I watched it happen, heard it happen. I've been inside Saskia's head for months. I have full faith she's not a spy. If you want to discuss the fact that I've kept you out of the loop, then let's talk about that. Because I'm to blame for the secrecy."

Vivian's words ring through my head again: *he wanted to keep you all to himself.* Heads turn to their neighbors, shoulders dropping, but no one speaks.

That is, until Gabriel mutters under his breath, "It doesn't matter anyway. If she doesn't have the key, we're back to square one. Like we've always been."

Lucan tenses behind me again, but thankfully, Vivian pipes up before another brawl can break out. "Not necessarily," she says, crossing her arms from across the table. "Saskia has insider information about the vampires and the nature of Xantera. This whole time, we've only been able to guess what's been happening within that Wall, but now..."

Every head in the room turns back to me, blinking expectantly. I swallow, realizing they're waiting for said insider information. The details of my everyday life back in Xantera are unfathomable secrets to these werewolves who have been living on the outside for centuries. And Lucan, it seems, hasn't told them anything about the information he's gleaned from our previous conversations.

I glance over my shoulder to find his eyes pinned to me, and when he reads the question brewing in my own eyes, he nods. A strange sense of gratitude swells in my chest over the realization that he chose to keep our entire relationship private up until this point. Letting me take the lead on what I want to share or not.

Clearing my throat and digging deep for more courage, I address the rest of the room with my chin a little higher.

"The vampires breed us carefully to achieve the perfect number of humans to satisfy them. Not just their needs but their greed. They control every aspect of our lives—from who we're supposed to love to where we work to what we eat—and they make it seem like an honor to give our blood. There's this thing called the Choosing..."

Over the next hour, I spill everything to every listening ear, watching the mixture of expressions morph from shocked to appalled to outraged all over again as I spew the details that sit in my stomach like rocks. The Cardinal Rules. Sanctuary Sunday. "Keep your spark alive." Even Gabriel's mistrustful twist of his mouth ends up in a clenched jaw when I tell them about our names and how they're chosen—something I've never thought was abnormal until now.

"Your parents really don't name you?" Soren asks, wrinkling his nose.

"Not often. They can request a name, but the Guardians would have to approve it. Usually, baby names are chosen from a random approved list right after birth."

I clamp down on my bottom lip, wondering, for the first time, if my mother requested my name for me or not. Just another thing I won't be able to ask her now that she's a stone statue in Arad's garden. Blood wells in my mouth before I realize how hard I'm biting down to keep from crying, and I swallow it, my throat somehow drier than before.

"What about your last name?" someone else calls out. "How are those chosen?"

"Last name?" I repeat, swallowing again.

"Yeah. Your family name?"

I blink. "I... I don't have one. It's just Saskia."

A grumble emits from behind me, and I don't have to turn around to know that Lucan isn't pleased with the phrase "just Saskia." But it's the truth.

"Wait. So *you* have a family name?" I ask, turning to frown at him.

The room goes quiet, as if I've just asked the most obvious question in the world. Something I can't quite place sparks in Lucan's eyes, but he recovers with smooth precision, the spark gone before I can truly make sense of it.

"Yes. It's Veradel," he answers evenly.

"Lucan Veradel," I whisper. "So your father and mother had the same last name?"

He nods. I didn't know family names even existed. I've never been more than a random citizen to the Guardians, and I never will be. Arad might have developed some kind of weird obsession in his efforts to get me to bend to him, but even that's just a game to him. A fleeting chase. To the vampires, we are nothing more than resources for them to cultivate, consume, and destroy.

I wish I could change that.

I need to change that.

And maybe the only way to do that is to ask some more questions of my own.

"What I don't understand," I begin, "is the nature of the Wall itself. How come none of you can touch it but I can?"

"We don't know," Taika says, and even though his voice is on the quieter side, everyone gives him respectful silence and attention—even the children. "There was already a wooden wall around the capital of the kingdom before the war, but when the vampires invaded, it... changed. Now, it causes us excruciating pain when we touch it, so we can't climb it, and it's too strong for any weapon or tool to so much as make a dent in it."

Something about his tone makes me wonder if he knows more than he's letting on, but Vivian speaks up before I can fully analyze it.

"A few hundred years ago, we tried to build a scaffold that would be tall enough to jump off onto the ledge, but the Guardians spotted us and shot it down with flaming arrows until it disintegrated. So I doubt that would work again."

"Maybe we can build another scaffold more discreetly," a werewolf near Gabriel suggests.

"That would take months," Vivian says. "The citizens need our help *now*."

"We could try to tempt the vampires into coming out so that we can just kill them out here," Soren muses.

"Tempt them with what, though?" Merrick asks.

"My perfect naked body dancing in the moonlight, of course." Soren winks at me, and a growl rises up from Lucan's chest.

A few of the children giggle, and a smile pulls at the corner of my mouth, but another frown pulls it right back down.

"What about other people?" I ask, glancing at the wall of the town hall as if I can peer through it, to the rest of the world I've never seen. "Is anyone else out there to help?"

"Not other werewolves. We are the last of our kind on this continent as far as we know, and the vampires attacked most of the other human villages before they invaded the palace, leaving them dead or injured until they all died out." It's Taika who answers this one, his face crumpled with grief and shame, as if he blames himself for not saving them all. "It's up to us."

My heart burns at the enormity of the Guardians' cruelty—destroying countless lives except for the ones they could contain, control, and benefit from. Still, I feel a puzzle brewing beneath all these words, as if several pieces are floating just beyond my grasp of comprehension as the rest of the pack bursts out with more ideas that all come down to the same grim facts.

We don't have the key, so we can't unlock the doors of the Wall. It's too strong for weapons to knock it down, and the werewolves can't climb. If we try to build something, the vampires will see us coming. What other options are there? Surely, the answer lies in the nature of the Wall itself. In what made it change.

Just then, the doors to the room burst open, and a few middle-aged werewolves barge in with platters of food: smoking slices of what's surely elk meat—the same one Vivian, Merrick, and Soren killed earlier—more bowls of sparkling berries, and freshly-baked bread with steam dancing from the slits in the centers.

It's not the overabundance of food that I faced in the palace, but there's definitely something more heartwarming about it than the bland trays of food I used to get in my housing unit as all the children jump up to grab a helping and everyone else thanks the werewolves who brought it, the spell of intensity momentarily broken.

In the shuffle, though, one of the little boys trips on an uneven floorboard and flies forward across the dusty floor.

Without thinking, I leap up and hurry forward, crouching at his side. "Are you okay?"

Sprawled out on his stomach, the boy's eyes widen when he looks up at me with a frightened look that burns into me and makes me recoil. He cranks his head sideways and connects gazes with one of the middle-aged werewolves, who rushes forward to help him up instead.

And just like that, the food on the table doesn't look quite as heartwarming anymore. I hurry back to my seat, fully aware that I'm only really welcome here because Lucan would demolish anyone who said otherwise. But you can't force a kid to fake pleasantries.

Lucan leans into me, taking advantage of everyone's attention now focused on the food to ask me in a low voice, "Are you all right?"

I realize he's spent the second half of this pack meeting in silence, letting me speak over him even though he's apparently their alpha. It makes me feel almost... powerful, and I allow him a smile to cover up the sick pit sinking low in my gut.

"I'm fine." When he glowers at me, I relent with, "I just feel like I'm missing something. If I could find out more about how vampires and werewolves *function*, then maybe I could figure out the link between the Wall and the pain you feel when you touch it." I sigh and cast my gaze around the room, watching everyone else fill up plates with food that fill my own stomach with queasiness. When I realize Lucan's still staring at me, the hues of his face paling slightly, I raise my eyebrows. "What?"

"I think," he says under his breath, "you need to read my father's journals."

After Lucan dismisses the meeting half an hour later with orders for everyone to brainstorm our predicament, he takes me, not to his well-maintained house, but to another one farther down a beaten lane, sagging under the weight of a moss-slick roof. Overgrown trees bow over either side of it, casting it in dark, jagged shadows.

"Um." I stop in front of the house, staring at the two broken windows that look like empty eye sockets bordered by glass teeth. "Are you sure this isn't haunted?"

"I'm about seventy-five percent sure," Lucan responds without even a twitch of his lips to indicate he's joking. "Although it *is* where I used to live with my mother and father until he died. Then my mother and I both moved out, claiming other houses, because we couldn't stand living in a place that smelled so much like him."

"Oh." It's about all I can think of to say, especially when Lucan marches to the front door and the deck beneath his feet nearly splinters at his weight. He doesn't even need to turn the knob, because the door doesn't appear to be able to latch anyway. He simply pushes it with a flat palm, and the hinges squeak as the door slowly swings open.

"I've maintained his office over the years, but the rest..."

Lucan gives me an apologetic wrinkle of his nose as I follow him into the house that only has a seventy-five percent chance of being haunted, him brushing away cobwebs dangling from the door-frame before they have a chance to touch me. Chivalric, honestly. But I'm too on edge to give him more than a whispered thank you as we step inside.

Inside, abandoned furniture forms dark shadows in every corner—a sofa with clawed legs, a large, standing clock no longer ticking, a cabinet filled with trinkets covered in dust. More cobwebs sweep from the ceiling, and I swear I can hear the small pattering of rats racing along the walls somewhere. The walls themselves are covered in faded, peeling wallpaper and portraits that dangle lopsidedly, too cloaked in dust for me to make out their pictures.

"Office is this way," Lucan says, gently leading me past a staircase I'd never want to climb and down a short hallway, where an open doorway leads to...

"Oh, this is much better." As soon as I step into the brightly-lit room, where late sunlight streaks through a clean window facing west, I feel each of my muscles relaxing again. A large, polished desk sits on the other end between wooden cabinets, several old, leather journals scattered on its surface.

"Your father wrote in these?" I ask, grazing my fingers along a cover.

"Most of them." Lucan watches me with an indecipherable expression. "Some of them are from my grandfather, actually, chronicling the rumors of vampire attacks on nearby villages leading up to the final invasion—Taika managed to steal them before he escaped with some other werewolves after my grandfather was killed. But my father wrote his journals after the Wall turned to stone. They're what I was reading when you were in the Blood Moon Palace, trying to find a cure for..."

He stops, and the horrible truth seems to press into us from every wall: there is no happy ending for us, even if we can tear that Wall down. I'm still infected with vampire venom. Still going to become nothing more than a statue, sooner or later.

The thought makes me clutch the edge of the desk, my knuckles white, in an effort not to collapse. Lucan's gaze lands on my fingers, and his brows tighten.

"We don't have to do this right now. You barely ate anything at dinner. Maybe you should go to—"

"No, I'm not going to sleep," I say firmly, and plop myself into the leather chair in front of the desk, already beginning to rifle through cracked, yellowed pages. In my schooling phase, all of our textbooks were glossy, pristine, and printed. These feel like the words are breathing between the pages, some ancient secret brewing just beneath my fingertips. "Maybe you missed something..."

"That one," he says, nodding at a slightly smaller journal than the others. "Read that one."

For the next several hours, I read while Lucan leans against the wall with his arms folded, watching me. Most of the entries just give me a sense of who his father *was*: loud, proud, and full of the same vengeance that brews in Lucan himself. The actual content about the Thirteenth Guardian I already knew because Lucan told me.

Until I get to an entry that reads more like a clinical study.

"You're telling me you had this information right under your nose and you *skipped over it*?" I hiss, staring down at the words that swim before my vision.

I drag my finger over the worn page as I read.

October 28, 52 AX

The Thirteenth Guardian has been telling me more

*een telling me more about the nature of his kind as
we plan for my pack to breach the Wall. Everything
makes so much more sense than it used to.*

*Vampire venom, for instance, is a magical substance
that interacts differently with a variety of objects or
subjects.*

"I was so desperate to get back to you that I started to rush
through them," Lucan admits in a grumble behind me, but I
shush him with a flap of my hand.

*In regular humans and animals, vampire ven-
om slowly fossilizes the organs from the inside-out,
turning the victim to stone.*

*In some creatures such as ourselves—werewolves—it
simply causes excruciating pain, due to our antibodies fighting it off.*

I stare at those last words. Antibodies. *Antibodies.* My mind
races at a dizzying speed, and my fingers quake over the pages
as thoughts and ideas flash through me faster than I can grasp
them. Of course, if the immune system was activated to such
an extent, it would cause pain...

Pain. My own stomach clenches with pain right now, hunger
ripping through me at such an inopportune time. Although, I
suppose I've only eaten a handful of wild berries over the last
few days, so that would be expected.

As soon as I finish reading this, I'll find something to eat. But
for now...

*In inanimate objects, vampire venom strengthens
and fortifies, effectively turning the material into
something impenetrable as long as the venom resides
in the material in an active state.*

"That's it," I breathe as Lucan reads over my shoulder. "The
Wall. It was wood, but the vampires injected it with their own
venom to turn it to stone."

"But how? Just by biting into the railings or something?"
Lucan asks.

"That, or maybe they found a way to concentrate their venom and inject it somehow." My voice seems to be slurring
against my will. My blood sugar must be dropping, but I don't
want Lucan to worry about me, so I try to push through.
"Lucan, if those veins in the Wall are filled with vampire venom,
then it hurts you to touch it because your immune system is
being activated every time you do."

I drop my eyes to the next passage in the journal, realization
after realization coursing through me.

And in someone with the vampire gene...

My vision blurs. My head spins. My stomach roils, like the
riot of Xantera has invaded my very bloodstream. I snap the
journal shut and rattle in a deep breath.

"Is everything all right?" Lucan narrows his gaze at me.

"Yes!" My voice comes out about two octaves too high, but I
clear my throat. "I just need to pee. I'll be right back."

Before he can peer too closely at the mask I just so haphazardly
constructed, I jump up, totter on my feet for a moment, and hurry
out of the study, through the skeletal remains of the house it resides
in, and out the door. Just in case Lucan is moving to a window to

watch me, I veer in the direction of his own house, where I skirt around it—

And into the woods beyond.

The truth of everything that journal just revealed is hammering itself against my skin, the words so glaringly obvious right in front of my eyes, but I don't want to let it in. If I let it in, my veins will wilt, my bones will crack, and the entire foundation of the world will turn upside-down. Even now, the trees around me swirl, like I'm flipping anyway, despite my best attempts to push the dizziness away.

All I know is that I cannot stay here. I don't belong, and I never will. The entire city of Xantera and everyone in the ghost town here are better off without me. *Lucan* is better off without me.

He'll see. He'll figure it out when he reads that passage in the journal. He'll be glad I left.

Still, I don't let the truth in. I just push forward, past tree trunks that warp around me, and soon enough I'm doubling over from the *need* that pierces inside me.

Need. I need...

My palms crash against the ground, grinding against rocks and pine needles. I crawl forward, desperate to get as far away as possible, retching as I go. When the last of my vision snags on a crisscross of fallen logs up ahead, I use all my remaining strength to haul myself into the dark, cavernous space between them, slathered in ferns.

Maybe I can't run from the Monster, but I can hide.

Right?

The last thought that whispers across my mind is that at least it was nice, getting to experience life beyond the Wall. At least I got a few good memories with Lucan to carry with me to wherever I go next. I hope he can say the same.

Then I slump sideways, my cheek slamming into moss-slicked ground, and darkness gobbles me whole.

LUCAN

I just need to pee.

The phrase rebounds in my skull, discordant and off-key. The look on her face before she left just now—hell, the look on her face all day, as if she's two gags away from spewing all over my shoes—pushes new adrenaline into my veins.

I need to pee is the excuse she gives to men like Tristan. But I'm not fucking falling for it a second longer. If she's trying to hide the fact that she's sick, that Arad's vampire venom is affecting her more than expected or something...

In five strides, I'm out of the house, surging down the road in the direction I saw her take off. A few of the children are out, playing with a ball in the patches of mud that have accumulated between houses, but they all give me a quick nod of attention as I pass.

Usually, I simply smile back at them, but right now my alpha status has good use.

"Did you see Saskia pass?" I ask them.

By now, everyone knows her name. Several of them nod eagerly. The oldest, a thirteen-year-old kid named Milo, points toward my house down the road. "Yes, sir. She went that way. Around back."

"Around back?" I question, my blood frosting over.

"Yeah." The youngest giggles between little fingers. "Do humans have bad hearing like their bad sense of smell? We asked her what she was doing, and she didn't even answer!"

I don't answer either, striding off again with panic fraying at my edges. Fortunately, I *do* have a good sense of smell... and I just caught a whiff of her trail, strawberries and roses lingering over that underlying scent of decay.

"Saskia?" I call, my feet thundering as I barrel into the woods.

Her scent zigzags, like she was staggering, and my pace quickens into a run. The farther it goes, the more a new fear begins to crack somewhere in the vicinity of my sternum.

Was she trying to run away? From me?

No sooner has that question raced through me than her trail ends near a pile of moss-eaten logs. A flash of red hair on the ground has me thudding to my knees in a flurry.

"*Saskia?*"

Before my mind can even process what's happening, my arms shoot out with lightning speed to scoop Saskia up against my chest.

My free hand grips her shoulder, shaking it slightly. "Hey, hey, hey, wake up. Come back to me, baby," I plead, but her head only lolls to the side, her face ghost-white, her lips parted, and her eyes closed like she's merely sleeping.

But she's not. Something is wrong—I can smell it lurking beneath her skin. That scent that makes bile rise in my throat. It's even stronger than it was ten minutes ago, as if Arad is somehow speeding up her fossilization process from within the Wall, trying to take her away from me sooner.

Gathering her in my arms, I can hear the faintest *thump, thump, thump* of her heart, so slow it makes my own halt in its tracks.

But the rest of my body is already moving, sprinting through the woods and up the street with Saskia cradled against my chest.

In under a dozen panicked breaths, I reach Taika's clinic, leaping up the ramp and pounding on his door so hard the hinges whine.

"Taika!" I bellow, the desperate plea leaving my throat like a wounded animal.

But there's no time to wait. Seconds are precious. I kick the door, and the frame cracks from the force just as a light finally flicks on in the downstairs window.

Raising my boot again, Taika swings open the door in a flurry before I can flatten it to the ground.

He rubs his glassy eyes, adjusting to the sight of us with a few extra blinks.

"Help her," I get out on an exhale, nearly knocking him over when I brush past him in my panic.

With a quick survey of Saskia in my arms, he steps back and closes the door, not bothering with the fact that it's barely hanging on the hinges. "In here. In here. Tell me what happened."

He shuffles around, pulling a pillow and a blanket out of the closet while I lay Saskia down on the first bed I find. I'm not even sure if it's Taika's personal bed or a patient one. I don't care. Not when her head falls to the side like a rag doll as soon as I lay her over the sheets.

"What happened?" Taika repeats firmly, lifting her neck to slide the pillow under her head.

"I don't know." Without her in my arms, my knees tremble, my hands shake. My voice comes out ragged and hoarse. "I don't fucking *know*. We were reading in my father's office, then she left to use the bathroom, and I found her passed out in the woods."

I can't get my breathing under control, and each breath I drag in reverberates in my ears, drowning out the sound of Saskia's heartbeat.

But with each second she doesn't wake, my anxiety only rises, and my lungs only fight harder for oxygen. Why is the venom affecting her so much so soon? I thought we had *years*. Could the world really be so cruel as to take away this woman a mere day after I finally got to lay eyes on her?

Beside me, Taika makes fast work of gathering his equipment, checking the pulse on her wrist with his fingers, opening an eyelid and shining a flashlight into her pupil. Her arms hang limply at her side.

"She's going to wake up, right?" I ask.

Taika ignores me with that damn stethoscope back in his ears. My mind whirs, watching him go eerily still as he presses the bell of it against Saskia's chest, right next to the gold chain around her neck.

"Did she hit her head?" he asks.

"I don't know! She was trying to run away from me, dammit."

His eyes flick to mine, dark and tired and troubled. If another second passes without me knowing whether she's going to be okay—

I reach out, my mind uncontrollable, to snatch the stethoscope out of Taika's hand and heave it across the room. Then I grab hold of the necklace's vial tight in my fist, waiting for that spurt of electricity to connect our minds like usual. Something swells in my bloodstream, but it's not like light—it's like darkness.

Saskia! I roar into the void, tugging on the necklace as if I can tug her back to me.

Nothing answers back.

And the vial on the necklace snaps off.

SASKIA

Before I stepped foot in the Blood Moon Palace, I'd never taken a bath. I'd never even seen a large body of water until I saw the rivers from the top of the palace's balconies and the snow-capped mountain this morning, so I've never had any need to wonder what drowning might feel like.

Until now.

Now, my lungs explode with need, like oxygen has completely vanished from the world. Darkness encircles me, but it's not a comforting kind. It's restrictive, a white-hot band wrapping around my throat and chest and squeezing tighter and tighter.

Somewhere far above me, a familiar voice shouts my name, but I sink lower and lower toward the bottom of my torment. My *need*.

I need something, but I don't know what. It's like a ravenous hunger raking long, jagged claws down my body from the inside-out. Not for food, exactly. But not for touch, either. *What do I need?* Why do I feel like I'm going to die if I don't get it? The answer hovers somewhere just out of my grasp, but even though I try to reach for the light, I only sink lower.

And lower.

And lower.

Until I *thump* against a solid ground.

"Not possible," a deep, male voice echoes, like a whisper through the room.

What's not possible?

Blinking rapidly, I open my eyes, expecting to find myself in bed with the people I love hovering over me, all concerned expressions and relieved smiles when they see me wake. But I forgot who it is I love, and when the darkness ebbs away in watery ripples, I find myself back in the housing unit from my childhood. I'm a girl again, just like in my last nightmare.

"Saskia," that same voice pleads, closer this time.

I look up, only to find someone completely different smiling gently at me. Not a statue in a cruel garden. A flesh-and-blood human being with an olive complexion and freckles dotting her nose just like mine.

But it's the wrinkles around her eyes I always loved the most. She used to compare them to a bird's feet, but to me, they etched a map of all the smiles she'd ever given me. A map of comfort and love that so many other children my age never got from the parents who were forced into having them.

"Saskia," she says again, this time her familiar tone like a song to my heart.

"Mom!" I cry, and race forward.

She enfolds me in an embrace immediately, warm strong hands grabbing my frame so that I don't fall apart. She smells sweet and tangy, like some kind of fruit and flower mixed in one.

"My girl," she breathes, brushing away a strand of my hair. "How I've missed you."

"I-I've missed you, too," I say, sniffing up tears before they fall all over the front of her shirt. "When I saw you in the garden, I thought it would be the last time. I thought I'd failed you."

"Never." My mother lifts a finger and wipes at my cheek. "If anything, it's I who failed *you*. By omitting the truth, thinking that you'd be better off not knowing." She sighs. "Thinking that as long as you weren't Chosen, you'd stay safe and live a normal life."

I rear my head back, confusion tugging my lips together. "What do you mean? You thought I'd be better off not knowing what?"

She doesn't sigh again, but she does peer at me with a frown, the wrinkles around her eyes pulling tight as she appears to contemplate. Then, with a swift nod of her head, she gestures toward the kitchen table, where a kettle and two steaming mugs have suddenly popped into existence. "Come. Have some tea with me."

As soon as we take a seat across from each other, the housing unit dissolves into startling blues and whites that immediately make me squint. When my eyes adjust, my mouth falls open at the scenery spreading all around us—the kitchen table, chairs, tea, and my mother all perched quaintly on the snow-capped top of the mountain from earlier, the sky wrapped all around us.

The first prickles of uneasiness tug at the back of my mind, reminding me of something pertinent I still have to do. But then—

"Drink up," my mother says, smiling at me as if teatime at the top of the world is a perfectly normal Sunday occurrence. "It's your favorite. Remember?"

I glance down at the steaming liquid in my cup, some kind of red-tinted tea that smells like the woods outside the Wall. As soon as I lift the mug to my lips and take a sip, that need in my throat seems to melt. Just a little bit.

"Saskia," my mother says, gazing off into the depths of the sky now that she's satisfied I'm nourishing myself. "Do you remember why you wanted to become a healer?"

"Because you were sick—"

"No." She shakes her head, attention lost somewhere among wisps of clouds. "Because your father was sick first, but you seem to have blocked him out." When I startle, she lays a comforting hand overtop mine. "I don't blame you, my girl. If anything, I aided you in forgetting him. I never answered your question the one time you gave me one, and you never asked again. It was against the Cardinal Rules, of course, to pry. But I saw that event spark an interest in you for the first time in your life, and I remember thinking it was the only good thing to come of it."

Her smile droops like a withering flower, and I shake my head.

"I still don't understand."

"Let me show you, then."

The mountaintop around us dissolves, reforming into walls that rise up on either side of the kitchen table in uniform lines: the alleyways between complexes.

My mug shakes in my hand as I see my father walking toward us from the end of it.

"Dad," I whisper, but my mother shakes her head.

"Just watch. He can't hear you from there."

I do as she says, assessing every detail of my father that I've forgotten over the years. His straightened posture. His long, sharp nose. His dark, auburn hair a stark contrast to his pale complexion. He's merely ten strides away from walking right into my mother when a shadowy blur barrels into him, knocking him into the alleyway wall with a resounding *crack*.

A scream of warning tears out of my mouth, but I'm too late, and my mother's right—he can't seem to hear me, anyway. He tries to shout as his attacker pins him to the ground, but a pale, marble hand clamps over his mouth, and then a pair of fangs sinks into the flesh of his neck in a flash.

The Eleventh Guardian. I'd notice that stupidly prominent Adam's apple in his throat anywhere at this point. The same one who attacked Odette, attacking my father right in front of me.

My father gasps for help, and my mug of tea nearly cracks in my grip. Just as I stand to try to help him, though—not caring whether he can sense me or not—the alleyway dissolves, reforming into our housing unit once more. Silence settles over the kitchen as if my father's shouts never left his mouth at all.

"He was bitten. That's why he got sick," I say to my mother, who lifts her mug to her own mouth and takes a sip. "Just like you. Only, he was never Chosen. But the Guardians have been taking more than they promised they would take for a while now, using the catacombs to drink from people in the dead of night."

"Yes," my mother says. "And no."

"What?"

"The Guardians definitely take more than they promise—or need—but your father didn't get sick because he was bitten. The vampire venom didn't work the same way for him. It... activated a different side of him, a gene he never even knew he had until weeks later, when he..."

Here, my mother cuts herself off, that faraway look stealing her focus as she gazes into the corner of the room.

"When he what, Mom?" I press, my voice rising as agitation nips at my chest. "What did Dad to do you?"

In response, she sets her mug of tea on the table with a clink, then scoots her chair back and stands abruptly, just as my father stumbles into the room and casts her a dazed look.

"You have to," she says, her voice shaking and scared.

"I can't keep doing this to you, Maribel." My father's own voice takes on a harsher tone despite the way he's clutching his own chest. His eyes roam over my mother's figure, and for the first time, I realize how wan she looks again, just like how she used to. "You're sick."

"I'm fine."

"You're *not* fine," my father protests. "You're going to die if it happens again."

"Well, *you're* going to die if you don't."

They stare each other down for a moment, two sick people trying to win a battle in order to save the other. And I think I start to understand, as my father's eyes flick toward my mother's neck, toward the same spot the Eleventh Guardian stole blood from him. He *needs* it. Needs the same sustenance I'm currently lacking in order to keep living. But the more he takes from my mother, the more her internal organs begin to fossilize.

She was already turning to stone years before the Guardians picked her out of the crowd.

Bitten by my father before she was Chosen by them.

But my father shakes his head, a determined film clouding his eyes—his *crimson* eyes. They're not as deep of a red as Arad's, but pink-tinged with popping blood vessels, as if they're getting there. To his fellow citizens, it might look like he just needs a better night's sleep, but if they get any redder...

He'd look just like a Guardian.

"Then so be it," he rasps at my mother. "I can't hurt you just to help myself. It wouldn't be living anyway."

I don't need to relive him dying all over again, even though now I know... he was dying of starvation. Of thirst. Of refusal to drink from the innocent people around him. The housing unit dissolves before he can crash to the floor, and suddenly, we're sitting on top of the blood moon itself: a cratered ground the color of blood with endless space spreading beyond it.

"Dad was a vampire?" I breathe. Heartbroken. Horrified. Hating what it means.

My mother nods from across the table but doesn't speak.

"How?"

Her voice twists, dropping into a low, guttural growl again. "The Thirteenth Guardian."

"Mom?" I whisper, confused. It looks like her but doesn't sound like her.

She shakes her head, clears her throat. "We never understood. Never could figure it out. The Guardians limit our resources and prevent us from learning about our past, present, or future. But it only made sense that your father had some kind of biological difference that responded to vampire venom by... becoming one. Because he didn't change until after he was attacked in the alleyway."

I exhale, inhale, exhale again, feeling that treacherous burn slowly crawl up my throat again. Need. Need. *Need*. I needed the right kind of sustenance, and I failed to get it in time.

"I'm dead, aren't I?" I ask my mother. "That's why I'm able to talk to you right now. I died like you and Dad?"

She stares at me for a second before swallowing thickly. "Not yet. You know what you have to do if you want to survive this, little nightmare. Drink."

I cock my head. Little nightmare? She's never called me that before. "I don't want to. I don't want to be *that* kind of monster."

"My dear girl." My mother reaches across the table and clutches my hand. "Whatever monster you become is the monster you *choose* to be. Nothing more, nothing less."

"Choose," I repeat.

"Choose," she confirms with a nod.

And then the crimson of the moon washes over us, crashing into the kitchen table, knocking over both our mugs of tea, and sending my mother scattering into mist. I try to scream, but water fills my mouth, and waves knock me back down into a state of drowning.

Only this time, that drowning smells a lot like blood.

13

LUCAN

S he's a vampire," Taika says.

"No," I manage to exhale hoarsely. "That's not possible."

The elderly healer stares at me for a beat before his eyes slice to Saskia's pale face. "Lucan," he says simply, lifting up one side of her lips. "Look."

My throat closes. Taika exposes four normal white teeth sitting in a row between...

Two elongated canines. Thinner and sharper than mine. Sharp enough to pierce tough skin and delicate veins.

Fangs.

How long have they been like that? I swear, they weren't there the last time she smiled at me merely a couple hours ago.

Shock wells in my chest, but in the back of my mind, all the pieces begin to click together. The reason Saskia was able to traverse the catacombs without any of the other vampires detecting her—because she was one of them all along. The reason Arad's venom seemed to give her a high rather than a low like her fellow Chosen Ones—because it was affecting her differently. The reason she was able to survive the fall from the top of the Wall—because she's not human.

But she doesn't look like she's surviving well now.

With a newfound urgency thrumming through my body, I turn back to Taika. "There's a journal on my father's desk. I need it now."

He blinks. "What?"

"Please. I think it'll help."

He roves a concerned look over Saskia before he nods.

"Saskia," I whisper when he's gone, crouching beside her and tucking a stray strand of her hair behind her ear. "I'm going to figure this out."

Her painfully slow heartbeat is the only response. I count them—three for every minute Taika's gone.

A vampire. A vampire?

But she can't be. Vampires are parasites. Cold leeches who prey on innocents. Saskia is the complete opposite in every way: warm, giving, compassionate.

By the time Taika limps back through the door, I've only reached nine, and her heartbeats only seem to be getting slower and slower.

Panic replaces the doubt caving in my chest cavity.

Leaping to my feet, I grab the leather book from his grip and sit beside Saskia to pick up where she left off.

And in someone with the vampire gene, the venom activates their vampirism. The process takes a few weeks, but eventually, their body will transition from needing food as sustenance to needing blood. Their heart rate will slow to barely a beat a minute, their teeth will elongate and sharpen, and their eyes will start to turn crimson upon their first drink. This is why the Guardians are careful to never impregnate a Chosen One. Doing so would create a vampire offspring—another contender to one of the limited thrones.

"She has a… a vampire gene," I stutter, trying to wrap my brain around it. A gene that Arad unknowingly triggered from the moment he first sunk his teeth into her.

Taika pulls a chair up next to the bed in silence, eyes glued to Saskia. His eyebrows pinch deeply until he finally asks, "How?"

I flip back to the earlier entries. The ones where my father talks about a vampire in love.

*He claims he's fallen in love with one of the humans…
And he's afraid they'll kill his lover if they find out.*

"The Thirteenth Guardian," I tell him. "They never found out he loved a woman. A *human* woman, who must have been pregnant with his offspring."

"Who was born with a dormant vampire gene that was never activated," Taika breathes. "All his descendants must have carried the same gene, until…"

"Saskia's father," I say, remembering how she'd described her father's peculiar death. "He had to have been bitten, even though he was never Chosen. And then Saskia…"

Taika sighs, picks up her wrist to press two of his fingers against her pulse. "All that time, and none of the Guardians ever knew."

I listen to Saskia's faint pulse, my mind stretched in a million different directions.

This woman isn't just a woman born on the other side of the Wall. She's my mortal enemy. Has been all along, apparently, although that side of her has stayed dormant until now.

And yet…

"She's going to die without blood," Taika warns, shifting uncomfortably in his chair before he rises and walks out the door, giving us privacy. Room for me to make a decision.

An alpha werewolf giving a vampire his blood—it's ludicrous. Risky in and of itself. A betrayal to my pack. Not to mention the excruciating pain I'd be putting myself through.

Despite every warning bell telling me to never touch her again, my hand reaches out of its own accord and skims her cheek. Her skin feels cold, and my heart skips when her eyes dart around beneath her eyelids.

I take a deep fucking breath. Mortal enemy or not, Saskia isn't preying on innocent people or taking more than her body needs. In fact, she *helps* innocent people and hasn't turned to blood, even when hunger has probably been gnawing on her for days now. Her own father refused to drink any more from her mother—died from starvation—and her ancestor, the Thirteenth Guardian, tried to help my kind rebel against his fellow Guardians.

So I don't care if the others hate me for this, rebuke me as their alpha, or want to kill me.

She's not dying on my watch.

"Little nightmare," I whisper, slipping into the bed beside her, wrapping one arm around her neck and lifting the forearm of my other to her mouth. "Drink."

For the first time since she fainted, Saskia's eyelashes flutter. Her lips press against my pulse, and she lets out a moan—

Moments before her teeth puncture my skin.

And as Taika returns with a *thump, thump, thump* of his cane, I feel her venom overtake me like a searing brand, setting me on fire, burning its way through my system.

Claiming me.

SASKIA

Relief floods through me as the warm liquid fills my mouth, parching all that thirst and starvation in my throat. There's something vaguely bitter about it, like I'm swallowing the earth itself, but I don't care. Not as the nightmare leaks away and all my senses slowly return to me.

Sound first. A rough, masculine voice saying, "That's it. Keep drinking. There you go, baby."

My eyebrows furrow as I obey instinctually, trying to understand who it is, what's happening—and why I suddenly feel ashamed. But the hunger overpowers me, forcing me to keep drinking, to keep sucking on...

Then the sensation of touch, of me *touching*, jolts through me.

With a gasp, my eyes flash open, and I wrench myself away.

"Lucan!" I cry, blinking rapidly as my vision finally clears.

His face looms over mine, tight with concern and something else I can't place at the moment. One of his arms circles my neck, and the other is held out in front of me, two thick streams of blood trickling from his forearm and plopping onto my chest.

At the sight of that blood, a peculiar ferocity steals over me. Mine. This male is *mine*, and somebody fucking hurt him.

"*Who?*" I ask sharply, struggling to sit up.

"Who what, Saskia?" Lucan asks, a trace of amusement flickering over all the strain on his face. *Pain*. That's the other expression I'm reading besides concern. Lucan's in pain, despite the hardened mask he's trying to wear for me right now.

"Who did this to you?" I hiss, nodding at his forearm and surprising myself with the venom spitting from my tone. My head pounds. My gums ache. And that hunger is welling up again, confusing me even though the knowledge from my nightmare begins to nudge at my brain.

Lucan exchanges a quick glance with Taika over his shoulder, then squints down at the blood streaming down his arm, eyebrows ticked up as if surprised. "Well, *you* did. But it's okay," he adds quickly when my face crumples. "You need it."

"No."

The word is barely a breath wafting out of my lungs as everything comes crashing back. What I learned about myself from my dead mother who must have derived from a figment of my imagination. What I suspected about my lineage as soon as I read that last passage in the journal, right before I fainted.

But there's no way. It's not possible. I don't need to drink blood to survive. I need a simple tray of food and water. Like a normal human. Like always.

I'm supposed to heal, not hurt.

My chest heaves as I drag in breath after shaky breath, and my mind spins with panic. I can't take in enough oxygen, which only makes me more frantic, more lightheaded.

Maybe if I deny it hard enough, this will all go back to normal.

"No," I say again, this time louder, and I hoist myself up so quickly that Lucan actually jerks back, letting me rise into a sitting position on the bed, even though he keeps his good arm around me. I look wildly around the room, as if a solution to this awful new reality might be hiding in the cracks of the windowsill or in the tears in the wallpaper surrounding us. My eyes land on the bedside table, where my necklace lays in a sad heap—the vial snapped off the chain.

How did that happen? I don't know, can't remember... but the brokenness of it seems to signify a severed bond between Lucan and me. How we can never go back to the way we were before.

I look at Taika, who only smiles at me sadly, then return my gaze to Lucan. "I don't want to hurt you," I whisper.

"If you don't," he says plainly, the amber in his eyes cracking open with emotion, "you'll die."

My breath comes out ragged as my eyes rove over his clenched jaw, the tendons straining in his forearm as he curls his fist, the rigidity of his posture. "But you're already in pain."

"But I'm giving my permission," he argues immediately, as if he knew that was the retort hovering on my lips. "It's not going to damage me long-term, like it would a human." His voice takes on an edge of a growl, authority lacing through each syllable as we size each other up. "Now, I don't want to ask you again, little nightmare. Drink from me until you're fucking satisfied."

Staring at him, I consider all my options.

I could bolt. That seems like the safest one—just run away in my new body now thrumming with a different kind of energy, until I collapse from exhaustion and starvation all over again.

But Lucan would catch me if I did, of course, and then we'd be right back in this same situation. And even if I *do* have the potential for more strength now than I did as a human, every one of my bones and muscles scream in fatigue and weakness at the present moment, hunger still licking the lining of my throat.

I didn't get enough blood. Not nearly enough. And until I do, I won't be strong enough to defy his orders.

"Drink," Lucan commands again, holding his bleeding arm out to my lips.

As soon as the smell hits, I can't help it anymore. Denying it doesn't stamp out the fire building in my chest, the deep urge to *bite*. His utter dominance over me coupled with the need for *more* join forces until I'm sinking my teeth back into his skin, pulling in the nutrients, gulping life back into me.

His blood doesn't taste good, exactly, not sweet like how I imagine a human would taste, but it tastes *right*. If this is going to be my life from now on, I don't want it to taste so sweet that I could get addicted. This bitterness seems to anchor me to the earth, giving me exactly what I need and nothing more.

But my stomach still buckles at the reality of what I'm doing.

Finally, when it feels like some strength has returned to the very tips of my fingers and toes, I wrench myself away again and wipe his blood from my mouth.

"I'm satisfied," I lie.

Lucan peers at me for a handful of seconds, as if assessing my honesty. Apparently, he decides he's satisfied, too, because he jerks his head at Taika, who hobbles forward with some kind of cottony material to press against his wounds. I open my mouth to suggest that they just wrap it, but when Taika removes the material seconds later, the pinpricks in Lucan's skin melt away. As if his body healed it that fast.

"How do you feel?" Taika asks Lucan.

"No different than all the hundreds of times I've tried to climb the Wall." Lucan's gaze reverts back to mine. "How do *you* feel, Saskia? That's the more important question."

I flex my fingers, glancing down at my body. I'm still in that dress from Vivian, albeit with bloodstains streaking the front of it now, but otherwise, I feel like I've been doused with cold water and electricity all in one. Energy hums in my veins, a sense of invincibility whispering at me to run, jump, tackle the male before me to the ground and...

No. Not letting myself finish that thought with Taika in the room, although I'm vaguely pleased at the notion that I'd still rather kiss Lucan than kill him.

Aren't we supposed to hate each other on an instinctual level? Maybe he does hate me now that he thinks I've turned into one of them—the Guardians. I look up and meet the amber of Lucan's eyes, and I can't read the worlds of emotions behind the mask of his tight-lipped face.

"I feel," I start hesitantly, honestly, "like I'm truly awake for the first time in my life. But Lucan, I swear, I didn't know. I don't even know how this is possible—"

"The Thirteenth Guardian," Lucan answers gruffly, picking up the fallen journal I hadn't noticed until this moment. "He must have been your ancestor..."

"Who passed the vampire gene to my father, who passed it to me," I finish, sliding a hand through my sweat-dried hair. "Arad said he didn't want a bunch of little Guardians running around, but he didn't realize he already had one—maybe several—right under his nose."

"*Don't*," Lucan growls.

Taika stiffens at the sudden charge in the room, but I merely cock my head at Lucan. "Don't what?"

"Say that parasite's name in front of me. I only want mine coming out of your mouth."

Every particle of my new body seems to freeze, as if the world hangs in the balance of his next answer. "Still?" I ask carefully. "You still... want me? Even though..."

"Still."

His answer isn't just firm. It's the center of gravity itself, anchoring me to him even more than before. "Why?" I whisper.

When he leans toward me, the air crackles. "It was never a question of why, Saskia. It was only a question of how long. Because mere hours ago, I thought you were going to be nothing more than a stone corpse in ten years' time—the blink of an eye, for my kind. Ten *minutes* ago, I thought you were going to be dead by the end of the night. Now?" His lips drag up in a smile. "Now you're mine forever, little nightmare."

Tears well in my throat, but before I can figure out why he would *want* to have me forever now that we're enemies, Taika clears his throat.

"The others in the pack, however, might need some convincing."

The others. Shit. I've only known I'm a vampire for five minutes, and now I've got to think about how I'm going to face dozens of angry, ferocious werewolves who already think I'm a traitor once I step out this door. They've been thirsting for a Guardian's blood for centuries, and now I'm fresh meat served to them on a shining platter to abate their hunger for justice. Even if I feel ten times stronger than I ever have before, I'm not stupid enough to think I could fight all of them by myself.

But Lucan rounds on Taika, practically vibrating with restraint. "The pack won't touch her, because they'll be unconscious before they can so much as lift a finger in her direction. Our target is the Guardians, and she is not a Guardian."

"But she is…"

"Not a Guardian," Lucan repeats firmly. He turns back to me. "Do you have plans to kill the Third Guardian just to replace him? Take his throne and Choose an unwilling sacrifice every blood moon?"

"No!" I cry immediately. "What? No!"

"See?" Lucan jerks his head back to Taika. "Not a Guardian. Not our enemy. The pack will just have to get used to her smell."

"My smell?" I exclaim, quickly dipping my head to sniff my armpit. "You think I stink?"

"Not exactly." Lucan wrinkles his nose, but a smirk plays across his mouth. "You're just... extra sweet now. Like strawberries and roses but condensed into a bottle and then sprayed up my nostrils."

I cross my arms and huff at him, feeling that energy rise up my bones again, urging me to run, climb, tackle him, so much more. "You're not exactly the most heavenly-smelling creature yourself." I inhale dramatically. "I'm getting... dirt. Just like the taste of your blood. What do you do, roll in mud in your free time?"

He takes a step closer to me, the air snapping between us, and glances at the bob of my throat.

"Last I checked, you were the one on all fours on the forest floor like a dog."

Every synapse in my brain seems to ignite and explode, and my fingers tremble with my own restraint. I enjoyed him being dominant in the past, but now my own urge to dominate fills me to the brim, and I can't *think* straight with him glowering down at me like that.

Taika clears his throat, and we glance at him.

"I'm prescribing you both a run. Right now. We're never going to figure out a solution to the current problem until Saskia gets her newfound energy out of her system. So run far away from here, both of you, before the pack comes to investigate, and then come back when you're ready to face them all." He uses his cane to turn and peer through a sliver of a gap between the curtains, exposing an early dawn sky. "No one's out, so if you go out my back door, I doubt anyone will see you. And I won't tell them what has occurred until you're here to tell them yourselves."

I break eye contact with Lucan long enough to lay a hand on Taika's shoulder, who stiffens for a moment before relaxing at my touch.

"Thank you," I say earnestly. Because he's right. I don't know how to move forward until I test out the new limitations—or lack of limitations—of my new body. I need to face myself and whatever I have with Lucan before I can face the others.

But I do know one thing as I cock an eyebrow at Lucan, silently daring him to chase me again. Xantera doesn't have time for me to run away forever.

So I'd better be fast.

I am. Wind whistles through my ears as I cut my own path through the forest behind Taika's house, this time carried by my own two legs. My own strength.

But running side by side with Lucan, just like I'd daydreamed about on one of the balconies of the Blood Moon Palace, I'm astonished at just how fast I really am.

In his werewolf form, his leaps match three of my strides, but I'm still able to keep up. My muscles feel like cold marble, impenetrable. My lungs don't get winded, nor do my joints scream.

For the first time in my life, I'm as strong and capable as the monsters I used to fear.

I turn my neck to look at Lucan, his dark, mottled hair slicked back in the wind, his amber eyes glinting at me in amusement.

My smile hurts my cheeks.

She looks happy, he thinks.

That's when I run face-first into a boulder.

The world jostles as I slingshot across the forest floor, like rock bouncing off rock, and land on my back.

I blink up at the brightening sky until Lucan's panicked human face materializes above me.

"Shit, Saskia. Are you all right?"

A laugh bubbles up into the air. "Yes," I promise, shrugging him off. "Think something again."

"What?" he asks, furrowing his brow, his gaze scouring over me as if checking for injuries.

"Think something again," I repeat, and wait for a beat before I remember. "As a werewolf. Shift."

Lucan cocks his head like I'm insane, but his legs elongate, fur sprouts instantly from his skin, and his face morphs into a wolfish one.

She hit her head too hard, he worries, looming over me. *Fuck.*

Placing my palm against my sternum, double checking that my chest is still necklace-free, I reply mentally, *I'm completely fine. I'm a vampire now.*

He audibly gasps as his eyes fly down to my neck, confirming for himself what isn't there.

My blood...?

His voice doesn't exactly latch onto my heartbeat. Instead, it swells from inside me, tracks down my core, rises along my spine. It's everywhere.

I nod, hope blooming within me once more. *Your blood. Since I drank it, it's in me... so I guess we're connected by more than just a necklace now.*

Incredible, Lucan says, and I agree.

Maybe we can't go back to the way we used to be, but we could create a new bond. One that doesn't require a chain around my neck. My mind swirls with the possibilities. Surely, he and I can't be the first vampire and werewolf couple in all of history. But I'd imagine it's so rare and rebuked that this isn't something that has been observed or studied very often.

Too bad...

Just as quickly, the hope seeps away. As I get to my feet, I do my best to bury the sadness poking holes in my joy so Lucan won't pick up on it.

He tilts his head anyway, sensing the shift in the air between us, but before he can question me or pry further into my mind, I'm running.

More like sprinting at full speed. And full speed for a vampire is a *blur.*

Further up the mountain, rockier ground begins to roughen the landscape. Lucan's paws thunder behind me, but he can't quite close the gap since I had a head start—not like the first time he chased me. Now, we're evenly matched.

Saskia, he growls through me. *What's wrong?*

I force my feet to move even faster, trying my best to distract myself from thinking anything at all, but all I'm really doing is tiring myself out faster.

Lucan slowly closes in until he's nipping at my heels, his thoughts pressing into my back.

Tired already, little nightmare?

I whip around at his accusatory tone, and Lucan skids to a halt.

You can't read my mind every time you want to know something, I shoot back right before he slams into me.

Again, I'm flying backward. This time, though, it's a controlled fall as Lucan pins me down against the rocky ground, his hulking form panting over me.

A splitting crack of rage that doesn't belong to me rips through my chest, the mood shifting so suddenly it gives me whiplash.

His eyes bore into mine. *You think I need to read your mind to figure you out?* And with a snap of his canines, he's human again. His chiseled jawline could cut stone. His muscular thighs press down against my hips when I start to wriggle beneath him. "I don't," he says, without breaking stride. "I *know* you. Inside and out."

My own anger flares when I can't manage to free myself from his grip. "Good for you." I let out a huff. "Now get off me."

Lucan chuckles darkly, running the pad of his thumb over my lips. "Maybe if you would have drunk enough, you'd have more strength to fight me off."

I tense every cold muscle in my body, and with all of my remaining strength, I push Lucan in the chest, launching him ten yards into the air.

He lands against a thick tree trunk with a boom. The tree shakes violently, pine needles raining down around us as Lucan slides down to his feet almost effortlessly.

Blinking, I scramble to stand up, and all the fear and denial and self-loathing I've felt since the moment I woke up bursts to the surface. "I don't want to be the reason you're in pain ever again," I seethe.

To my surprise, Lucan's face doesn't crumple. No flash of understanding crosses his expression. If anything, he only looks even more determined, his jaw clenching and his eyes narrowing. Maybe we really *are* enemies now, because all his sympathy for me seems to be gone.

"So, what then?" he asks, taking a step toward me. "You're going to starve yourself?" His voice is like rough gravel rolling over my skin, taunting me. "Resist this?" A claw shoots out of his index finger, and he drags it over his palm, slicing open a thin, fine cut. A bead of blood appears, and its scent fills my nostrils. My mouth waters, desperate to taste it on my tongue one more time.

I take a step back, remembering myself.

"Yes," I hiss. "I'll resist."

I already decided that I won't drink from him again. If what the journal said was true, I'll have until the next blood moon to live before starvation takes over me again and I die like my father did. Lucan and I won't ever get to explore a new bond because that would require me continuing to take his blood.

"I won't be a parasite," I say out loud.

Lucan begins to circle me, head cocked. "Parasites take without giving back. You can take as much as you want from me, and you'll give back tenfold. Therefore, you are not a parasite. What we have is symbiotic."

I laugh humorlessly, twisting to keep him in view. "Symbiotic? Is that so? What exactly do you think I give you back?"

He doesn't hesitate. "Life. Meaning. Everything."

I snort, crossing my arms and glancing away, despite the way those words make my stomach flutter. "You're just saying that to be nice."

With a growl, Lucan leaps forward. Adrenaline fuels me, my earlier exhaustion melting away as anger lashes back. I jump, colliding with him and sending both of us through the trees—straight into another boulder.

It cracks from the force, the sound echoing around us like an explosion, but I barely feel a twinge of discomfort.

Lucan smirks inches from my mouth. "Do I look like I'm being *nice* to you?"

"No. You look like you're being infuriating," I say, digging my nails into his pecs. Leaving marks I didn't realize I could make. Possession ignites through my spine. Infuriating but *mine.*

Heat builds between my legs, where his erection presses against me, pulling tight behind my belly button. I arch my hips ever so slightly just to feel the feather-light friction.

Lucan wraps a hand around my throat, squeezing so tightly that if I wasn't a vampire, I wouldn't be able to breathe. But I don't need to breathe nearly as much now, and he pulls my mouth to his.

His kiss is rough, sending a bolt of electricity straight through me, just like before. Becoming a vampire hasn't made his touch any less igniting. If anything, my body burns for him even more, desperate to explode against him.

I can't help the moan that escapes me. At the sound, he takes my bottom lip into his mouth and sinks his canines into it. Blood fills my mouth. *My* blood. It doesn't taste nearly as good as his, but the sting is a welcome shock to my nervous system.

"Did you like that?" Lucan asks before he soothes my lip with his tongue. When I nod desperately, he doesn't bite me again but pulls his head back an inch, exposing his own throat. "Make me burn, too. Give it back to me, baby."

I suck in a sharp breath, the need to *take* and *take* almost blinding. His pulse hammers in excitement when I run a finger along the vein across his neck.

"No."

I know what he's trying to do: goad me into biting him again. Give me just enough pain and fill me with just enough rage that I'd be willing to hurt him once more and finish my fill of blood. All of this teasing and taunting is his careful way of trying to play a game against me to force me to survive. But I can't fathom surviving like this.

Lucan doesn't give me time to fathom anything, though. In a flash, he's up and slamming me against a tree.

Then we're a fury of undressing—if you can call it that—between kisses. My dress is hiked up around my waist, my underwear ripped and hanging by a thread around one of my hips. His pants are at his knees, his shirt on the forest floor, his bare chest heaving.

The bark digs into my spine as Lucan spreads my legs wide to the point of pain and fills me so quickly the stretch is almost too much.

I cry out, delirious from the pleasure, as my breath is pushed forcefully from my lungs with every punishing thrust. Watching his abs contract as he ruthlessly slides in and out of me brings me so close to the edge that stars shimmer across my vision.

"Lucan," I moan over the obscene sound of how wet I am. This is primal, dirty.

"Remember, there are no rules here with me, Saskia."

Lucan tears my dress off, exposing my breasts. Then, burying his head in my chest, he teases my nipples too softly with his tongue before pulling back. With each of his thumbs and forefingers, he pinches them just hard enough to make a moan rumble up my throat.

But not hard enough to make me come.

I claw at his lower back, begging, "More."

He twists slightly, the pressure in my core building so chaotically, I'm on the verge of the most intense orgasm I know I'll ever experience. And then he releases the pain, replacing it with another soothing suck of his warm tongue, and disappointment wrings in my belly. "I can edge you forever, Saskia. Just build it and build it and never let you come. Like a monster."

"Destroy me then," I plead. My mind twists darkly. Another pinch of his fingers, another twist, and he has me right back where I was. On the edge. Wild. Out of my mind. Then he switches to using his canines, stacking feelings one on top of the other with a sharp ache followed by a warm lull.

"Look how fucking beautiful you are," he says when I arch my hips into him. "My little nightmare. My little vampire."

Then he takes every sensation back again, and I'm left panting, unable to speak. Of course, only for a second. Because he gives it all back mercilessly.

Slamming his cock into me with one long stroke, he laughs wickedly under his breath, his eyes roving over every part of me.

Again and again, Lucan gives and takes. Until I'm a sweaty, shaking, out-of-breath mess against a tree, whimpering for any sort of release.

"You're completely wrecked," he rasps, emotion glimmering in his eyes as they graze up and down my body. "Just like I like you. Now wreck me back. Please, Saskia. Wreck me back."

This time, I cave to his pleading and sink my fangs into his neck. No thought. No decision. No rules.

Just Lucan's warm, salty skin against my lips and his blood coating my throat, both of our moans floating into the crisp forest air.

"Fuck," he grunts. "That hurts so good. Don't stop."

Drinking him in, I feel his life force slide down my throat, settle in my stomach, and start to seep into my own bloodstream like we're becoming one, and my body might combust from the sensation of him inside me in so many different ways.

His entire body tenses, the antibodies in his system working hard to combat my venom. But I know the feeling, the pleasure in the pain that he's already given me. I can't pull away, knowing through our connection that he doesn't want me to. That somehow, this is different than him touching the Wall, because it's *me*.

"If you need my blood for the rest of your life, Saskia, it's yours," he breathes. "We're equal now."

Equal, I think, arching my hips, trying to feel him deeper as I swallow more and more of him. Never imagining how sensual this could be. *We're one.*

Like he can still read my mind, he whispers, "I already can't live without you, and now you can't live without me. We're *alive*, but only together."

And when we finally come apart, our bodies tremble so hard that the ground quakes.

LUCAN

L et's run away together," I say, slumping down against the pine needles littering the ground.

Saskia nestles against my chest, both of us trying to catch our breath. She closes her eyes, and even without our connection, I know she's imagining it: the unknown.

The color has returned to her cheeks. She looks healthier than I've seen her since she fell into my arms, and her sweet scent is magnified, like all of Arad's venom has completely dissipated, leaving nothing but *her* behind.

And the truth swells in my chest, so hard and fast I can barely breathe. She's not turning to stone. She has more than ten years to live. *Centuries.*

"We could explore the world," I add. "Find a new home. A better one."

She sighs as she opens her eyes and lets reality back in. "Xantera is the only world I've ever known. The only world that all of us have ever had. And I need to face your pack."

"I don't think it's a good idea to go anywhere near them right now," I tell her, a growl vibrating in my chest at the very thought. In truth, I'm not sure I *ever* want Saskia to be anywhere near my pack. In the last three hours alone, my entire world has split in half, where I'm the alpha of the last werewolves on one side and eternally tied to a vampire on the other.

I don't know how those two halves could ever join. But I know if I have to pick one...

Holding up her hand to inspect it, Saskia bends her fingers, flexes, like she's gained a sixth sense. Technically, maybe she has.

"If any of them wanted to attack me, I don't think they'd be able to catch me right now," she says, grinning. Then she drops her hand and peers up at me playfully. "But if you need time to recover from that, I understand. You must be wiped out."

Something about her new vampiric self inflates even more of a sense of competition in me than ever before. "Don't underestimate my stamina, Saskia. We'll see who the superior species is. Ready for round two?"

She pinches me under my arm, making me squirm, and rolls over on top of me until she's straddling me with her thighs. When she presses her lips to mine, a zing lights up my nerves.

"Maybe just give me a second," I concede with a low growl. "Venom. My blood. Antibodies. Mixing. All that."

She pulls back and blinks, mouthing words I can't make out. A gasp shoots from her lungs, and before I can register what's happening, she's throwing her dress back on and running off.

"Saskia!" I yell. In the blink of an eye, she's fifty yards down the mountain.

"That's it! Lucan, you're a genius!" Her voice carries back, high-pitched, excited, and I know she isn't going to stop.

Shifting, I bound after her. My body screams in protest, still stiff and aching. *How the fuck am I a genius? What did I say?*

Saskia's reply is only a giddy, *Yes, yes, yes,* like she's not even aware of me at the present moment.

Care to fill me in?

I thought you could read my mind, she teases.

It's going a mile a minute, I complain, *just like the speed of your legs.*

And maybe the venom is going to my head, making me a little rusty. I can make out blood and needles. Some term I've never heard that must be healthcare related. She's thinking about being a healer—or thinking *like* a healer. There's nothing I can grasp onto.

I need to talk to Taika, Saskia says hurriedly before she's back to chanting, *Yes—yes—yes,* with every enthusiastic footstep all the way back to the ghost town.

Taika's there when we turn onto the dirt road—along with the entire pack, their anger pressing like lead against my mental block. Most of them stand as werewolves, a few rows deep, like a wall of resistance. As if they were preparing for an attack.

Saskia skids to a halt, her thrill quickly replaced with uneasiness.

Maybe I didn't think this through, she tells me, and I hate the way her excitement—whatever the hell caused it—is so easily stifled.

I stalk around her until I'm standing in front of her, shielding her from the fury of the pack. Only Taika, Vivian, Soren, and Merrick, in the back, remain in their human forms. The rest are poised, lips curled, canines bared.

No. One. Will. Touch. You, I assure Saskia, lowering my mental block long enough for each of my words to land heavily into the minds of every single werewolf facing us. It's not a suggestion. It's an order from their alpha, which means they'll have to fight me to try to overpower me before they lay a single paw on her.

Reluctantly, they shift one by one until I can't hear the cacophony of their angry thoughts anymore.

Fucking Gabriel elbows his way to the front. I glance at Taika, who gives me a sorrowful grimace and raises his palms. "I didn't tell them. The children saw you carrying Saskia into my clinic, and when the rest of the pack came to me for answers, they smelled the change."

"Is it true then?" Gabriel's chest heaves as he sets his sights on Saskia. "She's really a vampire?"

I cross my arms. "She is, but it isn't what you think."

"She's a *traitor*," Gabriel snarls. "I knew it!"

Merrick and Soren grab him by the arms as soon as he takes a step forward. He thrashes to no avail, but his outburst gives others the courage to speak.

"Lucan trusts her, so we should too," Ashe says from the back.

"If Lucan's trusting monsters," Kyra argues, shooting a glare at me, "then maybe he shouldn't be our alpha anymore."

My anger spikes when she shifts that glare to Saskia. I step forward, my muscles aching with restraint, and roll up my sleeves. "Go ahead and fight me for the position, then, Kyra. When you're defeated, I'll just remind you who the *real* enemy is."

I point toward the Wall, and a few eyes flicker in that direction, warring expressions on all their faces. I get it. I really do. If I wasn't so head over fucking heels for the woman behind me, I'd probably have reservations, too.

But no one hates the Guardians more than I do—*no one's* tried harder to break down that Wall than me—so they should know I don't take her presence lightly.

In fact, I take her presence heavily. Like it's the entirety of the world.

But Gabriel won't let up. "*Look* at her," he snarls, still fighting to break free. "She's their spawn."

"And she's *our* salvation!" I roar, so loudly that a flock of birds takes flight from the tree beside us.

Gabriel stops struggling and snorts. "You're right, Kyra. He's lost his touch as alpha." He glances at Merrick and Soren, still holding him back. "If you value the rules of our pack, you'll let me fucking challenge him. Right now."

"Peace," a warm, familiar voice floats out from behind everyone, and a sense of calm washes over me. The pack parts down the middle, allowing my mother to walk through.

"You've challenged my son dozens of times before now, Gabriel," she says, not even deigning to glance in his direction as she wafts past him, "and you've always lost. Your chances of winning this time are even slimmer now that he's fueled by something else entirely."

My mother's eyes shift to Saskia, and soft wrinkles sprout around them as she smiles. "Hello, dear."

"Hello," Saskia whispers beside me, although I feel her body relax ever so slightly, and my own heartbeat steadies as Gabriel pulls his face into a literal pout.

"I believe you had something you wanted to tell us," my mother tells Saskia encouragingly, "before all these puppies started squabbling."

Merrick and Soren smirk. Gabriel and Kyra look ashamed. Taika's mouth twitches.

"Y-yes." Saskia clears her throat. "I just..." she starts, louder this time. "I might know of a way to try to bring down the Wall." At that, she has their full attention—and mine. "Would that prove my loyalty?"

No one dares make a sound... until Gabriel pipes up with a sarcastic quip. "Go on, then. How do you suggest accomplishing what we've been trying to do for centuries?"

"You all make special antibodies," Saskia says before I can decide whether to rip his head off or not, "when you're bitten because you're immune—unlike humans. And Lucan has been trying to climb the Wall for decades, coming into contact with it again and again, but not in high enough doses. And then today..."

Taika's eyes widen. "An antivenom," he whispers. "That's genius, Saskia."

"An antivenom?" I ask, looking between the two of them.

They're on the same page, but a chapter ahead of everyone else. A chapter ahead of *me*.

Saskia nods, smiling. "If we can use the antibodies in your blood to make an antidote, then it should counteract the venom laced in the Wall."

"And turn it back into wood?" I breathe, shocked that even such a thing is possible. If the Wall became wood again, I'd be able to splinter through it in a heartbeat.

"Yes. That might actually work," Taika confirms. But his eyes go from a blazing yellow to a dull burn, his shoulders falling. "Though, I don't have a centrifuge, Saskia, among other things we would need."

"A centri-what?" I ask immediately.

"A centrifuge," Saskia repeats, her eyes trained on Taika as she worries at her lip with her new fangs. "It's a little machine that separates substances based on their density. We'd need one to filter out the plasma." There's a short pause where Saskia's shoulders tense. "I know exactly where we can get one, though."

For a moment, the pack and I glance between Saskia and Taika as they exchange a significant look...

And then understanding punches me in the throat.

"Fuck no. Don't even think about it, little nightmare."

Saskia still refuses to look at me. "There's a centrifuge in the Healing Center in Xantera. I know exactly where it is, and now that I'm a vampire with all this strength, I'd be able to climb back over the Wall to retrieve it." Finally, she turns and lowers her voice. "It's the only way to prove I'm on your side."

Fury bubbles in my chest at the pleading expression on her face. "You don't need to prove shit."

She shakes her head. "Not to you, but to them."

The pack doesn't dare speak. All of their eyes are trained on the two of us, not wanting to miss a millisecond of how this plays out. My mother observes the both of us with sharp understanding brewing in her eyes.

I change tactics. "Can't I just... stir the potion really fast?"

Saskia folds her lips in, trying so hard not to laugh in my face. "It's not a potion, Lucan. It's an antivenom. And no."

"*I* thought it was a valid question," Soren pipes up.

Taika shakes his head. "We're fast, but not plasma-separating machine fast."

Saskia nods, her now serious stare darkening. "Lucan, it's the only way."

I sway on my feet. Saskia wants to go back into her cage to unlock it for everyone else, but how can I ever be okay with that? She might be our salvation, but who's going to save her?

Like a true Monster, I would rather watch everyone else perish than find a single scratch on her.

But when she places a gentle hand on my shoulder, and I stare into the new shade of her eyes—eyes she hasn't even seen in the mirror yet—I'm reminded that I can't keep her locked away from the rest of the world, or I'd be just like Arad.

"Promise me one thing," I croak.

"More promises?" she asks, though her beautiful lips quirk in a smile.

I nod and kiss her on those lips. Right in front of everyone. "You go in prepared this time."

SASKIA

According to Lucan, being prepared means taking a bath—his way of delaying the inevitable, I'm sure.

To be fair, though, I haven't washed a single part of my body since the Blood Moon Palace. So when I slide into the water he boiled and poured into his own tarnished, silver tub in his bathroom, I can't help but emit a groan of relief and sink as far as I can into the steaming warmth.

Lucan himself isn't here to move my fingers along my body this time. I can hear the faint grumble of his voice through the closed door to the right of me, having some kind of conversation with the few werewolves he invited into his home after the pack confrontation. I have no idea what he's talking about with Vivian, Merrick, and Soren downstairs, but the deep tone of their muffled words tells me it's serious.

Maybe his friends are trying to get him to see reason with me. Fling me back over the Wall, right into Arad's waiting arms, and forget Xantera entirely. It would certainly make more sense than this. *Us.* A werewolf and vampire... well, I'm not even sure I can say *in love.* Has that word ever crossed either one of our thoughts yet?

Maybe mine, like a whisper of a secret fluttering across my heart when I look at him, but I haven't heard it from him. So why didn't Lucan kill me as soon as I woke up with these fangs ripping from my gums?

I use them to gently pierce my bottom lip now, testing the sharpness and strength. Unlike Lucan's thick canines, these feel more like the needles I've used so many times to stitch up a cut in the Healing Center. I halfway wish I could pluck them from my mouth now, so that they could only be used to help and never hurt.

I already can't live without you, and now you can't live without me. That's what Lucan told me, right before we came undone together. As if somehow, he *likes* that I'm dependent on his blood now, that I can pierce his skin in the same way he can bruise mine. I'm just not sure if he actually means it, or if he's pretending for my sake.

Sighing, I glance around his bathroom, inspecting the details of it with renewed fascination. Unlike the plain identical ones in Xantera's housing units or the grand, gold-lined bathroom in my private suite in the Blood Moon Palace, this is purely and utterly *him.*

Half-used bars of handmade soap litter a shelf jutting from the wood-paneled walls, ranging in smell from mint to cedar to charcoal. A single bath mat that looks like it's about three hundred years old sits beneath a lone, tattered towel that looks even older, hanging by a wooden knob that Lucan must have nailed in by hand. A candle sits by an unused sink on the rustic wood counter, currently unlit; enough leftover light streams in through the window for me to see what I'm doing, although even that is certainly fading fast.

Before it gets too dark, I grab one of the bars of soap and begin to lather it in between my hands, massaging every inch of my new body and marveling at how *strong* I feel. My skin doesn't so much as dent under the pressure of my fingers. And I swear, my fingernails themselves have grown longer and sharper in the span of twenty-four hours, as durable as miniature blades. I could probably take a chunk out of the wall behind me, if I wanted to.

Of course, I don't. There's only one Wall I want to destroy.

At that thought, I sink under the water to soak the rest of my hair, then lather the soap onto my head and wash out every single ounce of grit and dirt. When I'm done, I rise out of the bathtub, water dripping all around me in echoing plops, and step out to wrap myself in Lucan's tattered towel.

Only then do I allow myself to look at the bottom frame of the cracked oval mirror hanging above the sink.

"Here goes nothing," I whisper to myself, and finally look up at my reflection.

A gasp shoots down my throat.

My eyes aren't the deep crimson of Arad's, exactly, but pink-tinged, like a red film slathered over the hazel and green. My eyelashes are darker, my eyelids nearly purple, as if Vivian's makeup from earlier is permanently stamped onto my face. But it's not. This is just how I look now—as ethereal and otherworldly as all the Guardians.

"I am not a Guardian," I tell myself, repeating Lucan's words from earlier. Trying to find conviction in them. "I am not one of them."

Suddenly, something rattles from downstairs, and Lucan's raised voice passes through the walls. So quickly I almost slip on the small puddle of water around me, I wrap his towel more firmly around me and race out the door, down the tight, spiral staircase, and into the kitchen.

"Is everything okay?"

Five pairs of amber eyes flick toward me. To my surprise, it isn't just Vivian, Merrick, and Soren in the kitchen with Lucan, but his mother, too, assessing me with both warmth and sharpness in her gaze. She's the only one sitting down at the moment, her arms crossed in a chipped wooden chair while the other four stand, facing each other.

"Hi, Saskia!"

The words come from Vivian. Lucan himself has his jaw hanging all the way to the floor as he stares at me, and a flush crawls up my neck when I realize I'm still naked, wrapped in just a threadbare towel, water beading on my skin and rolling off onto his floor.

Shit. If I was ever going to impress his mother, I've missed my chance. But I suppose gaining her approval was already a lost cause as soon as Arad's venom activated my vampire gene.

Soren, on the other hand, looks more than impressed enough.

"Well, *hello*." He rounds his lips as if to whistle, only for Merrick to slam a hand over his mouth before the first note can escape his mouth. Good thing, too, because Lucan turns to him with canines bared, claws already shooting from his fingers...

"Is everything okay?" I repeat, determined to prevent a fight that could very well demolish Lucan's entire house.

"Saskia." Lucan turns back toward me, his claws retracting, his jaw twitching. "I laid out some clothes for you right outside the bathroom."

"Oh." I glance down at my bare neckline, the swell of my breasts beneath the towel. From my periphery, I can see Soren smirking and Merrick looking away, while Vivian and Lucan's mother exchange glances. "I didn't see them," I say firmly, lifting my chin. "I heard shouting and wanted to make sure everything was okay."

I push out a little warning in those last words, wanting everyone in the room to know that I will *not* be locked outside of an important conversation. I've been locked away for too long. If everyone else in this ghost town wants me gone, I need to know.

Lucan rakes a hand through his hair, disheveling it.

"I was just trying to convince them..."

He trails off, glancing uncertainly at his mother, who raises a slender white eyebrow. My heart twists. *Trying to convince them not to hate you. Not to kill you. Not to think of you as the enemy,* I'm sure he means. Because they do. They hate me now. They want to kill me.

Vivian strides toward me, and my muscles tense in preparation for a blow. Her hand raises.

And then she lays it gently on my shoulder. "He was trying to convince one of us to fight him for the alpha position." She shoots a glare over her own shoulder. Not at me. At Lucan. "He was just going to hand it over, as if any of us want it."

"What?"

I crank my head toward Lucan, trying to read the stoic expression plastered over all his emotions. He hauls in a deep breath and meets my eyes.

"Better the alpha position goes to one of them than Gabriel."

"But..." I don't know much about the system of were-wolves—or *anything* about it, in fact. But I haven't seen a single other pack member who's as strong, or as determined, or as brave as him. "You're a perfect alpha, Lucan. Why would you want to give that away?"

Now, his eyes drop to the floor, and it's his mother who answers from her chair. "My son here thinks that his duties as an alpha—as a king—directly contradict his feelings for you. And that he has to choose one over the other."

The tone leaking from her words couldn't be any clearer: she disagrees. But I turn toward Lucan again, every promise and declaration he's ever given me swelling in my chest, nearly bursting. I can't tell if my stomach flutters with soft, delicate butterflies or if those butterflies have razor-sharp wings, threatening to shred me apart from the inside-out.

"You want to choose me over your pack? That's absurd, Lucan!"

"No." He lifts his head, and the entire kitchen seems to drop several degrees until I'm shivering in place. "What's absurd is that you'd think I'd choose anything *besides* you, little nightmare. I've told you over and over that I'm not leaving you, so when are you going to fucking hear me?"

When he eats the distance between us in two enormous strides and crowds into my space, everything else disappears except for the two of us. Just me and him, yellow and red pupils locked on each other.

"Do you need to hear the actual words before it gets through that beautiful mind of yours?" he continues in a softer growl. "I love you, Saskia. I loved you before I even laid eyes on you. I fell in love with your thoughts. Your worries. Your joys. Your fears. The way you talk and observe the world and fight for what's right, no matter what. What runs through your blood doesn't matter to me when I already know what runs through your heart."

I stare at him, unable to lock down the feelings swirling through me at his conviction. I know I should be saying something back right about now, but my jaw seems to lock up when I try to move it.

Lucan shakes his head, his eyes dusting over my face with the gentleness of a feather. "No need. I'm not expecting anything in return. I just need you to understand that yes, I do choose you over the rest of the world. You don't have to like it. But there's nothing you can do to change it."

His mouth sets in a firm line, and I have half a mind to take him right here, in this very kitchen, to soften the harsh lines written all over his face. But someone clears their throat and knocks some very important sense back into me.

"*Fortunately*," Lucan's mother says, "what's best for the pack and what's best for Saskia aren't mutually exclusive." Lucan and I both whip our heads toward her, the bubble popping around us. She grips the live edge of the kitchen table and hoists herself to a stand. "So you don't need to give up your alpha title at all, son. Not when both sides of the coin need you."

Lucan holds his breath, glancing between his mother, his friends, and me, his eyebrows pinched slightly.

Soren rolls his eyes. "Do you need to hear the actual words before it gets through that beautiful head of yours?" he taunts, and raps a knuckle against Lucan's head before Lucan can fend him off. "We *need* you, man."

"Oh, fuck off." Lucan pushes Soren away, but Merrick's clutching his stomach with suppressed laughter, and a smile twitches in the corner of Lucan's mouth.

Vivian beams at me. "Now that that's out of the way... come on."

She extends her hand out to me, and I take it, finding more solace than she could ever, ever know in the fact that she's still willing to touch me even though our skins are so different—mine as hard as marble, hers flexible enough to shift.

"Let's get you dressed. Not to impress this time, but to kick some ass."

I certainly *feel* like I could kick some ass in this garb.

Vivian managed to find some old hunting leathers that fit me perfectly, sculpting to my body with an elasticity that moves with my bones. She also gave me a special belt that I strap around my waist, fitted with various knives.

"In case you need something a little sharper than your new claws," she says now, admiring my appearance in the doorway with her arms crossed.

I glance down at my hands, flexing my fingers and feeling the sharp points of my nails pierce my palms.

Vivian watches me carefully, her eyeline following as I repeat the motion over and over.

"Feel different?" she asks curiously.

I nod slowly before a nagging feeling tugs on my heart. "Do you view me differently?"

Vivian blinks, then a laugh bubbles out of her chest. "Human. Vampire." She shrugs. "Same difference. You're still not as cool as me."

"I never will be," I joke, but I still feel the heaviness of the moment, a seriousness that lurks just below the surface of our moods. My tone changes to match it. "Thank you for still being my friend, Viv."

"Yeah," she says nonchalantly, waving a hand through the air, "I've always wondered if vampires are inherently evil or if the ones who stole our kingdom are just assholes. Pretty sure I have my answer now. You and I aren't actually that different. We want the same things. Love the same people."

My cheeks heat, the embarrassment flooding for multiple reasons: what Lucan declared in the kitchen and the fact that I didn't respond in kind.

"You love him back, don't you?" Vivian prods.

When I don't answer but my face reveals enough, the shadow of a smirk forms across her lips.

"What if the Guardians catch and kill me?" I whisper, a fear spreading in my belly like fire—not for myself exactly, but more for him and what my death would do to him.

Vivian cocks her head at me, her eyes pinning me with a stern look I don't quite understand. "Would you rather experience true love and lose it or never find it at all?"

My heart squeezes, goosebumps cascading up my arms. "That's profound."

Vivian bursts out laughing. "God, that's so cliche. I forget you've never heard things like that." But her laughter fizzles out as she leans against the doorframe, her brow furrowed in thought.

"Cliches hold truth though, I guess. Lived out again and again—by everyone, even if we're all 'different.' We all share something in common. Just something to think about."

Which, of course, I do. I think long and hard.

Guilt pricks in my chest. I can't tell Lucan I love him just to turn around, jump back down into Xantera, and then meet my demise at the Guardians' feet. It will only destroy him further.

And if I don't tell him I love him now, it will be even more incentive for me to survive.

More importantly, incentive for me to return.

LUCAN

S askia stares up at the looming height of the Wall, and I stare at her.

A slight breeze whistles in from the woods, picking up the ends of her hair and sending her scent straight into my nostrils. As soon as her essence invades my senses, I have to lock my limbs to keep myself from pouncing on her. From throwing her over my shoulder and running far, far away, where she won't ever be able to crawl back into this cage ever again.

It would be wicked, yes, but half of me doesn't fucking care.

The other half, of course, cares more than a million worlds put together. The way Saskia still looks at me like I'm the only thing orbiting her existence makes me yearn to be good for her. To be the exact opposite of a Monster in any way she needs.

"I can see the veins better now that I'm a vampire," Saskia breathes, and I move up behind her to follow the direction of her pointed finger—toward the glassy cracks in the Wall that writhe and twist ever so slightly, like live vines. "I never saw them moving before. Not as a human."

She can see better now. I should have suspected, but there's still so much more for us to learn about this new way of life. When she finally rips her eyes away from the Wall and back to my face, I wonder what else she sees in me now that her senses are so heightened.

"Don't do this." The words tumble out of my mouth before I can stop them.

Behind us, Vivian snorts. I'd almost forgotten she was even here with us, the rest of the pack gathered on the opposite end of the Wall, per my orders. "You'd throw me over the Wall if you could, Lucan, tell me to go get it, and walk away without a second thought."

I wrinkle my nose at her as Saskia laughs. "Don't tempt me."

Vivian swats a hand through the air. "She'll be fine, you love-sick puppy."

I groan at Vivian's smirk. She's probably going to remind me about my earlier heartfelt declaration for the rest of our goddamn lives. And honestly, as long as Saskia comes back, I don't care. But she needs to come *back*.

"You need to come back," I reiterate, ignoring Vivian again as my eyes slam into Saskia's.

She steps up to me and cups my face with soothing palms, the world shrinking into a cocoon around us until it's only me and her. "I escaped as a weak little human," she whispers. "I think I have an even better chance of escaping now that I'm... like this."

Her eyes flicker down to assess her body again, but I extend a single claw and use it to tilt her chin back up. Back to me. "You've never been weak, little nightmare."

But my weakness is her, so I'm a trembling mess when I fit my lips against hers, slowly this time, savoring the feel of something I wish I could stow away and hoard forever.

Us.

All too soon, though, a cacophony erupts from the distance, and we break apart. The rest of the pack members on the northern side of the Wall fling their howls at the moon at the same time for the first time in any human's memory. Hopefully scaring the shit out of the Guardians and the sentries who are so loyal to them.

"It's time." Vivian wrings her hands, all traces of her earlier humor gone. She glances at Saskia's leathers and knives. "Remember, if anyone sees you, they'll know you don't belong."

"So I won't let myself get seen, then." Saskia flashes her fangs in a dazzling smile.

My entire body quivers with the effort it takes to restrain myself from holding her back as she turns to face the Wall again. A sharp inhale singes my throat when she raises a hand toward the thing that has caused me so much pain over the last few hundred years.

Will it hurt her, too, now that my blood pumps through her?

As soon as her palm lays flat against it, I track the shiver that makes its way up her body.

"What's wrong?"

She jolts at my tone. Shakes her head. "Nothing. Just thinking about how this used to be wood. How once upon a time, you could have burned *it* instead of the other way around."

I dip my chin in understanding. "Get that centrifuge and come back to me, little nightmare, and then we *will* burn it. Together." I lift one of my fingers in a gesture she's no doubt never seen before. "And if you get the chance, throw the Guardians one of these for me."

She nods before reaching up, digging her fingernails into the imperceptible grooves of the Wall, and launching herself upward with a strength and speed that makes me dizzy.

But this time, instead of watching her fall, I watch her climb.

SASKIA

E very point of contact with the Wall sends faint echoes of pain
through my body.

But I don't slow. Don't stop, as I pull myself up and up and up,
knowing that it's only Lucan's blood in my system, reacting to the
vampire venom in the Wall. I'm sure his pain is usually a hundred
times worse, so I can't reveal so much as a flicker of discomfort.

Or I have no doubt he'll leap up and drag me away.

Finally, I break through the mist above my head, higher than
the treetops now. I can't believe I'm admitting this, but being a
vampire is fun—everything almost *easy*. As if I'm as nimble as a
spider.

Besides, it's funny how the Guardians never anticipated that any
of their cattle would actually become one. Arad doesn't know it,
but he gave me the power to do this.

Within minutes, I pull myself up onto the top of the Wall between spikes. With my newly sharpened sight, I'm still able to make out Lucan's dark shadow as it shifts beneath the mist down below, his presence swelling in my veins.

See you when you get back, he tells me. *And remember, I love you.*

Then he throws up the mental block around my mind, leaving me alone with myself in order for me to focus.

Instantly, regret slams through me at the echoing silence. I should have said it back—in case I *do* die. In case I don't ever get the chance to say it at all. But I don't want the first time I tell him to be mind-to-mind.

Swallowing down my stupidity, I turn and crouch, analyzing the twisting of streets down below, calculating how far I'll have to jump to land in the shadows.

With a deep breath, I spring upward and fly.

It *feels* like flying, at least. Because when I land stealthily on my feet, the impact barely reverberates through my body. But I have no time to process the exhilaration of freefall without fear.

Dozens of sentries line the nearest street, more than I've ever seen out all at once, their heads all cranked in the opposite direction as Lucan's pack howls and howls until even my own ears are ringing.

I creep along the shadows at their backs, listening to their low mutters of confusion and shock with a smirk twisting my lips.

"What's *that*?"

"The Monster, obviously."

"More like a hundred Monsters."

Fifteen, I correct silently. Fifteen werewolves decided to form a distraction for me tonight, including Gabriel and some of the older ones. But I'm glad the fear of the unknown is already making these sentries exaggerate the threat in their minds.

Then one of them whispers something that wipes the smirk right off my face.

"Maybe it's a bad omen for what we did."

What did they do? I peer around at what I thought would be bedlam judging by what Lucan and I saw from the top of Eversnow Peak, but the streets are empty except for the sentries. No rioting citizens. No unrest. Just a ghostly stillness.

Mapping out the quickest way to the Healing Center in my mind, I choose the third alleyway to my left and zigzag through Xantera.

The more I walk, the more my worry builds.

Signs of a dead riot stain the city. Boarded windows, glass littering the ground beneath them. Splatters of blood that I have to avoid every handful of steps. Some buildings are nothing but a pile of ash. And the usual flags and statues of the Guardians that adorn major points throughout our society are either torn or crumbled.

Fuck. Malcolm, Walter, Gaia, Eleni, Claudia... Did they leave anyone alive? Or is this the beginning of another ghost town? My chest constricts, my slow heartbeat thudding like a drum against my ribcage.

Just as I reach the main street, I poke my head around the corner to see a Guardian, the Ninth, stalking through the night back and forth across the Blood Moon Palace courtyard.

The actual Guardians patrolling along with the sentries? Unheard of.

Breathing heavily, I time his steps and the sentries' flanking him, watching their routine. But just when I think I've got it down, the Ninth Guardian snaps his neck in my direction.

I suck in a breath as I fly back into the alleyway, hoping like hell it was too dark to have seen me. But now I know just how sharp their eyesight truly is.

Turning on a heel, I choose a new path, eager to get off the street as soon as possible in case anyone chooses to investigate. Twisting through the night with a little extra speed, I'm finally here.

Not the Healing Center, but my old housing unit. I'm hoping against hope the detour won't take more than a couple minutes. I just need to make sure Malcolm is still alive.

Please don't be dead, please don't be dead, I pray, and I turn the unlocked knob.

The door squeaks open. Everything still sits in its usual place, only darker than I remember. No moonlight cuts through the shuttered window.

I search for the dim red light of the camera along the back wall but find nothing. Squinting, I see wires hanging from a rough hole in the wall where the camera used to sit. What happened here? Did Malcolm do that, or did a sentry? Or a Guardian? My blood runs cold when I realize that Arad might have come straight here to take his frustration out on my old partner immediately after I jumped off that Wall.

Curling my fingers into fists, I sneak across the room and open Malcolm's bedroom door. It creaks slowly, echoing in the tiny space.

"Malcolm?" I whisper into the dark. The lump under the covers doesn't move.

I tiptoe forward, dread filling my gut, knowing without a doubt that whatever lies under those covers isn't alive. There's no breathing, no heartbeat, no subtle movement.

"Malcolm," I nearly cry, ripping the covers off, knowing I'll find a dead body.

Instead, I'm blinking at a configuration of pillows—

Just as a large, grunting shadow charges at me from the dark corner with raised fists.

I shriek, my first instinct to cower starting to take over before I realize I don't need to do that anymore. At the last second, I stand up straight, rooted to the floor.

"Malcolm, it's me," I say after he lands a punch to the side of my head that feels surprisingly like a subtle bump—and makes me feel incredibly stupid for thinking a vase would make any impact against Arad's head.

I scrabble behind me and flip on the light.

"Saskia?" Malcolm splutters when his eyes land on my face and widen.

I release a breath. "I thought you were dead."

He rubs his eyes, as if convinced I'm a ghost. "I thought *you* were dead. Is it really you? How are you here? When's the last time you slept?"

"Slept?" I repeat, frowning at the odd question. The last time I slept was during that nightmare where I found out I'm a damned vampire, but I'm not about to tell Malcolm that. Maybe one day, but right now...

"Your eyes," he says. "They're bloodshot. Really, really blood-shot."

Oh. Right. Maybe he'll figure out I'm not a human sooner rather than later.

Malcolm's face pinkens at my silence, and he mutters, "I'm sorry. I shouldn't have pointed that out. It was rude of me."

"No, no." I wave a hand in the air. "It's fine. I haven't had a good night's sleep in a while." *Do my eyes really look that bad, though?*

No, a rich, deep voice answers, making me jolt.

Are you eavesdropping on me, Monster? I try to tease.

Only because you sounded distressed.

I swallow a sudden lump in my throat. I only got to look at the true color of my eyes a handful of times in my life before it was ripped away from me forever.

They're still the same eyes, Lucan says gently. *Just like the sky is the same sky even when the sun begins to set. Still just as beautiful. Just a different shade.*

I give a watery laugh, which makes Malcolm cock his head at me, confused. I clear my throat. "Look at us," I say, attempting to cover it up with a quick joke. "Both still alive and well, back in our old housing unit together. Who would've guessed?"

At the sight of his face, though, my happiness drains away. Malcolm might be alive, but he's not well. Both of his eyes are swollen, the purple bruises surrounding them only a few days old. Above his left eyebrow, a deep cut splits his skin, still red and inflamed and ready to bleed again at the slightest touch. And his crooked nose... definitely broken, by the looks of it.

"What happened to you?" I whisper.

Malcolm's shoulders slump, and he backpedals to sit on the edge of his bed, massaging his bruised temples. "The sentries, of course. I swear, as soon as we started questioning the Guardians or breaking any of the other Cardinal Rules, they just seemed to multiply."

I press my lips together, knowing time is ticking and that I really need to get to the Healing Center for that centrifuge. But Malcolm looks so broken—both physically and spiritually—that I can't just leave him here to break apart even more.

"That requires stitches," I say, reaching out to brush his hair back. He winces in pain. "Why didn't you go to the Healing Center? Gaia could have helped you."

"I don't trust anyone. Not anymore."

I motion to the bed, hoping that 'anyone' doesn't include me. "Lie down. Let me see if I still have some extra supplies in my old room."

When he does, I hurry across the hall to my old box of a room, the plain bed and lamp still sitting in their exact same spots as the morning of the last Choosing. My wardrobe door hangs ajar, my old uniforms and cloaks still hung up in neat rows. And when I jerk open the bottommost drawer, my few belongings rattle against each other.

I breathe out a sigh of relief. Alcohol pads, bandages, the embroidery needle from our standard-issue sewing kit, a half-used spool of thread.

Grabbing them all, I sneak back to Malcolm's room and pull over the chair in the corner to sit beside him. "It's going to hurt," I tell him, not bothering to lie. He knows there's nothing here to dull the pain.

Malcolm takes a steadying breath as I thread the needle and bend it into a crescent shape, but nods. He turns his face to the side, away from me, when I rip open an alcohol pad and sterilize the needle.

Just as it pierces his skin, he whispers through a groan, "I got your letter."

My hand pauses briefly, but I stay quiet as I resume.

"Not long before, every screen in the city came alive with static, and the loudspeakers squealed. The feedback so intense people were covering their ears. But then it went quiet, and those statues flashed across the screen. Everything I've ever taught my students, a lie." His voice cracks. "People's loved ones frozen in time. Others' lying in those beds about to kiss death. It kept replaying over and over on a loop. That is, until you came into view."

Malcolm flinches when my needle pokes a little too deep. "Sorry," I breathe, steadying my hand. "Just a few more."

He clenches the bedsheets and mutters under his breath, "You're right. That hurts."

"Might I suggest a nice 'fuck?' Saying bad words works wonders."

He chuckles through his tense jaw. "That's when the feed cut off, you know. We all watched you taunt the Third Guardian, heard him reveal the truth about everything and threaten to kill you. And there you were, defiant as usual, telling him to go fuck himself."

His eyes glaze over, as if remembering every detail, before he continues.

"I thought you were dead, and then I found your last letter in my dinner tray, explaining everything. So, Walter and I, we started the rumblings of defiance, whispered in people's ears, inciting riots until enough people started to fight back. We took to the streets, tearing down cameras and statues. We burned essential buildings, tried to storm the palace."

My eyes go wide, a tear threatening to spill. Pride and heartache claw at my chest.

"Why?" I whisper. "What really made you decide to do something?"

Malcolm frowns, chewing on his lip, before resolve tightens his skin I'm still stitching, and he winces again. "Because you were right, Saskia." With a great breath, his gaze latches back onto mine. "I... I love him. Walter. In a different way than I love you. And I don't think the Guardians should take away anything from us, but least of all love."

I beam, tying a square knot to finish the suture. He's right—and I'm so proud of him for acknowledging and fighting for it.

But Malcolm turns to look at me with concern still stamped all over his face. "How, Saskia? How are you alive? How did you get out of there? I saw you jump."

For a moment, I have an urge to lie down next to him and spill every single detail over the past several months, including everything the so-called Monster has ever said to me. But I'm not even supposed to be here right now, and time is bleeding away.

"I'm sorry, Malcolm. It's a long story and one I don't have the time to tell at the moment. But I'm bringing in help. It's the only way to defeat the Guardians. Humans are no match for them alone."

"I know," he says. "Our riots were quickly contained. The sentries took in hordes of people to throw over the Wall, and they beat the rest of us." He gestures at his face, now freshly stitched. "Thankfully, they didn't know I started it, but I keep thinking it should be *me* they fed to the Monster. All those people dead because I actually thought thousands of us could stand a chance against twelve Guardians if we united."

I lay a hand on his elbow and squeeze. "It's not your fault for trying. All we can do is try," I add, thinking of Lucan's earlier words. "And they might not even be dead."

I know for a fact that the rioters weren't thrown over the Wall, so where are they now? The same place as Diggory? Or did the

Guardians simply lock them in with the other Chosen Ones, drinking their blood until they became complacent and lethargic?

Another round of howling, this time from the east, makes both Malcolm and me jump.

"It's weird," he says, "we never knew there was more than one Monster."

"We never knew a lot of things," I reply, arching a brow. "And there's still so far for us to go."

From the belt around my waist, I pull out two daggers and place them next to the candle on the nightstand. He needs them more than I do, and I have plenty more.

Malcolm does a double take, his bottom lip dropping open. But he doesn't ask where the weapons came from or how I was able to acquire them. He just closes his mouth and looks back at me with resolve.

"Now, keep your wound clean, and lay low for a little while." I kiss his good cheek before pressing my forehead to his.

He smiles. "Thank you, Saskia."

"I'll be back, Malcolm. I promise. And next time, I won't be alone."

Back in the minty night air—this time wrapped in one of my old cloaks I plucked from my closet in order to camouflage myself a little better—I find the sentries scurrying around like ants, shouting useless orders as the pack continues to howl and howl and howl.

As I approach the end of the alleyway and stick my neck out to look up and down the main street, I can't help but smirk again, watching them panic.

Though, it makes things harder for me to get across, where the entrance to the Healing Center sits thirty yards in front of me.

I debate how much of my speed to use, and whether or not I'll need to use it.

Lucan, can you move the pack back to the north, behind the Blood Moon Palace? Make the sentries think something's happening there?

Done, he replies instantly, and the pack's howling ceases abruptly.

The sentries freeze and look between each other wildly.

One minute of silence passes. Two.

Just as the sentries start returning to their patrolling rhythm with a spooked look in their eyes, the howling bursts back into life, right behind the Wall where I first jumped into Lucan's arms.

The sound electrifies me.

All of the sentries turn toward it, half of them starting to sprint in the Blood Moon Palace's direction.

Pulling my hood over my head, I step out into the open at a quickened pace. I'll have to pass right behind a sentry, frozen in his tracks by the roaring of Monsters.

But as long as they keep howling...

Twenty yards. Ten.

That's when I lift my eyes and my heart cripples with intense shock.

"No!" I gasp. Cry. Wail, really. Forgetting where I am, the urgency of the situation, my knees buckle as I take in what I so desperately wish wasn't real.

A body stretches out above the Healing Center doorway, wrists and ankles tied with rope that strains against the cinched knots. Each limb is pulled out tight, the head lolling unnaturally. Still, I recognize the face—the thick eyebrows and dark hair—and my entire body goes rigid as pain rips through me at the realization.

Claudia.

LUCAN

A blast of emotions rocks me, coming from Saskia herself. First is shock, so swift and powerful that I almost collapse alongside her.

This brutality wasn't committed in secret, not behind the walls of the palace, but out in the open, in front of the very place that people go to be healed. It's a mockery and a warning and a threat all wrapped in one—the last piece of this facade of a utopia peeling away.

Revealing the true nature of Xantera for everyone to see.

"No," Saskia cries again, and then her grief—and mine, too—hit me square in the chest. You don't have to be a healer to know that Claudia is dead. Through Saskia's eyes, I can see dark, dried blood caking the rope hanging her up, soaked into the woven fibers and staining them a deep, almost black, red.

It's all my fault, Saskia thinks in horror. *If I hadn't asked her to broadcast incriminating videos to all of Xantera...*

It's nobody's fault but the one who took her life, I cut her off, pacing along the Wall and wishing for the thousandth time I could kick it in. This time, not for revenge. This time, I just want to comfort, to be there for her and let her cry into the crook of my neck. But right now, I'm only a warm presence in this chilling reality. *I'm sorry*, I whisper.

Saskia heaves out her own, "I'm sorry," but it's not directed at me. The pain cracks through her chest, the regret pricking her like a thousand needles.

"I'm sorry. I'm sorry. I'm sorry," is all she can manage to get out as it echoes through the night back into our connection. *Lucan... do you think Eleni's okay? She helped Claudia get to that tech room. What if she got caught, too?*

I can't answer that despite how much I wish I could.

And that's when anger explodes out of Saskia, stacking on top of the sadness, one after the other, oscillating back and forth until pure rage wins out.

Rage at the Guardians. Rage at the system. Rage at the lies and deceit and cold-blooded indifference.

Her gears click into place, a shift that slams into me with an overwhelming force—and I know.

I know she's not just a healer anymore. She's a healer who is now willing to kill the parasites that killed Claudia. Willing to destroy the vampires that have officially pulled the veil of perfection off of everyone's eyes with every countermove made against her.

But I see this for what it is—desperation. The Guardians have no other option but to instill fear in the humans. Fear of *them*, not just me as the Monster.

Problem is, Saskia is no longer human.

SASKIA

I know I need to steal the centrifuge before I get Claudia down. But seeing her strung up like that, murdered for sharing the truth... it only strengthens my purpose and the deadliness coursing through my veins.

Gagging, my furious tears well as I take a step back.

The automatic glass doors stretch open before me from the motion, just as the sentry whips his head in my direction.

"Hey!" He grabs my arm, twisting me around forcefully and pulling me right into the line of the camera I was trying to avoid. Hopefully, the Guardians are distracted just as much as the other sentries. "Do you have permission..." Recognition dawns across his face as he peers under my hood, and his mouth curls into a disgusting smile. "You're that Chosen One who—"

Swinging my free arm, I land a fist to the side of his head, knocking him out without letting him finish his sentence. Before he can crumple to the ground, I lower his body and drag him until he's slumped against the wall, cringing at what I just did despite the necessity of it.

He almost ratted you out, and you're feeling guilty for silencing him? Lucan asks incredulously, still lurking in my head.

Well, I probably gave him a concussion. But more than that, I can't bear the thought of taking someone's life while Claudia's dead body hangs overhead. The only ones I want to kill right now are the Guardians themselves. Which I will do. I'm sure of that now.

Good thing he's right next to the Healing Center, Lucan grumbles.

Without glancing at the camera, I whisper a promise to Claudia, then slip inside the building as the doors seal closed behind me.

Apparently, the rioting, beatings, and execution didn't touch my old favorite place, because it's business as usual here. Or at least the facade of business as usual.

Two patients sit in the waiting area, eyes cast downward, while an information clerk sits behind the desk, her blonde head buried in her computer. Before any of them can look up, I disappear behind the first door to my left.

The hallway is empty, but I pull my hood down tighter around my face. The cameras here blink from every corner, operable as always.

I stick as close as I can to the walls, trying to act as normal as possible as I navigate the maze to the laboratory.

Each healer I pass politely nods their head without looking too hard at my face. They don't peer too hard at anything. They don't question or think. The Rules are ingrained too deeply, I realize, and Claudia's death just makes them too frightened to look up and peer even closer at the truth.

Which is why when I turn the corner and see Gaia, I swallow my nostalgia and keep my head down.

"Good evening," she says as she passes me.

My ribs clench. It's so good to hear her voice, to know that she's alive. I wonder if she participated in the riots, or if she kept her head down and clung to the Cardinal Rules. Probably the latter, judging by the lack of bruises or scratches on her face.

Masking the tone of my voice into something slightly higher-pitched, I repeat, "Good evening."

Then her footsteps recede, unaware that anything is amiss, as I slow.

The laboratory door looms ahead of me, closed. The frosted glass distorts my view of the inside, so I have no other choice but to take a deep breath and swing it open.

Instantly, cold, sterile air hits my face. Several refrigerators hum on the far end of the room, while other analyzing machines whir and clink and emit a high-frequency pitch that my new vampire hearing can't block out.

I can smell the blood, too. Old blood, new blood, blood in vials, blood everywhere but nowhere in sight at the same time, locked away in one of the many metal cupboards lining the wall above a counter that spreads across the room...

Where one man, hunched over a microscope, looks up to find me still standing in the doorway.

"Hello." He blinks rapidly, as if trying to adjust his eyesight. "Can I help you?"

It's him—the healer who turned me in for arguing with Gaia what feels like a lifetime ago.

Making a split-second decision, I say casually, "Dr. Edward asked me to get him a few things. Would you be able to show me where they are?"

Dr. Edward, I know, is the Healing Center's leading pathologist, so it's not like I'm pulling a random name out of my ass. It *could* be true.

The healer, however, squints at me, rubbing at his eyes with a frown as he takes in my cloak and hood—not healing scrubs. Shit. Maybe I should have just knocked him out like I did the sentry, but I really don't want to give a second person a concussion in the same night. Even if he kind of deserves it for reporting me to the Guardians all those months ago.

"I'm sure if Dr. Edward needed anything from the laboratory," the healer says coldly, abandoning his microscope and standing up to face me slowly, "he'd know that all lab equipment *stays* in the lab. Now come a little closer and tell me your name."

I sigh. If he insists...

In three powerful strides, I'm in his face with the tip of a dagger pressed under his chin. Two days ago, I wouldn't have even dreamed of doing such a thing, but Claudia's body strung up in front of the Healing Center door lit every fuse in my body. This man had to have walked under her corpse to get to work today, and he's worried about who I am? Maybe he should be worrying about who *he* is, deep down.

"Name's Saskia," I say with mock brightness. "I believe we've brushed shoulders before." The man gapes as he takes in my face, my eyes, and the cold touch of metal against his skin. "And right now, a very talented doctor needs some equipment to *leave* the lab, so I'd appreciate it if you could direct me to where I can find them."

That's my girl, Lucan coos.

I wouldn't actually use this against him, I argue, glancing down at my blade.

You wouldn't have to. You could use your bare teeth to rip him to shreds.

I swallow thickly, trying not to inhale the sweet scent of blood pulsing through the scared, trembling man in front of me, and some of my anger deflates. *I wouldn't do that either.*

That's my girl, Lucan says again, pride lighting up his voice.

My attention returns to the healer, who finally manages to splutter, "What does this doctor of yours need, then?"

"A centrifuge to start with," I answer immediately.

The healer wets his lips nervously. "What kind?" I blink at him, and a slow, triumphant smile spreads across his mouth. "Benchtop, gas, high-speed? Surely, your *doctor* specified the type you'd need."

I dig the dagger just a tiny bit more into his neck, until his smile bleeds away.

"Anything portable," I say, and pray that's the right answer. "One with a back-up battery."

The healer raises his hands and takes a step back, so I follow him, dagger still pointed an inch away from his chest, around some tables in the center of the room and to the opposite side. There, he nods over his shoulder—

At a small, cube-shaped machine with digital buttons lining the bottom and a circular porthole on the lid up top. A centrifuge.

I snatch it up with my free hand and manage to squeeze it into an inside pocket of my cloak, although the bulge of it presses against my waist. "Great! Thanks! Now I need..." I silently recall the list of other requirements Taika gave me earlier. "Sodium hydroxide, sodium chloride, pepsin."

Too slowly, the healer takes me to various cupboards, and I stuff my pockets with bottles of liquids and powders with labels that I make sure to check, just in case he's trying to lead me astray. But he doesn't, and the laboratory doors don't fly open. Nobody storms in to stop me.

Finally, I have everything I need.

"Well, it's been a pleasure working with you," I say politely, giving the healer a mock bow and finally removing my dagger from his space to twirl around.

"Now, wait a second!"

I don't wait a second. I burst out of the laboratory door and pick up my pace in the hallway, using all of my restraint to not break out into a run. He keeps shouting at me, but I don't stop, don't glance back, just keep twisting and turning my way through the Healing Center until I'm almost to the main entrance again.

That's when the loudspeakers crackle.

"Saskia."

Arad's maniacal voice fills the hospital, vibrating through my bones along with Lucan's growl of warning in my mind. One of the cameras' blinking red lights slowly swivels toward me, training its sights directly on me. A few passing healers stop in their tracks, eyes widening at the intercom in the corner.

With no time anymore to spare, I finally break into a sprint.

"My favorite Chosen One," Arad laughs through the speaker, his voice following me around every corner. "So eager to return to me."

The centrifuge in my pocket thumps against my thigh with each step. When I burst out into the main entrance of the Healing Center, every head cranks my way and the information clerk shrieks with a hand on her heart, but I don't slow. Out the double doors, I don't hesitate for even a moment.

Twisting, I find the closest foothold and heave myself upward with all my vampiric speed and strength, scaling the metal doorframe, up, up, up, until I reach Claudia.

Then, grabbing my knife again, I saw through the ropes until they snap, one by one.

Claudia's body slumps into mine. I gather her carefully in my arms before launching myself back down to the ground, all in the matter of a few blinks.

Then I jump past the still-unconscious sentry and skirt around a herd of other sentries converging onto the main street.

They shout after me, demanding I stop, threatening to kill me as I start to run faster.

Slow down, baby, Lucan says soothingly. *Right now, the sentries by themselves are no threat to you. But if you run too fast, you'll show your hand. And all twelve Guardians will come after you in a heartbeat if they realize you're more than they think you are.*

I don't look back. Running south, I force myself to stay at a pace equivalent enough to that of a human, but just out of reach of their swords. Claudia's head lolls against my chest. Air swishes against my back as the sentries swing.

When I reach the farming fields, sprinting down a column of high-rising stalks, a cloud passes in front of the moon, shrouding the night with more darkness.

I'm so close to the Wall, only one giant leap away.

But the sentries' sudden silence makes me wheel around.

At the edge of the field, they surround me in an arc like they've got me well and truly cornered, their swords drawn and a gleeful gleam in their eyes as I press my back against the cold, veiny stone that sends those vague echoes of pain shooting through me.

Then Rosalyn's simpering face sharpens across my vision as I home in on her grinning back at me.

"Saskia," she says politely, as if we're back in my housing unit with Malcolm, hiding threats behind pleasantries all over again. "So good to see you again."

I scoff in her face. I won't play this game any longer. "Sorry. I can't say the same."

Rosalyn flushes, but then her smile grows wider as her eyes rake over Claudia in my arms.

"So sad," Rosalyn tuts, "to see a Chosen One go feral like that one did. I don't know how she got into the tech room, but she was as wild as the Monster himself when we tried to stop her." She sighs heavily, placing a hand against her heart as if the memory weighs on her, even though I can see the pleased gleam in her eyes from here.

So I give Claudia the only thing I can in death: glory.

"Seems to me that if she still got the truth out to all the citizens with you and four others trying to stop her, she wasn't just wild. She was strong. Stronger than you."

Now Rosalyn's smile slips.

"Not strong enough to survive my blade through her throat, unfortunately. I do hate to give consequences, but the Guardians rewarded me for it. As they will when I do the same to you."

She raises her sword as if she's actually going to charge me, and I take a step back. Not because I'm worried about my own life, but because I don't want Claudia to be mutilated any further.

But before she can, the other sentries suddenly sweep apart, parting down the middle, and an overwhelming presence fills the gap. The same presence I've felt during every Choosing, magnetizing in all the wrong ways.

Rosalyn stops abruptly, her hands slamming into her sides with doe-eyed obedience. Compared to who just arrived, she's no more of a threat than a spider or snake.

Arad takes one lazy step toward me, the sentries fill the hole he left behind, and then it's just me and him surrounded in a ring.

He crosses his arms over his chest, not threatened in the slightest, cocky even. But I swear, there's the faintest hint of confusion and fear brimming beneath that expression.

"You survived that fall?" he asks, tracking his eyes down my body as if trying to see through the cloak and the shadow of my hood. "And without hurting yourself? What did the Monster do, throw you back over?" He laughs, the sound like nails scraping stone. "Even *he* didn't want to mess with my scraps."

Lucan responds by howling out loud, right on the other side of the Wall against my back, and Arad actually flinches. Especially as the cacophony of the rest of the pack continues on the other side of Xantera.

I clutch Claudia's body tighter against me. "I'm nobody's scraps. But I *am* a nightmare. Haunting you forever."

Arad forces out another laugh, piercing through the heavy, hushed breathing of the sentries. "I don't actually believe in monsters, Saskia. So, tell me, how did you get back in? And why? Feeling nostalgic for your old life? Did you realize how well I treated you in here? How much better it is than the real, cruel world?

Wanted to see if I still have the city under my thumb after the stunt you and your friends tried to pull? Or were you coming back for this?"

From beneath his velvet cloak, he pulls out that same key I searched so long for, swinging it before me like the pendulum of a clock. Taunting me. Trying to bait me.

It doesn't work. I know that if I get close enough to grab it, he'll grab *me*, and then I won't be able to get these supplies to Taika. So instead of lunging for it like he expects me to, I scoff.

"Do you ever actually wait to hear an answer after you ask a question, or do you just like to hear yourself talk?"

For a moment, Arad keeps dangling the key out in front of me, as if he hasn't quite processed that I'm not falling for it. Then with a wrinkle of his nose, he tucks it away and waves his hand lazily. Like I'm a bug he'll squash easily. One that isn't even worth exerting his energy over. "Bring her to me."

The sentries lunge.

Easily, I swing out a leg faster than humanly possible, knocking two into the rest until they all tumble backward. Only Rosalyn manages to sidestep the chaos, leaping through and swinging her rapier toward me, toward Claudia—

Until I grab a knife from my belt in a flash. I've never handled a weapon before, but even without training, my sharpened eyesight and agile movements send the blade whizzing right on target, sticking into her shoulder and jerking her sword backward.

A scream of pain tears out of her mouth. The sound floods me, but my usual healing propensity doesn't so much as cringe with guilt. Because *she* killed her. She killed Claudia.

The remaining sentries scramble to a stand, hesitating.

Just like Arad. His nostrils flare, eyes bulging, as realization dawns on him that I'm no longer someone he can bully around.

He crouches, his face mottled with rage, and spits, "They turned you into a werewolf?"

"I wish," I laugh, which only makes me grin harder and bear my fangs, revealing the truth. I can't help myself. This moment is so sweet, I can taste it on my tongue. To bolster it, I lower my hood and shoot him a glare with my new crimson eyes. "Try again."

Arad gasps, too stunned to move.

With the extra second, I raise my middle finger just like Lucan showed me.

Then I scoop Claudia up over my shoulder and clamber back up the Wall.

It only disarms Arad for a moment. I can feel the air stir as he leaps, flying up behind me, cursing me, or maybe himself, as I pull myself up, faster and faster and faster.

When I reach the top, I don't hesitate. Launching myself off the edge, I soar through the air and land perfectly on my feet, right between Vivian and Lucan, still in their werewolf forms. Instantly, Lucan leaps in front of me, putting himself between me and the Wall with his back arched, teeth bared, and claws digging into the earth in preparation.

Far above us, Arad hesitates on the top of the Wall between two spikes.

Do it, Lucan thinks. *Jump, motherfucker.*

But the clouds clear, causing moonlight to spill over all of us, and he jolts back just as quickly, clinging to the spikes.

"One vampire who can touch the Wall still doesn't mean anything. Come back again, and it'll be twelve against one." Even from way up high, Arad's voice carries to us on the crisp night air. Or maybe that's just my new vampire hearing at work. My eyes also detect how he zeroes in on Lucan, lifts a lip in a sick, one-sided grin. "And next time, I'll gladly take her away from you. Give her something to really scream about—"

I stop listening, blocking the rest of Arad's words out, because his idle threats don't matter. Neither he nor the centrifuge matter right now, with the weight of this body in my arms.

We need to bury her, I tell Lucan instead, choking on my words.

He half-turns toward me, his hulking silhouette more terri-fying than anything else in these woods, but his ears twitch, and the amber in his eyes seem to melt when they look at me. Relief fills them, but all *I* can feel right now is guilt and grief.

Of course. Vivian?

Yes, alpha? Vivian's tail flicks.

Guard the Wall until Arad slides back into his lair. Have the others run the perimeter with you. And if a Guardian tries to come after Saskia... tear them to shreds for me.

Would be my pleasure.

At that, Vivian flings a howl up at Arad, one that seems to bite at the air with jagged teeth. I don't look up to see if he flinches or not, or even if he's still there. I just turn my back on the Wall, Claudia in my arms, and put as much distance as possible between her and her former cage that she never got to escape alive.

We march through the brisk night air until the dirt road turns into grass, through the wrought-iron gate circling the graveyard.

"This way," Lucan instructs me as he veers to the left.

I follow on his heels, weaving around tombstones, an iron bench, a worn statue of an angelic woman with wings.

Lucan stops in front of a group of headstones laid out in neat rows.

Each one is blank. No names. No dates.

He steps carefully between them, stopping on the last row, all the way to the right. There, Lucan gestures for me to lay Claudia's body at the end.

"These are the graves of every citizen who has jumped before you," he says, wrapping a comforting arm around me as soon as I straighten, his thumb rubbing circles against my shoulder. "I don't know their names, but I was born to protect each of them. Just as I was born to protect you."

The emotion comes on suddenly, knifing up my throat. I swallow the sting, but the tears still fall.

"While you dig," I say, blinking through them, "I'll clean her."

Lucan nods and shifts without a word.

Leaving him behind to claw through the dirt, I race at full speed toward the river, collecting a bucket and rag from Lucan's house along the way.

When I return, the top of Lucan's monstrous head barely pokes out of the hole he's already made. I drop to my knees before I dip the rag into the bucket of fresh water.

I start at Claudia's wrists, washing away the dried blood, trying to soothe the raw skin. Next, I switch to her face and neck to wipe away the dirt caked into the lines of her skin. With my nails, I tame her knotted hair and tuck it behind her head, then smooth out her clothes.

"There," I say quietly when I'm done. It takes another beat for me to speak again, the words stuck like a pit in my throat. Nothing justifies or makes up for this. "You won't be forgotten," I whisper to her. "I'll make sure of it. I'll tell everyone how brave and courageous you were. How you stood up for what is right and how much you sacrificed for others. How you helped end this. How you were the one behind the camera, giving them the truth."

I halfway expect her to say something back, but of course, her lips remain still. When Lucan hoists himself out of the hole, he helps me lower her down onto the soft earth.

At least I can give her this: a place of eternity to rest instead of a stone garden where she'd be a decoration for the Guardians, like my mother. I think she would have preferred it this way, even if I never really got the chance to get to know her within those palace walls.

"I'm sorry," I whisper again, for the last time. Because even if Claudia knew the risks, I was the one who told her about the

Chosen Ones turning to stone and came up with the idea to reveal the truth. The only way I can avenge her death now is by making sure she didn't die in vain.

When Lucan and I are done blanketing her in the loose earth and placing a stone overtop her grave, he sucks in a breath and brings out something pinched between his fingers.

The crimson vial that used to hang from my necklace, before he snapped it off.

"Taika gave this back to me, and I've been hanging on to it, just in case..." His eyes rove over my chest, where the vial used to sit. *Just in case this new communication between us quit working and you needed it back,* he doesn't have to say. "But now," he continues, "I think it's time to put my grandfather's blood back where it belongs."

As the wind makes the branches beyond the graveyard creak, Lucan leads me to a pair of gravestones a few rows away from Claudia's. They're weathered from time, patches of algae growing in various spots despite the fresh bouquets of wildflowers lying at the base of each one. Unlike the nameless Chosen One graves, these ones are labeled.

WARREN VERADEL
ADRIAN VERADEL

"My father's body is buried here," Lucan says, nodding at Warren's headstone, "but we didn't have anything to bury my grandfather with. Until now."

Slowly, he bends and places the vial of blood in the middle of all those wildflowers, and it looks... perfect. Exactly where it was always meant to be.

A rustle sounds behind us. I whip around, my nerves still on edge, but it's just a couple dozen pairs of amber eyes blinking at us from the edge of the cemetery. The other pack members, come to pay their respects to their ancient king who is finally resting in some semblance of peace.

Swallowing the scream I want to fling back at the Guardians for all they've taken away, I turn toward Lucan, something much different hovering on my lips.

Half of me feels like now isn't the right time to be declaring anything heartfelt, when we just buried a woman who might have been my friend in another life.

The other half of me knows that it's *always* the right time to tell someone you love them.

So I do.

"I love you, too," I declare, raising myself on tiptoes to press my lips to his. Lucan captures my kiss with a surprised widening of his eyes before closing them, gripping me tighter, the centrifuge in my cloak's inner pocket pressing between us. "I love you," I mutter against his neck, "and I should have said it earlier. Life is too short, too fleeting not to—"

I choke on those last words, and Lucan pulls back to swipe a gritty thumb along my cheekbone, wiping away the single tear that spilled over.

"Then we have a weapon the Guardians could never see coming," he whispers back.

Realizing what he means, I suck in a breath and nod. Arad might know I'm a vampire now, but I'm willing to bet he could never predict the depth of the love I have for the Monster. Or how much he has for me.

And together, we're going to avenge Claudia and all the others who have suffered.

I just hope like hell the object in my pocket was worth it.

LUCAN

J ust as the new morning sun crests above the Wall, Saskia places a handful of bottles and a little machine on the workbench in Taika's patient room.

I hover, crowding her and staring at it in awe.

It's not much. Just a foot long, a foot wide, maybe half a foot high. It has a few buttons on the front screen, and the little gray door on top is transparent. But apparently, it spins really fast.

"Sit," Saskia demands, wheeling around. She pushes me down by the shoulders into the woven chair, and I obey upon contact, the backs of my knees knocking against the hard wooden edge.

"Is this how you treat the people you love?" I tease, trying to coax a smile onto her face.

We only had a few hours of sleep before the birds started their morning chirps outside our window, so dark circles haunt her undereyes... although that might be from the dead Chosen One, too. My own chest is a raging battle, rage over what the Guardians did clashing against the flurry her words created last night, my heart trying to hammer itself out of my skin to get to her.

She *loves* me. She loves *me*. If making this antivenom wasn't so pressing...

Saskia rolls her eyes with the faintest smile lifting the corner of her mouth and glances at the syringe already laying on the counter. Taika, however, shakes his head.

"You need to bite him again so we can take advantage of the immediate immune response."

Saskia stiffens, her gaze switching longingly to my neck, but she makes no move toward me or my endless supply of lycan-thrope blood.

I narrow my eyes before I tip my chin up. "My blood is yours. For the rest of our lives, I want the privilege of keeping you alive." I'm already half-hard thinking about her fangs piercing my skin. "Oh, not to mention that there's zero fucking chance of me not contributing to bringing down the Wall—so bite me, little nightmare."

She doesn't need to be told again. As Taika turns away to busy himself with preparing the needle, she slinks onto my lap, the delicious pressure of her thighs clamped tight against my hips.

This time it's slow. Methodical. Her palms skate up my chest, and even though they're technically cold, the contact leaves me electrified. My hands wrap around her hips, trying to pull her even closer.

Those two sharp pricks against my neck sting so good that I have to repress a moan. Hers vibrates against my skin like a whisper.

I know she can feel just how much I like this, and there should be no doubt left in her mind about whether or not she's causing me pain. There's no denying how intimate it is, but we're both restraining ourselves for Taika's sake.

Too soon, she pulls away, standing up. The absence of her body leaves me even colder than before.

"Was that enough?" she asks Taika, licking her blood-stained lips.

My blood.

"It should be," he replies, interrupting my wandering lewd thoughts with a long needle that he holds up in front of his face. "Which arm would you prefer?"

I debate rolling up my sleeves before shrugging and just yanking off my shirt entirely. Then I plunk my left arm down on the table before Taika connects a thin rubber hose to the needle and then some sort of vial onto the end of it.

"Big breath," he says gently. "This might hurt a little."

"I'm not afraid of a little nee—OW! Dammit, doc."

He shoots me an apologetic eyebrow twitch and mutters, "It's just a blown vein. Haven't done this in a while."

"It can't be any worse than my bite," Saskia offers, sliding her hand over mine.

My blood slithers up the hose like a bright red snake and fills the collection tube within seconds. Taika pops the full one off and replaces it with another.

"Your bite means your mouth is on me, which is all I can ever ask for," I tell Saskia as Taika keeps his rhythm, filling three more vials, one after the other. "This is a cold piece of metal in my vein."

"Not anymore." Taika eases the needle out, a bruise already forming—and already healing—where he punctured me. "You're all done. Now, Saskia and I will centrifuge it, and your plasma will rise to the top, where we can extract it."

The words sound like a foreign language, but I trust he knows what he's talking about. "And what do *I* need to do?"

Taika and Saskia share an amused moment before he shrugs. "Go away so Saskia can focus. You're distracting her."

My eyes find Saskia's, and I want to bask in the hint of pink warming her cheeks. She's trying not to look at my abs, I realize. Or the bulging muscles in my arms. Or my pecs.

"Fine," I say, trying not to let my smirk touch my lips. "I'll leave."

But not before I rise to my feet, slide my hand around Saskia's throat, and kiss her over her slow, steady pulse that picks up ever so slightly at my touch.

Satisfied, I stride out the door and step outside, where the pack all scrambles to their feet, like they've been waiting for me on the front lawn. Which, I guess, they have.

Gabriel steps forward with an exasperated sigh. "Well? Does it work?"

"We won't know for a while," I grunt, already pissed off just at the sight of him.

"That's convenient," Gabriel scoffs. "She could just be tricking all of us. Especially you and Taika. Maybe it's a ruse to—"

This time, it's not me who pummels him. A tiny brunette blur whizzes across the lawn and slams into Gabriel, tackling him to the ground. He grunts out in pain when his body pounds into the dirt.

After the initial shock wears off, Gabriel swings a fist into Vivian's side. She returns one to his temple before they're a rolling heap of groans and curses.

Much to my delight, Vivian eventually gets a knee into Gabriel's balls, and she uses the moment to pin him down.

"I'm tired of your inflated ego," she spits. "Saskia is the first real hope we've had in centuries. Don't you want to have hope?"

"Of course I do," Gabriel splutters. "I just—"

"Then pull it out!" she screams.

"Pull *what* out, you crazy bitch?"

"That stick you have shoved so far up your ass that it's choking you."

Vivian doesn't wait for his reply. She knees him in the gut and stands up, leaving Gabriel to curl into the fetal position in pain.

"Anyone else got anything to say about Saskia?" she asks, dusting herself off.

I fold my arms, beaming. Not a single pack member dares to annoy Vivian any further. A few shake their heads, one slow claps, another few smirk at Gabriel, and I try to swallow my laugh as he spits out a mouthful of dirt.

Merrick, however, stalks up to Gabriel and presses his boot into his cheek, grinding his face against the dirt once more. "Call her a bitch again," he says, his voice as calm and quiet as ever, "and I'll rip out your tongue just to shove it back down your throat."

Understanding settles in my chest—that protectiveness and possessiveness over the one person who means most to you. Honestly, I'd do worse if anyone called Saskia anything I didn't like. But all this rage of ours has nowhere to go. No real outlet for centuries, forcing us to turn on each other, again and again and again.

So when Gabriel scrambles to a stand, puffing his chest out at Merrick, I use my alpha tone of command to halt him.

"Save it, Gabriel. Save it, Merrick."

Both of them turn their glares upon me.

"For what?" Merrick demands.

"For them."

Once again, I point toward the Wall, toward our real enemies and all the people within that cage that need to be freed.

Because even if Saskia's plan works and we get inside...

We'll still have twelve vampires to slay.

SASKIA

Taika and I work through the day, isolating the active ingredients in Lucan's blood and adjusting the pH of his resulting plasma. I'm in awe over the process, at how carefully Taika describes every step, showing me and then allowing me to try.

"And now to add the pepsin solution," he practically hums, snatching up the little glass bottle. "I'm glad you managed to get the liquid kind rather than the powder, since we don't exactly have distilled water anywhere nearby. Here." He hands me a small, clear pipette before I can respond. "We only have ten milliliters of plasma to work with right now, so let's dissolve one ounce of pepsin in it."

I close an eye, sucking up the appropriate amount of liquid. "How do you know what the right amount is?" I ask, eager for more information. In our schooling phase, they skimmed over the processes of... well, everything. There was no point in going into detail when the Guardians would ultimately choose our careers.

"I don't know," Taika admits. "A long time ago, I developed some snake antivenom for the kingdom using sheep blood, but *vampire* antivenom using *werewolf* blood... it's an entirely new process. An experiment, if you will."

My heart drops, even as I squeeze beads of pepsin into Lucan's plasma and watch it dissolve among the thick, yellowish substance. An experiment? We don't have *time* for an experiment. But I suppose testing it out on a Wall is better than testing it out on a human.

Still, my mind wanders to the possibilities...

If we can get this right, could we inject it into those stone statues in Arad's garden?

Could my mother wake up?

"What would happen if we just used the raw plasma?" I ask, glancing at the empty bottles scattered around us. If we fail at this, we won't have any more chemicals to purify the antibodies with. Only the centrifuge to filter out the plasma.

"In human patients?" Taika muses. "They'd probably die, due to some unwanted components in the plasma. Toxins that would shock their system. In the Wall? Probably nothing, because the antibodies wouldn't be concentrated enough. Okay, now let's bring this pH back up. Hand me the sodium hydroxide?"

By the time the sun fades once more past his clinic's window, we have several sterile vials of an opaque liquid that no longer resembles or smells like Lucan's blood whatsoever.

"Do you actually think it'll work?" I whisper finally, staring at the vials that look so inconspicuous.

"There's only one way to find out," Taika says gently. "But we'll have to let this incubate for a few days, and in the meantime... even vampires and werewolves need sleep. I daresay you haven't gotten much since you fell off the Wall the first time."

I flex my fingers, still feeling the foreign sense of power thrumming beneath my skin and remembering how Lucan said he once ran around the perimeter of the Wall for days and days before he finally fell unconscious. "Apparently, I don't need as much rest as humans do."

But Taika gives me a pointed look, peeling off his gloves, so I take that as my sign to leave. Maybe some real, solid rest after everything that's happened in that time frame wouldn't be such a horrible idea.

"Thank you," I tell Taika. "For trying this with me. And teaching me."

He bows his head. "Thank you for giving us the idea. I'd like to think we could have done it without you, but I'm not sure contact with the Wall would have created enough antibodies in any of our systems. And I never would have been able to acquire the right equipment."

I nod and cast one last long look at the little centrifuge on the counter before bidding him goodbye, crossing my arms against the nip of the nighttime as soon as I open the front door. It looks like everyone's gone to bed, the wind warbling through an empty street, so I ease the door shut as quietly as possible and hesitate on the clinic's ramp.

"You didn't think I'd be able to sleep without you, did you?"

Lucan's shape dislodges itself from the shadows across the street, and I instantly feel my chest loosen as I breathe a sigh of relief. He waited for me—for hours, judging by the crumpled, dirt-streaked state of his clothing.

"You've slept without me plenty of times before," I say, taking his outstretched hand as he steps closer. His large, warm fingers thread themselves through mine.

"Never again," he promises, and chills graze along the back of my neck at the intensity of his words. For the next five minutes, we walk hand-in-hand to his house—where the world suddenly tilts off its axis as he scoops me up off my feet.

"What are you doing?"

Lucan doesn't even glance down at my best attempt at an affronted expression. He simply marches inside, me against his chest, as if I weigh no more than a rag doll.

"Replacing a bad memory with a good one," he says simply.

It isn't until we're up the spiral stairs, through his bedroom, and toward those glass doors I've tried not to look at that I understand: the balcony. *I'll show you how beautiful it can be the first cloudless night we get*, he told me on my first night. Is it a clear sky tonight? I forgot to look, so consumed with my thoughts about antivenom.

Placing me on my feet before the glass door, Lucan swings it open.

I step out first, quiet, almost reserved. A heavy weight seems to pull my eyes downward, past the railing, where the dirt road stretches between rows of houses in varying degrees of degradation. A strange sense of fear spreads in my stomach, as if every person still trapped within Xantera might rise from the ground and wave up at me with jerky, skeletal arms. As if I've already failed them and left them behind to rot.

Lucan's presence steps up behind me, though, magnetic in the opposite way of the Guardians'. I feel his thumbs grip the sides of my face. And tilt it up.

Finally, my eyes lift to the sky.

For a few seconds, I blink, adjusting to the blanket of rich, velvety black speckled with bright lights. The stars. They look far enough away to be separate universes, yet my hands twitch upward anyway, as if I might be able to touch them. What would they feel like? Soft and silky like fabric? Warm and sticky like honey? Or something else entirely?

"You are not a Chosen One anymore, Saskia," Lucan says from behind me, his warm, rough hands still cupping the edges of my face. "And you don't have to keep looking down."

I lean my head back against his chest, wishing I could cement that declaration into my heart, but something keeps tugging at my peripheral. What if no one else ever gets to experience the stars like this? What if all my friends I left behind never get to see the night sky with no Wall around their entire world?

"What if..." I start out loud, swallowing thickly and squeezing my eyes shut. "What if it doesn't work?"

"The antivenom?" he questions me as his rough palms skate down my arms.

I nod, trying to loosen the tension in my body, but somehow, my muscles cord further into cold marble. Lucan carefully slides the straps of my dress down my arms before his thumbs press into my constricted shoulder muscles, working their way between my shoulder blades. The light pressure feels a little like heaven.

"All we can do is try," he says finally. "And keep trying. Over and over again, until the world caves."

We're both silent for a beat as his words settle heavily on my heart. If that's what it takes then that's what I'll do, but the weight of it all, being the one who has success or failure resting on their shoulders... it's a lot.

"I know what that feels like, to feel responsible for others' well-being. To lead despite not asking to be a leader," Lucan continues, dragging a pleased moan out of me as he works out the tension in the muscles framing my spine. His fingers move to my lower back, then hips—and when he hikes my dress up a few inches—my glutes.

I feel like a sculpture he's molding out of clay, leaning heavily against the railing now. One where he occasionally presses his lips into my curves and hums against my skin.

And then murmuring, "If we fail, Saskia, then we fail. But it won't mean that you didn't try or that you don't care. I've failed thousands of times. Trying to bring down the Wall, obviously, but also as the alpha. I've had to make hard decisions, ones that have helped us and ones that ultimately hurt us, even though there was no way of knowing at the time which. One thing I can guarantee is that not everyone will agree with you, but when you know that you've done everything in your power to do the right thing, then there's nothing to worry about. And I've *always* done what I think is best for us, *collectively*, just like I know you will."

He pauses and crouches behind me. His hands drop to my thighs, massaging the tips of his fingers in slow circles along my hamstrings.

"Well," he amends, "until you, that is."

"Wha..."

Again, my words melt into a moan at his touch, louder this time, echoing into the night air. I freeze, suddenly self-conscious of the fact that we're outside, and that anybody could be looking out their window to find me pressed against the railing with my straps pulled down and my dress hiked halfway up. I scan the streets nervously...

"What did I tell you?" Lucan asks me, rising back to his full height and twirling me around so that I'm facing him with my back to the railing. He puts a finger beneath my chin. "Look *up*, little nightmare."

I do, basking my sights in the blanket of stars once more. With my neck now fully exposed to him, Lucan's lips find the skin just above my collarbone.

My mood shifts. Suddenly, the air turns sticky, like honey dripping from the sky. I want more than just a massage as his mouth trails along the curves of my breasts. But we're still outside, still out in the open. Nobody else is out, but...

"Can you be quiet, baby?" he asks, a smirk lacing his tone.

This might be the biggest break-the-rules moment of my life, and my first instinct is to put my head down and say no, we can't. But Lucan's eyes turn molten as they grip mine, and I remind myself, just like he told me, that I'm not a Chosen One anymore—even if we've chosen each other.

So I glance over my shoulder one more time to make sure the streets are empty before I practically melt. "Yes, I can be quiet."

LUCAN

S he can't be quiet.
  That much is clear as soon as I spin Saskia around, pressing her stomach against the railing, and hike up the hem of her dress. She gasps into the night, and I've never felt so smug or proud of a sound in my entire life.

With her round, perky ass exposed, I run my palms over the curve of each smooth cheek before I crouch to my knees behind her and sink my canines into one.

She gasps even louder, then smothers her moan into the back of her hand.

Swiping my thumb between her legs, I swirl it against her clit in a tight circle, testing her.

Still moaning into her hand, Saska grips the edge of the railing with the other. Her knuckles turn white from the pressure.

The rest of her body, though, goes from hard clay to putty in my hands, just like I wanted.

"That's it," I praise her, keeping my voice in a deep whisper. "Relax."

I want to worship every inch of this body, study every curve and dip, catalogue every goosebump that I bring to the surface. And the Monster in me wants to destroy her.

Ravage her so that no male could ever get the scent of me off her.

She lets out a satisfied breath, her body responding to my touch with an arch of her hips, and it takes every ounce of restraint in me not to slam my cock into her here and now. But my goal isn't to coax any screams from her lips tonight.

Despite my nature, tonight, I'm going to melt her into a puddle.

Under the stars that she never got to bask under until now.

Her perfect ass arches again, desperate for the friction. Chuckling, I oblige with two of my fingers. I fill her slowly, stretching her just enough, until the tight warmth has a string of curses falling quietly from my mouth as I watch them slide in easily up to my knuckles.

Saskia moans in response, so eager and wet for me.

My cock is equally as desperate. Straining against the zipper of my pants, I rub my hand over the bulge. It's not enough to even take the edge off, but I like to torture myself just as much.

"You see," I start to explain through Saskia's muffled moans, pumping my fingers in and out, "I may have once done what was best for the collective. But now, after you? 'Collective' isn't in my vocabulary anymore. Like I said earlier, I'll choose you over anyone and everyone, again and again. You are the light, and I am your dark. I'll be a Monster whenever you need one. So save Xantera, little nightmare, and I'll save you. Always."

If she'd play along, if I'd let myself, I would fuck her against this balcony and drive her to the brink of insanity. I'd make her scream my name so loud, Arad would hear her delirious pleasure from the other side of the Wall and know he would never get to experience my nightmare.

But not tonight, I tell myself. Tonight, I'll behave. Just a little.

When she looks back at me over her shoulder, my eyes shoot to hers with a threatening heat, picking up the pace with my fingers to guide her right to the edge.

And I keep her there.

I press my lips into the supple skin of her left ass cheek, reveling in how tight her pussy grips my fingers. As my teeth skate across her skin, her legs begin to quiver.

"Please, Lucan," she begs through her hand. "I need you."

I need her, too, more than she will ever know. But I don't say a word.

Instead, my eyes fuse to her gaze, watching every detail.

The lines of pleasure crease across her forehead, her full lips parted, struggling to take in enough oxygen. Her head falls back. Then her eyes start to roll back, fluttering closed.

"Open your eyes and come with stars in them, little nightmare."

Finally, I curl my fingers in the exact I spot I know will take her breath away completely—because I can read her mind even without a necklace.

Her body reacts violently for me. Shuddering against the balcony, her limbs like jelly, she cries out my name into the cool air until I press my palm against her lips and smother it into my skin. Her fangs prick my skin, a sting I want to wrap myself in, as she struggles to control the sounds coming from her mouth.

A satisfied smile twists up my cheeks watching her come undone for me, but I'm not going to let her recover. Even I have my limit with how much I can behave.

She whimpers, somewhere between longing and exhaustion, when she realizes I'm not going easy on her.

The head of my cock teases, presses slowly into her, and pulls out, slick from her arousal.

Again, I repeat my movements, achingly slow and driving an inch deeper with each new controlled thrust.

I want to slam into her up to the hilt, but agonizingly, I restrain myself, tensing my forearms as I grip her hips like my life depends on it.

Running my hands over her ass, I groan when she starts to ride me, trying to take back control. Her hips move rhythmically, sliding my cock in and out of her warmth.

"Look at us," I murmur, pulling out completely, then pressing into her fully. My breath whooshes out of my lungs at the feeling. "A werewolf and a vampire in love. Defying the world."

I press my lips into her shoulder, dropping kisses down her spine. Soft and sensual, just like the way I make love to her. I don't always have to be a Monster.

There's no urgency in this moment. Just heavy breaths shared, both of us trying to control the sounds crawling up our throats.

My fingers lace into her hair, pulling her head back to gaze at the wide-open sky. Nothing will ever cage her again. Nothing will prevent her from living her life freely, as long as I'm alive.

And when we come together with smothered moans, it's like we're shattering with shards of starlight before putting each other back together, piece by piece.

SASKIA

"S o, how was your night?"

I choke on nothing but air at Soren's question the next morning. We're all in the town hall, Lucan, Soren, Merrick, and Vivian eating breakfast while I *watch* them eat breakfast. Unfortunately, none of the eggs, bread, or fruit looks even remotely appetizing anymore, but I'm nowhere near hungry with Lucan's blood still running through my veins.

"W-what?" I ask, as Lucan shoots a daggered stare his way.

"You know..." Soren's eyebrows lift. "Your first night sleeping as a vampire. Or is it your second? I lose track with all the excitement going on." He shovels some scrambled eggs into his mouth and freezes. "Wait, do you even sleep? Or do you just lie in a coffin like the rumors say?"

My shoulders relax as I realize he *doesn't* mean he saw Lucan and me making love against the railing last night. "Oh. Yes. I definitely found a coffin to lie in last night. It was wonderful."

In truth, last night was probably my best bout of sleep I've ever had. After cleaning ourselves up, Lucan and I stumbled to bed completely exhausted and ravaged, and I woke up this morning to find myself curled into his body as if the hardships of life molded it just for me.

Thankfully, Soren doesn't press me for details about what happened *before* that as Vivian wrinkles her nose at him from across the table.

"You know you're supposed to *eat* your eggs, not wear them."

I have to agree with her. Lucan's friends eat like... well, wolves, scarfing down everything in the vicinity as if chewing is merely a suggestion. I didn't notice it before, while I was so nauseous that I couldn't focus, but now I steal glances at the other tables around us: how the children practically inhale their breakfast, how Gabriel's fork stabs his plate with enough force to break it—although that might be due to the death glares he shoots toward me whenever Lucan isn't looking.

Soren looks down at his chest and shrugs at the bits of egg clinging to his shirt. "I call it a sexy scramble."

"Where do you even get all your eggs, anyway?" I pipe up, imagining a bunch of poor mother birds flying back to find their nests empty. I've never actually seen an egg before it was cooked and pushed through the slat in my door, but I know from my schooling phase that wild birds lay them in little circular beds of twigs and leaves.

"There were plenty of farm animals here in this town before the Wall turned to stone," Merrick answers, his arm around Vivian's chair.

"Yeah, and Lucan's mom has made sure to keep breeding and taking care of the chickens." Vivian wipes at her mouth and gives a burp without looking even mildly ashamed. "It's made breakfast the easiest meal of the day, because we don't always have to hunt for it."

"Unfortunately," Soren adds, "the cows died out. Poor bastards."

My gaze drags to Lucan, who's already observing me with the same wonder that I'm observing everything else. As Vivian, Merrick, and Soren plunge headfirst into another conversation about cheese, I lower my voice. "Where does your mother live? I haven't heard any chickens..."

Not that I even know what a chicken sounds like, but surely they chirp or croak or howl or something?

"Last house down the row, by the meadow." Something indiscernible passes over his face. "She hasn't liked crowds ever since my father died."

"Well, then, she definitely wouldn't like Xantera," I half-laugh, picturing all the thousands of bodies crammed together during the Choosing.

And just like that, my mood drops again, especially as Lucan murmurs, "Veradel."

"What?"

"Before the Guardians took over, our kingdom was called Veradel."

"But Veradel—that's your last name." My mouth pops open before I snap it shut again. "The kingdom was named after you and your family?"

"No." He presses his mouth in a firm line. "*We* were named after the kingdom. My ancestors took on the name Veradel as a reminder that we would always be tied to the people we were sworn to protect. The Guardians knew that, so they changed the name to Xantera—meaning 'protector of the earth'—to mock and defile it even further."

My hands tighten into fists in my lap. I shouldn't be surprised that Arad and his fellow vampires would disrespect Lucan's old kingdom like that, but it seems like they did a thorough job of squashing every part of the true history underfoot. I bite my lip, forgetting, once again, how sharp my new teeth are as the sting of their pointed ends makes me jolt.

"You okay?" Lucan asks, eyebrows furrowing.

"Yeah, I was just thinking…"

Around me, Vivian, Soren, and Merrick fall silent, obviously listening in, and even the rest of the room seems to pause mid-chew, as if they've somehow sensed the direction of my thoughts.

"When the vampires invaded," I begin quietly, "they had the element of surprise, right? But there were still only thirteen of them, and how many of you?"

"Nearly one hundred," Lucan admits. "But that's including the children and those nearing the end of their millennia, like Taika. So half of them couldn't fight anyway."

Still. That was fifty werewolves to thirteen vampires, and the vampires still won. I don't *feel* like I'm stronger than Lucan or any other werewolf here, but how did so few vampires manage to best so many werewolves, even with the element of surprise?

Vivian lays an arm on mine. "You have to remember, Saskia, before the invasion, vampires were near myths to us. We knew we existed to protect our people from those monsters of legend—um, sorry, no offense—should they ever show up on our doorstep, but we'd lived for generations peacefully, mingling with and protecting humans without incident."

Lucan nods. "My grandfather had no way of knowing how a vampire fights or moves. We knew nothing about your speed or agility." His eyes skate down my body for a brief moment, and I know he's imagining our clash in the woods, the way the very ground quaked at how we came together. "Until now."

"Well, that's just it, then." I scoot my chair back and stand up, feeling Gabriel tense as if I'm poised to attack him. But I don't even spare him a glance as I smile at Lucan and extend my hand. "I think it's time you all learned how to fight a vampire."

Vivian looks downright gleeful as Lucan and I circle each other in the meadow behind the old church.

My steps are light, but for some reason, I feel no need to match Lucan's stance. He stalks me in his werewolf form with his chest nearly brushing the ground, ready to pounce at any moment.

Scared to attack first, baby? I taunt him, even though I'm the one with nerves fluttering through my belly. Why did I even suggest this? I've been a vampire for a grand total of what... three days? And Lucan has been a werewolf for centuries. He'll probably have me by the throat in no time.

Right on cue, Lucan himself snarls. *Scared you'll like my canines against your throat a little too much?*

I swallow my insecurity and force out a smirk, taking a wide step to my right, mirroring Lucan's movements.

Need a heads up? I ask. *Three... Two...*

"Wait—" Vivian tilts her head before a gasp rolls off her tongue, noticing for the first time that I'm no longer wearing the necklace. She whips her head back toward Soren and Merrick. "What the *hell*? Are they communicating right now?"

Shrugging, I risk a half-turn to her, keeping my eyes trained on Lucan. "Drinking werewolf blood has its advantages, apparently."

"No way!" She grins, then morphs from bottom to top, her nose elongating into a grinning snout, that dark fur the color of her hair sprouting over her body, her fingers sharpening into claws. Two seconds later, you'd never guess a petite, innocent-looking female was just standing in the werewolf's place. *Oh, I gotta listen to this.*

Fine by me. I smile.

Don't encourage her, Lucan rumbles, but there's a hint of amusement in his voice.

Afraid she's going to side with me? I tease.

No, he chuckles. *I know* she'll side with you.

Kill him, Saskia, Vivian confirms, amber eyes sparkling.

As I turn my head for a split second to laugh with her, Lucan uses my apparent distraction to pounce.

His body flies through the air at me, but it's like time begins to ooze, slowing to a snail's pace. I track every millisecond out of the corner of my eye with ease, and then sharp new instincts take over my limbs, and I leap faster than I ever knew was possible.

A boom claps like thunder when I connect with his hulking form, but with my element of surprise, I clearly have the advantage.

At least, for a second I do. Wrapping my legs around his mid-section and my hand around his throat in midair, I twist and throw my body weight down on top of him right as we hit the ground. He'd be able to use his strength to throw me off of him within half a second, but I already have my mouth against his neck, my fangs grazing his pulse.

You're dead, I say playfully, pleasantly surprised with myself.

Vivian hoots. *That did* not *disappoint.*

Lucan scrambles to all fours after I release him. *How did you know exactly where to grab me?*

I press my lips together and try to replay the last twenty seconds, remembering the thrill of those instincts rising up inside me. *Well, for starters, my peripheral vision is 20/20 now,* I explain. *20/10? Maybe 20/0? Whatever it is, it's good.*

More like perfect, he mutters.

Exactly. If you're in my line of sight at all, it's like I can anticipate your next move. Unless you're directly behind me, change tactics.

We're back to stalking each other in a wide perimeter, when I hear Merrick and Soren's voices join the fray of our minds.

We had to experience this for ourselves.

Yeah, Lucan. It's not every day we get to see your ass get handed to you. This might be the highlight of my life.

We're going to have an audience soon, I laugh.

Then we'll give them a show.

Lucan doesn't bother with a surprise attack. In this makeshift ring, he'll never get behind me anyway. He lunges, this time keeping his paws on the ground so that I can't get to his midsection. I see his plan unfurling, and honestly, it's not a bad one.

Just as he's about to barrel into me, I juke him with an agile shutter step, not even thinking about what I'm doing, just following the movement my body wants to perform in the face of my enemy. Lucan can't adjust quickly enough to my lithe movements, and he misses sinking his teeth into my arm by half an inch.

We spin together, him kicking out his hind legs to throw me down onto the grass, me baring my fangs to rip off his head.

I grab hold of his fur at the last second and manage to pull him with me to the ground, where we spiral until I end up on top with a grin, showing off my fangs.

How many lives do werewolves have? I joke, barely out of breath. No wonder the original Thirteen Guardians were able to take down Veradel with the element of surprise. Fighting a werewolf doesn't require any training at all. It's just second nature.

Merrick whistles. *Damn, she's fast.*

I already know that, Lucan reminds us.

But you're stronger, I say, climbing off of him. *If you had anticipated my move half a second before it happened and adjusted, you'd have ripped my arm clean out of the socket.*

Lucan snaps his teeth hungrily. *Got it. Somehow anticipate what you're about to do, even though you're doing a damn good job of blocking it out mentally right now.*

I can't explain it, I add, *but it's like I can see everything in slow motion. Maybe if you try to be a little less predictable, do some more feints, it would be harder for me to keep track of your movements.*

Noted, Lucan growls. *Again.*

Oh, hell yeah, Soren hoots. *We've got ourselves a lovers' quarrel.*

Just as Lucan springs off his hind legs without warning.

I swing out an arm, but Lucan twists in midair before my fist can connect and lands two inches away from where I anticipated.

His momentary triumphant smirk splits through me, which only fuels my competitive edge. I manage to twirl in a circle around him until I'm at his monstrous back, hooking my fingernails into his fur to throw him to the ground. But instead of fighting me on that, he turns his head and clamps his teeth around my right wrist. Not hard enough to break my new marble skin, but just enough to fling me sideways, off of him.

That's all you've got? I tsk breathily as I land on my feet in a crouched position.

Funny you think I'm using my full strength, he replies, already circling me again with a glint in his eyes that suddenly makes me feel like prey in the best way possible.

Don't go easy on me then!

Just as I'm about to launch myself at him again, he does it first—and leaps completely over my head. Before I can spin around to face him, I feel two large, human hands grab me and push me to the ground until I'm face-first in the grass, spluttering.

I try to kick back, but Lucan's already on top of me, pinning me down with his giant human body, one hand wrapped around my throat as his canines brush the shell of my ear.

"You look good pinned down beneath me," he says, licking my throat.

I laugh and squirm against him, although pride bursts through me when he releases me and I turn around to view his triumphant face framed by the halos of the sun above us. "What took you so long?"

"Took me a minute to figure it out," he observes with an arched eyebrow before he beams and extends a hand to help me up. "How you maneuver. How you calculate your next step and how I should time it. You're graceful, but in a reactive way. Like your next move is only based on what you think I'm about to do. And knowing how well you can see, I may as well just stay on offense."

"My turn!" Vivian shouts, bursting our bubble.

Lucan grins, but not before he warns, "Hurt her for real, and you'll have to answer to me."

Vivian rolls her eyes, but gives him a sarcastic, "Yes, alpha."

I turn my focus on her. She's quicker on her feet, using her small size to her advantage, and manages to pin me within two tries. Merrick is almost as strong as Lucan, but he moves better in the air and manages to pin me in three. Soren, on the other hand, could use a little work.

"Behind you!" he shouts at me a few hours later, pointing over my shoulder, but I shake my head and parry.

"Not falling for it this time." Not that I should have fell for it *last* time, either, but I'm not about to tell him that.

Soren strokes his chin in apparent contemplation, and I use the opportunity to take a swing at him. He catches me by the wrist, twists, and nearly manages to fling me down before I kick him in the shins. As soon as he releases me with a groan, I pin him to the ground.

Lucan whistles. "This might be easier if you'd just shift into a werewolf, Soren. She's going to beat your sorry ass every time if you don't."

"Listen." Soren sighs at the first signs of sunset in the sky. "My mother used to say, if you ride bareback first, using a saddle will make it ten times easier." At my confused expression, he adds, "That's back when the kingdom had horses and shit."

"I have no idea what you're talking about," I pant, getting up.

"Nobody ever does!" Vivian laughs from the sidelines.

Soren hoists himself up and plants his hands on my hips, sweat glimmering on his forehead. "You know, I should have paid more attention when Mrs. Wright tried to teach us ballroom lessons. You move like you're dancing, Saskia."

I wrinkle my nose. "Dancing?"

"Yeah? No need to look so offended. That's a good thing."

"She's not offended." That's Lucan, stepping forward and crossing his arms as he observes my expression. "She just doesn't know what dancing even is. Do you, little nightmare?" His last words are a soft whisper masking some deep layer of pain that I can't decipher.

When I shake my head, Soren's mouth drops open until *he's* the one who looks offended. "All right, those motherfuckers have done a lot of cruel things in there, but taking away dancing? I can't wait to kill them. But until then..." He swings around and snaps at Vivian and Merrick. "We're having a street dance tonight."

Merrick sighs. "I'll tell Ashe to bring out his violin."

Vivian beams. "I'll start the fire!"

Soren claps me on the back, even though I'm pretty sure I've never been more confused in my life. "Don't worry. No ballroom. Plenty of alcohol. You can even step on Lucan's toes."

By the time the sun dips into a pinkish horizon, the dirt road that cuts through the ghost town looks completely transformed.

A fire blazes in the center, hotter and brighter and wilder than anything I ever saw flickering in the catacombs. The heat bats at my face as Lucan and I step closer, smoke billowing up into a cloudless sky above us. The children chase each other with sticks, shrieking and laughing while their mothers yell at them to watch their step, and someone strung beautiful, glowing... *things* up and down the street.

"Lanterns," Lucan says softly, gazing down at me with a small smile. "I never got to experience it, but my father said Veradel used to have huge celebrations in the streets, and people would make their own lanterns to put out in front of their houses. It's one of the traditions this pack has tried to carry with us. Keep alive."

I take in the lanterns and the soft, colorful glows they cast. Some are rectangular, others round, but they all look as delicate as butterfly wings. The concept of everyone getting to make something different and show off their creation flips the Cardinal Rules completely upside-down.

And I like that.

"What did Veradel celebrate?"

Lucan chuckles. "The start of summer. The start of winter. The king's birthday. *Any* birthday, really. If a baby was born, the neighborhood would host their own special celebration, and pretty soon all of Veradel would catch wind of it and join."

"Sounds like they'd use any excuse to celebrate," I tease, although longing for something I've never had twists a sharp knife through my stomach.

What would it be like, to embrace what makes us different? To have fun whenever we want rather than the mandatory Sanctuary Sunday? To *dance*?

Even though our minds aren't connected in the moment, Lucan watches all the emotions ripple across my face, and he holds out his hand with a smile.

"Let's go find out."

I take it, my soft, smooth fingers threading through his giant, callused ones. We drift even closer to the fire, where the rest of the pack mills about, talking and laughing. True to his word, Soren is handing out tiny glasses—like vials—of amber liquid that I watch people drain in one gulp.

"Want one?" he asks us as we approach, wiggling his brows.

I look to Lucan uncertainly, who frowns at my reaction.

"You don't need my permission, Saskia. If you want to drink, I'll be here to take care of you."

My cheeks warm as I realize that I *was* waiting for permission. A habit drilled inside me since the moment I was born that I'll have to figure out how to break. Because despite all my defiance during adrenaline-induced moments over these past few weeks, I still find myself slipping back into the Cardinal Rules during normal interactions like this.

But I want to make my own rules now.

"It's just…" I scramble for a reason to explain the hesitancy. "I'm not even sure I can consume anything other than… you know…"

I glance at Lucan's neck, where the indents of my teeth still mark his skin.

"Only one way to find out." Soren winks at me. Lucan growls, and he laughs.

"Okay, then." I grab the little glass and bring it to my nose, sniffing. The contents make my lips purse, sharp and sour.

Just as I'm about to take a sip to test it out, a high-pitched cry cuts through the smoke. I jerk my head up to witness one of the children tripping as he runs after his friends, sprawling out on his hands and knees—the same boy who fell in the town hall several nights ago.

This time, I resist the urge to rush toward him, despite the pang in my heart rattling through me, begging me to do something. If the boy didn't want my help that first night, he certainly won't want it now that I've got scary crimson eyes and fangs.

As his mother bends to lift him up by the elbows, however, I spot the scraped knee, dripping with blood that I can smell from here and imbedded with small chunks of gravel and dirt.

And I can't help it.

"Just a second," I murmur to Lucan, shoving the glass back into Soren's hand.

In a flash, I'm down the road in the opposite direction, knocking on the door of Taika's clinic. A cane thumps on the other end, and Taika's weathered face appears behind the door when he opens it a sliver.

"Saskia!" He opens the door wider. "The antivenom is still…"

"No." I shake my head. "It's not that. Do you have a bandage I could borrow? And maybe some kind of disinfectant?" If nothing else, that boy needs to wash out his wound with some clean water, unless werewolves are naturally resistant to infections or something.

Taika smiles. "Of course."

Two minutes later, I'm back at the bonfire site, this time with a wet washcloth and a clean strip of fabric. The back of my neck prickles as Lucan's eyes trail my every move. Trying to keep my own eyes downcast and my lips pressed together to hide my fangs, I softly approach the mother and child, still crying as he clutches his knee in the middle of the road.

Both of them stiffen when they look up to find me looming over them.

"Here," I mumble, holding out the washcloth and fabric.

The boy glances at his mother, tearstains striping his cheeks, then at me, then at his mother again, who gives an encouraging nod.

And the boy sticks out his leg in my direction.

"T-thank you," he stutters.

For a moment, confusion parts my lips, but I catch on when neither of them moves to take the supplies out of my hand. Bending with a small smile, I gently dab at his blood—an earthy smell, just like Lucan's—and wrap the strip of fabric around his knee before tying it together.

"There. That should do it," I say, and the boy hops up to rejoin his friends as if none of it ever happened.

Before I stand up, his mother eyes me with renewed interest. She's nearing middle-aged, with a few strands of gray streaking her dark brown hair and soft lines around her eyes... although I can't be sure if she's forty or four hundred.

"You didn't have any urge to taste it?" Her voice is low, just for me. "My son's blood?"

Oh. *Oh*. I almost press a hand against my chest at how repulsive the thought is—not blood, necessarily, but taking something from the most precious and innocent in our society. "No." I shake my head firmly. "I don't need to drink a lot, but even if I did, I would *never* take from anyone who didn't ask me to."

She seems to read the earnestness in my eyes, not flinching away from their color, because her muscles suddenly relax. As if she's been on edge until this very moment. My heart pinches over the fact that Lucan's entire pack—save for maybe Vivian, Soren, and Merrick—has been living with the fear that I might attack them at any moment.

Now, though, the boy's mother smiles and nods over my shoulder.

"I think you deserve to experience a different kind of drink, then. It doesn't sound like your Guardians ever let you have fun like this."

Turning around, I find that Lucan and Soren have drifted over. This time, when I grab the drink, I don't hesitate before knocking it back like I saw the others doing.

Instantly, fire pours down my throat and lands in my belly. I cough, gasping, eyes bulging.

"That's disgusting!"

Vivian and Merrick appear at his side, and Vivian snorts. "You won't think that if you have one or two more. Come on." She grabs my hand, pulling me away from Lucan. "Let's dance!"

I have no idea what I'm doing, but soon Ashe does indeed start up a sharp, jaunty tune on a funny-looking instrument, and the notes settle into my bloodstream. Vivian moves my hands up and down until my shoulders loosen, and I begin to mimic the sway of her hips.

"That's right! Follow the music." She lowers her voice with a giggle. "Lucan's looking at your ass."

Like an idiot, I jerk my head over my shoulder to find that Lucan's eyes are snapping back up to mine. Grinning, I mouth some words that he waves away with a smirk twitching in the corner of his mouth.

But I don't stop swaying my hips.

I like the feel of his eyes on me. The burn that cascades down my body.

Smoke infuses my senses, a warm, woodsy scent that fills every space in my head. The crackling of the fire adds a layered rhythm to Ashe's song, and my eyes get stuck for a moment, mesmerized by the orange embers flaming like they're alive. I almost feel as if I'm one with the smoke, twisting around, lingering in the air.

Vivian moves sensually against me, and I mimic the ribbony flow of her torso as the music slows and drags its notes.

Twirling, I come face to face with Lucan to find that his smirk has deepened. He pulls me into him, folding his body into mine.

"Dance with me, little nightmare," he breathes against my temple.

I glance back at Vivian, making sure she isn't left alone, but Merrick is already scooping her up into his arms with a kiss.

Lucan spins me, his fingers digging into my hips as he nestles my ass against his front. I follow his lead with each turn and dip and let my head fall back against his shoulder.

My body starts to warm, a slow tingle spreading up my arms as I reach behind me to clasp the back of Lucan's neck and just move with the flow.

It's slow at first, a soft tempo that our bodies keep time to. Our body parts meld together. Our body heat rises. His hands fan out over every inch of my exposed skin. And we just dance together through the soft smoke from the fire.

After who-knows how long, Soren appears in front of my face with another little glass of amber liquid. Lucan chuckles as I squeeze my eyes shut and throw my head back, bracing myself... but it stings a little less going down the second time.

Then the music picks up, and we're twirling. Lucan lifts me in the air, and laughs tumble out of my mouth as my arms rise above my head.

Until I'm breathless and lightheaded, all wide toothy smiles.

"So, do you like to dance?" he asks me eventually when the music slows into more somber, soft notes.

When I pause, unsure what to do, Lucan situates my left hand around his shoulder and places his right palm on my waist before taking my other hand in his.

I tuck into him as he maneuvers my body and nod against his chest, deciding in the moment that yes, I do like to dance. It's care-free, energetic, like a string of pure happiness weaving throughout your body.

But my mood shifts suddenly and solemnly with a sigh on my lips.

Looking up at him, I pout. "I've missed out on so much."

All this time, he was dancing and hunting and learning and doing... *everything* that we couldn't.

Lucan cocks an eyebrow, eyeing my dramatic bottom lip, before he brushes my hair back and kisses my neck.

"You have so much time," he says, "to discover everything. Everything you never knew existed. Things you'll hate. Things you'll love. I promise I'll show you."

I suppose I will if we make it that far, but it's a strange concept to not even know your true self at twenty-three. I assume that before the Wall and the Guardians, most people began experiencing things like this when they were much younger. And I've experienced nothing.

Lucan traces a finger up and down my arm as we stare at each other, lost to the outside world.

"What was it like?" I ask. "Your childhood. Growing up here."

His eyes trace the ground in front of us, almost guiltily. "It was good."

"Andddd..." I tease.

"And it was fun." He pauses, presses his lips against my fore-head. "I was a free-range child. Viv, Soren, Merrick, and I, we've explored every inch of these woods, every mountain peak."

"Did you have a school here?"

"Sort of," Lucan laughs. "One of the older werewolves here tries to get the kids gathered to learn math and reading. But Merrick and I used to ditch all the time to go swimming and fishing in the river. I thought I was such a little bad-ass. We'd jump off roofs, pretending we could fly. We'd steal apples from Mrs. Wright's orchard."

My eyes widen as I stare at his lips. So pretty. Smooth. Full. "Drove my mom so crazy, she blames me for her white hair. And, of course, my dad would threaten to skin me alive."

"That sounds *really* fun, though," I say, my heart thumping in a weird pattern of emotions, wondering what it would be like to have such a carefree childhood. "Your parents loved you—love you."

He nods. "We've always been close. And it's like I have dozens of parents. Everyone watches out for everyone, and no one can keep a secret for long. Holidays are always big affairs, with elaborate meals and dancing, even though there are less than fifty of us now. In true Veradel fashion, we continue to celebrate the little things, the big things. Births, birthdays, first werewolf shifts, the first night of summer, the first snow."

"I couldn't imagine getting to do anything remotely close to that."

"I know, baby." Lucan places a finger under my chin and tips my head up to look me in the eye. "But this is your family now."

"Lucan!" Soren's laugh cuts through the haze in front of me. "Why're you making our girl cry? Is she a sad drunk?"

I blink back the tears threatening to spill, which only causes two to roll down my cheeks, before I let out a wet laugh. "I'm not sad. I'm happy."

Lucan snarls. "Call her 'our girl' again and you'll be crying, too."

Soren holds up his hands in protest, each with another glass of what they call alcohol in his grip. "Don't get your damn balls twisted. I come bearing more gifts."

Lucan shakes his head at it when Soren holds one out to him.

"You're no fun anymore," I joke, taking the other from Soren's hand and shooting it back as he does the same.

"That's my—" Soren darts his eyes to Lucan. "—Lucan's girl."

Before Lucan can snap at him, Ashe strikes up another song, this time one that makes me jump up and down in excitement. How fast the notes change. How fun it sounds.

Then the world tilts, and I stumble back into Lucan's chest with a squealing laugh.

"Is this drunk?" I marvel up into his striking face. He nods, smirking as I run the tip of my nose along his jawline. He smells delicious. Not in a way that makes me want to drink his blood, but in a way that makes me want to put my mouth and lips and tongue all over him.

"Feel good?"

"Great," I confirm, eyes stuck to his lips. I lift my chin to try to reach them with my own. "I want to have sex with you."

Shit. Did I say that out loud?

Apparently so, because Lucan pulls his shoulders back, wetting both of his lips before one of his canines snags on his bottom one. "Not tonight. You'll have to settle for more dancing," he says, standing with me in his arms and placing me back on my swaying feet.

Disappointment flutters through me, but my body still crackles with... fun.

So I settle, but I can't help myself from touching him. My hands snake under his shirt as we move. Over his biceps. Along the top of his ass.

Why won't he kiss me?

"I know you want me," I murmur into his neck after I twist and rub my ass over the hard bulge in his pants.

"That's not a secret, little nightmare."

"Then take me," I beg.

Lucan's mouth hovers against the shell of my ear. "Not while you're drunk."

"I'm not *that* drunk," I say, immediately knowing it's a lie. Whatever this is, I don't feel normal. But it's so *good*.

My hips grind into him, wanting more each time a desperate groan rumbles from the back of his throat. And every time he scolds me and restrains himself, his fingertips digging into my hips, a thrill shoots through me.

But how much restraint can he possibly have?

LUCAN

This woman will be the death of me. Send me straight to hell and back.

As I unlock my front door, Saskia cups my crotch and tries to nibble up the column of my neck.

She's run through every emotion possible tonight until she's peaked at insanely horny.

And how much fun it's been to watch her. Living carefree, letting go, dancing in the smoke and moonlight, laughing.

Pushing her gently to arm's length, I offer her a sympathetic smile. "I know, baby. But for the millionth time, not tonight. Now, tomorrow... you'd better brace yourself, because you won't be able to walk for days."

Saskia sighs dramatically as she whisks past me and takes the stairs, giving me the perfect view of her ass while she swings her hips back and forth.

I run my hand over my face. My dick is straining in my pants to the point of pain.

Keeping a vampire woman off of me has proven harder than I anticipated. Her movements are always just a little too quick for me to stop her before she gets her hands on me. And she's frighteningly strong with liquor coursing through her veins.

Even now, I blink, and she disappears from the top of the stairs.

"Saskia," I call out to her as my bedroom door clicks shut. "I'm sleeping on the couch."

Her muffled giggle fills the stairwell as I turn around, then a thump reverberates through the walls.

Shit. I fly up the remaining stairs two at a time and throw open the door.

Instead of finding her knocked out like my mind convinced itself, she's fully naked in the middle of the room with the most seductive smile I want to lick right off her sexy face.

"This is pure torture, Saskia," I groan.

She sure looks pleased with herself when I cross the room, which only makes me chuckle, but her face falls when I divert to the closet.

Ruffling through my drawers, I find one of my shirts before I return to face her and slip it over her head. The hem falls to her knees, and I pull her arms through the holes gently as she whines my name.

"You're really not going to touch me?" she whispers.

"Really," I whisper back.

Saskia huffs.

"But when you wake up," I add, "*sober*, it's going to be a different story. You want my head between your legs?" Saskia shifts on her feet, tensing her thighs. "I'll spend the entire day there. You want me to fuck you fast? Slow? Upside down? I'll teach you every position you didn't know your body could twist into." I point to the bed. "But right now, it's time to sleep that off."

She nods, a sparkle shining in her eyes, and immediately, I know this isn't over.

Crawling across the bedspread with the shirt hiked up and her back arched so I have a full view of her glistening, she tsks, "Lucan, that must hurt."

Before I can ask her what she's talking about, she settles against the pillows and drops her eyes to my raging erection.

I look down at my dick straining against my zipper. "Yes," I confirm. "It certainly wants to be buried inside you right now. But it can wait."

This deliciously feisty fucking woman is *mine*. And I love her with everything I have. It's going to be fun to give her exactly what she wants in the morning.

When I look back up at her, shock hits me square in the chest. Her knees fall open before she dips her fingers between her legs.

"If you're not going to touch me," she says defiantly, "then I'll just have to do it myself."

Fuck. It's going to be a long, painful night.

26

SASKIA

I stretch out my sore body from head to toe and open my eyes, a smile already on my lips.

That was one of the best nights of my life.

But when I crane my neck to tell Lucan so, his glower hits me square in the chest. His face is etched in hardened lines, his eyes dark and sunken.

"Finally awake, little nightmare?"

I smile uncertainly. "I slept like the dead."

"I'm glad," he replies, though he looks anything but glad. "Do you feel all right?"

"Feel great," I confirm, then ask cautiously, "Did you sleep well?"

"Oh, no, definitely not." He gives a dead laugh. "Didn't even close my eyes."

"You stayed up all night...?" My voice trails off as hazy memories float to the surface—dancing that felt like sex with clothes on. I caress a hand across his cheek before I sit up. "You stay in bed and get some rest. I'll make you breakfast."

After I tuck Lucan in tight while he watches me with a gaze intense enough to slice the air, I'm up and out of the room in a flash, leaving him in a heap of sheets and fluffy pillows.

Beyond his kitchen window, the woods fan out, glimmering in the sun that is just starting to peek through the canopy in different shades of orange and yellow.

Moving closer to the stove, I light the gas with a set of matches Lucan keeps in the drawer, then turn to grab one of the pots that hangs on the hooks above the adjacent counter...

Only to gasp and almost drop the pan on my foot when I catch Lucan leaning against the doorway, his glare stronger than ever.

"You're incredibly quiet for someone so large," I say as the spurt of fear subsides.

"What are you doing?" he growls.

I look down at the pan in my left hand and the spatula in my right. "Making you breakfast?" Even if I don't need anything besides blood from here on out, Lucan still needs to eat normal food. And I'm sure I can figure out how to cook.

But his eyebrows lift.

"What, exactly, are you planning to make?"

"Uhhh..." I gaze around his kitchen for any detail that might help, because I didn't actually think this far ahead. A few browning peaches sit in a fruit bowl, and several strips of dried meat hang over his smoking fireplace. "You tell me." I pop a hip against his cabinet. "What do you have that I can cook with?"

Lucan clicks his tongue, then surges forward and crowds into my space.

"Do you remember last night?" he asks, peering into my eyes.

I blink. "I think so, yes. I drank. We danced. We had sex."

"We did *not* have sex."

I blink again. The memory of me splayed out on the bed with my fingers exploring between my legs... and then it goes blank.

"I had to force myself to turn around, and when you were finished, you begged me to sleep with you," Lucan growls, "so I slept by your side. But I never touched you in that way."

"Oh," I breathe. "You're mad."

"No," he seethes. "I've just been stuck with *this* for about ten hours now." He gestures down at the noticeably large and hard bulge in his pants.

Confusion pulls through me. "Then why didn't we have sex?"

Something flits across his face that looks a lot like anger. Not directed at me, but... "You can't consent to sex when you're drunk, Saskia."

"What?"

Again, that anger flashes across his face, and now I know where I've seen it before: it's the same look he always gives when he talks about the Guardians. Like he wants to murder them and puke on their shoes all at the same time. But he doesn't raise his voice at me when he explains calmly, "Alcohol lowers your inhibitions and impacts your decision making. And I was sober, in a position of power over you. I was taking care of you, not taking advantage of you."

"So the lines were blurred." It's a statement and a question. My mind pieces together his reasoning, the way I felt last night, completely uninhibited. And how easily consent was taken from me every Sanctuary Sunday. How Malcolm had to have sex with me when he wasn't even interested.

Lucan nods slowly, his face so close to mine, I could stick out my tongue and lick his lips for him. He smells like pine and smoke from the bonfire, and my body starts to itch from the heat it's creating on its own.

"That's actually hot," I murmur, biting my lip. "And I can consent now, can't I?"

He wraps a hand around the pan and practically throws it on top of the stove. Then he takes the spatula from me and lets it fall to the ground.

"What do you want, Saskia?" My breath hitches. His voice is a deep baritone, thrumming through my core. "Tell me."

I don't have to think about it for long. I still want what I wanted last night, just now with a clear mind. "Touch me, Lucan."

He hovers his lips over mine and brings the tip of his finger up to my nipple but doesn't quite touch me.

"You'll have to be more specific than that." His breath travels across my jaw and down my neck.

Goosebumps rise on my flesh in his wake. I whimper.

And then I decide to flip on him because my defiant little fantasy to take control isn't just a drunken one.

"Where'd we leave off?" I ask, backing up until my butt hits the counter. I place my palms on the cold edge and drag myself up so I'm perched right on the edge.

This time *he's* the one who whimpers.

I'm still in the shirt Lucan dressed me in last night—no underwear—so I simply spread my legs while Lucan watches with an inferno of a stare. His hands clench into fists as my finger circles my clit twice, then slides into my wet heat.

"What was it you said a while ago?" I taunt him before throwing his past words back at him. "'Once I'm inside that Wall, you'll be crawling after me of your own accord'?"

Lucan's eyes blaze, never breaking away from where I continue to pleasure myself. His chest heaves, trying to drag in more oxygen.

"Well, we're on the *out*side of the Wall... Lucan."

His nostrils flare, pupils blown. "Tell me what you want and it's yours."

"Crawl to me."

Lucan doesn't hesitate. His knees hit the wood floor with a thunk before his palms flatten out in front of him, and he crawls on all fours until his face is settled in the space between my knees.

"*Now* touch me."

He presses his lips to the inside of my thigh and hums as his fingers glide up my delicate skin to replace my own. His thumb swipes over my clit in tight circles before two of his thick fingers fill me. His other hand slips under the hem of my shirt and pinches one of my pebbled nipples.

I let out a strained breath as a current pulses through me in waves.

He moves his mouth closer to me, but I braid my hand into his soft hair and hold him back.

"Can I taste you?" he pleads.

Tugging harder on his roots, not letting him move his head an inch, I nod.

Lucan smiles in understanding before he extracts his fingers and brings them up to his mouth to clean them off.

He groans as he closes his lips around them, savoring the taste of me as he slides them out slowly.

"So good," he moans. "I want the real thing."

And because I can't take another second of his tongue not on me, he smirks as I guide his mouth exactly where I want it.

With a flat tongue, he licks all the way from bottom to top before he inserts his finger again and curls it. His lips capture my clit, teasing me, sucking me, biting me, until my hips have a mind of their own.

They arch against his tongue, matching his rhythm, and I fall apart, panting his name in shockwaves.

When my body unfurls from the snapped tension, now putty in his hands, Lucan tugs at my ankles, and I follow his lead, sliding to the floor.

But I'm not done with what *I* want yet.

Slinking to my knees between his legs, I reach out and inch Lucan's shirt over his head. Each tense ridge of muscle reveals itself as I peel it off and fling it to the side. Next I slide my palm down his shaft bulging in his pants with a sly smile.

Lucan hisses through his teeth.

I waste no time unbuttoning and unzipping to let his cock spring free. Wrapping a hand around him, my mouth waters when my thumb runs over the wet tip.

"I've never done this," I whisper.

He covers the back of my hand with his, stopping my slow strokes. "Saskia—"

I cut him off with a firm voice. "I want to."

His hand rises to my face, and he sweeps his thumb across my cheekbone as his eyes bore holes in mine, then laser across my lips, an understanding passing between us. He presses his thumb along the seam of my mouth, so I part my lips to let him slip it in. My tongue swirls around the rough pad of his fingerprint.

"Beautiful," he coos.

I release the suction around his thumb, wanting to look beautiful with something else in my mouth.

Teasing his cock with one long stroke of my tongue along the bottom, I savor the taste of him as a rush of heat twists below my belly button.

He's warm and heady, filling my throat as he presses into me gently. My tongue works itself over every vein, trying to memorize the way he feels, how large he is.

I moan when our eyes connect and Lucan thumbs my hollowed cheek. He watches himself slide in and out of my mouth through half-lidded eyes until they flutter closed.

Then it's my turn to watch him through my eyelashes, power building in my chest at how wild and crazed he looks. Proud of how much of an effect I have on him.

Lucan sucks in a sharp breath before his voice comes out hoarse. "Does that make you wet, little nightmare? Having my cock in your mouth?"

I nod, the gush between my legs undeniable, and wrap my full lips around him now.

Up and down, I work my lips and my tongue as Lucan gathers my hair in his fist and mumbles curse words under his breath.

Instinctually, I know what to do, and it's easy to follow his cues whenever he groans for me or his legs tremble. I quickly learn that he especially likes it when I take him deep enough to hit the back of my throat.

"Fucking hell, this is the most gorgeous view I've ever seen," he whispers to himself when I'm able to take him to hilt. Words flow out from under his breath. "The sunrise lighting up those red lips locked around me. You're a dream, Saskia."

I hum appreciatively for him, lost in the sensation of bringing someone else such an immense pleasure. Never before have I *wanted* to bring someone else immense pleasure. My fingers find my own clit, which makes Lucan moan out my name.

Suddenly, his thighs tense, and he tries to pull himself out of my mouth. I shake my head, wrapping my hand around the base of him to keep him right here.

"Is that what you want?" he asks. "You want to swallow?"

I reluctantly tear my mouth away for a moment. "Yes," I confirm, and when he hesitates, I practically beg, "Lucan, I want to taste you in a different way."

He captures my mouth with his for one long kiss where our tongues meet fervently before he guides me by my hair back to the head of his cock.

I brush my lips over him, slick with my saliva. Then it takes only a few strokes before a hoarse sound rips from his chest as he spills into my mouth.

The salty, slightly sweet, and heady taste of him ignites my core. It might even be better than his blood. He shutters when I pull my head back.

"Not yet," Lucan commands me, tugging on the roots of my hair to tilt my face up to his. "Open."

I obey.

A smile curves up one side of his face, dark, wild.

"You're mine." His thumb dips into my mouth, gathering some of his come that I have on display for him before he runs it over my red lips. "Now swallow."

His eyes follow every contraction of my throat as I do what he says, and when I lick my lips, he's already growing hard again.

I stare, but Lucan only chuckles as he slides his pants down and kicks them to the side.

"Werewolves have stamina," he says, voice low, locking my knees around his hips. "And you make me want to do this for the rest of the eternity we have together."

His fingers find the hem of the shirt I'm still wearing and slide it up as he plants a kiss on my bare skin with each new body part he exposes: belly button, breasts, sternum, collarbone.

The mood shifts from a lust-filled, desperate need to a lovingly soft caress, a content exhale, like the two pieces of our souls are calling for each other.

"I love you." His breath skims across my shoulder. "How did I get so lucky that you fell into my arms?"

"And I love you," I sigh, letting my head fall back as his lips pull my sensitive nipple into his mouth. "I love you because I want to. Because I choose to."

His callused hands work over my breasts, then cup around my waist to lift me up and bring me down onto him. With adoration clouding his eyes, he kisses me, hard, a sound echoing in his throat as I slide down fully.

"Lucan," I moan into his mouth, completely satiated.

Wrapping one hand around the back of my neck and the other around my ass cheek, he presses his forehead against mine.

My fingers lace through his hair before I lift myself, angling to hit the perfect spot, and come back down with a sigh. Lucan and I find the perfect pace as we work together.

With each up and down movement of my hips, our souls converge like a whisper of unsaid words: *I love you. I love you. I love you.*

I've found my strength, my world, my own personal Wall that doesn't lock me in but builds me up. And everything I can't say in this second, I say with my eyes.

Nose to nose, we can't look anywhere else but at each other as our breaths become labored. Two opposites, two natural-born mortal enemies, blending together as one.

When we've regained enough strength, Lucan gets to his feet, tinkers around at the water bucket, and comes back with a wet kitchen towel.

He swipes the warm cloth along my inner thighs as I watch silently, reveling in the softness that's such a contrast to his rough nature.

"What?" he asks quietly.

I shake my head, biting back a smile. "Nothing."

"Taking care of you is the bare minimum, even as a Monster," he huffs playfully under his breath as my eyes wander to the oven.

The little black spiraled handle juts out from the tiny door, soot covering the now-opaque window.

"Will you teach me how to cook?" I ask suddenly.

Lucan arches a brow, smothering a smirk. "Is this a backgammon, poker, 'men love to teach women things' thing? What information are you trying to pry out of me?"

"No," I laugh. "It's a meals-through-a-door-slat-my-entire-life thing."

His canines freeze in a grin as realization flickers over his face. I'm not human anymore, but just this once, I want to pretend to be one—to experience the things I should have had the opportunity to experience before the Guardians took that away from me. Not just the thrilling whirlwind of drinking and dancing, but simple moments like these. Cooking in a kitchen together, as if we're *not* two types of monsters trying to tear down a Wall...

And besides, he still needs to eat, even if I don't.

"Okay," Lucan says finally, pupils hardening in determination. "Then I'm going to teach you how to make the best damn breakfast in the world."

After he tosses the towel in the washroom, we both scrub our hands with clean water before he starts pulling things out of a square container packed with snow and ice: a glass jug of milk, a dozen oval-shaped objects stacked carefully in a basket, and a yellow, waxy-looking substance on a platter.

One after the other, Lucan switches to the cabinet and plunks the remaining items down in a row on the counter.

"What are all these?" I ask, eyes wide.

He holds up the basket with a confused pinch of his brows. "Eggs?"

"*Oh*. So *that's* what they look like!" I've eaten eggs, of course, but I've always seen them as pale yellow scrambles. Not these delicate, oval objects, speckled and untouched and perfect. At the incredulous look on Lucan's face, I point to the platter with a sly smile. "And what about that?"

"For fuck's sake, they didn't even give you *butter* in there?" Lucan exclaims, massaging his temples. "We hand-churn cream to separate the butter from the buttermilk. Merrick's father is the best at making it in Veradel."

"And what's that?" I point at the glass jug, smirking as Lucan's face deepens a shade, anger palpable in the twitch of his jaw. "I'm just kidding. Don't blow a gasket. I know what butter and milk are."

"Oh, you wicked thing." Before I can blink, Lucan dips his finger in the soft yellow butter and swipes it down the bridge of my nose.

The next thing I know, my vampiric senses take over me in a competitive race to best the male who should be my enemy. I grab a handful of butter and smash it into his face.

"Oops," I say when he blinks through the slick, greasy substance sliding down his features.

Then we're both bursting into laughter, Lucan burrowing his face into my neck.

"We're going to make fried eggs," he tells me, planting buttery kisses down my collarbone. "It's the superior way of making and eating them."

"Fried eggs," I repeat breathily, trying to sound serious. "Eggs that are fried. Got it." I frown at them, though. "There aren't any baby birds in these, are there?"

Settling next to me at the counter, Lucan grabs a large bowl, then an egg, and holds it up in front of our faces.

"No. These come from my mother's female chickens, which she keeps separate from the males. So they're not fertilized. I can show you her coop after this, if you want." Catching my eye as I grimace, he hooks a finger under my chin in understanding. "Hey, you're not in there anymore."

"I know," I whisper.

"And you don't have to feel guilty for being out here. Living your life. You're doing everything in your power as fast as you can do it. You're making a difference, but you're also allowed to enjoy yourself. You only get to experience this life once."

He's right. I'm not sitting idly by. A little bit of warmth replaces the chill when I choose to smile.

"And right now," I say eagerly as I watch him, "I want to experience cracking an egg."

"Okay. So here's what you're going to do." After Lucan settles an iron pan onto the stove and lights a match beneath it, he gently taps one of the eggs against the edge of the pan and uses his thumb to separate the shell, until the interior plops inside in a perfect circle. "Now your turn."

Gingerly, he places another egg in my outstretched palm. I take a deep breath...

He chuckles.

I glare at him, my determination solidifying, before I tap the egg against the side of the pan just like he did, press my thumbs lightly against the crack—and it completely crumbles.

Egg shells and gooey yellow and clearish liquid ooze out from between my fingers.

I pout, but Lucan only grins.

"Not used to that strong vampire body." He winks. "It's fine. No one saw. Try again."

My next two attempts don't go any better, but I focus on the pressure of my fingers, how much strength I can exert through them, and finally on my third try, I successfully crack one open cleanly.

The yolk, as Lucan calls it, slides into the pan perfectly intact, suspended in the egg whites. Beaming, I raise my head to find that his smile matches mine.

"Again," he says, and I do it one more time, until there's three perfect eggs sitting in the pan. The fire crackles beneath it and soon, I watch, mystified, as the eggs begin to sizzle and form golden edges, bubbling in the orangish middle.

"Now for the best part," he says, bringing out two little glass shakers from the cupboard, one filled with what looks like white sand, and the other black sand. "I save salt and pepper for special occasions, because they're hard to come by."

"Are you saying I'm a special occasion?" I joke.

"I hope not," he tells me seriously. "I hope you're a forever occasion."

Forever. It's a real possibility for us, now that I know I'm not fossilizing. We don't just have a few years left together, but all of eternity.

If we can survive what happens next, that is. If we can truly bring down that Wall and liberate our people.

When Lucan shakes the salt and pepper over our eggs, he finally turns to me with pride spread across his face. "There you have it. The best breakfast in the world."

My mouth waters uncontrollably, but not because of the smell wafting from the sizzling pan. There's something about the way he always captures my gaze so wholeheartedly that makes me feel hot, separate from the heat of the wood-burning stove—confident, carefree, purposeful.

"Well? What are you waiting for?" I grab a knife and fork and hand it over to him. "Did I do okay for my first time?"

Lucan snags the fork and cuts off a piece right from the pan. He closes his eyes when he takes a bite and nods, smiling. "You did perfect."

At his expression, pride bursts within myself that I helped *make* this. Created it. But I don't need human food anymore, and sadly, I likely won't enjoy it, even if it does taste good to Lucan.

Hope still brews in my chest—maybe I'll become just a tiny bit more human if I take a bite...

Nervously, I stab the fork into the eggs and bring it to my mouth, the salty taste coating my tongue in a weird, tingly new way.

Trying to savor it, I close my eyes.

"Well?" Lucan asks eventually.

But I know, nothing will ever compare to *him*. Not anymore.

I smile, never more sure of anything in my life. "You're still my favorite. Always."

By the time we're done eating, it's time for me to venture back out to meet Taika.

Today, we're further purifying Lucan's antibodies with a filtration method. We work diligently through the day, adding the acid to precipitate out the non-antibody proteins, then running the liquid through a filter from Taika's old laboratory. When we have enough to fill two large vials, we slip them into our snow and ice-packed cooler.

Hours later, I finally look up to find that frost kisses the edges of the window.

"Winter's going to be a harsh one this year," Taika remarks, and I shiver at the thought of everything freezing over. In Xantera, I only ever had to deal with snow when I was walking from my housing unit to the Healing Center or Blood Moon Palace. Here, I imagine that the cold will seep into every wall, through every door.

There might not be any electricity out here, but at least I'll have Lucan to keep me warm.

A peal of laughter and shouting jerks my head upward again. Through the frosted window, I can just barely make out a group of werewolves crowding around the edge of the meadow down the road. Including the children.

Taika smiles. "Looks like they're waiting for you to start training again."

For some reason, I blush. He makes it sound like I'm some kind of professional trainer, when in reality, I'm just a new vampire listening to my base instincts. I glance down at our spread of supplies and liquids, still in the process of cooling down.

"Go," Taika says, waving me away with a gnarled hand. "I'll let you know when it's ready. There's nothing more we can do at this point besides wait."

I nod, but right before exiting, I spot the broken necklace that Lucan snapped in his efforts to wake me when I fell unconscious.

Even though we're connected through more than just a vial now, I find myself reaching toward the coiled gold chain itself, lifting it over my head, and settling it against my neck once more.

"I like the way it looks," I tell Taika, even though that's only a fraction of it. In truth, I like the way it reminds me of how I met Lucan. Where I come from. And what we still have to lose, if this doesn't work.

He bows his head in understanding, and after waving good-bye, I make my way out the door, down the ramp, and toward the meadow with my arms crossed over myself against the biting cold of the air.

Just as I'm about to step back onto the main road, however, a voice slithers out from the shadows between two dilapidated, lopsided houses.

"I've got to admit, vampires are really clever."

I whip my head toward the source, crouching in a defensive stance as my eyes make up horrible shapes in the darkness: the Guardians, coming for me at last. But after a few blinks and steady breaths, I inhale sharply as I realize it's just Kyra standing in an alleyway, her hands on her hips...

And Gabriel with his arms folded, leaning against a brick wall behind her.

"W-what are you two doing?"

My voice comes out in a quiver. I glance toward the meadow, but one of the houses is blocking my view of all the others.

Kyra's lips pull up in a smile, her nose wrinkling as her eyes trail the gold chain looped around my neck once more. "Just wanted to have a little chat with you. It's hard to get a word in with our dear alpha always hovering, not letting us talk."

The phrase *not letting us talk* seems to rebound in my skull. It reminds me too much of the Cardinal Rules, and Kyra's eyes glimmer as if she knows it.

I swallow thickly. "I'm sure Lucan would be happy to hear what you both have to say." I shoot a glance at Gabriel behind her, and he meets my eyes with a hardening of his own.

"See, that's where you're *not* so smart," Kyra says with a sigh, tossing her hair back and taking a single step toward me. "Or maybe you're just a really good liar. Because Lucan's obviously not happy with anything we have to say if it's not *Oh Saskia, you're so perfect, Saskia, you're our salvation, Saskia.* If we're not kissing your ass, then he's quite literally pommeling us. So tell me—does that sound like good leadership to you?"

My face flushes with a blast of humiliation. My breathing feels like it's shrinking, forced through a narrow tunnel. I want to defend Lucan like he's defended me, but all the Cardinal Rules seem to swirl around and around my head, and I know I can't do anything besides allow Kyra the freedom to speak her mind.

Otherwise, I'd just be proving her own point.

"So tell *me*." I try to force a modicum of calm back into my shaking voice. "What do you really think?"

This time it's Gabriel who lifts himself off the brick wall and takes a step forward, and the air seems to tighten as I face these two werewolves who hate me.

"I think this is all a ploy," Gabriel says with sharp, vicious quietness. "Not that you're with the Guardians—I don't think you'd go to such great lengths to bring down the Wall if you were secretly on their side—but I do think you want to replace them."

"Replace them? *What*?"

"Oh, please," Kyra scoffs. "You somehow get *Lucan Veradel* to fall in love with you, something every female in this pack save for his own mother and cousins have tried to do for centuries now, and you want to help him reclaim his throne? You know full well you'd be the one to sit by his side if that ever happens."

I take a step back, sucking in a lungful of brittle air as the implication of what they're accusing me of hits me right in the chest. "No. I don't want to be queen."

"Prove it, then," Gabriel snaps. "Help us defeat your Guardians, and then *leave him*. This pack and that entire city in there—" He points in the direction of the Wall. "—will be better off without a vampire in charge anyway. Just look what your kind has done."

Silence falls between us, heavy as a snowstorm. A chill snakes through the alleyway, pebbling my skin. *Leave him.* Leave him? I could never leave Lucan, even if I wanted to.

But what if Gabriel's right? What if I help them kill the Guardians, just to end up replacing them? I can't put myself in a position where I might hurt innocents or take away anyone's freedom. But I can't hold Lucan back from his rightful place as king, either.

"Prove it," Gabriel hisses again.

And then he grabs Kyra by the arm, and they leave me standing at the lip of the alleyway with a heart that would be hammering against my chest if only I was human.

LUCAN

The first thing I notice when Saskia joins us in the meadow is that gold chain hanging around her pretty little neck again. I'd be lying if I said it didn't fill me with some sort of twisted, smug appreciation that she picked it back up. That she wants to be marked as mine.

Then my eyes rove up to her face, and I know something's wrong. I can see it in the tense lines of her face, even as she tries to hike up a smile when all the children run up to her.

"Ask her!" one of them cries, pushing the oldest, Milo, toward her.

"Yeah, do it, do it!"

I try to catch Saskia's eye, but she won't look at me, so I exchange a bemused glance with Merrick and the others instead. Milo peeks back at his mother, hovering on the edge of the meadow with the other parents, before he shuffles up to Saskia and murmurs, "Will you... um... can I fight you, too? Just to practice?"

"Milo!" his mother calls, her voice stern and melodic. She was one of the few werewolves who lived in Veradel back when it was still a kingdom, just a child herself when the vampires invaded. I remember how overjoyed she was when she and her mate found out she was pregnant with Milo thirteen years ago. "You can't even shift yet."

Milo rounds on his mother, his arms crossed. "But if we're attacked, then I should learn how to fight a vampire with what I've got. I'm still strong and fast and—

"We're not going to be attacked, Milo."

"We might if *she* manages to bring the Wall down like all you want her to." The boy doesn't have to nod at Saskia for everyone to know who he's talking about. Once again, I try to catch her eye so that I can detect what kind of emotion is brewing in them, but she won't look at me. She's just standing there, wringing her hands together. Did something go wrong with the antivenom?

"Even if the Wall comes down," Milo's mother bites back, "there's no way *you're* going to fight."

"Maybe not, but what if the vampires decide they don't want to fight, either? What if they run away... toward us?"

The kid's actually got a point. The Wall has protected my pack from the Guardians just as much as the Guardians try to tell the humans it protects them from *us*.

"I say go for it!" Soren calls with his hands cupped around his mouth, breaking the silence. "Give the pup a chance!"

Milo doesn't like being called 'pup' apparently, because he wrinkles his nose, but his mother sighs and glances at Saskia.

"I'll go easy on him," she mouths with a nod. My chest tightens, then warms, as I realize how everyone—besides maybe Gabriel and Kyra, not here at the moment but surely watching from some window—have finally accepted her as one of the pack.

"Okay." Saskia seems to steel herself with a deep breath, locking away whatever's bothering her, and turns toward Milo. "You might have the upper hand when it comes to smell, but my eyesight can detect and analyze every movement you make, so you're going to try to surprise me. Act errat—"

Before that word can even leave her lips, Milo shouts and barges toward her. The other children cheer from the sidelines, but Saskia easily sidesteps him, twirls, and grabs him from behind—gently, I notice. Taking it easy on him. The little shit responds by twisting in her grip, kicking backward, and landing a hit to her shin.

Which makes me have to swallow a growl.

Graceful as ever, Saskia hooks her foot beneath Milo's ankle and tries to push him forward, but he crouches and yanks them both sideways. She stumbles, he grabs her arm, and the small crowd goes wild as he throws her sideways.

I lurch forward without thinking, but before Milo can fully pin her down, Saskia pops back up and evades his hands with quick, dancing steps backward. Good girl.

"That was really nice!" she calls to Milo. "But maybe this time, don't shout when you charge me?"

Milo's mouth parts, then snaps shut again. I barely have time to register the moment he barrels forward without warning when something peculiar happens. Saskia freezes, her mouth dropping open in shock.

But I know what this is. I've seen it before—*felt* it before.

Milo keeps stumbling forward, his shoulders growing and hunching, his neck broadening, his nose lengthening. Fur rips from his back with a sound like medical tape tearing itself off skin. An animalistic growl erupts from his throat as he skids to a halt—

In wolf form.

True, his wolf form isn't nearly as domineering as mine, and his tufts of hair are sticking up in rough, thin patches... but everyone in the meadow blinks at him in utter shock and silence.

Until we burst into cheers. A round of applause from me. A holler from Merrick. A long, shrill whistle from Soren. The other children run to Milo, screaming and immediately pressing their small, stubby hands over every inch of his new body.

Saskia herself claps her hands off to the side, as if she's unsure whether or not she should be celebrating with all of us. My heart twists, and I stride toward her, but Vivian gets there first—stalking up from behind her and pushing her into the excitement. Milo nuzzles her in appreciation.

Saskia beams, truly radiant. For the first time, I think she might feel like she belongs.

Then Milo's mother is there, leaping forward, pride engraved in her smile as she cradles her son's new lupine face in both hands, kissing him on his snout as he wags a bushy tail and turns in a quick circle.

That's when I look back at Saskia and notice the moment her own smile slips.

Shit. An emotion I can't even name presses against my sternum. I'd gift Saskia the whole damn world ten times over, but I can't give her her mother back. The whole reason she wanted to be a Chosen One in the first place was because of her mother, and yet now she's *here*. Helping my family instead of her own. Watching another mother embrace her child.

And fuck if that doesn't haunt me.

So I push past the celebratory chaos, right to her.

"Hey."

"Hey!" Her voice comes out high-pitched, but she still won't look at me.

I run my hand down her arm, lacing my fingers through hers. Finally, she raises her eyes to mine.

"I'm okay," she insists.

But another voice cuts me off before I can respond.

"What a wonderful thing, to witness a first shift. And what an even more wonderful thing to be the reason it came about."

We both whip around to find my own mother extending a hand out... and not to me.

Saskia's eyes widen a fraction. I give her hand an encouraging squeeze before releasing her, thankful for my mother's appearance and hoping like hell that she can give Saskia everything I can't.

Hesitantly, Saskia loops her arm with my mother's, and they walk away from the meadow, toward her house across from the old church.

When they disappear, I turn back to Soren and give his shoulder a friendly shove, pushing him into Merrick.

"Let's see if you've learned anything from her, too, or if I can still beat your ass like usual."

As Vivian rolls her eyes, the three of us begin to laugh and slam into each other. Even Milo joins in, proud of himself, and the other children shriek with giggles as they root for different werewolves.

Taking in the sight before me with a pinch in my chest, a single thought glows within me despite the chilly air settling over the town.

After centuries of howling and prowling around the Wall, I feel more connected to my pack than ever before.

As if Saskia has already healed a gaping wound I never even realized these last remnants of Veradel had.

SASKIA

The wind rattles around us, causing the shutters along the side of Lucan's mother's house to slap against the brick, as she leads me around to the backyard.

Stretching out in neat rows before us, leaves in all shades of green and purple burst from wooden-looking boxes. Toward the back, there's a mini house painted red and white with a ramp leading up to a square opening and walls of wire. Chickens in a variety of speckled colors peck at the ground, soft clucks echoing into the woods beyond.

So *that's* what they sound like.

"I spend most of my time here," she comments with a wave of her hand, "among my plants and animals."

"It's beautiful," I say. Even in the chilly temperature, her plants are thriving.

Lucan's mother steps around one of the boxes teeming with what I assume is cabbage and makes her way to what looks like a bucket tied to a string that's hanging over a circular stone wall.

She turns a crank, and the bucket drops into a hole before she heaves it back up by the rope. The bucket, now filled with water, sloshes as she heaves it over the edge.

"I can help you," I tell her, rushing forward, my feet grinding into the gravel pathway.

She waves me off and laughs. "I didn't bring you here to put you to work. Besides—" She winks. "—I may be old, but I'm stronger than you."

So with a blush, I watch her, wondering why she *did* bring me here, as she waters her garden.

"These are all my winter veggies," she explains as the water soaks into the dark soil. "Carrots, cabbage, kale, fava beans. I've got to keep the goats away from them." She laughs. "They're our only source of milk, but they'll demolish my garden, so I keep them in a pen behind the chicken coop."

"It's beautiful—all the colors," I say.

Pride lights up her eyes as she steps up to another wide box teeming with yellow flowers. "This here is yellow jasmine, and I'm hoping my camellias bloom soon. They come in as beautiful shades of red and pink and white."

When the water bucket is empty, she places it down on the gravel path, wipes her hands on her flowing skirt, and asks, "Now, would you like some tea?" then winces. "I guess you don't drink tea anymore."

Heat creeps up my neck. *Nope, just your son's blood.*

"Anyway," she rushes on lightheartedly, "come in. I want to show you something."

Curiosity blooms as I follow her up the porch steps, her long waves of white hair cascading down her back, and into her sitting room.

One wall is covered by shelves with books—so many that I think she may have collected them all from every abandoned house remaining in Veradel. Dried flowers, I assume from her garden, are pressed into frames and hung up around the room. And there's so many blankets and pillows on every seat, that I imagine she reads a book every night, cozy in the firelight from her hearth.

I settle wordlessly next to her on the small floral-patterned sofa. A small, round box sits on the table in front of us. As she stares at it, her eyes well with tears before she quickly blinks them back.

"This is one of the only things I have left from Veradel," she says softly.

"I'm so sorry," I say. *For what the Guardians did, who they are, what they destroyed,* I don't say.

Five centuries of hatred brewing. Five centuries of staring at that Wall from the outside, just as I've been staring at it from the inside. Five centuries of pain that could be avenged in a matter of hours.

I don't know what else to say, what else to do, except let my actions speak for themselves.

"It isn't your fault," Lucan's mom says simply, patting my leg. Her long, slender fingers curl back into her lap. "Besides, how can I think ill of you when it was your ancestor who saved my life?"

I blink at her. "What?"

Lucan's mom nods, eyes glazed over as she peers into a memory. "Everyone remembers it as a war, but it really only lasted one night. When the vampires invaded the Blood Moon Palace, we were having a feast in the dining hall—laughter and music and dancing, all the lanterns in the world lighting up the whole place. There were humans there, too, mingling with the royal family, so many that there was hardly any space to move. I was trying to sneak away with Lucan's father, to steal a kiss from him in the rose garden."

She smiles softly, and I inhale at the picture she paints. So many innocents, not knowing what was about to happen.

"They seemed to appear out of nowhere," Lucan's mom continues in a hushed voice. "We'd heard rumors about vampire attacks, of course, but we'd never actually seen one before. Until then. Lucan's father and I had just made it to the rose garden when the screaming began." She pinches the bridge of her nose. "We could smell the blood and death and started to rush back into the palace when something stopped us. Or rather, some*one.*"

Her eyes flit to my face, and her lips lift slightly. "I can see the resemblance. He had the same dark red hair as you, and similar features, the Thirteenth Guardian. We were so stunned by how beautiful he was that we stopped in our tracks. Both he and Warren tensed, readying for a fight, until the Thirteenth hesitated. 'You'll die if you go in there,' he told us. 'So go beyond the Wall. Save yourselves.'"

"And you listened to him?" I ask, frowning, trying to imagine anyone with Lucan's stubborn blood actually obeying an enemy who invaded.

"Of course not," Lucan's mother chuckles. "We told him to go fuck himself, so the Thirteenth Guardian charged us. We ran as other werewolves began to flee into the garden, shouting at us, but then the vampire got Warren by the shoulder... and instead of fighting, threw him over the spikes of the Wall before he did the same to me. We survived the fall only because of our werewolf blood, and by the time we tried to get back inside, the wood was already turning to stone." She sighs. "That's when we met up with the few others who had escaped and gathered in the nearest town to try to form a plan to reclaim our kingdom. Only, the plans never worked. Over time, the lifespans of the remaining humans who lived in this town passed, and our own numbers dwindled. Life moved on, as it always does, but our goal remained the same."

I twine my fingers together, trying to understand why she's telling me this.

"The Thirteenth Guardian still invaded your kingdom, though. He wouldn't have needed to save your life if he'd just... I don't know. Not endangered it in the first place."

Lucan's mom huffs another laugh. "Oh, I know. But he could have killed us right then and there instead of forcing us out—which tells me he always had a kernel of goodness inside him. I didn't even know he was the same Guardian my husband ended up communicating with through letters until you showed up. Then, I suspected, based on the resemblance."

My mouth falls open incredulously. "You suspected I was a vampire descendant when I first showed up? And you didn't want to chop my head off upon first sight?"

"I could never in a million years forget his face. And why would I? You've already done so much for us, and most of all, my son. That kernel of goodness the Thirteenth Guardian possessed... you've nurtured it until it's grown into something so much better."

Heat creeps along my cheeks, and I wonder briefly if the actual blush can even make an appearance beneath my skin.

"Oh, but I haven't done anything," I insist. "Lucan didn't need my help. You raised an amazing man, ma'am—I mean, Mrs. Veradel. Did I use that right, your last name?"

She nods, laughs under her breath. "I gave him life, but so did you. Just in a different way. And please, call me Stella."

Tears well in my eyes, burning the back of my throat, but I look up at the ceiling, studying the cracked paint, and blink them back.

"He's lucky to have you," I whisper. "I miss my own mother so much."

To my surprise, Stella turns to me and gathers me in a maternal hug, the kind I've missed and craved for so many years. A knot builds in the back of my throat as she rubs her palm in a soothing circle along my back, rocking me back and forth, and whispers, "What was your favorite thing about her?"

The question surprises me even more, but I'm grateful for it, because it drives me to think about her, my actual mother, rather than the absence of her. After a few moments of thinking, I say resolutely, "How she loved others. The Guardians chose her partner and forced her to have a baby, so you'd think loving my father and me would have meant she caved. That she let them control her. But it almost seems like the opposite, actually."

I think back to how she let herself bleed for my father over and over, even though she could have just turned him in. How she made up extra lyrics just for me, even though creating such a thing broke all the Cardinal Rules.

"Her love was her own kind of rebellion," I finish. "I just wish it was still here."

Stella pulls me back by the shoulders to look me straight in the face, and I can't miss the sincerity shining from her amber irises that look so much like Lucan's.

"A mother's love never ceases, Saskia. It still thrives inside of you, shapes you. And I know, just from knowing you, that she was an amazing woman. She would be proud of all that you have accomplished. How you fell. How you rose."

She reaches for the box in front of us, placing it on her lap gently.

"Now," she says, "the only things I have from before the invasion are the dress I was wearing—which hasn't fit me in longer than I care to admit—and what the few werewolves who escaped managed to gather with them before the Wall closed, like the journals and this..."

Stella slides the top of the box off, revealing two glittering, gem-encrusted pieces of jewelry large enough to slide an arm through.

"The king's and queen's crowns," she says, smiling softly at my expression. "The only family heirlooms we have left. Lucan's father placed this one on my head the moment that Taika married us a few years after the Wall turned to stone." She nods at the slightly smaller, more delicate one. "And *this* one belongs to Lucan."

I stare at the other crown, imagining Lucan taking his rightful throne and dipping his head for someone to place this on top, just like Gabriel and Kyra said he would. A sharp, sad feeling twists in my stomach at the thought that we're not just a werewolf and a vampire—two species meant to be enemies—but a king and... definitely not a queen.

Leave him rings through me. This pack and that entire city in there will be better off without a vampire in charge anyway.

Stella, however, picks up the queen's crown and hands it out to me.

"I'd be honored to pass this on to you."

My mouth falls open. I meant what I told Kyra—that I don't *want* to be queen, a fact that clings to my heart and buries roots deep into my stomach. But Stella's not just offering me a crown, I know. She's offering me maternal love, acceptance, and a place in her family.

So the fact that I cannot accept this gift makes my stomach crumple with pain.

"Oh, come here." Stella puts the crown back in the box and pulls me into another hug that feels so good and warm and right that tears actually swell in my eyes this time. Over and over, I whisper a muffled thank you into her shoulder, and Stella just holds me, until finally I'm pulling back with a laugh, trying to compose myself.

"Sorry," I say finally, eyeing the wet spot on her shoulder with a grimace.

She waves a hand with a scoff. "Are you kidding? I'm used to puppy slobber. A few vampire tears are nothing."

"I didn't realize Lucan slobbered," I say with another laugh, "but now I'll have to make fun of him for that."

"I do no such thing."

We both whip our heads around to find Lucan standing in the open doorway in human form, his dark, mottled hair pushed back. But he's not alone. Standing next to him, leaning heavily on his cane, is Taika, with all the other werewolves gathered behind them in Stella's garden.

There's only one reason they could have all followed Lucan here. I glance down at the medical bag in Taika's hand, and he nods at me as Stella squeezes my hand in her own.

The air around us becomes magnified, electric, heavy, as if the full weight of the world is finally crashing down.

"The antivenom is ready."

By the time we make it to the right part of the Wall, the moon hangs like a sickle in the sky.

I'm glad it's not a full blood moon tonight. According to the journal entries of Lucan's father, I would need to feed if it was, but as of right now, I feel just as energized and powerful as I did this morning, Lucan's blood still singing through my veins. Like I could fight in a war.

"You're sure you want to do it here?" Taika asks, leaning his cane against the crooked edge of a nearby stump to grasp the handle of his medical bag in both hands.

I glance back at him and all the other members of Lucan's pack behind us. Vivian is practically bouncing on the balls of her feet in excitement, Merrick with his arm slung tight around her, and Soren rubbing his hands together in anticipation. Gabriel and Kyra lurk in the back, arms folded with skepticism, but several of the others look openly hopeful.

Even Stella followed us here, watching from a distance in the shadows of the trees.

"This is where we first almost met," Lucan tells Taika, tugging my eyesight forward. "Just the Wall between us," he whispers to me, and I think back to that day in the catacombs when I ran into the edge of the city, trapped, just on the other side. Now, we're both standing on the outside together, the forest floor dipping down to that same stone door that's locked shut. "I wanted so badly to claw every piece of it apart to get to you."

I swallow the thickness in my throat and squeeze his hand. "Now we get to claw it apart together," I tell him, and nerves squirm in my belly as I glance at the medical bag. "If this works."

"It will, Saskia."

I stare straight at the door, at the slowly-moving veins of venom writhing in the fossilized wood. "I wish I had your confidence."

Lucan leans in close to murmur in my ear, his voice tickling against my hair, "That's ironic, considering you're the only thing I'm truly confident *in*."

I close my eyes briefly before turning to Taika with a nod. He unclasps the medical bag, setting it on the crown of the stump and dipping his hand in to pull out one syringe, then another—then finally a vial filled with a bright, clear liquid.

Turning the vial upside down, he slides a needle through the top and extracts the liquid slowly, filling the syringe carefully as if he's about to inject a living, breathing soul and not a Wall that we want to completely destroy.

Finally, he hands a now-filled syringe to me, and I take it with a steady hand, my years as a healer overpowering the tremble that might otherwise fill my fingers.

Taika repeats his steps before he tries to hand the second syringe to Lucan. "Alpha," he says with a proud dip of his head.

Lucan only stares at the needle pointed directly at him.

"I—I don't think I can. It wasn't my idea. I didn't make it with you."

All too aware of every pair of ears listening behind us, I lay my free hand on his wrist. "These are *your* antibodies, Lucan. *Your* fight. Every time you tried to climb this Wall, every time you tried to tear it down to save your people, to save me... it resulted in *this*." I nod at the syringe still in Taika's hand. "This is literally your blood, sweat, and tears at work. So you can."

The whistle of the wind though tree branches twirls around us. Somewhere in the distance, an owl hoots as Lucan stares and stares and stares at me.

Finally, an awed smile spreads across his face, and he outstretches his hand, his fingers closing around the barrel while his eyes never leave my face. "Look who's confident now."

I laugh and nudge him with my elbow. Then we both take a deep breath and turn back toward the Wall.

It looms so high above us that the air goes cold as we step into its shadow, descending down the needle-strewn ground, where Lucan's old pawprints already scar the forest floor. This close, I can also make out the faintest gouges in the door where he once clawed at it—and no doubt burst with pain upon contact. Pain that we'll now use against the Wall itself.

"Are you ready?" I breathe, eyeing a particularly thick vein in the doorway and placing the tip of my needle against it.

"I've been ready for a few hundred years," Lucan murmurs, and he does the same. "All I do is push?"

I place my thumb against the tip of the plunger and nod. "Just one last push."

So side by side, eyes locked on each other, we plunge the needles into the Wall.

And push.

For several minutes, nobody speaks.

I squint at the Wall, hardly daring to breathe, as if I can make those veins of venom dissolve just by concentrating hard enough. They undulate as slowly as ever, giving the stone a ripple effect that messes with my vision the harder I look.

Slowly, Lucan and I hand the empty syringes back to Taika, who puts them back into his medical bag before retrieving his cane from the stump and waiting.

And waiting.

And waiting.

"It can take more than thirty minutes for antivenom to work in human patients," Taika finally says, breaking the silence shrouding us like a heavy cloak.

"What about in a Wall patient?" Soren asks out loud.

Everyone—even Stella—turns to shoot him an exasperated look, and Soren scrunches his nose.

"Right. You wouldn't know, because you've never had a Wall patient before. I'll shut up now."

"That's the smartest thing you've said all day," Vivian murmurs.

Still, the exchange seems to have broken the spell of silence gripping us all by the throat, and soon murmurs rise among the werewolves at my back. I stare straight ahead, gripping Lucan's hand with enough force that in any other male, I might have squeezed his fingers off. But Lucan squeezes me right back, anchoring me to him as my heart drops further and further down, the minutes dragging by with painstaking slowness.

By the time half an hour passes, the moon shifting in the sky above us, the Wall still hasn't changed. As much as I try to imagine it into existence, the stone isn't melting back into wood. It stands just as impenetrable as always, looming over us like a hulking monster rooted deep into the earth, refusing to budge.

"Maybe I should check—"

Lucan moves before I can hold him back, reaching out to brush his fingertips against the stone... and immediately jerks back with a curse.

A pit sinks so low into my stomach, I want to fall to my knees. Behind me, Gabriel speaks the words I can't bear to say out loud.

"I'm not waiting around for this shit any longer. It didn't work. It's over."

I can hear pine needles crunch underfoot as he turns to leave, and worse, the sound of several others turning to follow him. Taika passes me a sympathetic glance, and Lucan wraps his arm around my shoulder, pulling me in tight.

"It's okay," he whispers. "Remember, we try over and over again until the world caves."

I shake my head, tears burning images of my mother as a statute into my retinas. Images of Malcolm and Gaia, Eleni and Sylvia, all the people I have failed who might not live long enough for the world to cave. For the first time since my mother was Chosen, there's a gaping wound in the world that I can't heal, that I can't fix.

And I don't know what to do.

I don't know how to keep trying.

I don't know what the point is.

"It's over," I repeat, the words like ash on my tongue.

Lucan grabs my chin and forces me to look at him. "Listen, Saskia..."

"No. It didn't work." I jerk away. "It wasn't enough. I—"

"You stubborn woman." Lucan grabs hold of me by the back of the neck, amusement and exasperation clashing on his face. "Haven't you learned to obey me yet, or do I need to teach you a few more lessons?" He smirks as I splutter. "I said *listen.*"

My mouth pops open to protest, until I realize his own mouth has already snapped shut. His eyes narrow in concentration, and I realize what he means by *listen*.

I do, straining to pinpoint all the sounds of the night. The hooting of owls. The whirring of crickets. The creaking of tree branches in the wind. The breathing of the pack members who stayed, still watching this very exchange. The subtle beat of Lucan's heart beside me.

And something fainter. Something so faint, it's almost undetectable beneath the layers of everything else, like the crackling of frost as it melts under a piercing streak of moonlight.

"Is that...?" I whip my head toward the Wall again and lean forward, until my nose is nearly brushing the stone—or what's left of it. The veiny, hardened material looks thinner, practically translucent in two blooming areas around the injection sites.

"I told you it would work," Lucan says smugly.

With a great collective gasp, the rest of the pack members surge forward to see for themselves, elbowing and bumping into each other to get a good look. Right before our eyes, the stone continues to dissolve, revealing two cloud-shaped sections of gnarled wood, each about the size of a fist. Then the size of a dinner plate. Then bigger and bigger, until the sections merge and spread, and a door stands in front of us surrounded by a halo of stone.

A very *wooden* door.

The mood in the air quickly spikes from excitement to something sharper as everyone stills, each of us probably imagining how easy it would be to kick that door in. Our way inside. *Their* way inside, finally, after five hundred years of being locked out, is right here.

"Saskia." Lucan's voice cracks. "You did it, baby. You did it."

He turns, clutches both sides of my face, and fits his lips to mine with a kiss that spits fire into my bones. Then he turns to his fellow pack members, and I can hear the alpha overtaking his voice as it turns deeper, more commanding, like he was born for this moment.

And maybe he was.

"Merrick, Vivian, go get weapons. Soren, get torches. Mom." His eyes flick over all the heads to meet Stella's. "Get the children and the elderly into the bunker and do *not* come out until we're back."

Stella looks like she might try to argue, but at the set of Lucan's jaw, she squeezes her eyes shut and nods. Opening them again, she surges forward to gather both Lucan and me in a crushing hug.

"Be careful, my children. Come back to me in one piece. Both of you."

Then she casts us a longing look before turning back toward the woods, her long white hair winking in the moonlight. Without hesitating, Merrick, Vivian, and Soren spring into their werewolf forms and follow, their silhouettes quickly swallowed by the trees as they hurry to obey Lucan's commands.

"The rest of you." Lucan's eyes glide over the remaining werewolves—including Gabriel, who must have whipped around when he heard the commotion. "Are you in?"

"Absolutely," Ashe says immediately, and several others express their instant agreement, cracking knuckles and loosening shoulders. Kyra glances over her shoulder at Gabriel, whose eyes flick from the Wall to me.

I hold his stare, knowing what he's telling me without words: *prove it.*

Then he inhales and jerks his head at Lucan.

"I'm in, alpha. Of course I am." He hurries toward us again, averting his eyes, but Lucan's attention is already back on me.

"You've done your part, my dream." He brushes a strand of my hair out of my face with astonishing tenderness. "If you want to go with my mom, no one would—"

"Not a chance," I cut him off, catching him by his wrist. "I'm coming with you."

He gives a sigh. "Of course you are. But I had to try, didn't I?"

I flash him my best grin and turn to Taika, who's definitely staring at the wooden door with misty eyes that I pretend not to notice as I cup a hand on his shoulder.

"I wouldn't have known how to do it without you."

He blinks back at me, wiping at the glimmer of tears on his cheeks, and says, "You make an excellent apprentice, dear. When those bastards are dead, we'll be able to make antivenom for everyone they've ever hurt. So make sure you win."

"I will," I promise, my words coming out about ten times more confident than I feel.

But there's no time to shake my nerves, because Vivian, Merrick, and Soren bound back mere seconds later, carrying more weapons and torches than should be physically possible. Everyone grabs a knife or pitchfork or ax and straps them to their backs and limbs, even though I have a feeling our best assets will be our teeth and claws. I myself take a familiar belt filled with knives in sheaths. This way, we'll be prepared for anything.

All too soon, Lucan's using a match to light the torch in Soren's hand.

Flame flickers against the night, ripping light into shadow. Lucan takes the torch, hauls in a deep breath, and turns to look at me with a questioning gaze as he holds the fire a breath away from the wooden door, the antivenom slowly dissolving more and more of the stone around it. I doubt it'll dissolve the entire Wall, but this is enough for now.

I nod. "Burn. It. *Down*."

Lucan doesn't need to be told twice. He presses the torch against the door, and we all watch as the flame catches the wood. Black spreads across the surface, and smoke begins to waft out in tendrils, until finally, Lucan can't hold back anymore.

He kicks the door inward, and it comes crashing down in a pile of splinters and ash.

A breath of cold air blows out at us from the tunnel within, making the torchlight stutter. We all stare at the opening for a second. Then everyone else backs up, and I feel the shift in the air as they change forms.

When I turn around, twelve werewolves stand in a semi-circle around me, their weapons strapped to their forearms and hind legs, all of them so large that I know the catacombs will be a tight squeeze for each of them.

It's okay. I'm used to having to squeeze into tight places, Soren's voice fills my head, and the others groan before Lucan throws up his mental block until it's just him and me.

Whenever you're ready, little nightmare.

His monstrous form pads up next to me, amber slits observing me from his towering height. Even after everything we've gone through, the sight of the Monster in the flesh still shoots exhilaration up and down my body.

The Guardians have no idea the wrath they are about to face. From him *or* me.

In answer, I throw up my head and do my best impression of a howl at the moon.

The others catch on, splitting the air with their own howls, and I smile knowing that the Guardians have heard this before. They have no way of knowing that tonight, it's different. These aren't howls of desperation, of rage, or of agony, but of eagerness. Excitement.

Joy, judging by the pealing ring of Lucan's, loudest of all.

Then he springs forward, into the tunnel and the darkness beyond.

LUCAN

My limbs have never felt so free, bounding down the cata-combs with Saskia on my heel.

I can feel her presence right behind me, even more than I can hear the other dozens of thundering paws of my pack. Something about her energy feels like static electricity, causing every hair on my werewolf body to bristle with anticipation—as if she's the one I should be running toward.

The dichotomy of having her by my side as we approach an inevitable war and the primal need to scoop her up and protect her from every horror in this world is thrilling in two very different ways.

She's in her element, free, wild. Her exhilaration palpable against my back. I would never deny her this moment or become a Monster that hides her away from the world. But that doesn't mean I won't do everything in my power to keep her safe, because I *will* become a Monster the second anyone threatens or harms her in any way, no questions asked.

My heart swells, basking in the fact that I'll be whatever she needs me to be. That she can just be *herself*, a privilege she's never been granted.

But I keep my eyes forward, my vision cutting through the darkness and taking in every damned dust particle that swirls in the tunnels we zigzag through.

Left, Saskia murmurs to me when we come to a fork, but I already know. I spent months sketching out these tunnels from the outside, and now I know the way to the center by heart.

To think that right above our heads are all the people I've always dreamed of saving...

To think that at any second, one of the Guardians could zip around any corner...

It's only when we come to a cavernous opening, several archways circling the area as fresh torchlight flickers in brackets around us, that I skid to a halt, the others stopping in a crowd around me to listen for any signs of life. Or death.

A steady *drip, drip, drip* of water leaks from the ceiling, plopping into puddles of shimmering, red-tinged water on the ground. By the sudden alarm bells ringing in Saskia's head, I can tell that she smells blood. And frankly, so do I.

The scent of death, like metallic rot, permeates these very walls.

That tunnel right there. Silently, Saskia points toward the gaping mouth of an opening directly across from us. *That one leads to the dungeons of the Blood Moon Palace.*

Every cell in my body screams at me to follow that direction, to invade immediately, but I can't shake an equally loud feeling that we need to stay basked in shadows for a moment longer. There are no cameras down here, but it's like the tunnels themselves are watching our every move.

Let me go first, I tell Saskia and the pack, lowering my mental block so that all of our minds are connected. *As soon as it's all clear, we run again. But I just want to check.*

Thankfully, none of them argue, even Saskia. I place a single, large paw out into the cavern, then another, until I'm treading silently into the very center, splashing through the puddles. All that flickering light illuminates me, and the air in the catacombs seems to fall utterly, deathly silent.

I think we're good to— Merrick starts.

Just as a blur of marble white rushes at me from one of the tunnels at my back.

30

SASKIA

I scream Lucan's name as the Seventh Guardian grabs him by one of his monstrous forearms, tearing at his flesh, and lunges at his neck with her fangs.

But Lucan's already moving. Twisting. Thrashing. Throwing himself to the ground and rolling on top of her. I can tell that he's taken our earlier training to heart, because as soon as he pops back up to his feet, the Seventh Guardian has lost her hold on him.

"Monster," she spits. "How did you get in?"

Lucan can't respond, of course, not in his werewolf form, but something protective and possessive overtakes me at the way her eyes gleam hungrily in his direction, so enraptured by his presence that she hasn't even noticed the rest of us still hiding in the shadows over here.

No, thank you. This male is *mine* to hunt and bite and taste. Nobody else's.

So I answer in Lucan's stead.

"That's for you to die never knowing, *Guardian.*"

The Seventh Guardian twirls around at my voice, practically spitting with fury when she lays those crimson eyes on me as I step out of the shadows, into the light. If I were still a human, I might drop to my knees in surrender right here and now, but I'm not something she can suck dry anymore. And she knows it.

"*You.* You treacherous, Chosen *bitch*," she hisses at me. "Arad told us you'd turned into a vampire, but we all laughed at him. Told him it was impossible." She begins to prowl in a circle around me, and I spin in place to keep her in my sight. "Now I'll have to apologize to him... after I torture you like I tortured your friend."

Fear punches me in the gut at her words, nearly halting my spin. "What friend?"

"Oh, what's his name? I lose track when there's thousands of you. Oh, right!" The Seventh Guardian snaps her fingers with a mock laugh before narrowing her eyes in a glare. "Diggory."

I can hardly remember to breathe as that name rings through me. "Diggory's alive?"

She can't keep the twisted smile off her face long enough to keep me guessing.

"Where?" I manage to whisper through my shock, but she only revels silently in it, smirking at my obvious distress.

"I have to admit, he's a stubborn one. Wouldn't give up your name even though we already knew you had spoken to him. Tell me..."

She cocks her head, still prowling in circles around me, and I just barely manage to make eye contact with Lucan behind her. He's holding back, trying to give me time to collect information while she's in a talkative mood, but I can sense the vibration of his restraint in our shared blood.

The Seventh Guardian, however, remains oblivious. "Where's the rest of the necklace he gave you?" she asks, crimson eyes flicking down to my chest, where the gold chain hangs. "I don't know how you managed to hide it for so long, but Arad put all the pieces together after you jumped. Every step you've made since you were Chosen, we have on camera."

I scoff. "The Third Guardian didn't put any pieces together. He didn't want to believe a Chosen One could keep any secrets, have any opinions, become anything powerful, until it was staring him right in the face. And even then, he underestimated me. Just like you are. So I'm going to give you a choice right now, even though you didn't give your citizens one: leave this city and never look back... or die."

The vampire throws back her head and laughs at the catacombs' ceiling.

"You think you can kill me, *Saskia*? You don't even know how. And I'm not underestimating you. You are just as spineless as the Thirteenth Guardian was. Soft for humans. Afraid to take what you can." She crouches, as if preparing to pounce. "And you will be just as easy to turn into a corpsssssssse."

Her last word catches on the blood that spurts out of her mouth, splattering my front.

With a thud, she drops to her knees at my feet. Behind her, Lucan—back in his human form—pulls his ax out of her back with a disgusted wrinkle of his nose.

"How dumb can you get?" he mutters as the rest of her falls forward, her forehead cracking against the stone floor. "Turns her back on me for a solid five minutes while insulting and threatening the love of my life? Did she forget I was here?"

"I don't know, but that was the coolest fucking thing I've ever seen."

It's Soren, hurrying forward in his human form with Merrick and Vivian, while the rest of the pack members stick to their werewolf shapes. All of them circle the Seventh Guardian's body, though, sniffing at the sweet, dark liquid that spreads in a blossoming circle around her.

"I don't think that's her own blood," Vivian says, plugging her nose.

"No." I shake my head with a grimace. "That's definitely a mix of human blood she must have drunk recently." My stomach twists, hoping like hell it's nobody I know.

But even if it isn't, the fact is she chose to drink human blood. Even if the sight of a dead body feels wrong to look at on so many levels, I know this is the only way we can save Xantera—by killing them all.

"Well," Soren says with a happy sigh. "At least that was easier than expected, right? Not even a hair out of place, alpha." He claps Lucan on the back. "Only eleven to go."

As soon as the last word leaves his lips, however, the Seventh Guardian jerks.

"You were saying?" Vivian asks with raised eyebrows.

A gurgled hiss leaves the Seventh Guardian's mouth. Her head snaps upward. She shoots to her feet before any of us can grab her, but the werewolves work quickly to surround her in an impenetrable wall of muscle and fur. She spins, the wound in her back already healing—

And then Kyra rips off her head.

I wince as the decapitated head hits one of the walls with a squelching *thud*. The Seventh Guardian's body crumples to the ground a second time, and Soren whistles.

"Scratch what I said earlier. *That's* the coolest fucking thing I've ever—oh, come on. Really?"

The headless corpse jerks again, the fingernails scratching at the floor in an effort to drag itself toward the head across the cavern. Gabriel steps forward and pins it down with a single, giant paw, but one of the arms whips around to scratch him, and he yelps.

"Enough with this shit," Vivian grumbles. She marches forward to snatch one of the lit torches from its sconce on the wall. Before the Seventh Guardian's body can crawl its way to the head, she brings the flame down upon it.

For a moment, nothing happens. Then another moment passes, and still nothing happens. The flame licks the Seventh Guardian's body, and although her clothes catch on fire, her marble skin remains unaffected.

Worse, one of the arms swings up to snatch at the torch, and Vivian has to wrestle it out of her grip with a grunt.

"No wonder she turned her back on you," Merrick mutters to Lucan. "She knew she wouldn't die."

Panic seems to settle over us like snow. If we can't even kill one vampire when all of us are circling her, how are we going to kill the rest of them? Are they—*we*—completely immortal? No, that's not possible. The Thirteenth Guardian died, I just have no idea *how*.

And what if Arad or any of the others comes down to the catacombs to investigate the noise we've already made while we're trying to figure it out?

"Saskia." Lucan closes the distance between us in two strides and cups my face in his hands. "Can you think of anything that will help us? Anything Arad might have told you in the past?"

I close my eyes, straining to scrape anything useful from my memories, but... nothing. I spent so much time trying to escape Arad's presence that I never paused long enough to glean any useful information from him, dammit.

My heart beats in my chest, slow and steady as ever, but that doesn't stop it from feeling everything. Fear. Terror. Horror, as the werewolves behind Lucan try to keep the Seventh Guardian's body from rejoining her head to no avail.

My useless heart.

My useless human heart.

With a gasp, I open my eyes.

"That's it! In the garden, right before I jumped, Arad told me our hearts can't turn to stone." More accurately, he said, *I am going to drain you dry until you are just as much of a stone as your helpless mother. Well, except for your heart. The only thing that can't turn to stone is your useless human heart.* "And since we all started off as humans—"

"Even a vampire's heart would still be vulnerable." Lucan snaps his fingers and kisses my forehead, but before he turns around, he casts one last look at my chest. As if even more scared now that he knows how I might die as well.

But I push at his shoulder. "Go!"

He spins on a heel, dripping with murderous power. Just as the Seventh Guardian's body reaches her head, fitting it back onto her shoulders so that sinews begin to reconnect, Lucan's claws shoot out of his fingers, and he punches through her chest.

When he rips out her heart, the Guardian falls to the ground for a final time.

"Burn it," Lucan says with obvious disdain. The thing clutched in his fist isn't a pulsing, bloody organ like I'd imagine, but a sad little lump of charcoal gray, the color of the ash we left behind at the door of the Wall. Obviously something that hadn't been used in a long, long time.

Without looking over his shoulder, he tosses the heart toward Vivian, who shrieks and bats it at Soren. "Ew, I don't want to touch that thing!" he hollers, but catches it anyway before it can land in the puddle at his feet, grimacing as he holds it out. "Fuck, get it over with."

Merrick pinches the bridge of his nose, grabs the flickering torch from Vivian, and holds the flame out to the heart. With bated breath, we wait...

And then it bursts into flames.

I swear, I can hear the Seventh Guardian's final shriek fade into silence as her once-human heart crumbles away into gritty embers, her ashes mixing with the bloody water on the floor. The rest of her remains in a heap, utterly still and lifeless, as if she truly became nothing more than stone.

"*Now* we're one down, eleven to go," Merrick says with a grim twist of his lips.

In his werewolf form, Ashe whines toward the tunnel leading to the Blood Moon Palace, but Lucan already seems to know the thoughts spinning through my head. "We can't." He shakes his head. "Not yet. The vampire mentioned that she's been with Diggory, which means..."

I'm already sprinting, no time to contemplate it, taking the tunnel that the Seventh Guardian came out of. If I remember correctly, this one leads to a locked door that I always thought of as a dead-end. In my human form, I was never able to open it, but now that I'm a vampire?

I smash through the wood as if it's nothing more than paper, splinters exploding all around me as I burst into what looks like an underground chamber made of a single, narrow stone passageway bordered by iron cells. There aren't any torches to light this place, but my vision uses what little light still bleeds from the cavern behind me to take in my surroundings.

Prisoners by the handful are crammed in every cell, their space containing nothing but a bloodstained stone floor and a pile of rags in the corner. The smell of piss and vomit permeates the air even thicker than the blood. Moans and coughs fill every inch of the space, and heads turn to look at me with reactions ranging from panicked to sluggish—some of them near death.

All of them covered in too many bruises and seeping wounds to count.

These are where the rioters were taken. These are all the people who tried to fight after Claudia revealed the truth... and failed. Now they're suffering for taking a stand.

But when I rush toward the first cell to try to help, the man gripping the rusted bars backs away, his eyes flying open in fear.

"No," he stutters with a hoarse voice. "Please don't."

My throat closes like a vise, and the only thing I can feel is the sadness wrapping around my heart.

He's afraid of me—of my marble skin and crimson eyes and darting movements.

"I'm here to help," I reassure him, but he cowers in the corner. So do all the others as I walk past each cell in a daze, until a groan rises from one of the last ones in the back.

The heap of fabric in the corner of the cell moves shakily as a bruised arm appears out of the folds to lift itself and then flop back down. I catch a glimpse of a swollen face covered in fresh, oozing cuts.

"Diggory!" I gasp, grabbing the bars and rattling them with all my strength. They creak, the sound straining through the stone dungeon, but they're just as locked as the Wall once was. No veins of venom writhe within the iron bars, but I'm still not strong enough to get to him. And once again, I don't have a damn key to open it.

Diggory peers up at me through the bars. His face is likely unrecognizable to anyone who knows him, but to me he looks the same as his one night in the Healing Center... only worse.

Both eyes are swollen slits, brownish purple skin hangs off his cheek in strips, and dried blood mixed with fresh blood has stained his lips in various shades of red. I wonder if he can see me, if he even remembers who I am. He's been at the forefront of my mind with every step I've taken, but to him, I might just be the healer that took care of him for less than a day.

"I'm trying!" I promise him, my voice cracking. Panic shoots down my limbs, causing my entire body to tremble. He's right there, within an inch of death, but I can't get to him. I don't know what to do, and after all of this he's going to die on my watch. "I'm trying!"

"Saskia," Lucan says from behind me, and I jump, not realizing he followed me in here.

But he just anchors his hands around my waist, lifts my shaking body off my feet, and sets me down two feet to the right.

Then he places his massive hands where mine just were, gripping the bars so tightly that his tan skin turns white. His forearms tense, lines running along the ridges of each muscle, and with a grating screech, the entire cell door pops off its hinges.

Lucan tosses it to the side like it weighs nothing, leaving a gaping hole for me to step through.

"Diggory!" I cry, rushing inside, all of my anxiety melting away as it brings back every ounce of the healer in me. Cradling the elderly man against my chest when I fall to my knees, I keep the tears at bay. "He needs to go to the Healing Center. Right now," I tell Lucan, throwing a wild gaze over my shoulder to find that the rest of the pack has filtered in, looking more than confused about this change of events. "I'll go while you—"

"No." Lucan steps forward and fills the doorway completely with his enormous frame.

"You need to stay with your pack," I start to argue.

Lucan shakes his head. "You were alone within these Walls for far too long, little nightmare. Now that we're in here together, we *do* it together. Every step." And he gives me no time to counter. Wheeling around to face them, his commanding tone is like the swish of a knife. "Work on getting all of the prisoners free. Saskia and I will be right behind you as soon as we get back."

At his words, all of the other prisoners begin to limp or crawl to their iron bars, jaws dropping as they take in their potential rescuers. I see blackened, swollen eyes widen when they land on those still in their werewolf forms, and some immediately retreat into their shadowy corners once again. Others begin whispering to each other with hopeful tones, and my heart twists as I clutch Diggory to my chest.

They all risked their lives to protest the Guardians. And now, maybe, just maybe, they'll get to keep their lives despite it.

Vivian, Merrick, Soren, and the others nod and get to work.

Gabriel and Kyra, however, exchange glances with curling lips and sneering expressions that I understand immediately.

Just like he promised he would, Lucan is choosing me and my wishes over the pack and their mission. I'm already rotting his position as alpha and king. Already compromising everyone else's safety.

But Diggory...

After another snarl from Lucan, Gabriel and Kyra jolt into action, closing their jaws around the bars nearest them and yanking the cell doors off their hinges.

As the prisoners stumble out, Lucan whispers, "Let's go."

With Diggory still in my arms, we move through the catacombs, trying to find an exit. I follow Lucan blindly with each turn, knowing he memorized this maze like the back of his hand.

Two rights and a left. Then a hollow cave that splits into five additional tunnels. Lucan doesn't hesitate when he takes the second to the right. And within a minute, we're ascending up to an alleyway lined with identical doors and eaves blocking the moonlight above.

Long abandoning the idea of being quiet, I sprint past Lucan, down the alleyway, toward the main street with Diggory groaning against my chest. In the back of my mind, the Cardinal Rules are clanging together, and I can't help but hear echoes of that stupid female voice spouting out the curfew warning every night.

"Citizens of Xantera, please return to your individual housing units. Recreational time is over. Citizens of Xantera, please return to your individual housing units."

If my patient wasn't two steps away from death right now, I'd laugh at the absurdity of this. We're *definitely* out past curfew.

But my vampire speed is too fast for anyone to catch me, so when I burst out onto the main street, I don't pause even when a line of sentries crank their heads in my direction.

"Halt!" one shouts, twisting from his lookout on the balcony of the Sentries Station half a block up toward the palace.

The others surge toward me, five sets of footsteps pounding pavement as if they actually have a chance at getting to me when Lucan emerges from the alleyway, a warning growl rumbling off his chest.

"I wouldn't go after her if I were you. Just a little advice if you want to live."

At that, I can't stop myself from twisting my head to watch over my shoulder as the sentries skid to a halt and turn to face this new threat. I can practically smell their bewilderment when he steps out into the moonlight, not in his werewolf form, but larger and stronger than any human in Xantera could ever get, the muscles cording on his neck as he clenches his jaw.

"Y-you are not allowed to be out this late," one of them stammers, as if trying to convince himself that Lucan is merely a citizen when everything about him screams otherwise—strapped with weapons, with no cloak or badge in sight.

"Oh?" Lucan cocks an eyebrow. "Then come put me back to bed."

His ruse works. The sentries change directions, charging him with their rapiers instead of me. Lucan barrels into them as if they're nothing, sweeping them off their feet in one fluid movement of his arm that makes me suck in a breath—knocking them out before their heads even hit the ground.

Which is why I don't see the sentry leap out of a darkened alleyway to my left, his rapier slicing through the air.

Every millisecond seems to tick by slowly as the blade comes crashing down toward Diggory in my arms.

Instinctively, I raise one of my hands to meet it before it does, catching it by its sharp edge. The metal doesn't completely slice through, but it imbeds between my fingers like a blade cracking into marble, sending a bolt of pain up my arm. "Saskia!" Lucan cries from behind me.

He's there at my side before the sentry can even blink or process what just happened, and I rip the rapier out of his grip by the blade. Lucan takes it from me, his amber eyes darkening as they zero in on the new, spiderwebbing gash in my hand.

It's already healing, my skin stitching itself back together, but Lucan gives an icy laugh.

"That was a colossal mistake."

And he uses the rapier to slice off the sentry's hand by the wrist.

"Don't touch what's mine," he seethes as the sentry falls to his knees with a scream, his hand thudding to the ground in front of him and blood spurting from the stump. "She doesn't deserve even a scratch."

I don't have time to admonish him for it. More sentries, dozens of them, are sprinting toward us now, and Diggory has gone much too still against my chest.

"Go." Lucan presses a quick kiss against my forehead again. "I'll keep them out."

He pivots on a heel to face the flood of sentries with that bloody rapier still in his hand, and this time, I don't turn my head to watch.

I rush up the next block and burst through the sliding glass doors of the place I once considered home... without a cloak and hood to hide that it's me this time.

No matter what happens in Xantera, it's like you can always count on the Healing Center to stay the same. The sterile smell still stings my nostrils. The light bulbs still buzz with an obnoxious current. The information clerk still sits at the front desk, currently helping a patient check in with an excessive shuffling of paperwork.

"Help!" I hurry forward, and the information clerk looks up with a surprised widening of her gaze. "He needs immediate attention!"

"I..." She gives Diggory a once over before her eyes graze over my face, alarmed. The patient in front of her presses a hand to her heart and nearly faints at the sight of us. "You're..." Her eyes move back to Diggory, and I can see the cogs working in her mind, piecing together who and what we are. Rebels. "And he's..."

"Dying," I finish for her, my impatience bubbling to a breaking point. "He's dying, so get someone out here to help right now!"

All around us, doors crack open as healers emerge from hallways and locker rooms to see what all the commotion is about, stopping in their tracks when they take in Diggory and me. All of them are familiar faces, people I've nodded at or said good morning to hundreds of times before today. I'm not sure what, exactly, they've been told about me and the rebels, but none of them surge forward to take Diggory from my arms.

And he's... he's stopped breathing.

"Please!" I cry, depositing Diggory onto the waiting room floor and beginning chest compressions, horrified to hear his ribs cracking beneath my palms. I'm too strong—haven't had enough time to figure out the strength thrumming through my veins. "I need a defibrillator right now!"

"You are both traitors to the Guardians and Xantera," a vaguely familiar voice spits, and I look up to find that same male healer I stole the centrifuge from. He recognizes me, bitterness lining every inch of his face as he gazes upon my efforts to save Diggory.

If I weren't busy with chest compressions, trying to employ just enough force to keep his blood pumping, I'd probably strangle the male healer with my bare hands.

But another voice answers in my stead.

"Step aside, step *aside*, you miserable fool."

Gaia pushes her way to the front of the crowd, where she immediately drops to her knees on the other side of Diggory and locks eyes with me.

For a moment, a world of unspoken words passes between us. I see shock and sorrow in hers, but also relief and maybe even joy. To be honest, I never thought I'd see her again either, but here she is now, gazing into my new crimson eyes without fear or disgust curdling her expression.

Only acceptance.

"We are healers!" Gaia shouts over her shoulder, her eyebrows narrowing. "We swore to protect the sickest and neediest and most vulnerable of our citizens! Regardless of whether or not they agree with you. Regardless of how you feel about them. *Regardless* of the Rules."

Pride bursts from me as all the other healers wither under her expression. Maybe she didn't expressly join the rebel movement, maybe she wishes she had, but it's clear that she regrets sticking to the Cardinal Rules so stubbornly before I was Chosen. And I couldn't be more grateful for her change of heart.

"Now someone get a gurney so we can take him back right this INSTANT!" Gaia screams.

Miraculously, two of the healers obey, scurrying off and returning moments later with a bed on wheels. The healers get their hands beneath Diggory and hoist him up, one of them immediately continuing the chest compressions as the other wheels him away.

Gaia takes one last look at me, standing empty-handed in the middle of the waiting room with blood smeared across my front. She reaches out to squeeze my hand, and I squeeze hers back as tears slip from the corners of my eyes.

"Thank you, Gaia." If anyone can save Diggory from this point on, it's her.

She swipes at her own eyes and pulls away. "I'm sorry I ever doubted you, dear. I never believed one person could make a difference, but now I'm starting to think otherwise. So go make them pay for it." She nods at the portraits of the Guardians hanging on the waiting room wall above our heads. "It looks like they've finally met their match with you."

Then she's gone, pushing through the swinging doors after the gurney.

I stand there for a moment, staring at where she disappeared as the information clerk and everyone still in the room stares at *me*.

The male healer has his hands clenched in fists, so purple-faced with anger that he can't even speak. Dozens of heartbeats tick in chaotic melodies, and dozens of breaths go in and out, but otherwise, you could hear a badge drop in the silence.

Until, that is, the alarms begin to blare.

LUCAN

The sentries keep coming from every direction like a multiplying horde of ants.

I try my best not to kill them, just to maim or knock out cold, reminding myself what they really are: only humans, appointed to this position by the Guardians. They're just doing their job.

Still, I keep seeing them charge at my woman with their rapiers, and my anger swells until there's a mountain of unconscious bodies growing around me. The shouts and cries that stab the night are surely going to attract the Guardians themselves, and I can already see several citizens of Xantera pressing their faces against their windows that border the main street.

Just when I'm wondering what the hell is taking Saskia so long, the alarms start going off.

They ring throughout the city from every loudspeaker, so piercing and echoing it's like the sound is coming from inside my skull. Like all of Xantera is wailing in pain.

"Shit." Just as three more sentries charge at me, I use my own stolen blade to clash against theirs, twist, and morph back into a werewolf. The remaining sentries freeze in place, eyes popping out of their heads. A few of them shriek and back away. But my canine teeth bare themselves in a grin, because that electric bolt of Saskia's presence floods my veins.

You okay? I ask her.

Yeah, she answers immediately. *Diggory's with Gaia now. But Lucan—they must know we're here.*

The alarms overlap now that we're connected, as if I can hear them through her perspective from the end of a long tunnel. My teeth grind together at the sound, but honestly, I'm only surprised it took the Guardians this long to notice our invasion.

Satisfied that Saskia is momentarily safe, I dissolve my mental block until I'm streamlining with the entire pack.

Everything good in the catacombs?

Yes. The voice belongs to Gabriel, which tells me that Vivian, Merrick, and Soren must be busy talking to the prisoners in their human forms. *We've freed most of them, and Ashe and Kyra are on guard right outside the prison.*

No signs of any more vampires so far?

None.

Good. That means they only know about me and Saskia. I can feel the authority in my voice threading through the connection that binds us all, a strategy unfolding itself in my mind. *I'll try to lure them out here in the open if you and the pack want to sneak out of the catacombs and divide into groups of twos. Surround the city if you can, then slowly close in.*

You've got it, alpha, Gabriel says, and my heart swells for the bastard. Despite all the times he tried to fight me for this position in the past, now that the moment has finally come, he's all in.

Just in time, too, because a *BOOM* sounds in the distance, overpowering even the alarms. When I look up, it's to find three humanoid shapes bursting through the doors of the Blood Moon Palace up ahead and whizzing toward me with a speed that blurs their features.

I stand my ground, tail flicking, digging my claws into the road beneath me.

For a moment, I'm certain they're going to maintain their speed and pounce on me at the same time, but then they screech to a halt right in front of the enormous pile of sentries at my feet.

The alarms die with one last echoing blare.

"Well, well, well," one of the Guardians huffs, his long throat lengthening even more as he lifts his chin. From all the times I've been in Saskia's mind, viewing the world from her perspective, I know they call this one the Eleventh. "If it isn't the Monster in the flesh."

I chance a glance at the other two Guardians, both of them giving me eerie smiles with crimson hate dripping from their eyes. One of them is the Fourth, a female with skin and hair whiter than her fangs. The other is the Tenth, a male with a dark skin tone as smooth and alluring as silk.

All three of them begin to stalk closer.

"And would you look at that?" the Eleventh Guardian continues, his voice growing loud enough to reverberate up and down the road. "You've killed our people, just like we knew you would if you were ever able to claw your way in."

He jerks his head at the pile of bodies between us. I don't take the bait, don't feel the need to tell him that every single sentry is still alive when I know he can hear their hearts beating as surely as I can—until the Eleventh Guardian cranks his head left and right and I notice the people watching from the alleyway.

Dozens and dozens of Xantera's citizens have crept out of their housing units, still clad in their identical issued nightgowns, to investigate all the commotion. And now hundreds of eyes widen at me in horror as they bounce from me to the bodies before me.

No, I want to tell them. *I'm here to save you.* But in my werewolf form, all that comes out is a growl that makes several of them gasp. Somewhere to my left, a baby begins to cry.

Well, fuck. That didn't have the effect I was going for.

"Don't worry," the Eleventh Guardian continues, and I catch the smirk lifting the corner of his thin lips, even though he tries to keep his face a careful portrait of concern. "We'll protect all of you from this vile abomination. Just like we did before."

And all three of them pounce.

I throw myself forward, leaping over the pile of bodies and catching them by surprise as I slam into the Eleventh.

The collision of our bodies sends a *crack* through the air, and he slams into the ground beneath me. I don't waste time sinking my canines into his chest to rip out his heart...

But before I can, razor-sharp nails dig into my shoulders and spine so hard that I roar.

A pair of fangs sinks into the back of my throat, tearing through my flesh. Vampire venom shoots through my veins like hot poison, setting my body on fire. I thrash, twisting to tear the two other vampires off of me just as the Eleventh scrambles to a stand again.

"You really think one Monster can defeat *three* Guardians?" the Fourth Guardian laughs in my face.

She kicks me in the stomach, knocking the air out of my lungs. I double over, dropping to all fours, but then immediately use the momentum to swipe my head at her legs and send her sprawling.

My relief is short-lived, though. The Eleventh Guardian jumps onto my back from behind, curls an arm around my throat, and squeezes.

I rear upward, toppling backward so that he smashes against the ground beneath me. It works, but then the Tenth Guardian is on top of me, slashing at my stomach with his fingernails like claws. I snap at his neck and toss him off as far away from me as I can.

Just as the other two vampires close in on me again, the Tenth Guardian's body slams into one of the power lines, making it crash against the nearest housing complex. Sparks ignite. Flames burst to life. The rooftop catches on fire, and several people scream.

Double fuck.

On a whim, I jump up and melt back into my human form, relishing the way all the watching humans suck in a breath as they witness my shift. Maybe now they'll rethink everything they've ever been told. Even the Eleventh Guardian pauses behind me, caught off guard.

The Tenth is already back without a scratch, narrowing his eyes at me next to the Fourth. I was trying to get all three of them herded together, but these two will have to do for now. "What's this? Surrender? Ready to get on your knees and bow?"

"No," I rasp, the pain from their nails and fangs searing through me even more in my human form. I swear, they carved out entire chunks of my flesh. "But you're about to."

A sound, wet and sticky, squelches through the night.

Before the two Guardians can even turn around, their eyes flash open in shock. For a moment, they stare at me, mouths gaping, blood leaking from the corners of their lips.

Then they fall to their knees and keel forward, faceplanting at my feet.

"What?" the Eleventh Guardian cries behind me, but I smile up at the glorious sight that will be painted on the canvas of my brain for the rest of my life.

Saskia. A terrifying, beautiful nightmare haloed in a backdrop of flames, splattered in blood...

Holding a shriveled vampire heart in each fist.

32

SASKIA

The hearts are spongy in my hand, like old pieces of meat that have long begun to rot.

Lucan beams up at me with such a breathtaking look of adoration all over his face that I almost drop the hearts just to jump into his arms. While the Eleventh Guardian stands there, staring at the vampire corpses in shock, Lucan strides toward me and brushes a finger beneath my chin.

"Such a good girl. Thank you."

I swallow the dryness in my throat at what I just did—how I snuck up behind the Fourth and Tenth Guardians and punched my hands into their backs until my fingernails found the right organ. "Do you know how hard that was?"

He frowns. "Ripping out their hearts? I know it's not in your nature."

The whole time he was fighting the three vampires, we were communicating mind-to-mind, forming a plan of attack where he was the distraction and I was the element of surprise. But loitering in the shadows of the Healing Center, watching them creep closer to him three on one...

"No." I shake my head and step closer to him, inhaling his woodsy scent that permeates all this too-sweet blood surrounding me. "It was hard to wait until their backs were turned before I helped you." My eyes flick to his neck, where a gash wraps around the back of his throat. "They hurt you."

It's the only reason I was able to do what I did. Part of me still can't fathom that I actually destroyed a living—no, *two* living bodies—like that.

But we're not done. The Eleventh Guardian stands motionless, staring at the lifeless body of the Fourth Guardian in disbelief. At the weight of our attention, he drags his head up, blinking at us while the rest of his body remains frozen in shock. Just like the vampire in the catacombs, his eyes trace me, putting the pieces of Arad's claims together.

"How dare you?" he exhales finally, stepping closer. Lucan throws an arm in front of me, but the Eleventh Guardian doesn't even seem to notice him anymore. "You think you can turn on us and win? We *made* you!"

"No," I hiss, clutching the vampire hearts even tighter. I'm afraid that if the Eleventh Guardian gets ahold of them before we can burn them, he'll stuff the organs back into the marble corpses at our feet to revive them. "You do not *make* anything. You hurt and take and destroy."

The apple in his throat tightens with anger before he puffs out a humorless laugh. "You know nothing about pain and selfishness and destruction. We've shielded you from the true horrors of the world. You should be thanking us. You *owe* us."

"She owes you nothing but death," Lucan scoffs.

The Eleventh Guardian cuts his eyes to Lucan as if suddenly remembering he's there. Then he changes tactics, his arms stretch widely out to the sides as he spins in place to address the horrified crowd.

"Citizens of Xantera. *This* is what we have shielded you from. This Monster who piles bodies at his feet. And once again, my fellow Guardians and I will slay him—and anyone who aligns with him—to teach you all a valuable lesson: we cannot be defeated."

Some citizens, however, eye the two vampire bodies with doubt reflecting back in their eyes. The Eleventh Guardian's confidence slips. Despite Lucan's protective stance in front of me, he drops into a crouch, eyes trained on my chest, right where my heart is.

"No! Don't hurt my healer."

The voice is high-pitched, young, and completely disorienting. I swing my head toward the source, where a small girl scurries out from the shadows of an alleyway.

Before her face even hits the light from the flickering flames licking across the rooftops nearby, I know who she is.

"Odette, stay back!"

I've never seen such a stubborn clenched jaw on someone so young. Odette ignores my command, hurries out in front of me, and throws her skinny arm out just like Lucan.

That's when the Eleventh Guardian's gaze flicks hungrily down, and my vision goes red when I remember what he did to her.

He was the vampire who snuck out through the catacombs and took her blood in the dead of night. *He* sent her to the Healing Center with lethargy and dizziness that no one could explain and everyone wanted to ignore.

He's set her on a track toward a shorter life. So now I have to end his.

But once again, the Eleventh Guardian turns to address the crowd that has begun to form around us, his arms spread wide as if to comfort them. If I attack him now, who knows how many bystanders would get hurt in the fight bound to ensue?

"Do you see how the Monster works?" He jabs a finger in Lucan's direction. "Stealing our Chosen Ones from us." He nods at me. "Murdering our sentries and Guardians." He nods at all the bodies around us. "Manipulating frightened, young girls into joining his cause." He nods at Odette. "Burning our city down?" He doesn't even have to nod at the fire, swelling in size and sending plumes of smoke toward the moon. "We told you to beware his eyes and resist his howl for a reason!"

Nobody says a single word, but I can taste the fear and uncertainty slicing through the air. Just in the last few weeks, these people saw televised evidence that their Guardians were turning Chosen Ones to stone, yet the evidence is stacked against Lucan, too.

The Eleventh Guardian turns back to us with a sneer, but only for a moment.

"You think you've won," he hisses in a voice low enough that only we can detect. "But I can assure you, this battle is far from over." His next smile rips across his face. "You might have our humans… but we have your pack."

Then he's a blur of motion as he zips back up main street toward the Blood Moon Palace, leaving his fellow Guardians in heaps at our feet.

We all stand stark still, watching his figure get smaller and smaller until the door booms shut again in the distance as he closes himself in, no doubt barricading it so we can't follow.

Lucan and I stare at each other with eyes full of fear.

The pack.

He doesn't waste time shifting, much to the further shock of the people around us. Some scream or shout, but we ignore them. Tethered to Lucan's mind once again, I try to spear toward the pack, but we both slam into a barrier so thick and wide that it's only silence on the other side. No sign of Vivian, Merrick, or Soren. No hint of what might have happened to them in the catacombs, or of how the Guardians found out about them down there.

No indication of whether they're alive or dead.

"How is this possible?" I ask, struggling to maintain my hold on the vampire hearts when my body begins to tremble. "How could a vampire block their *minds*?"

As Odette stares upward in awe, Lucan collapses back into his human form with an unmistakable ripple of grief crossing his eyes.

Grief? Oh no, who...

"It wasn't a vampire who blocked them," he says, his tone low enough to split the earth itself. "Only werewolves can do that."

"But... why would one of the pack block us out?"

The truth whips me in the face, stinging my eyes. Someone in the pack has betrayed us... and I think I know who.

Lucan's lip curls. "Every mind has its own style, its own signature. I'd recognize that mental block anywhere."

He doesn't have to say the name out loud. It clangs from his mind to mine, so loud and crippling that I want to beat it away.

Gabriel.

Hurt and anger punch through me in waves, but I know it's only an infinitesimal fraction compared to how Lucan feels. Gabriel may have hated me from the very beginning, but he never respected Lucan as alpha, either. And now the rest of the pack is suffering for his treachery.

But how did he defy Lucan's orders? What does he even have to gain from this? Where's the pack now?

With a shriek of frustration, I lob both vampire hearts toward the fire spreading from rooftop to rooftop. They sizzle on contact, crumbling to ash, but the satisfaction of successfully eliminating two more vampires never comes.

Not when our friends, our family, our *people*, are still in danger.

"Odette!" a panicked, fatherly voice calls from the throng of people surrounding us, and snaps Lucan and me back to the present moment as the girl's parents push to the front. "Come back here right now." His eyes stay trained on Lucan, untrusting, wary, and scared.

When Odette shakes her head defiantly, her mother shrieks, "He's the Monster, Odette! Get *away* from him!"

Murmurs travel across the crowd, and Lucan swivels his head, trying to pick out voices from the sea of faces.

"He's not the Monster. He's just a man."

A few women sigh. "A *gorgeous* man."

"No, didn't you just see him change? He's a Monster with claws and teeth and fur!"

"I don't see claws or teeth or fur."

"Because he's tricking us, somehow. It's an illusion!"

"No, he's just a human. But *she* helped him!"

"Yeah, she's *definitely* not human. She clawed out both of their hearts!"

"Good. The Guardians deserve to die after what they've done to our Chosen Ones."

Some people are shuffling backward, trying to get away from us. Others are pushing their way forward to try to see the Monster with their own eyes.

I lace my fingers through Lucan's, both of us unsure how to start—how to explain. The chaos around us intensifies like a wave of uncertainty, all of their varying voices like an explosion of flames crackling at the sky.

"Can they be trusted?"

"They might just kill us, too!"

"Or they might save us."

"We have to save ourselves."

"No, remember what happened when we tried to do that last time?"

This is nothing like the polite greetings carefully echoed back and forth each morning and night like we've always been taught. These are personal opinions. Unsolicited questions. Disagreements. Thinking. Engaging. Trying to change.

Despite the fact that Lucan and I are getting the brunt of it, my heart swells with painful pride to see how far Xantera has come.

And then a voice I'd recognize anywhere speaks up.

"We've seen the truth! We know that the Guardians have been lying to us for centuries about what happens to our Chosen Ones. We know they steal our blood under a false premise."

Malcolm steps out of the mob, passes Lucan a curious glance, and gives me the smallest smile before turning to address the crowd again.

"So why would we believe anything they've ever said about the Monster?" His confident tone carries over the hushed whispers, and I catch Walter's face, beaming from within the crowd. "Maybe we should decide if this so-called Monster is good or bad for ourselves."

Some nod. Some shake their heads. Others continue staring at Lucan, as if determined to catch him shifting again. But none of them look convinced *enough*.

And Lucan is so, so quiet in the face of the people his grandfather used to rule. Frozen in the gazes of the people he has spent centuries trying to get to, trying to protect.

I squeeze his hand, and he sucks in a breath, snapping out of it. After a large swallow, he says, "I'm not here to hurt you. I know those are just words, and I know you've been lied to in the past. I know that my actions will be the only way to prove my truth."

If the crowd was quiet before, now they're not even breathing. Only the crackle of the rising flames permeates the night as the people of Xantera look upon their rightful king.

I decide to break it by telling them more of the truth. They deserve to know all of it.

"It's true, he's the Monster," I start, a little too loudly. "But the Monster has a name and a family and a story. A life outside of this Wall that was stolen by the Guardians centuries ago." I swallow down the emotion edging into my voice, trying to sound firmer. "His name is Lucan, and they killed his grandfather and his father. Stole their kingdom and trapped us here for the sole purpose of feeding off our blood." People exchange frowns and looks of disgust. "Yes, we turn to stone after being bitten, and the Guardians haven't just been biting the Chosen Ones. They've been taking more than they need. Stealing from our children and neighbors in the dead of night."

"What about you?" a silver-badged teenager pipes up. "You say the Guardians are bad, but you look exactly like them! Red eyes and fangs..."

The words stick in my throat, uncertainty taking over me again. What if I *am* exactly like a Guardian, deep down? What if I should be killed alongside them?

Lucan opens his mouth angrily, but it's Malcolm who says, "Anna, you were in the Healing Center for a week after your stroke." He points to a middle-aged woman who looks vaguely familiar. "And Saskia nursed you back to health."

Tears spring to the woman's eyes as she nods. If I remember correctly, I also helped her for months afterward in rehabilitation after the right side of her body was paralyzed.

Then Malcolm spins to find a man I cared for after one of his operations.

"Daniel, Saskia's the reason you still have all ten fingers after that machinery accident, isn't she? She helped during your operation, then changed your bandages every day until you were discharged."

Daniel hangs his head, then looks up at me and smiles softly as he wiggles his fingers like a thank you.

Lucan's smile gets wider, more adoring, as Malcolm continues around the circle, pointing out people that he knows I've healed in the past. I'm not sure vampires can blush, but if they can then my face is probably as red as my hair.

I never realized that Malcom paid that much attention to our conversations at the dinner table, when I would tell him about my day at work. I always thought of those times as forced formalities, but maybe he valued them all along.

Just as he's pointing out a fifth past patient of mine, someone sarcastically calls out, "Let her speak, Malcolm!" and the crowd chuckles in unison.

This time it's Lucan who squeezes *my* hand in reassurance.

I take a deep breath to steady myself. "I am... like the Guardians, but in an entirely different way. The Thirteenth Guardian loved a human, and he was killed for it. But not before he fathered a child, apparently, making me his descendant. I was just as shocked as you are now. But I promise you that I don't want to live like they do. I want to defeat them."

A lot of faces in the crowd register hope, but from the back I hear, "If you're not like them, whose blood do you drink to stay alive then?"

Well, shit. If the world could open up and swallow me whole right about now, that'd be wonderful.

"*Mine,*" Lucan supplies for me as my face heats. "And since my blood is different than yours, I don't turn to stone when she does. Problem solved."

More opinions and questions explode into the night, but we're running out of time to keep answering them. The pack needs our help *now*.

"What are we supposed to do now?" Walter asks, louder than everyone else as he steps up next to Malcolm.

"Hide," I say immediately, "in your housing complex while Lucan and I try to breach the palace."

"We want to fight!" a man yells.

Others whoop in agreement, the energy in the crowd intensifying.

Another man yells, "Besides, my housing complex is on fire, anyway!"

"But you're human, and you don't have any weapons," I argue. "You're no match for the Guardians."

"Maybe not," says Malcolm gently, "but there will be more sentries in the Blood Moon Palace, Saskia. You're going to need all the help you can get."

"And besides..." a high-pitched voice adds. Odette bends at her waist to swipe a rapier right off one of the stirring sentry's belts. With a swift kick to his face, she knocks him unconscious once again and raises an eyebrow at me. "Who says we don't have weapons?"

LUCAN

As all the citizens who want to fight rush forward to pick the swords out of the pile of sentries, I murmur to Saskia that I need just a moment to myself.

She nods, but I can see the concern in her eyes. I plant a quick kiss on her cheek before bounding into the nearest alleyway opposite of the fire, until I'm bathed in shadows, alone.

Then I shift again.

This time, I don't just spear toward the pack with my mind, but barrel into that barrier again and again. Trying to find cracks. To hear *anything* on the other side.

After a solid two minutes of me pacing back and forth, exerting all of my mental energy toward the dead-end connections, a familiar voice breaks through the silence.

Stop, Lucan. It's over.

My blood boils at the sound of Gabriel's tone. All those times he challenged me in the past, I won and let him live. When really, I should have ripped his head off his neck.

You're not just defying an alpha's orders, Gabriel. You're betraying the entire pack.

And there's only one way he was able to do that.

Oh, now you want to give the pack attention? I renounced you as my alpha, so I no longer take orders from you, he sneers into my head, and it hits me what he's done: become his own one-werewolf pack, in the hopes that *my* members will join *his. Your whole life, you've only cared about the strangers within this Wall, not us. And now, you only care about* her.

My teeth snap, as if I can bite at him through thin air. *The funny thing is, I almost believed that, too. But you know what I realized as soon as I caught on that you're a traitor?* I don't wait for him to answer. *That it's possible to care about* all *of you. I choose her over the world, yes, but only when assholes like you force me into a choice. The truth is, I care about the humans of* Xantera *and* Saskia *and* the pack.

Gabriel huffs out a cold, dead laugh. *If you had truly cared about us all along, we would have relocated and forgotten this place long ago. Left it all behind and found somewhere else to build a new life. But instead, you let us fester in a rotting shadow for* centuries.

So why didn't you leave? I snarl back, and a real snarl escapes my chest, rumbling through the alleyway. *I never held you hostage. You could've formed your own pack long before now. Found your own new life to build from the ground up.*

Because I still had hope! Gabriel roars. *Until she showed up, that is. And then I clung to false hope that you'd realize what a parasite she is, just like the others. But you didn't. When we finally got close to reviving our lost kingdom, you chose to follow her out of the catacombs, away from our goal, just because she loves some old, half-dead human.*

I freeze, my hair bristling, my senses crackling. *Some old, half-dead human is just as worthy of our protection as any other. Young, old, able-bodied, weak-bodied, man, woman, anyone in between—they're all worthy of freedom, and Saskia knows that. She's always known that. Do you?*

Gabriel's silence gives me all the information I need.

No, you don't. Because you're lying to me, and to yourself, I growl. *This isn't about freedom for you or for anyone else. This is about your need for control. For power. Why else would you be blocking my access to my pack unless you were trying to force them to join yours? You never managed to beat me in a fight, so you're finding another way to become alpha. Enlisting the help of our greatest enemies just so they can achieve what you could never accomplish alone. Killing me.*

I swear, a flicker of guilt ripples between us before Gabriel yells, *For their own good! They don't realize how you've been dragging us down. And when the Guardians finally kill you, I can give them the leadership and direction they deserve.*

As if his emotions are cracking his mind, little snippets of his most recent memories bleed through, and I catch glimpses of what, exactly, he did. As soon as Saskia and I left those catacombs, he snuck away while the rest of the pack tried to free those prisoners and found his way to the Blood Moon Palace—then found the remaining Guardians in the throne room.

"One of your kind is already dead," he said immediately, before they could jump upon him, and that made them freeze long enough to hear the rest of his words. "But I can help the rest of you live as long as you help *me*."

Several of the Guardians all crouched to pounce on him anyway, but Arad lifted one pale white hand from the seat of his throne. "Wait. Let him finish."

Gabriel lifted his head. "The Monster and your Chosen One are on their way to the Healing Center right now. Alone. You can ambush them and end this battle before it's even begun."

Arad's eyes flicked toward one of the cameras in the corner of the throne room, every limb of his body taut with sickening anticipation, and I know he was eager to catch *my* little nightmare again. "And what do you want in exchange for this information, wolf?"

Gabriel eyed one of the empty thrones in the middle of the row—the Seventh, to be exact. The one that's available now that its owner is dead. "A seat among you. Xantera can be better than ever if we join forces. And you must only get rid of the current alpha and his vampire lover. No one else."

Arad's face stretched into an impossibly-wide smile that revealed every one of his fangs.

"Deal."

The memories leak away, and I curse at Gabriel.

You really think that parasite is going to keep his word? Let you rule alongside him? Not kill any other member of the pack? Panic twines around my bones at the thought of any of them getting hurt.

As long as they behave... Gabriel starts, uncertainty filtering through his tone.

I cut him off, having heard enough. No way in hell is Vivian, Merrick, or Soren going to behave in the face of our most ancient enemies. Nor any of the others. So I hurl a last thought against the barrier that Gabriel has up, hoping the message gets through to them anyhow.

We're coming for you.

34

SASKIA

By the time Lucan bounds back out of the alleyway, every willing citizen has a weapon of their own. The rest of the children have been ushered back into the safety of some housing complexes on the other side of the city, far away from the fire, by teachers and caregivers. The only one who remains is Odette, currently arguing with her mother and father.

"But I want to help!"

"No, Odette." Her father stands over her with his arms crossed. "You're too young. Too small. And you've been weaker, ever since..."

He doesn't have to finish that sentence. Ever since the Eleventh Guardian drank her blood and sent her to the Healing Center. My chest burns at the injustice, but Odette tilts her chin up.

"Which is why I want to kill him." She balls her little hands into two tight fists, and I can't help but feel like if we're lucky, she'll get to meet a young werewolf with her same temperament. Despite being different species, I'm sure Odette and Milo would be fast friends.

"Hey." With Lucan watching me, I bend down until I'm at the same level as her and gently hand her one of my knives from my belt, watching her fingers wrap around the hilt. "I need you to go protect all the other children. Don't let a Guardian get into those housing complexes. Okay?"

Odette stares at the knife with gleaming eyes that reflect the firelight. "This is for *me*?"

"For you," I confirm with a nod, shooting a glance up at her parents, who sigh. "Because you're a warrior. Brave and fearless. And they are going to need you."

I don't tell her that if we win this, I'll do everything in my power to make more antivenom and give her a second chance at a full lifetime.

With a tightened jaw, Odette nods, finally turning to follow her mother and father back into the safety of the alleyways. But she casts one last look back at me and says, "The Wall might suffocate you in your dreams, but it looks like you're bringing it down now."

I follow her pointed finger to where smoke is swelling around the borders of the city, knowing she's right. Then she disappears into the shadows after her parents.

Finally, Lucan and I face the line of people waiting for our say-so, Malcolm and Walter in the front. Part of me wants to scream at them to run, hide, take cover... but I know I'd be here, too, even if I'd never turned into a vampire. Defending my city. Defending the innocent and weak and young.

And there's nothing else to say to them. They've decided this for themselves.

Unlike the Guardians, I will never take away their choice.

With a final nod at each other that fills my heart to the brim, stretching it beyond its perimeters, Lucan and I break into a run.

The housing complexes, Childcare Center, Educational Institution, and Sentries Station blur past us. Within seconds, we're bounding and leaping over the courtyard where the Choosing takes place, whizzing beneath the shadows of all the empty balconies.

As we near the front double doors where two sentries usually stand guard, I can see the first signs of vampire venom stealing over the wood, like frost overtaking a leaf. Cowards. Trying to block us out by fossilizing the Blood Moon Palace itself.

But they're too late.

With a final leap, Lucan shifts in midair, his form growing until he's the Monster through and through, smashing through the parts of the door that are still wooden.

We both land in that long, glamourous hallway on the other side...

But it's not empty like it was when Arad walked me in after the Choosing. Now, it's crammed with hundreds and hundreds of sentries, all pointing their rapiers at us with shaking hands.

In the very front, Rosalyn has abandoned her mask of doe-eyed innocence, raising her blade with a heavily wrapped shoulder. Oops. I almost forgot I threw a knife at her the last time we met, but I'm unlikely to forget again any time soon. Two slits for eyes glare at me from within her helmet, sizzling with hatred.

Well, right back at her.

"*Charge!*" she screams.

They all storm toward us, a dozen swords slashing in my face, and not even my new shiny eyesight can keep track of all of them at once.

I duck. Whirl. Try to kick the sentries down or push them to the side without actually killing any of them. A slash of pain erupts against my arm, and I cry out, glancing down to find a blade against it, tiny fissures in my skin sprouting from the line of impact.

I send my foot through the sentry's stomach, but two more blades crack against my back—not slicing all the way through me but landing against me like heavy blows that knock the wind from my lungs, splitting my skin just enough to send vicious stings zinging up my body.

Saskia! Lucan's vicious snarl fills both my mind and the hallway. My peripheral vision catches him ripping a sword out of a sentry's grip with his canines, clamping down on his neck, then swinging his body until three or four fall over at once, his fury exploding outward like a physical force.

I'm okay, I pant. *They're not strong enough to get to my heart.*

Because that's the only thing that really matters. The rest of me can crack and bleed all it wants as long as my heart is okay, but I can't ignore the fact that these sentries are slowing us down significantly. Where the hell are the Guardians? The way they're hiding behind an army of humans instead of coming out to meet us face to face... it fuels the rage pounding through each of my movements.

Again and again, I twirl and kick and jump and dance, trying to make any kind of headway against the horde of bodies and weapons that just keep coming and coming, until—

CRACK.

My vision stumbles. As if from the end of a long tunnel, Lucan roars my name. I sway on my feet, my fingers drifting upward to touch the blade lodged halfway through my neck... and then my gaze slides upward to find Rosalyn panting in my face, a triumphant glimmer shining through the slit in her helmet as her hands grip the pommel of her sword that she used to kill Claudia.

"Got you," she says sweetly.

My vision begins to grow dark frost around the edges, and I teeter backward, trying to mouth Lucan's name. He's barreling toward me from the other end of the hallway, but several blades are sticking from his shoulders and hide, slowing him down. At the same time, a new sound rolls into the hallway from behind us, rattling into my eardrums like a distant storm: stomping and shouting and the clanging of new metal as the citizens catch up to us and join the fray. A safe, familiar face charges into view.

Malcolm.

His eyes widen as he takes in Rosalyn and me, and then he's roaring just as viciously as Lucan, sweat already gleaming on his face as he swings his own sword toward her.

"Get your hands off my partner, you bitch!"

Rosalyn sucks in a breath, wrenches her blade from my neck, and tries to turn it against him. Through the last of my narrowing vision, I watch the tip of her rapier slice against his leg—

But Malcolm's already sending his straight into her chest.

I don't watch Rosalyn fall, but I feel her body thump to my feet, and the soft fingers that belong to Malcolm gripping my face moments before warm, rough hands replace them.

"Saskia." Lucan shakes my shoulders, human again. "Stay with me, baby."

"Okay." It's all I can think to say as I blink away the fog. Strangely, his face is coming back into focus as my tissue stitches back together like jagged pieces of tile.

Lucan gingerly runs his thumb over the wound when it closes.

"Amazing," he breathes.

I blink at him, rallying a deep breath and noting the wounds peppering his own body with clinical awareness. "Good thing yours heal just as quickly." I nod at how each of them is already clotting over. "None of those blades hit anything vital?"

Lucan shakes his head. "Nope. Tough werewolf skin." He turns to Malcolm with a fond, "Thank you."

Malcolm nods, panting through clenched teeth. His leg, I notice, is dripping with trails of blood that smell a lot sweeter than Lucan's, but he just says, "Go. Find the Guardians. We'll handle the sentries from here."

With a last glance back as the citizens fight the remaining sentries in a cacophony around us, Lucan shifts back into a werewolf, and we hurry onward.

Where the hell are they? he asks into my mind.

We skid to a halt in the domed antechamber, where two spiral staircases swoop up and around the door to the dining hall. Those paintings of the Twelve Guardians stare down at us from the ceiling, as if watching us get closer and closer.

In answer, I march forward and kick down the door to the dining hall.

Lucan and I step inside, but the place screams of emptiness. Platters of half-eaten food still sit on the table, chairs pushed out haphazardly. No sign of any servants or Chosen Ones. Or Guardians.

This way, I say on a whim, and lead Lucan back out into the antechamber, where the din of the battle between sentries and civilians swells with screams and clangs of metal that make my stomach writhe. The faster we can get rid of the Guardians, the quicker we can stop the fighting behind us, too. *Left, then right,* I tell Lucan, already sprinting away. *This hallway should curl around the dining hall and lead straight to the entrance of—*

The north wing. I'd bet anything the Guardians have the pack somewhere in there.

Just like the last time I was here, the massive double doors rise high above my head, made of black and white marble etched in elaborate swirls of gold. In the middle of each door hangs one of those circular, golden knockers.

We don't waste time knocking or offering our blood, though.

Once again, Lucan uses his brute werewolf strength to slam himself against the doors. Since they're not wood, they don't come down immediately, but they do crack right down the middle.

He slams himself into them again. More fractures spiderweb up and down the marble. Again and again, he throws his whole force into it, until the walls themselves are shaking, and the marble comes crumbling down like chunks of black and white snow.

When the dust clears, we have a clear view of the grand hall lined with all those Guardian statues. Immediately, we veer left through the open doors of the throne room—

And stop dead.

Every member of our pack—in human form—is standing rigidly in front of a throne, with a Guardian pressing a blade against each of their throats and several sentries holding rapiers against their backs... preventing them from shifting. They'd be impaled on the spot if they tried. Gabriel's the only one who stands free, wringing his hands off to the side.

In the center of them all, the Third presses his own knife a little deeper into Vivian's neck, earning a whimper from her that makes me want to slice off the smirk on his face.

"Saskia," Arad purrs, his eyes roving over me, ignoring Lucan completely. "How lovely of you to finally join us."

35

LUCAN

Shifting so quickly my bones feel as if they're going to snap, I stand on two human feet.

"Let them go."

My voice rumbles through the ground, walls, and thrones. It vibrates the very air with the intensity of its command, strong enough to bend any werewolf to my will.

But Arad is not a werewolf. A smile twitches at the corner of his lips.

"Say please. Then I'll consider it."

Bullshit. I know it's fucking bullshit, but then he presses his knife deeper into Vivian's neck, and a small bead of blood begins to sprout from the indent.

"Please," I hiss through my canines as Merrick shouts Vivian's name.

"Hmm," Arad hums, swiping the tip of his finger through Vivian's trail of blood, making her suck in a breath. "Werewolf blood does taste disgusting, doesn't it? And I'm afraid you don't sound sincere enough."

That's when Kyra, held hostage by the First Guardian, breaks into a wail.

"Gabriel! Do something! This isn't what we—"

The First Guardian, despite looking as if he's as ancient and crusty as the earth itself, gives her a nick with his knife, and she falls silent with a whimper.

Gabriel twitches toward her, seems to rethink, and then catches my eye. *I told you* rolls off me in fiery waves, and he must understand, because he actually flinches. His shoulders hunch, his head bowing in the slightest tilt of submission before his eyebrows tighten and he turns to Arad.

"You said you wouldn't hurt the rest of the pack."

"Did I?" Arad presses a hand against his heart. "I seem to remember promising you the only werewolf I'd get *rid* of is their current alpha. Which means I get to *keep* the rest."

Gabriel's face goes wan, his fingers still twitching, and my inner Monster begs me to explode. But one wrong move could send any of those blades into the flesh of my pack members, and that's unacceptable. I have to control my bones and teeth and claws—play this game carefully.

"What do you want?" I grit out. "Name your price."

I half expect him to tell me to surrender myself, and I know deep down that I'd do it. If the only way to get Saskia and the pack out of here safely is to offer my own neck, I'd do so in less than a heartbeat. But it's not me that his eyes slide to. It's...

"Her," he says immediately, pupils grazing over Saskia so heavily I want to rip them from their sockets. "I want *her*."

My anger is like a flash flood raging through my core, a fire igniting my limbs, until my vision goes red. I should have predicted this. He's *always* wanted her, from the moment he approached her during the last Choosing and he realized how defiant she really is. But he doesn't want Saskia the person, I know. He wants Saskia the object. The prize. The win.

So I cock my head, about to tell him over my dead fucking body, when Saskia herself breathes out a single word that reverberates through the throne room.

"Okay."

"No," I say immediately, grabbing her arm when she moves to take a step forward. "You're not giving yourself up." I try to fill my voice with an alpha's warning, so that she knows this isn't negotiable. The last thing we need is to be arguing in front of these parasites.

"Lucan." Her lip curls up, revealing her fangs. "Let me go."

"No." *Never.* I wish I was in my werewolf form so that I could impale her brain with that word. Make her see reason. Still, she tries to jerk away, and I tighten my grip on her arm.

"Lucan, stop. You're *hurting* me."

I release my hold like she shocked me, horrified to find large fingermarks purpling her skin. Arad releases a chuckle from across the room.

"Well, isn't *this* a turn of events? Looks like you can't get her to obey, either, Monster, but I'll tell you what. If you stand for freedom as much as you say you do, why don't you let her choose? You... or me."

Fuck, fuck, fuck. As every eye flits to me—ranging from the amber of my pack mates to the crimson of the vampires to the varying shades of green, blue, and brown of the human sentries—I know that Arad has me backed into a corner. At this point, the only thing I can do to stop Saskia from giving herself up is physically restrain her.

Which I will. I *will.* That's what Monsters do.

"Saskia," I try again before I have to resort to that, softening my voice and reaching out to grab her hand instead. If she would just meet my gaze, I'd be able to read her better. "We can figure this out. Don't leave me."

At that phrase, she physically recoils. For some reason, her attention flickers to Gabriel, who gives a miniscule shake of his head that I don't understand. Saskia, however, sets her mouth in a grim line and wrestles her hand out of mine.

"I was wrong," she says, the reddish hazel of her eyes solidifying into something I've never seen in them before as she finally meets mine: repulsion. "Life outside the Wall... I thought it might be better on the other side, but it's feral and wild out there. No electricity. No order. No Rules. It wasn't until I experienced it and came back that I realized how much better it is in here."

Confusion ricochets across each face in this hideous throne room, from Guardians to werewolves to sentries... to mine. My heart no longer pumps.

She's lying. She has to be lying.

But Arad's grinning as if she isn't—as if he actually believes what she's saying. "We all make mistakes, Saskia. I'm glad to see you've finally arrived at the same conclusion as everyone else. So who's it going to be?" He pauses. "Guardian or Monster?"

Every breath seems to waver as Saskia glances at the thirteenth throne, an unmistakably *hungry* expression in her gaze. "I know I'm not human anymore, but my ancestor sat in that chair. And I want to come back... if you'll have me." She dips her head at Arad.

Who throws his head back up in a cackle.

"Is that so?"

Saskia's face pales. "Yes."

Arad grins with all his teeth. "Then *prove it.*"

Again, Saskia physically flinches at that phrase, glancing at Gabriel. Once again, he shakes his head, so subtly that I halfway wonder if them communicating is just a part of my imagination. And again, I reach out and snatch her hand.

"Saskia."

"Stop touching me!" she shrieks, ripping herself away. "I'll always choose my own blood." Warning seems to ring through each word.

My own dirty werewolf blood whooshes in my ears, and understanding barrels into me. If this is truly what she wants to do, then I have to respect and honor her choice, or else there won't be any difference between Arad and me at all.

But my vision still blurs when she unstraps her belt from her waist, letting her weapons clang to the floor. Vivian's eyes widen. Soren tries to shake his head at her. Merrick grunts. My claws extend from my fingers, digging into my own palms until blood wells from each mark. It takes self-control granted from an unearthly power for me to refrain from lunging forward to snatch her back.

Then, like a scene from my worst nightmare, Saskia drifts toward Arad.

Each of her steps claps against the floor. Every breath tightens.

Arad's eyes widen a fraction, as if he didn't expect her to actually do it. And when she gets close enough for him to touch, he removes his knife from Vivian, who stumbles away with a gasp.

Prove it seems to ring through the room.

Saskia does.

As the other Guardians and sentries lower their own weapons from the rest of my pack members, she raises her hands and cups Arad's pale face.

His entire countenance shifts, his eyes running over her neck where the gold chain hangs, as if she's still human. As if the blood that runs through her veins right now isn't *mine*.

Then he swipes a tongue along one of his fangs and lifts his eyes to her lips. She leans toward him with a tilt of her chin, closer and closer, but the second before their lips meet, my own curl up in a grin.

Because the moment Arad lets his eyes close in preparation for a kiss that he never won at all, Saskia rips his head off his neck.

SASKIA

All around me, the pack members shift back into werewolves and fighting explodes through the throne room as I take Arad's head by a fistful of that golden hair and chuck it to the side.

But before I can pull out his heart, his arms shoot out to grab me, and his foot—

It kicks out, hitting me in the stomach and sending me soaring into the opposite wall.

Saskia! Lucan cries, our connection re-established now that he's a werewolf again.

My back crashes into the wall, sending pain fracturing through my whole body while chunks of marble fall from the ceiling like jagged pieces of hail.

I catch Lucan's eye from across the throne room. He's already in the middle of a fight with the First and Eleventh Guardians, but the moment he turns toward me to make sure I'm okay, it gives him a disadvantage.

The First Guardian lunges for his back...

And I'm a blur as I race toward them, crashing into the vampire before he can sink his teeth into *my* Monster.

The First Guardian flies backward, and Soren's there to catch him by the throat.

You're going to kill me with your antics one day, little nightmare, Lucan says, towering over me in his monstrous form as the slits of his amber eyes glimmer down at me.

Like I said, I'll always choose my own blood, I tell him with a wink. *And my blood is your blood. On your left, baby.*

Lucan swings his head to throw off an incoming Guardian, then turns back to me. *Yeah, I caught on eventually. But it still almost killed me, having to let you go for even a minute. Behind you.*

I whirl around and swing my fist into the wall of lean muscle that charges at me. It's the Eleventh Guardian again, Odette's personal monster, and this time, I don't plan on letting him go.

Together, Lucan and I unleash ourselves upon him. As the Eleventh Guardian rolls to his side and swipes at my ankles with nails that rip off chunks of my flesh and pull a shriek of agony from my throat, Lucan closes his jaws around his arm and flings him off me.

Gritting my teeth against the pain, I twirl and catch his other arm, pulling with all of my vampire strength.

The Eleventh Guardian screams, but Lucan and I don't quit pulling him apart.

And with a sound like shattering glass, he cracks down the middle, from the top of his skull to the top of his legs, his innards spilling out until his shriveled lump of a heart flops onto the floor.

We need a fire, I pant, grabbing the heart before the Eleventh Guardian can stitch himself back up. I glance around the throne room, past the chaos of our pack members fighting against the remaining Guardians and sentries, and what I see on the other end makes my own heart freeze to a standstill.

Arad's corpse has reached his head, his arms extending to plop it back on his shoulders. I can't seem to do anything, think of anything, as I watch the sinews forge back together like mine did. Arad's eyes roll in his head before he blinks rapidly and sets his sights back on me.

A grin inches up his mouth.

WE NEED FIRE! I repeat, screaming into the pack's collective minds. We can tear these vampires apart all we want, but if we can't burn their hearts...

Retreat, Lucan orders everyone. *Try to draw them toward the Wall.*

But nobody is *able* to retreat. Vivian's trying to tear down all the sentries, ten to one, and she yelps as a rapier pierces her in the hind leg, another one in the front. Merrick howls in rage, but he can't get to her as the Ninth and Twelfth Guardians converge on him, pinning him down. Soren's still going head-to-head with the First Guardian, who's fighting with more stealth than I could have ever imagined for such an ancient being, rolling and twisting, throwing him off again and again. And the others are struggling with the remaining Guardians, their movements too quick to make out.

We've killed three of them, torn another one in half, but we're still outnumbered.

Still losing.

As if he knows it, Arad lunges for a discarded weapon on the floor. Lucan snarls and starts barreling across the room toward him, but Arad scoops up the dagger and brings back his arm. I scream Lucan's name in warning, and that's when Arad's gaze snaps up to me.

He wants to kill me. I can see it in his eyes, the hunger to conquer me once and for all.

Lucan rams into him, knocking him to the ground, but the knife is already whistling through the air with more force and speed than any human could accomplish.

Toward my chest. My heart.

Before I can move aside, pain ricochets through my entire being, white-hot agony flaring across my vision. Connected to my mind, the entire pack yelps in unison, and Lucan roars.

But when I open my eyes and look down, it's not to find the knife lodged in *my* heart.

Instead, Gabriel stands in front of me, swaying on his two human feet, blood bubbling from the corner of his mouth as he gives me a look filled with nothing but sorrow and regret.

"I'm sorry," he breathes out. "I thought you were... the Monster..." His eyes glaze over. "But I can see... I was wrong." For a moment, his body seems to try to shift, fur sprouting in patches over his body, bones snapping, canines dropping.

But the wound is too great. The blade hit his heart perfectly. I hold out my arms on instinct when Gabriel tilts forward.

Catching him the moment he takes his last breath.

LUCAN

When a pack member dies, we all feel the pain of their soul slipping away.

It slices through us as if *all* our hearts take a last beat—a piece of our bond crumbling to dust. I felt it when my father died, and I feel it now. Despite Gabriel's betrayal and his brief split from the pack, my heart squeezes into a ball so tight, I can barely breathe. Howls unfurl throughout the throne room, and Saskia gasps.

The Third Guardian uses that moment to grab my throat with both hands.

Even though my neck is as thick as a tree trunk in this form, Arad's strength supersedes anything I can shake off. His grip tightens, cutting me off from oxygen, and his nails pierce through my skin like ten mini daggers.

If he gets to my lungs, I know I won't be able to heal fast enough to live.

And I need to live for *her*. My reason for every breath that is slowly fading.

As my vision frays at the edges, I throw myself back, crushing Arad against the floor beneath my weight, but he doesn't release his grip on my throat. I shift out of desperation, morphing back into a human, but the change doesn't catch Arad off-guard either.

If anything, it emboldens him. I scrabble at his hands around my throat, managing to pry off a few fingers, and I can feel my blood spurting from the wounds he's inflicted.

"Take out any more of my fingers," Arad whispers in my ear sickeningly, "and you're going to bleed out, wolf. I'm holding you together now." He digs his nails deeper into my neck. "Aren't I?"

I can't speak with him clutching my throat like this. It feels like someone took a pitchfork and rammed it through my vocal cords. All I can do is try to end his life as he takes mine.

Instead of trying to pry off more of his fingers, I extract my claws, reach behind me, and plunge them into the sides of his neck, too.

Arad roars. From across the room, I catch Saskia's eye as she lays Gabriel down against the wall, as gently as possible. I see the moment her pupils darken as she takes in the position I'm in—how Arad won't let go of me, even if it kills him.

And vice versa.

Her mouth opens. I see her lips form my name, but I can't hear any sound come out. My ears are ringing, a calmness creeping over my bones like vines twining around branches.

The moon seems to blossom right before my eyes.

If death means I get to dream of her forever, then so be it.

I close my eyes.

SASKIA

L ucan closes his eyes, his pain ripping through our bond and shredding me apart.

I scream his name again, but even as I leap over Gabriel's body to get to him, I know I'll be too late. All Arad has to do is twist, and Lucan's dead—simply because the pack's connection to each other weakened us the moment that Gabriel took his last breath. Because we feel each other's heartbreak and grief like an echo chamber, hitting us again and again and again.

It's not fair, that love strips us so bare.

Just as I'm about to reach Arad, however, the doors of the throne room fly open again. I expect more sentries, more threats, more danger... but in floods a surge of something *else*.

Malcolm and Walter, leading the other citizens of Xantera who must have defeated the sentries. Other Chosen Ones, led by none other than Tristan. And servants in their uniforms, led by...

Eleni.

All humans. All the oppressed ones we've been trying to save, not running away or cowering in the face of their Guardians but facing them openly with weapons of all kinds. Not just rapiers, but kitchen knives. Iron candlesticks. Shards of glass. Fire pokers. In Eleni's case, what looks like a splintering wooden leg ripped off of the thick mahogany table in the dining room.

Which she rams into Arad's back now.

His face contorts, rage crumpling it into something pinched and ugly. Retracting his nails from Lucan's throat, he turns to rip her apart—

I'm already there, throwing him off her. Everywhere around us, humans surge toward the Guardians who are slowly squeezing the life out of my pack, and it gives them pause. Vivian, Merrick, and Soren use that second of hesitation to kick them off. Ashe and Kyra manage to scramble to a stand.

And the fight's back on.

"Are you okay?" I pant toward Eleni, clamping a hand on her shoulder as chaos unfolds once more. My heart doubles over in relief, finally able to process the fact that she's *alive.*

She breathes up at me, eyes widening as she takes in the color of mine, but nods. In that moment, a million words seem to flash across her face, words she'll never get to say because they took away her choice to. But I understand anyway.

"I know. Fuck them."

She nods, raises her chin, and sprints into the crowd with her makeshift weapon held high. I don't waste more time dropping to my knees and crawling up to Lucan, feeling my heart sink at the spurts of blood arcing from his neck, stinging my nostrils with his earthy, woodsy smell. Shit. This is bad. Worse than I thought.

"No, no, no," I cry, putting pressure on the wounds with my hands. "You're going to be fine, baby. These are going to clot over, just like your other wounds. Nobody dies on my watch."

But that's not true anymore. So many already have. My father. Gabriel. Claudia. And from somewhere over the heads of all the people fighting, horror rips through me as Tristan goes down with a bloodcurdling scream.

I can't save them all. I can't be everywhere at once.

All I can do is bend over Lucan with his life pulsing against my palms, trying to staunch the bleeding and telling him to hold on a little longer.

In the haze that whirls around me, a pair of gentle hands lands on my shoulder, and I look up through bleary vision to find two faces I never expected to see within these Walls:

Taika and Stella.

Lucan's mom drops to her knees next to mine, her eyes roving wildly over her son's wounds. Taika does the same with his medical bag, only calm determination on his face as says, "Your hands are shaking too badly for this, Saskia. Allow me."

Quickly, I remove my hands, letting Taika take over as a frigid numbness crawls over me. Lucan's mom wraps her arm around my shoulder and squeezes with a sniff. "We saw the fire and felt Gabriel..." Her voice trails off, and she swallows. "There was no way we could stay behind, knowing that you were in trouble."

"Thank y-you." I choke over the last word, watching Taika wrap Lucan's neck, the bandage blooming with crimson as soon as it touches his skin.

I cling to Stella, blinking through the agony, hoping that the next time my eyes open, the bleeding will have stopped—that Lucan isn't going to die.

Taika just keeps applying pressure where the blood continues to soak through the fabric, determination in his eyes to staunch the flow and allow Lucan enough time to begin to heal. But it doesn't. A muffled sob leaves Stella's lips.

Glancing up through my haze, I find that the rest of the pack is faring much better. Soren shouts as he finally manages to rip out the First Guardian's heart with his teeth. Vivian's shaken off the rest of the sentries, leaving them to the other citizens of Xantera, and locked her jaws around the Second Guardian's throat. Merrick squeezes the Twelfth Guardian's heart in his fist. And Kyra's on her knees, holding Gabriel's body.

Soon, every single Guardian's heart has been ripped out.

Except for Arad's.

From across the throne room, right next to the doorway, he sweeps his gaze over the destruction of his fellow brothers and sisters, his lips curled up in disgust. He knows he's lost. Knows that thanks to the servants and Chosen Ones he underestimated, he will not sit on his throne ever again.

But instead of fighting until his last dying breath, he passes me one last hateful glance.

And runs away.

Fuck. That. He hurt my Lucan, so he doesn't *get* to run away.

Removing myself from Stella's hold, I lean forward to plant a gentle kiss against Lucan's lips, savoring the slight waft of breath that escapes between them. He's still alive—barely—but I have to ensure that Arad won't remain so.

"Wake up for me," I whisper against Lucan's ear. "Please, please wake up."

Then I leap up, leaving him in the care of Taika and his mother, and race after the Third Guardian.

LUCAN

I never dreamt about anything until *her*.

Before her, my time asleep was spent in darkness, and my time awake was spent in wrath. I only wanted to destroy—the Wall, the Guardians, Xantera itself.

Now, I want to create—not just a new kingdom for my citizens to feel safe in, but a life with her. A home where we can figure out how to keep loving and dancing without a Wall looming over us. A better world.

So I'm pretty pissed when I feel death tugging me away from the light.

"No," I tell the dark, shadowy figure walking toward me from a deep recess of this dream. "She told me to wake up."

"Cool it." The shadowy figure raises his palms, his voice familiar. "I just came here to talk."

"Gabriel?"

A light washes over his face so that I can make out the details. None of those harsh, angry lines scrunch his forehead anymore, painting a picture of peace over his expression. He laughs.

"That might be the first time you've ever said my name with any fondness."

"Well." I clear my throat and throw my hands in my pockets. "This might be the first time you've ever looked at me with something other than hatred and envy. Is this death? Heaven?" I look around. "Or hell?"

"Neither," Gabriel says bluntly, offering nothing else.

"What do you want then?"

He glances around us nervously, eyeing the endlessness of this dreamscape I'm stuck in—nothing but darkness stretching in every direction. I don't even know where the light is coming from, how either of us are able to see anything.

"To make amends," he says finally, blowing out a breath. "For what I did."

My tone and posture both soften despite myself, whether this is a figment of my imagination or not. "I already heard you tell Saskia sorry through the bond. You saved her. That's enough for me."

"No." Gabriel shakes his head. "She might have never needed saving if I hadn't betrayed you and the pack, and if I hadn't..."

When he pauses for too long, I ask sharply, "If you hadn't *what*?"

"Well." For the first time in his life—death, now—shame clouds Gabriel's features. "I thought it would be better for all of us if she removed herself from you. Released you of the hold she has on you. I told her to prove that she cares about the pack and the humans by leaving you, but then when she tried to do that with Arad... I knew, in that moment, that it wasn't the right choice. I tried to tell her no."

In any other place, rage would have me pouncing on him, digging my canines into his neck and chewing right through it for that. But here, in this strangely calm and dark space, I find myself hauling in a deep breath.

Besides, I can't kill him if we're both already dead. And Saskia *didn't* end up leaving me.

Gabriel hangs his head.

"You were right. I can see that now. I was using any excuse to claim any kind of power I could put my hands on." He runs his hand over his face. "In a way, I was no different than a Guardian—just in a different form."

I can't believe I'm actually doing this, but I clap Gabriel on the back and pull the asshole into a hug that we never got to do when he was alive. "Anyone can be a Guardian or a Monster. But you chose to change, in the end. That's all that matters."

Gabriel sighs, a pain behind his eyes still haunting him. "Don't say that just for my benefit."

"I'm not," I insist. "We're all capable of evil. We all hurt others at some point in our lives. I'm no exception. But that doesn't mean we can't grow and learn. Choose something differently the next time."

The echo of silence that reverberates after I close my mouth is loud as hell. Because there won't *be* a next time for Gabriel. His last act was just that—his last.

"Well, at least I can say my last act was a good one," Gabriel says finally, and I replay the moment he threw himself in front of her. "A few minutes before my last breath, I felt myself slip into your pack, under your leadership, once again. And the moment I took that last breath, Saskia looked as if she was in as much pain as I was. You know what that means, right?"

"What?"

Gabriel smiles softly. "When a pack member dies, we can feel the pain of their soul slipping away. She felt mine, and I felt hers. Somehow, she's become a part of the pack, too, even as a vampire." He shakes his head with a chuckle. "Now go back to her. She needs you as much as you need her."

For a moment, we stand there instead, our arms locked around each other. Death tugs again, but this time, it doesn't touch me. Gabriel jerks away from me, drifting backward, and smiles.

"The light, alpha." His voice fades as the darkness begins to eat him. "It's coming from you."

I look down at my chest, finding a beam of what looks like moonlight, indeed, shining from where my heart should be. Pain begins to ebb back into existence, and I know that my wounds are healing rapidly enough to give me another shot at creating that better world.

"Well, it's been fun!" I holler at death, still feeling it hovering somewhere just beyond my eyesight. "But maybe next time!"

Why? my dream seems to ask me, a faint voice like wind whistling through the darkness. *Why choose the pain and heartbreak when you could simply... drift away?*

Before Saskia, I wouldn't have had an answer, but now the words spring to my lips as effortlessly as all the kisses we've shared and words we've exchanged.

Because I have someone to wake up for.

SASKIA

I just barely catch the tail-end of Arad's cloak flapping in the breeze before he disappears through the doors leading to the outside garden.

It feels like time has rewound and reversed itself. Now *I'm* the one chasing *him* through the rosebushes, up the stone staircase to the next terrace above us. And instead of streaks of sunset filtering through the clouds, it's light from the crackling flames that illuminates my path.

The antivenom must have dissolved more of the Wall, because everything past the garden, stretching from left to right as far as I can see, spits sparks into the night sky, smoke unfurling in great, black plumes. I underestimated just how well it would work. Heat blows into my face, but I don't slow down as I chase Arad up, up, and up.

"You can run!" I call after him, still keeping my promise—still refusing to give him the satisfaction of uttering his name out loud. "But I will catch you!"

I chase him through the fountains and hydrangeas on the second terrace.

"You can hide, but I will find you!"

Past the hyacinths and statues of old Chosen Ones on the third.

"You can scream, but no one will hear you!"

In fact, I'm pretty sure nobody would hear *either* of us scream, what with the crackling, snapping flames so close to catching the Blood Moon Palace on fire. Briefly, I wonder if it's possible for a vampire's marble skin to melt off...

And then we're on the topmost terrace, where the people who have turned to stone are crammed together, crumbling and fading. Arad finally swishes around to turn and face me.

His arm around the statue of my mother.

"What are you doing?" I ask, screeching myself to a halt.

Arad's entire face gleams wickedly, orange and red in the flickering firelight. He presses his head into my mother's frozen cheek, as if he's whispering against her ear. "I daresay her death would be irreversible if I..." He runs a single nail down her stone neckline, sending an explosion of fury through every atom in my body. But the meaning is clear:

If I move a single step closer, he'll break my mother into too many pieces to fix.

"What's your plan?" I ask incredulously, not daring to move a muscle despite my tone. "You obviously can't get past that Wall of fire, so how are you planning on running away?"

"Running away?" he scoffs, his nose scrunching. "Oh, no. I'm not running away from this empire I've built."

"All the other Guardians are dead," I say flatly.

Not technically true—their hearts aren't yet burned, but it's not going to be a hard thing to do with all this fire everywhere.

Arad, however, waves a moon-white hand through the air.

"I don't need the other Guardians. I'm still going to kill the dogs all on my own, just like I killed them five hundred years ago." His voice reaches a pitch bordering on insanity, and his grip tightens on my mother's statue until she wobbles. "But this time, I won't bother with the formalities of a Choosing. I'll drink from whomever I want, *when*ever I want, and then I will discard them immediately instead of wasting years letting them wither away to stone. And there will be nobody around to stop me, Saskia, because you will either die or join me."

Behind him, the spikes on the Wall break away, crumbling into ashes. Someone howls.

I tighten my hands into fists at my sides and spit, "I will *never* join you. That's a promise—and you know I always keep my promises, *Guardian*."

Arad's smile flickers over his fangs. Those crimson eyes tighten with the kind of loathing only someone who loathes themselves can achieve.

"Suit yourself."

It happens so fast, I don't have time to blink.

Arad's arm lashes out and knocks my mother's statue over.

A lifetime of lullabies and hugs and soft soothing flashes before my eyes as she tips, her eyes locking with me one more time before her stone figure crashes against the ground and shatters into several shards right in front of me.

My scream of horror lodges in my throat, suffocating me, making me double over as if grief itself kicked me in the stomach. Because this is it. All this time I worried she was dead, and now she actually is. The antivenom won't work on fractured pieces.

But I hit my knees and crawl toward her now, sobbing her name, begging her to come back anyway.

So many things I would fix if I could. Say if I were able. All of those moments I wish I could get back. I wouldn't take them for granted. But now, this is the end.

Right as I grab her dismembered stone hand, Arad kicks me in the shoulder, flipping me onto my back and planting his foot on my chest. My tears blur my vision of him towering over me, looking so smugly pleased with himself that vomit rises up my throat.

"Love," he hisses. "It makes you so weak. So foolish. All I had to do was shove over a silly little *statue* of someone you once loved, and you came crawling right to me, didn't you?"

"Not once." My sob cracks my words wide open.

"What?" Arad asks, annoyance etched into his hardened voice.

"I didn't love her *once*," I say, gripping my mother's stone hand in mine, the heat of the fire making it warm as if she's still alive. "I'll love her *always*. Forever. Something you will never understand, not because you're a vampire..." I cough as he presses his foot harder against my chest. "... but because you have chosen not to. Because you didn't use your human heart that you could have wielded like the greatest of weapons."

Arad throws back his head and laughs at the smoke-infused sky. "Greatest of weapons? Well, I'm going to enjoy ripping your *greatest weapon* out of your chest. Any last words, Saskia?"

Despite the grief weighing me down more than Arad himself ever could, I smile through my tears and blink at the two yellow lights glimmering above me.

"Yes, actually." I exhale. "There's a Monster behind you."

LUCAN

Before Arad manages to turn around to find me looming behind him, I've already caught his wrist, twisted, and ripped off his hand.

I'm in my human form, relishing how it feels to face him man to man. I used to wonder who'd be stronger if we were on even ground, but there's no doubt in my heart anymore. Watching him destroy Saskia's last hope for her mom has solidified my answer.

He screams. I toss his hand aside, rip off his other one before he can use it against me, and grab him by the neck one-handedly, holding him at arms-length as he spits and thrashes like some kind of angry alley cat without the claws to scratch anymore.

Pathetic.

I reach forward with my other hand, right into his open mouth, and rip out one of his fangs by the roots. He tries to bite me, of course, but I'm used to the pain by now, so I don't jerk my hand back before wrenching out the others.

One by one, I fling them over my shoulder until he has nothing left to bite *with*. Until his gums are a bleeding mess, and I'm clutching one more fang in my hand.

Holding it up in front of my face, I inspect the bone-white tooth with morbid humor.

"You know," I muse, "I always envisioned stabbing you with one of your own fangs. Turns out they're way too small."

I let it clatter to the ground before I extend my claws one by one. Arad's eyes widen, darting to each as they rise out of the tips of my fingers. Then I plunge all five of them into his chest, hitting between each rib—puncturing his body just like he impaled so many others over the last five hundred years.

His scream catches in his throat before I snarl, "And this is for putting your gaze on what's *mine*."

I switch to his eyes, digging my claws into his sockets one by one, plucking out his ability to ever look at my little nightmare again. Maybe it makes me more of a Monster than ever before, to drag out his death, but I can't help loosening my hold on his throat to drink in his sweet screams, and I swear Saskia shudders with relief when those eyeballs roll onto the ground far away from her, where she's still clutching her mother's dismembered stone hand.

"Saskia," Arad begs, trying to crane his neck to twist toward her anyway, stolen blood pouring from his empty eye sockets, but I keep a firm grip on his throat. "Don't let him do this."

Slowly, Saskia rises to a stand, glancing down at her mother's pieces all around her. Her own eyes are swollen, puffy, and glazed with tears that I wish I could kiss away when they spill onto her cheeks. The Wall blazes behind her, outlining her in furious, sparkling red.

"You're really going to let him kill all the Guardians?" Arad continues, his voice nasally and muffled now that he doesn't have fangs or hands or eyes. "You're really going to let the *Monster* take over again? He's going to destroy Xantera, Saskia, and you know it. Please."

The way he says that word, *please*, only ignites me with more fury that crackles in my bones. How many people begged *him* for mercy, only to be met with pain and death? And now, after everything, he's going to try to manipulate her?

But this is Sakia's call. I won't take that away from her, even if I know what her answer will be.

She floats forward, until she's close enough for me to count each blood-splattered freckle and to see my reflection in her irises. She doesn't look at Arad, only me, as she says, "Yes, I'm going to let the Monster take over again. And yes, he's going to destroy Xantera."

She bends at her waist, reaches out with a slender, graceful arm, and tears off the key to the Wall still wrapped around Arad's neck.

Behind her, even more of the Wall crumbles away as the fire devours it, leaving us a clear view of the forest spreading in waves beyond it. Mountains and rivers and *freedom*.

"But he will rebuild Veradel."

Then she plunges her hand into Arad's chest.

There's a moment where his face goes slack—where I'm certain he's aware that his death hovers moments away and he's surprised it ever came for him—before she rips her hand out.

I release him as his body falls, and Saskia holds up the tiniest, most rotten, useless thing I've ever seen.

Eyes misting again, she chucks it over her shoulder but doesn't bother to watch as it gets swallowed in the flames and smoke behind her. She simply rises to her tiptoes.

And we fit our lips together as the Wall comes down.

SASKIA

By the time Lucan and I finally break apart, soft flakes of snow begin to float down from the heavens all around us, landing on Lucan's hair and frosting everything around us—the terrace, the statues, and the last remnants of the Wall.

Lucan and I stare down at what remains, charred ash, embers, and the last of the stubborn flames a hundred feet below us.

Soon, our pack emerges from the top of the staircase to join us, forming a line along the edge of what used to be Xantera. To my left, Vivian smiles before tossing a vampire heart over the edge of the balcony. It soars through the air, dropping like a stone into the heat below.

When it hits the ground, a plume of black and white ash puffs into the air and the heart sizzles, letting out a shriek that eventually dies in the wind.

Everyone collectively shudders.

Merrick goes next, followed by Soren, Ashe, and the others, each shriveled gray heart plummeting to its finality.

How fitting, that the remains of the Wall are what destroys the Guardians once and for all.

After the last wail of a dying heart fades away, I turn to Lucan and inspect his neck wounds with a gentle fingertip, blinking away the snowflakes clinging to my eyelashes.

"Amazing," I marvel, running my touch over Lucan's scar tissue, already shiny and pink in the spots his body healed over.

"Good thing Taika stopped the bleeding fast enough to allow me to even start to heal," he replies with a disgusted scrunch of his nose. "Otherwise..."

Lucan wedges his boot under Arad's lifeless body and flips him over with a swift kick. Then hauling the vampire up by his clothes, he heaves him through the spikes, the very ones I stepped through before I jumped. It's like my nightmare from so long ago, but in reverse order: Arad falling, and me standing tall, never to fall again.

When the rest of the Third Guardian disappears, I actually smile. Soren slings an arm around Lucan's shoulder as everyone gathers around us in a circle.

"We did it," he says, hushed, in awe.

Vivian snuggles under Merrick's free arm, and the rest of the pack follows suit. Lucan loops his free hand around my waist, tugging me in close and planting a kiss on top of my head. Then we stand there in a huddle, limbs intertwined, staring out at the destruction of what doesn't imprison me anymore.

Until Vivian breaks the silence with a sarcastic grin and laughs between her own tears, "Soren, are you *crying*?"

Soren sniffles and runs the back of his hand across his cheeks and nose. "Damn right, I am."

We all do. The tears stream silently down our faces, plopping at our feet, where the pieces of my mother still lay like a wreath around me. The snow is coming down even harder now, covering each part of her in a soft, sparkling layer of white, until finally, I bend to pick up her stone hand again.

Lucan stoops to help me. Together, we retrieve every single fractured part of her, the two of us cradling her remains against our chests. Pain lashes against my heart again at the finality of it, but the stone feels almost warm against me. As if part of her will always remain right with that Monster in my heart.

"Come on," Lucan says gently, gesturing behind him. "Let's get her out of this place."

With the pack following us, we retrace our steps down through the terraces and back to the throne room, tracking snowy footprints through the hall.

A somber sight greets us when we step through the enormous double doors, now hanging off their hinges.

Blood spatters cover the floor and even some parts of the walls. Rubble, broken glass, discarded weapons, and bodies litter the ground. Hushed voices echo from all four corners, where those who survived are tending to the wounded on one side and respectfully draping sheets over the ones who sacrificed far greater on the other. At the far end, Kyra is still cradling Gabriel's body, her eyes puffy, but when she looks up and meets my gaze from across the room, her eyes trail over what I'm holding.

Her lips tremble, and she nods at me. Not an apology, exactly, but as close to one as she can get before she presses her forehead back to Gabriel's again.

Turning away, I find a spot near the other bodies, where Lucan and I lay out my mother's pieces, putting them together slowly.

Each piece is a memory—some happy, some sad, some full of regret. Memories echo in me with peals of laughter, but there were also moments of ridiculous tears and heart-wrenching sobs.

And all of that I bottle up to carry forward, to keep her memory alive in all the good times and the bad times, each just as precious, just as important. I can't go back and say sorry, but she knew. She knew how much I loved her through the happiness and the pain.

Finally, she's whole and looks like she's simply sleeping, like the others. But none of them are. They're not dreaming or stuck in nightmares. They can't wake up. And as I sit there, staring at the rows of them, I'm struck by how unfair that is.

Every single one of us only gets one chance at this experience called life, and for some, it's ripped away in a heartbeat. For others, it's stretched out, tainted, abused by those who don't care about how sacred and beautiful it should be. And we can't undo it. We can't give the people we love a second chance. We can't give them one more smile, one more hug, or one more goodbye.

But the lullaby that escapes my lips is still for them: an altered version to give them the end to the story they never got to witness themselves.

Round and round, the Monster prowled,
Starved for the rightful throne.
He used his claws, he used his teeth.
He tore down the ancient stone.

Even as Lucan listens, his face rapt with attention, I continue to sing for *her*, for the tiniest sliver of a chance that somehow, the light that once ebbed and flowed in this body before me can hear.

On the vaguest whisper of a hope that one day, we will all get an experience *beyond* life. To smile. To hug. To say hello again.

On and on the girl did march,
Starved for the mythical light.
She, a nightmare, he, a monster...
Together, they made it right.

I lean my forehead against her one last time, then finally pick myself up. Catching Lucan's eye, I sniff and give a half-smile. "I know. I'm a better healer than singer."

He shakes his head, nothing but that same rapt attention all over his face. "Your voice isn't about tone or cadence or pitch, Saskia. It's about the words you put out in the world when you have the freedom to do so. And I think your words..." He grazes a thumb along my cheek. "...are as beautiful as the rest of you."

I clear the lump out of my throat and give a shaky exhale. Then I nod.

"I'll admit, they're more beautiful than *that* sound."

We both glance over our shoulders as a few citizens start to drag the Guardians' heavy, lifeless bodies past us, the sound scraping across the floor like table legs.

Lucan winces. "Yeah, I'll go help with that."

As I watch, he strides over to the citizens who are already wiping their brows and throws two lifeless, marble statues over each bulging shoulder before marching toward the double doors again.

Knowing that he'll have plenty of fun throwing them off the balcony like he did to Arad, I finally turn to assess the room, squinting for any signs of...

"Malcolm!" I cry, rushing over to the figure Taika is bending over between the third and fourth thrones.

My breath whooshes out of me in stark relief when I see Malcolm's chest rise, and his eyes flutter open to give me a weak smile.

"You're all right," I tell him, my own smile wobbling.

"Better than ever," he grunts. "I got to see history in the making."

"You got to *write* history in the making," I correct him. "We couldn't have done this without you."

And he certainly paid for it. The gash Rosalyn gave him is a lot worse than I initially thought. As Taika busies himself replacing the bandages beneath a makeshift tourniquet, I see how deep it goes—all the way through muscle, to the bone—and flinch away.

Malcolm, however, looks haunted and proud of himself at the same time, probably remembering how Rosalyn used her power to try to control our bodies what feels like so long ago.

"I didn't realize it was so bad until the fight was over, but it was worth it."

He smiles, especially when a certain coworker limps over with a water jug. Walter, bruised and bloody but in one piece, brings the jug to Malcolm's lips and lets him take a few sips before he kisses away the droplets dribbling down his chin.

Satisfied that they're both going to be okay and finally together, I stand up again, casting my gaze around the throne room to all the tentative interactions that sprout between servants and citizens, Chosen Ones and werewolves. Vivian and Merrick are assembling makeshift stretchers, made from sheets they must have collected from the thousands of beds in this palace, to help transport the wounded to the Healing Center.

Soren's own voice drops an octave as he stares with blazing intensity across the room and says, "If I'd known how beautiful the women in here were, I would have tried to speed up the whole Wall destruction process."

I follow his line of sight, and crash into a familiar pair of eyes. Eleni.

When I speed across the room to her in a vampiric flash, Soren follows.

"Hey." I try to gently take the sheet out of her strong grip as she bends over the mangled corpse of a civilian, her chest heaving. "You've seen enough horror in this place. You don't have to do this."

Crouching down beside her, I take in the sight of her. She has dried blood caked into the lines of her face and sweat beading on her forehead, right beneath her bangs. A handprint-sized bruise mottles her neck—but it looks like she held her own regardless.

And despite how exhausted she must be, Eleni fights me with a firm shake of her head, but I uncurl her fingers and gather her into a hug. The sigh she lets out loosens her whole body.

"Have you ever been outside of this palace?" I ask. A question I should have asked her long ago.

Eleni pulls back, tears welling in her eyes when she gives me another shake of her head, this time more somber.

"Do you have a family?"

Her jaw drops as she sucks in a gasp. Maybe her sibling or a parent she hasn't seen in years. Maybe even a child.

I squeeze her and glance up at Soren, who's watching the interaction with an expression that gives the distinct impression he'd like to murder the Guardians all over again, his eyes on her mouth—realizing that she can't speak. "There's a town just beyond the... woods out there." Refusing to say 'Wall,' I cock my head in the direction of Veradel. "If you want to leave this city and never come back, I think there would be a place for you there."

Soren nods with more fervor than I could have imagined. "I can turn any of those old houses into your own damn castle, if you'd like. And I'm really good at catching rabbits and shit if... if you get hungry," he finishes weakly.

He grimaces, probably expecting Eleni to sob harder...

But instead, she *laughs*.

And maybe the Guardians took almost everything away from her—maybe their deaths can't bring back the life she could have had—but there's a glimmer of hope in that laugh. Like the sound of new bells ringing for the first time. I have no doubt that she'll be able to rebuild herself outside of these walls with people who will actually treat her like she deserves.

When Eleni finally nods, I successfully remove the sheet from her hand and nudge her away. "I've got this. Go wherever you want to go. You don't need to be here another second."

Eleni rises, but just as she turns, I scramble to my feet to wrap her in one last hug. "Thank you," I say. "Thank you for taking care of me and helping me."

She hugs me back, and with a turn of her heel and a curious glance at Soren, she's gone. I give him a look, my eyebrows tilting, and he shoves my shoulder.

"Shut up."

"I didn't say a word," I hum.

"You didn't have to. I know you're thinking I should stay away from her."

"Why?" I smile. "Because you're a Monster?"

For once, Soren doesn't pull a sarcastic remark out of his sleeve, so I turn to face him fully.

"Eleni was born in a true monster's lair and never had the chance to see what the skies look like beyond it. You are the opposite of everything she'd had to learn to fear. And by giving her a home where she can be free, you'd be giving her a future she never thought she'd have. Just like Lucan gave that to me."

For a half-second, I let my gaze cut to the far end of the throne room, where Lucan himself trudges back in with soot smearing his face, the Guardians' bodies officially gone. His muscles bulge beneath his tattered shirt, his hair disheveled, his hands bloodstained...

And I've never seen a more hopeful future. Every atom in my body relaxes in his presence, like the Monster is truly what gives me comfort, security, and that sense of home.

"Well, if you insist..." Soren says finally, a smile tipping his mouth, "then I guess I'll go help her pack."

"You do that. Although I don't know where her sleeping quarters are loc—"

"No need," Soren interrupts firmly and taps his nose. "Remember? We werewolves have a much better sense of smell than you, vampire. I can track her down."

Surprisingly, him calling me a vampire no longer sounds like an insult. It just is. Because it's our choices that matter so much more than what lurks in our blood.

Amused, I jerk my head at the doorway. "Get going, then."

He doesn't have to be told twice.

Over the next several minutes, my heart grows heavy again as I take careful steps to cover the remains of those who lost their lives—each one a story. A sacrifice to strive for something different for others: their children, their friends, their neighbors.

Covering Tristan is the worst. In death, he looks as still as the fossilized Chosen Ones, what would have been his future anyway. Now, though, no amount of antivenom can bring him back.

Just as I finish pulling back the last sheet, a new voice breaks through the hushed murmuring in the room.

"Diggory! Sylvia!" Belinda crashes through the doorway. "Diggory?" Her gaze flies around the room before landing on me and all the rows of deceased rebels spreading on either side.

She looks at me with fear, a question swirling in them.

Reassuringly, I shake my head. "He's not here." I don't even know if she can hear me. I'm too far away, so I stand up and rush closer as I say louder, "He's alive, Belinda, but he's not here."

She crumples in relief, stilted sobs racking from her chest. I manage to catch her under her arms and support her weight before she hits the ground.

I hold her until her cries become heavy breaths. Five long years of her daughter just out of reach, her husband fighting it in any little way he could.

Finally, it's come to an end.

"Diggory's in the Healing Center," I explain. "He was imprisoned in the dungeons, hurt but alive. He's going to be all right. His healer, my friend, will take the best care of him. I promise. And Sylvia..." I pause, unsure how to even begin to explain. "I found her—"

"She's stone, isn't she?" Belinda hurries out barely above a whisper, blinking in confusion at my appearance. "My baby's stone now. Gone, forever."

"No, not forever." I swallow a lump the size of a rock in my throat at the realization that while my mother might be gone, the rest of the fossilized Chosen Ones... they still have a chance. "Come with us to the Healing Center," I say firmly, "and on the way, I'll tell you about antivenom. Your partner and daughter both ensured that we still have hope."

Belinda nods.

And one day soon, I don't say, *all three of you will be reunited.*

Taika hobbles up behind me, overhearing our conversation. "That's right. We have a lot more to make for all the people on those terraces."

I smile, because I like the sound of that. I can finally shed my monster layer where I have to claw and kill to protect the people I love, and go back to my favorite thing to do.

Healing.

LUCAN

Hours later, the throne room is finally clean. Taika has taken those who need immediate medical attention to the Healing Center, while the rest of us who are relatively unharmed stand back, taking in the sight of the thirteen spiked thrones in silence.

Chills rack my body as I face them. My grandfather once sat in this room, until his throne and life were ripped away from him. My father should have sat in here. Now...

"Well," Vivian finally says, cutting through the silence. She tips her head toward the center throne and glances at me. "You're the rightful king of Veradel. That's yours now."

Not a single remaining human—citizen, Chosen One, or servant—mutters their dissent. They all saw what my pack and I accomplished. How we defeated the real enemy but didn't touch the innocents.

Finally, the world sees me as more. More than the Monster who prowls outside the Wall.

But I hesitate, my gaze sweeping up and down the gaudy seat as I imagine the equally gaudy crown waiting for me back at my mother's house. The corners of my lips twitch downward.

"No," I finally answer. "It doesn't belong to me."

The pack stares, brows furrowed, eyes bouncing between me and Saskia. My mother inhales but doesn't say a word. The humans glance at each other uncertainly.

"Lucan..." Saskia starts, raising her hand, as if she can pat some confidence back into my back.

"No, you don't understand. It doesn't belong to me anymore." I don't raise my voice as I turn toward her. It's softer than ever before, yet firm. This decision has been swirling in my subconscious for a long time now. "You're the one who got us to this point, Saskia. *You* brought down the Wall. Saved *your* people. Your citizens look to you to lead them, and they do so with respect. Not fear or anger or jealousy." I shake my head. "I can't sit there."

To my surprise, she shakes her head right back, my chest heavy as every eye turns toward me.

"I can't sit there either."

"Saskia, just because you're a vampire doesn't mean—"

"No." The words flow out of her mouth faster than I think she intended. "I can't even stay here."

This isn't about what Gabriel said to her, I realize, as yearning brews in her eyes—probably amplified by the fact that there's no Wall closing in around her anymore. Just woods and free space and air. Nothing stopping her from running and running and never looking back if she wishes. And I don't blame her. She needs that.

"I've been trapped in this city my entire life," she continues, "doing what is expected of me, somehow breaking every Rule along the way." I allow myself a deep breath and force myself to look her in the eye, regardless of the blow I can feel coming. "But after we administer the antivenom to everyone who needs it, after this city rises from these ashes," she says, "I want to see what's beyond the woods. Beyond Eversnow Peak. I want to experience the parts of the world I've missed."

She searches my pupils for a reflection of the sorrow that seems to have overwhelmed her suddenly: thinking that we can't stay together, because while I rule here, she will be somewhere out *there*. Not tied to anyone but herself.

"I'm sorry," she chokes out. "I just can't. I need you, but so do they. And I can't ask you to come with me, no matter how badly I want you to."

"What about what *I* want?" I ask her.

She swallows, her voice coming out hushed. "What do you want, Lucan?"

Silly, stubborn woman. She should know by now. "You, of course. I want to be wherever you are." I curl my lips up in a wicked smile. "Besides, I'm a Monster. I wasn't meant to sit. I was meant to prowl. To chase."

She lifts an eyebrow and teases back, "Chase your nightmare?"

"To chase my dream," I correct her. "Because that's what you are."

I can't help it anymore, excitement tingling up my limbs. I extend my hand out to her and cradle her into my chest. Reaching up on her tiptoes, Saskia presses her lips to mine.

Vivian squeals and claps. My mother smiles. The other werewolves hoot, but a few humans exchange confused glances.

"Who's going to lead us, then?" one of them asks, and I grin. How ironic and perfect that a single unsolicited question will be the very thing that sets into motion the future of entire generations to come. Because I know exactly how Saskia will respond. It's why I fell in love with her in the first place.

She turns to address the crowd.

"For five centuries, we have had every aspect of our lives controlled by someone else. But now, there is a chance to start over with thirteen empty thrones." She gestures behind her. "For us to decide what's best for us. I'm not sure whether that will be a king or a queen or a council or something else entirely. All I know is that our voices should be heard, our opinions considered, and our decisions our own."

She raises her chin higher, with me, the Monster, by her side.

"For five centuries, we have been Chosen. Now, it's time to let the people choose."

SASKIA
EPILOGUE

Darkness envelops me, but every other one of my senses is heightened.

I touch the fabric covering my eyes, a strip that Lucan ripped off his own shirt and tied around my head to blindfold me. It smells like him, pine and earth.

But the werewolf himself... I have no idea where he is. Behind me or in front of me or somewhere else entirely.

"Lucan!" I protest with a laugh, reaching my fingers out and scraping nothing but fresh, brisk air with a hint of something briny I can't identify.

It's been one month since we left Veradel, after I made sure every Chosen One was given an antivenom. One month since Taika, Belinda, a newly-healed Diggory, and I sat around a Healing Center bed with Sylvia's statue lying rigidly on the mattress, tiny, translucent veins of venom I was never able to see as a human crawling along her stone skin. I don't think I'll ever forget that scene, even if I *do* end up living forever.

The way we pushed the needle into one of those veins. The way Belinda's tears splattered her daughter's fossilized face as we waited. The way Diggory wrung his hands together, until color began to bloom in Sylvia's face again, and her own hands twitched.

It was those hands of hers that moved first, a single finger pointing out before both palms lay flat and moved in small, circular motions.

"What is she saying?" Belinda asked Diggory immediately.

His own gruff face streaked with tears as he said, "I'm here."

And then Sylvia opened her eyes. They *all* opened their eyes—every Chosen One who had fossilized to some degree or another. Even the purely stone ones, as long as they had turned to statues in this lifetime and remained undamaged, uncrumbled, unbroken, melted back into flesh and blood as soon as the antivenom found their still-human hearts.

My own eyes are still closed, though, blindfolded by the strip of Lucan's shirt. Over the last month, we've pushed farther and farther west, into wild terrain with nothing more than two backpacks and a tent. We've seen waterfalls, the raging water plummeting a hundred feet off a cliff. Animals I never even knew existed. Canyons and valleys and rivers and now?

I'm not sure, because I can't *see*.

"Over here."

I whip toward the source of the teasing growl, my entire body tingling in anticipation.

A claw caresses my opposite arm, and I jolt with a gasp, every nerve crackling.

"Stop with this torture, Lucan."

"Why? Isn't torture what I do best?"

I laugh and then suck in a sharp breath when his hand grips my waist, his other hand clutching mine. Every point of contact between us alights with electricity.

"Follow me," he whispers into my ear.

I don't protest as he leads me forward, up a sharp incline where high grass tickles my ankles. I just grasp onto him, relishing the feel of his warm skin and working muscles beneath my fingers.

Until we're descending again, and my feet step on something cold and wet and strange.

"Oh," I breathe, my foot sinking an inch. I wiggle my toes into the grittiness. Take another step. "What *is* it?"

"Keep walking," Lucan says, and I follow him, trusting him completely.

Slowly, I regain my footing, my confidence growing with each step. "It's cold... but hot? Soft... but gritty?" My nostrils flare. "What's that sound?"

Something huge is crashing and roaring, like a thousand were-wolves howling at the moon. Lucan chuckles when a sudden, unmistakable surge of *water* surrounds my feet. Taken aback, I hop on the balls of my feet with a squeal.

Lucan steps around me as he wraps his arms around the back of my shoulders and cages me into his chest.

"You should see how beautiful this is," he murmurs in my ear. The breeze of his words sends goosebumps down my neck.

"I can't *see* anything," I exclaim, pouting. "What are you looking at?"

"You," he tells me simply, beginning to untie the knot behind my head. "But there's another view for you to look at."

When the fabric falls away, I reel in a breath... just as a wave hits me in the shins.

"This, little nightmare, is the ocean."

The sound of my gasp is masked by the crash of another swell against the shore, the cold water nipping at my ankles, crawling up my skin.

"The ocean," I murmur in disbelief. Staring. Unable to tear my eyes away. "It's like the end of the world."

Blinking rapidly into the sunrise, I trace the horizon that cuts across the sky, separating the pink-tinged clouds from the deep blue, almost black, water. When I inhale, salt stings my nostrils, the taste of it lingering on my tongue.

Lucan stands there, smiling at me, until I finally wretch my gaze away. Then he scoops me up with a taunting laugh and barrels into the frigid waves.

"Lucan!" I shriek, a split-second left before he sends us through the white crest of a massive wave.

With my eyes squeezed shut, the water roars through my ears, the freezing temperature biting at my skin in a way that makes me feel more awake than ever before.

Lucan breaks the surface, shaking droplets from his hair, and kisses me. I cling to his neck, wrapping my legs around his waist until our bodies mold together. Just wet lips and slick skin and salty ocean water.

And love.

It radiates from every touch, every atom of our bodies intertwining. As his fingers tense, bringing me as close as humanly possible, I arch into him to notch myself into every angle of his body.

His tongue caresses my bottom lip, bringing it into his mouth and nibbling with his canines, teasing me with the sting.

This is how it's been, just me and him, so free to explore each other's hearts and minds and bodies like eternity would never be enough.

And with this stretchy fabric clinging to mere bits of me, it's easy access for Lucan's roaming hands. He groans when his fingers slip underneath my top. My nipples pebble, desperately anticipating that zap of electricity he likes to make me wait for. I grind into him, begging for him to appease me.

Luckily, Lucan's in a giving mood, rolling my nipples between his thumbs and index fingers, pinching. My core ignites with a delicious current.

He drops kisses down my neck as I lace my fingers through his thick hair, guiding him lower where I crave the feel of his canines.

The moment before my eyes start to flutter closed, a wave taller than Lucan rams into us.

"Oh, shit!" I shriek as Lucan loses his balance, and we crash into the water again, spluttering when we both come up grinning before I wrap myself around him again.

Lucan brushes back my salty hair sticking to my face, planting a soft kiss against my lips.

"Have you been here before?" I whisper.

He nods. "Once." For a moment, he gets lost to a far-away memory before he continues, "My father brought me. Right before he died, actually. Soren, Merrick, Vivian, and I played in the sand and rode the waves for hours. I felt so insignificant looking out at this vastness of nothing. But as usual, my father was so much wiser than I am."

Lucan closes his eyes while I trace his features with the pad of my thumb. Down his cheekbone, across his jaw.

"And why is that?" I prompt him softly.

"He explained how it made him feel—that when he looked at the ocean, it humbled him. Made him feel like he was a part of something bigger, and that this immense stretch of water didn't separate us. Instead, it connects us."

"Where do you think it goes?" I ask, peering out at the horizon, trying to imagine other people, other societies, other ways of life. "Do you think anyone else is out there?"

"There's only one way to find out," Lucan answers, slicing his eyes over my shoulder and dipping his head to gesture at something down the beach. "A boat for you, Saskia Veradel."

The name still makes my stomach flutter. Since I don't have a family name of my own, Lucan offered me his months ago, and I took it for the same reason he did: to remind myself, always, what our kingdom means to us. What our *people* mean to us.

Which is why my breath catches when I twist to find something bobbing in the water that I didn't notice before. Made of wood and painted white, it's curved with a long flag-like piece of fabric attached to a tall pole flapping in the wind.

I scrunch my brows when I turn back to Lucan.

"My father had it made in case any pack member wanted to leave and explore the rest of the world," he explains. I've sent some people to come out and maintain it over the last few hundred years. And last night while you were still sleeping in the tent, I came out and dragged it back into the water."

"A boat," I repeat.

"A sailboat, to be exact."

My eyes widen. "For us?" I ask. "To use?"

"That depends," Lucan says with a chuckle. "Only if you want. We can sail away. Find out what's out there." He cocks his head out toward the horizon, then swings it back to the shore. "Or we can go back to Veradel. Your choice. I'm okay with either one, as long as I get to be with you."

I chew on my lip, deliberating. Whenever I pictured my ideal future, I envisioned taking care of others in the Healing Center, aiding Taika as I learned everything I could from him. And I still want to do that, but I meant what I said in the throne room of the Blood Moon Palace: I want to see the parts of the world I've missed out on as much as I need to breathe. This freedom I've experienced over the last month has only just begun to mend the part of me that grew up suffocating, wrapped up in a band of others' expectations and control.

So before I can keep healing other people, I need to fully heal myself.

"One day," I say confidently, "we'll go back home. But not today."

Lucan smiles as he starts to wade us through the water and waves. "Good choice, little nightmare."

As we close in on the boat, it rocks against the shore, held tight by a rope that disappears into the dark blue water. With two enormous hands gripping my ass, Lucan hoists me up onto the deck before he scrambles up behind me. The wood beneath our feet creaks, and I grab onto the woven railing to keep my balance.

"Sea legs," he chuckles and waves a hand over our new temporary home. "Go explore. You'll get them eventually. Just in time for me to make them shake again tonight."

He winks and I roll my eyes, biting down on a smile as I walk the outer edge without falling. There's a wooden wheel with gold spokes that sits prominently in the back, a table and two chairs nailed into the deck, and ropes that jut out at every odd angle.

I stick my head into a doorway to see a few short steps that lead down into a kitchen, bathroom, and bedroom. There on the tiny dresser next to the bed, I can see a few of my belongings already sitting atop it: my handheld mirror, lipstick, the gold chain that first connected us, the key to a Wall that is no longer standing.

By the time I return, Lucan is busy tying knots and pulling the anchor up out of the waves.

Leaning against the cabin, I marvel as he works, his muscles contracting, his tan skin glistening in the sun, until the sail unleashes in the wind with a booming whoosh.

A gasp rattles out of me with force as I look up, enamored with the gorgeous cream sheet of fabric. My neck cranes up to the top of the mast that kisses the sunlight.

I blink back at Lucan, beaming, as my eyes adjust.

"Ready?" he asks.

I've never been more ready. To learn what's out there, to explore the world, to seek and find the unknown.

"Ready," I say.

Then together we sail toward the horizon, to whatever awaits us beyond.

T~~HE~~ T~~WELVE~~
C~~ARDINAL~~ R~~ULES~~

1. ~~Don't~~ question ~~your Guardians.~~
2. ~~Don't~~ seek ~~out attention.~~
3. ~~Don't~~ think ~~about yourself.~~
4. ~~Don't~~ ask ~~unsolicited questions.~~
5. ~~Don't~~ listen ~~to idle gossip.~~
6. ~~Don't~~ express ~~personal opinions.~~
7. ~~Don't~~ engage ~~in arguments.~~
8. ~~Don't~~ wish ~~for more than necessary.~~
9. ~~Don't~~ create ~~strife among neighbors.~~
10. ~~Don't~~ keep ~~secrets from authorities.~~
11. ~~Don't~~ change ~~without permission.~~
12. ~~Don't~~ venture ~~near the Wall.~~

ACKNOWLEDGMENTS

I can't lie, this duology was a challenge for me. How do you write about a "perfect" society without being boring? How do you write about a romance between two people who've never even met? How do you write an interesting character when she's not allowed to have a personality? These questions weighed on me in every scene.

That being said, I know for certain I never would have been able to get past my mental doubts and write the duology by myself. So thank you, first and foremost, to my co-author Grace Pearce for being the one to push us through to the end. It may have been hard, but accomplishing such a complicated task made us grow as writers. We did it!

A tremendous thank you to our incredible beta readers, Bri, Klara-Mei Li, Maddy, and Angelina for all of your critiques and comments that ended up helping us shape our revisions and rewrites. I'm so grateful for the time you've spent on our story and the energy you spent thinking about how it could be better. You ladies are the best!

Thank you to all of our ARC readers as well, for reading, reviewing, posting, and helping us spread the word. We couldn't have done it without you!

Thank you to my husband, as always, for being a constant support during this crazy journey. He's always there for me to vent and ramble to, two things that are a crucial part of the creative process for me. He claims to enjoy listening to me, but I'm pretty sure he's just really nice. Thanks for all the tea, babe.

And finally, thank you to YOU, for taking a chance on such a strange mashup of genres. I know dystopian books don't usually have vampires and werewolves, but I hope you enjoyed Saskia and Lucan's love story! You are the reason that indie authors get to keep writing.

Love,
Mariah

Acknowledgments

This book wouldn't exist without Mariah. From the moment she sent me the blurb, I have been overly excited about this book—much to her dismay. But when I love something, I love hard—and I truly love this duology.

The very first thing I said was "I want to write a mind-to-mind spicy scene," because when can you ever do that in contemporary romance? And boy, it did not disappoint. We worked very hard to blend our writing styles together to create a cohesive voice, and after countless voice memos, text messages, and calls, I'm so proud of what we've created—especially when it went from us thinking it would be a 90k word standalone to a 180k word duology.

So of course, she is the very first person I want to thank. I know you're itching to get back to your Esholian Institute series (and so are your loyal readers), but I cannot thank you enough for putting up with me through this story. For trusting me to co-author this with you. For everything. It has been one of the most fun years I've had writing and spending time with characters, and you've taught me so much.

Thank you to our beta readers, Bri, Klara-Mei Li, Maddy, and Angelina for helping shape this story. This wouldn't be what it is without you, and Saskia and Lucan's story is so much stronger because of y'all. Every thought and comment is appreciated more than you know!

Thank you to my family as always. You put up with me through all the boxes of books littering the house, and the time I spend in my head or with my face in my Kindle. I love you more than I can express.

And to our readers, thank you for taking a chance on our spin on vampires and werewolves. Thank you for rating and reviewing and sharing anything you can about this series. Even if you didn't love it, thank you, thank you, thank you! Just picking up an indie book makes all the difference.

Love,
Grace

ABOUT THE AUTHORS

Mariah Montoya has always spent her days imagining stories about the fantastical. She is the author of the Esholian Institute series and currently lives in Idaho with her husband, children, and wiggle butt named Posy.

Instagram: mariah_author
TikTok: mariah_author

Grace Pearce is the author of *Leigh Makes Three, The Ex List, Perfect Praise*, and the Guardians & Monsters duology. She lives in southern Louisiana, but her husband may one day get his wish to move to a state with less humidity.

gracepearcebooks.com
Instagram: gracepearcewrites
TikTok: gracepearcewrites

TITLES BY MARIAH MONTOYA

The Esholian Institute Series
By the Orchid and the Owl
By the Moonbeam and the Mist

TITLES BY GRACE PEARCE

Leigh Makes Three
The Ex List
Perfect Praise

The Guardians & Monsters Duology
Xantera
Veradel

www.ingramcontent.com/pod-product-compliance
Lightning Source LLC
Chambersburg PA
CBHW051949240626
47153CB00005B/1684